VIRAL VECTOR

MARCUS MCGEE

PEGASUS BOOKS

Pegasus Books
8165 Valley Green Drive
Sacramento, CA 95823
www.pegasusbooks.net

First Edition: January 2013

Published in North America by Pegasus Books. For information, please contact Pegasus Books c/o Marcus McGee (mmcgee@pegasusbooks.net)

Library of Congress Cataloguing-In-Publication Data
McGee, Marcus
Viral Vector/Marcus McGee – 1st ed
  p. cm.
 Library of Congress Control Number: 2013901903
  ISBN - 978-0-98332608-2-0
 1. Mitchell, Destiny (Fictitious character) – Fiction. 2. African American detectives – Fiction. 3. Political Assassination – Investigation – Fiction. 4. Viral Vector/DNA Sequencing – Fiction. 5. Political fiction.

10 9 8 7 6 5 4 3 2

Comments about *Viral Vector* and requests for additional copies, book club rates and author speaking appearances may be addressed to Marcus McGee or Pegasus Books c/o Ms. McGhee, P.O. Box 235, Neptune, New Jersey, 07754, or you can send your comments and requests via e-mail to marcus.media@yahoo.com

Also available as an eBook from Internet retailers and from Pegasus Books

Printed in the United States of America

For Willie Lewis Brown, Jr.

*For insights on life
and politics*

THE PERFECT WEAPON FOR POLITICAL ASSASSINATION

"WHITE HOUSE TARGET"

In this sequel to *Legal Thriller*, former San Francisco prosecutor/women's advocate Destiny Mitchell receives a call in the middle of the night from a condemned inmate, who pleads for her to save him from someone who is trying to kill him and dozens of other Death Row inmates.

Upon investigation, Destiny learns that Death Row inmates at San Quentin are indeed dying at unprecedented rates— seventy-five in two years! When the inmate dies and she receives a second phone call and a warning from a menacing operative, who demands to know what the inmate told her, she realizes she has become embroiled in a sinister intrigue that possibly involves state and federal government officials, the California prison system, a secret society and even her own husband, private detective Bryan Osaka.

In a desperate bid to save her own life and the life of best friend/Chronicle reporter, Kiyomi Yamakita, Destiny is shocked to discover the reason the inmates are being murdered and the contrived method, designed to provide a small, patriotic group with the power to control the world.

Utilizing new gene therapy techniques and a breakthrough viral vector, this powerful cabal, backed by billionaires, has created the "perfect tool" for discreet political assassination, beginning with a "White House target."

The viral vector has a near one hundred percent effective kill rate, carrying with it all the moral dilemma and implications of the President's drone program—only this weapon is discreet and undetectable, eliminating the need for transparency.

Enjoy twist after twist right down to the provocative conclusion!

13

You said in your heart,
'I will ascend to heaven;
above the stars of God
I will set my throne on high;
I will sit on the mount of assembly
in the far reaches of the north;

14

I will ascend above the heights of the clouds;
I will make myself like the Most High.'

Isaiah 14

The U.S. government is surreptitiously collecting the DNA of world leaders, and is reportedly protecting that of Barack Obama. Decoded, these genetic blueprints could provide compromising information. In the not-too-distant future, they may provide something more as well—the basis for the creation of personalized bioweapons that could take down a president and leave no trace.

Atlantic Magazine, November 2012

http://www.theatlantic.com/magazine/archive/2012/11/hacking-the-presidents-dna/309147/?single_page=true

VIRAL VECTOR

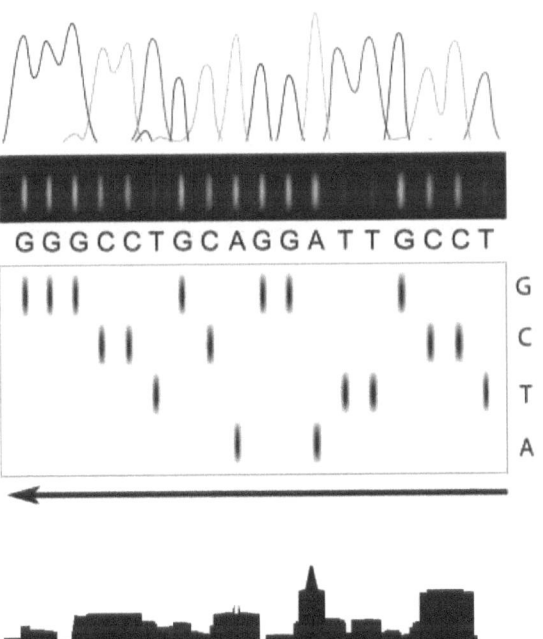

GGGCCTGCAGGATTGCCT

Viral Vector

By Marcus McGee

Chapter 1

"Words. Our words *matter*. We must be deliberate about what we say tonight. Our words will mean the difference between our commitment to *Country First* and the crime of High Treason."

In the weighty silence that followed, Wendell Greene's eyes fell on the masked faces of what appeared to be two men and a woman seated at one end of the long conference table in the spacious boardroom. A third masked man, former governor Hugh Gordon, sat with his head bowed, breathing to calm his thoughts, focusing to maintain resolve. Greene cleared his throat and continued from his place at the head of the table.

"You, Governor," he continued, "You are destined to be remembered most in all this. History will cast your lot with that of either Thomas Jefferson or Benedict Arnold. Make no mistake, your presence tonight and your involvement will help provide legitimacy for this necessary deed. You have our profound respect and admiration."

It was a scripted, secretive meeting, convened one minute after midnight in a dim boardroom, twenty stories above the steady, shimmering black flow of the Potomac River in the Rosslyn submarket of Arlington. The tower was mostly dark, and the night was silent. A full moon shone high above the city, bathing the darkened room in the tickly twilight of Selene. At the conference table, Governor Gordon writhed in his seat, uneasy, uncomfortable and increasingly unresolved.

Associate Supreme Court Justice Wendell Greene was a large man who wheezed when he breathed and always seemed to be out of breath. His large stomach, usually concealed under judicial black, rose above the table when he inhaled. His limp white hair, visible above his mask, was combed straight back, recently ruffled with splayed fingers. He spoke slowly, with a throaty, raspy voice.

"We are the last hope for America, brave patriots and understandably, reluctant conspirators. We know what must be done and derive no personal joy or gratification in doing what only we can do. The wheels at last are in motion. We will be heroes or martyrs."

He motioned toward a masked aide by the door, who in response, bowed her head and exited.

"Words, my friends. Let us not be betrayed by our words, now and in future discussions. While it is natural to be curious, it would be best to let me question our guests without interruption. The less any of you say, the better you'll fare in all this. I'm an old man. If we are discovered, I'll take the blame and I'll be the first to fall on my sword."

The aide reentered, followed by two men in suits, billionaire technology stock trader Helmut Wolf and Dr. Benjamin Rosecrans, founder of *Genengine*, a private genetic research company. The aide then exited, so that only the men she brought in and the group at the table remained. The doctor seemed nervous, but Wolf walked to a place before the group, standing in the shadows.

"Brave gentlemen and gentlewoman," he announced with an air of pride, "I appreciate the invitation to this impossible event. We have a great work to do, evidenced by the fact this meeting is even taking place. As no doubt our chair has informed you, what we speak tonight must never leave this room, and when it is accomplished, we must all be prepared to die to conceal what we have done.

"Let me introduce the brain behind this endeavor," Wolf continued as he motioned toward the door. "Our good doctor here has spent the last ten years perfecting a process we financed, a one-billion-dollar experiment very near its application phase. It's very narrow purpose: covert political assassination, on the global scale, reserved for the narrow and extraordinary aims of our enterprise. It is the *invisible hand*."

The governor squinted, trying to get a glimpse of the doctor's masked aspect through the murky gloom. Wolf paused to make sure his words had resonated.

"Our targets will die from natural causes, and no investigation initiated in the United States or elsewhere by any government or agency will implicate the process or the individuals involved. Through genetics, we have achieved perfect murder, which can be repeated over and over again as necessary, of course for the greater good. The question is not, who is going to *let* us?—rather it is, who is going to *stop* us? Thank you, Doctor."

The doctor gone and doors shut behind him, Greene nodded and cleared his throat.

"And at what point will your process reach its application phase, Mr. X?"

"Forty-five days. Beyond that, assassinations will, how shall we say, they will be final in no more than sixty days after we launch the vector."

"And you're sure you can gain access to our target?" the Justice continued.

"We already have what we need there. What we'll require from you is cover, and of course, compensation. I have confirmation half the money was wired this afternoon, with the balance due when the target is neutralized."

Governor Gordon, against Greene's advice, against his own good judgment, raised his face, staring in disbelief, blurting out the words before he even realized what he was saying.

"White House target?" he gasped. "So you're telling us you're going to murder the most powerful man on the planet and get away with it?"

Wolf was uncomfortable with the question. He glared toward the Justice, who had assured him in advance there would be no unscripted questions. Greene shut his eyes as he exhaled and glanced over at the governor.

"As Mr. X indicated earlier, he and the doctor are merely in the experimental stage of an experimental process," he sighed. "No one has indicated a specific target. *Words*, Governor."

Gordon sat back, discomfited.

"I'm sorry. I shouldn't have said anything."

Greene smiled to reassure his old friend.

"Don't worry, Governor. The die is cast."

"Destiny Mitchell! Is this Destiny Mitchell?"

The illuminated numbers on the clock face were still blurry, slowly coming into focus: 3:43 a.m.! She did not recognize the desperate voice.

"Who? Who *is* this?"

"It's me, Percy Grant!" the voice screamed. "You gotta help me! They're killin us up in here!"

Now she was awake. She sat up, checking the phone's caller ID.

"Who are you? I don't know you."

"Yeah you do!" the voice insisted. "You put me in here. Perseus Grant—double murder in '89, mother and daughter, Potrero Hill!"

When she remembered, she cringed, eyes widening, and almost hung up the phone, but she hesitated.

"Hold on. How are you *calling* me?"

"That's not important! You gotta help me. They're killin us in here!"

She flicked on the light.

"Wait a minute! Are you still at San Quentin? Are you calling me from inside the *prison*?"

"Yeah! I paid my ass to get your number and this phone! And I called you because no one *else* would believe me. I swear there's somethin up with this prison. They're murderin us in here! It's in the DNA!"

Incredulous, she took a breath.

"You raped and tortured two women. You're on Death Row. Of *course* they're going to kill you! Why are you calling me? I'm going to report this to the warden."

"If you don't help me, I'll be dead, so it won't matter. But listen, you know I kilt them women. I *deserve* to be in here. You were right to come down on me."

His voice broke.

"I always respected you for that. You're good people. That's why I knew you were my only hope, and not just for me, but for all of us."

"What are you *saying*?" she emphasized. "You're on *Death Row*!"

"But this ain't the state doin this! or maybe it is. Whoever it is, we still got rights. If you don't help us, no one will. They'll kill us all! Please!"

She took a deep breath and braced herself.

"Talk to me."

He rambled on for a minute and a half and suddenly stopped, whispering about hearing footsteps. He returned and continued for another twenty-five seconds and then he was gone again. After fumbling with the phone for a few seconds, he returned.

"Someone's comin. Fuck! Someone heard me. I'll call you back!"

Two days later, she read the story in the paper. It wasn't a big story, on the second to the last page of the first section. His picture was there, a photo from the trial. That ugly trial had been an ordeal she struggled to forget, but the sight of his face dredged up a torrent of long-buried, consciously blocked memories.

It was her second year in the San Francisco district attorney's office. Fresh off her third conviction, she had grown to love her job as a homicide prosecutor. She thought she was making a difference, putting the bad guys away, at least the ones who went against her. But she was unprepared for the details from that savage double murder in McKinley Park in November of 1989.

Perseus Grant, the accused, had kidnapped a woman and her thirteen-year-old daughter after dusk as they walked past the park, headed home from a neighborhood store. In his parked van, he raped and tortured mother and daughter for eleven hours. At dawn, he stabbed each in the neck through the carotid artery and left them to bleed to death on the sidewalk.

Grant was the first real monster Destiny had ever encountered as a prosecutor, and that made him the most memorable. Everything about him was creepy, sadistic and inhuman. His dark, sinister eyes, glazed over like a caged animal, suppressed extreme rage, never changing as they followed her around the courtroom. No one could penetrate past them. Stoic, he never spoke a word to his attorney and never took the stand.

But when the conviction was read, his head snapped toward prosecutor Mitchell as he lipped the words, "I'm gonna kill you, Bitch!" before guards roughed him up and forced him from the courtroom. Her knees became wobbly and she began shaking so erratically that she could not read the court document in her hands. She was unresponsive to the judge and had to sit to calm herself, never having been threatened so directly before, and this by a monster.

A week later, before sentencing, the judge asked Perseus if he wanted to go on record with a statement of regret. Destiny cringed as he stood. She had considered not attending the sentencing, but her boss insisted on her presence, asserting he would not allow the defendant to intimidate the district attorney's office.

"Walls can't keep me from her. I swear I'm gonna get out, and when I do, I'm gonna kill that ho right there. Yeah, I mean you, Destiny Mitchell! And if you think what I did to that bitch and her daughter was some sick shit, just wait till I get to your ass!"

For years, she had nightmares about Perseus Grant escaping and showing up somewhere. Freaked out about being alone at night, she took a roommate for three years and invested in a high-tech security system. But over the years, she realized how clever he had been. She had sent him to one form of prison, and he had sent her to another. Counseling helped. After nearly two decades, she had almost forgotten him.

But the phone call two days earlier brought back the emotional memories and the creepiness of the experience, the menacing, animal-like quality in his expression as his eyes followed her, studied her, the baritone in his voice when he threatened her and the crime scene photos of charred holes in that woman and her ravaged, mutilated daughter.

His voice however, was different during the phone call. It was lighter and more animated. She heard fear in his voice, but fear from what? She checked the next day, and there were still several appeals he could have availed himself to if the system began marching him toward the prison's death chamber. Despite his crime and sentence, the state was not threatening to kill him any time soon. She had thought to call the warden or make a report about the late-night call, but he seemed almost believable.

Her eyes returned to the newspaper. Perseus Grant was dead, two days after the panicked call from the prison, implying his life was in danger. It was just too eerie to be a coincidence. And while she felt great relief that he would never be coming after her, she was impressed that he had gone through so much trouble to call her. Monster that he was, he trusted her to save him from whatever had produced the terror evident in his voice.

The article under the picture said he died from a heart attack and that he had been suffering from delusions and having emotional problems over the last couple of years. According to the reporter, prison psychologists said Grant had the highest tested IQ of all the inmates at San Quentin: 161. In the final paragraph, the writer made mention of another death at the prison a week earlier. And another inmate died from a heart problem some eight days before that. Mind still reeling, she closed her eyes, remembering.

She had never met Dhara Rangarajan and daughter Lata, but over the course of the trial she got to know them better than most. Dhara and her husband, Haresh, owned a corner liquor store and deli in an adjoining neighborhood. Eighth-grader Lata worked in the store after school and on weekends. On two or three evenings each week, Dhara and Lata took walks that ended with a slow stroll past McKinley Park.

Evidence indicated Perseus Grant watched the women over a few weeks, noting they walked past the park at about 6:00 p.m. on most of the days they were out, which was usually at dusk. Dhara and her daughter, however, did not account for the daylight savings time shift affecting the first Monday of November.

A week earlier, and they would have been walking toward the sunset, slanted light glowing from the horizon, but the earlier sunset on that day took them by surprise. A bruise on the side of Dhara's head indicated Perseus hit her with a blunt object as she passed his van, knocking her unconscious. And Lata, terrified by the violence, hadn't put up much of a fight, though flesh from the defendant's face was found under three of her fingernails.

Both victims were raped, sodomized and burned in various places with a blowtorch. The pain was so extreme that Lata had chewed her tongue in two and Dhara cracked three of her molars. Destiny remembered viewing a portrait the two had taken a week before the incident in glaring contrast to the crime scene photos of their bloody and burned withered bodies, eyes sunken deep back into the sockets. He was an animal, but now he was dead, and the world was a better place without him.

"Read the paper this morning?"

"Three papers," Destiny answered. "Part of my morning routine."

"So of *course* you saw the article about Perseus Grant?"

Destiny nodded.

"Cried all *in* my milk!"

She looked across the table at Kiyomi.

"I don't think I told you yet," she began, hesitation in her voice, "but he *called* me two nights ago."

"Perseus Grant! Really? From inside the prison? How'd he pull that off?"

"Don't know," Destiny shrugged, "but it was a weird call. The anger was gone. He was actually begging me."

"Begging you to do what?"

"Not sure. He kept saying that some 'they,' some secret agency, was killing the inmates. He seemed desperate. I think he was begging me to help him."

Kiyomi's natural curiosity was peaked. Through instinct and training, she could smell a fluke in a bucket of bullshit. She had started as a reporter at the *Chronicle* when she was twenty-one. Over the years, she had moved through the ranks, becoming a crime scene reporter, a special features editor and a crime bureau chief before getting married and having a daughter.

At forty-six, she proclaimed fatigue and no longer wanted to work the typical "beyond full-time" reporter hours. So for the last four months, she had reported on innocuous daily events on a part-time basis, mostly boring stuff. Crime scene work was exciting, while the generic, metropolitan stories the paper assigned to her were unfulfilling and disappointing. She longed for the adrenaline rush she felt as an investigative reporter.

"What *specifically* did he say?"

Destiny shrugged.

"He was ranting mostly, repeating himself."

She thought for a moment.

"He said there was something up with the prison, that the prison was involved."

She closed her eyes.

"He kept saying, 'they're killing us,' and when I reminded him that he was on Death Row, he said it wasn't the state. He said he knew who it was and what they were doing. He said they were going to kill him and anyone else who knew."

Kiyomi nodded.

"And then he dies two days later?"

"From a heart attack."

Because the two had been friends since grade school, Destiny could almost read Kiyomi's mind, but she asked to be sure.

"Okay, so what are you thinking?"

"A lot of things could *cause* a heart attack—drug injection, poisons, chemical fumes."

"You think he was murdered?"

Kiyomi studied her best friend's face and body posture.

"You talked to him. What do *you* think?"

"I think whatever had him afraid was real to him, but the article said he was delusional."

Kiyomi laughed.

"That was a reporter writing what the prison told her to write. Zero research was done there. I know the lazy reporter. Did the number come up on your caller ID?"

"First thing I checked. He called from a blocked number," Destiny answered, rechecking numbers in the phone.

Kiyomi took a folded newspaper section from her satchel, placed it on the table and rescanned the article.

"Did you see the bit here about the other inmate, the one that died at the prison a week ago, and the one before that?"

"Yes, I saw that."

"Well, what do you think? You think the deaths could be related?"

Destiny wagged her head.

"You're the reporter. Me, I hardly noticed. Used to be a lawyer, but I run a foundation now, and I'm better off for it. Is that what you think?"

"I think Perseus Grant calling you from Death Row and then just suddenly dying two days later is a mighty strange coincidence. And if you add that to the fact two other inmates died over there recently, I think it's worth looking into."

Destiny shrugged.

"Well then, *you* look into it. As far as I'm concerned, the death of Perseus Grant closes the chapter and the book. The whole ordeal is over. Coincidence or not, the state, the system, you, me—we're all better off without him. He was a sicko. If someone killed him, he had it coming."

After ten years with the San Francisco district attorney's office, Destiny Mitchell was selected as executive director for the *Aegis Foundation*, an organization dedicated to defending, protecting and empowering women trapped in violent or oppressive domestic situations and work environments. In Destiny's final case as a prosecutor, she took on Jordan Alexander, one of the city's favorite sons, seeking to prove his guilt in the brutal murder of his wife, Lynette.

The jury hung and Jordan walked, but lawyers for Allegra Benson, Lynette's mother, managed to get a twenty-one-million-dollar civil judgment on behalf of Allegra, and Lynette's three daughters. When Jordan committed suicide twelve years later, the plaintiffs received another five million dollars. Allegra used her portion of the money to create the *Aegis Foundation* and chose Destiny to administrate it.

Destiny was forty-eight years old, but she looked much younger. Her hair was short and chic. She had recently stopped dying it, so there were subtle gray highlights. Her face was taut and pretty, her smooth brown skin still glistening with the freshness of youth.

When she married Bryan Osaka six years earlier, she was certain they would be happy. But she had no idea how demanding her job at *Aegis* would become. When the Foundation went national, she was required to be away from home five nights a week, and she was busy with constant phone calls in the balance of her time.

Bryan tried to be understanding. He took up golf and intensified his work schedule, but it got old after a few years. He loved Destiny too much to ask her to give up her work at the foundation. He knew how passionate she was about helping troubled women. So he just walked away.

His move to "San Diego" reflected the separation and distance he felt had grown between them. She was devastated when he left and offered to scale back her schedule, but both knew it was impractical. At some point she would have to choose between quitting the foundation and staying married.

When the phone rang at three o'clock that next morning, she froze for an instant, staring at the clock. Perseus was dead. Who could be calling at that ungodly hour? The number, just as it had been a week before, was blocked. Caution straining her voice, she answered.

"Hello?"

"Is this Destiny Mitchell?"

The voice was male and sounded menacing. She answered.

"Yes."

"What did he tell you?"

She sat up, turning on the lamp next to the bed.

"I have no idea what you're talking about. Who *is* this?"

"It would be better for you if you didn't ask me any questions. You talked to him for more than two minutes that night. What did he say to you?"

She reacted to the tone of his voice.

"It's three o'clock in the morning. How dare you call me and threaten me! Why don't you tell me who you are, and then maybe I'll talk to you. Otherwise, I'm hanging up."

"I don't have to threaten you, Ms. Mitchell. Perseus Grant has already gotten you involved in something far more dangerous to you than anything I ever could. So please, for your own good, tell me what he said."

She wanted to rebut, but she realized her disadvantage and the implied warning. He knew her identity, but she had no idea who he was. And if Perseus Grant's fears were not the product of a delusional mind, then this person on the other end of the phone was perhaps capable of murder, or at least he was in some way connected.

"As you obviously know, the call was very brief," she explained, nervous. "And he spent the better part of the call reminding me about who he was."

"That's fine. And when he got past the introduction, then what did he say?"

She balked, wondering if Perseus Grant's words were the only leverage that she had.

"It's like they said in the paper. He was ranting. He was delusional, and it was almost four in the morning!"

The voice interrupted.

"Just tell me what he said, goddammit! We both know he called you for a reason. He said something to you! He *told* you something! What was it?"

"He said,"

She drew a deep breath.

"He said someone was trying to kill him, and maybe some of the other inmates."

"He *told* you that?" he groaned.

She nodded.

"Yes."

"Did he say or tell you anything else, anything else at all?"

"No, nothing."

"Thank you, Ms. Mitchell. I appreciate your honesty. I trust you'll tell no one about either his call or mine, or you'll needlessly endanger other people. If you don't hear from me again, that will mean I've been able to resolve this matter without incident."

"And if I *do* hear from you?"

She could hear the man's breathy sigh.

"If you do, it just might be too late, for you. *And* for me."

When Kiyomi arrived at six a.m., Destiny was frazzled, seated on the couch in the living room, drinking oolong tea.

"I got here as soon as I could. Did you call Bryan?"

"He's flying up this afternoon."

She crossed her arms.

"I don't know. I'm just freaked out by the phone calls. First Perseus Grant, and then this *other* weirdo, whoever he was."

"And he threatened you?"

Destiny's eyes welled with tears.

"I don't know. He said Perseus Grant got me involved in something dangerous. It sounded like something life-threatening."

"You think the call was some kind of a prank? Maybe someone's trying to scare you?"

Destiny looked over at Kiyomi.

"Trying? Perseus Grant died, two days after he called me. When people start dying, you take that pretty serious."

Steadying her hand, she sipped the tea.

"What gets me is that other voice on the phone—he sounded like someone powerful, but he sounded scared too. I don't remember how he said it, but it seemed he thought *both* our lives were in jeopardy, his and mine."

"He obviously called from a blocked number?"

"Yes," Destiny nodded. "But what I don't understand is, Perseus Grant died from a heart attack. He wasn't murdered. He had a heart attack. Medical Examiner said in the paper his heart was in bad shape."

Kiyomi bowed her head for a moment and began.

"I told you I would be doing a little research on San Quentin. Well, you know me. It wasn't long before I found something there that's at least a little alarming."

"What's that?"

"Remember that article from the other day? It said another inmate had died a week earlier?"

"Yes?"

Kiyomi pried open her brown leather satchel and withdrew a folder.

"Well, I checked. That inmate died, and another had died a week before that. According to prison records over the last forty years, the Death Row attrition rate is about three or four inmates per year, and half of those basically die of old age."

She handed Destiny a document.

"However, in this last year, forty-one inmates have died, only one from old age. The rest are either from heart attacks or multiple organ failure, and that's along an eighty-twenty split. Thirty-four died the year before."

Destiny's mouth fell open as she read.

"Okay, so what does this mean?"

"I don't know, but something's foul. Something's *happening* over there, and I'm thinking Perseus Grant somehow discovered what it was."

Destiny stood, her left hand slicking back her hair.

"Why doesn't anyone *know* about this? Why hasn't the *Chronicle* reported on this?"

"No one's paid attention. It's the prison. They tightly control information coming out of there, and its Death Row inmates who are dying. It all flies under the radar. An inmate dies of natural causes and the family is quietly notified. In most cases, they're privately relieved it's all over, that it's an act of God. If there's no family, the body goes out for cremation. So the passing of a Death Row inmate isn't news, or at least it hasn't been, until now."

Destiny shrugged, wagging her head.

"So something's happening to these Death Row inmates? It's either some hazard at the prison or someone's killing them, or both. A week ago, I wouldn't have cared, but now I don't have a choice. What are you thinking?"

"Well, according to the man who called you a few hours ago, you're already involved in this. Whoever's behind it, if they think you know something, they might come after you."

Destiny sighed.

"Might? I have to expect that they will."

Kiyomi had gone to the kitchen where she was rummaging through the refrigerator. Her head appeared in the doorway.

"The way I figure it," she ventured, "after Perseus Grant discovered whatever he did, he didn't have many people he could trust. Probably no one. Then he remembered back to the trial. He remembered how far you had gone to see that justice was served in those murders. Maybe he was hoping you'd do the same for him."

"Or he did it to get revenge on me for sending him there. Either way, I'm involved now."

"*We're* involved," Kiyomi insisted, "but we're not going to sit here and wait for something to happen. We have to get to the heart of this. We have to find out who they are and what they're up to."

Destiny looked over at her friend, gratitude in her eyes.

"And how do we propose to do that, Girlfriend? We've got nothing to go on. We don't even have a phone number."

Kiyomi smiled.

"But we have something much bigger, and possibly better. We have a pattern. We have evidence that Death Row inmates are dying at San Quentin in unprecedented numbers. No one else is paying attention. We have leverage. We'll start at the prison."

Chapter 2

Jettson Turner did not seem extraordinary in any way, not unless he was running operations, his specialty. He was a short man with eyes sunk deep within their sockets. His skin was tanned and wrinkled, like worn leather. He smoked one cigarette after another from the time he got up at five-thirty until he succumbed to the seductions of fatigue at midnight.

He wasn't likable. In fact, his profanity-laced language offended most people, but he was good at his job. A former Chief-of-Staff for a previous White House administration, he was known as a man who could make things happen, a fixer. He was shrewd, organized and a stickler for detail. His focus was intense, indivertible, as he was always a few steps ahead of everyone else.

Turner scrutinized the three men seated at the table before settling into his chair.

"What's this about a fuckin containment breach?"

Cornell Cotton, in charge of Turner's debriefing and containment operation, hesitated before answering.

"I would hardly characterize it as a breach, Sir. Just a concern, pre-emptive."

"What the fuck! Concern my ass! A fuckin inmate called out and *talked* to someone!"

"That's true. On July 23rd at 3:41 a.m., Grant made a call from a disposable cell phone to a woman named Destiny Mitchell, and yes, it's the same Destiny Mitchell who runs the *Aegis Foundation* in San Francisco. The call lasted two minutes and fifty-seven seconds."

"What the fuck!" Jett sighed. "Any prior communication? Of course you *checked* that?"

"Naturally. No prior communication. Though it turns out she was the prosecutor who put him on Death Row in the first place. He threatened to kill her in court."

"So this bastard, someone gives him a phone, and with one phone call to make, he fuckin calls the bitch who put him away? Why her?"

Cotton typed a command on his laptop, glancing down at the screen.

"We have the phone. It was just that one call, so we're pretty much contained. Exactly one week later, I called personally to debrief her. She was spooked. This was a guy who threatened to kill her, calling her from prison Death Row in the middle of the night. He spent that two minutes and fifty-seven seconds trying to convince her who he was. He never got the chance to tell her anything."

"Fuck! And I thought we were done over there!" Jett growled. "Okay, Grant—was he the last loose end?"

The man on Turner's left shook his head.

"Well, there's Sutter, but he's a guard."

Cotton glared at his underling for interjecting out of turn.

"Sutter is on his way out."

Jett bowed his head, massaging his brow while thinking.

"I just don't get a good feeling about this. If there's any chance this thing has gotten out of the prison, I have to assume it has. I want surveillance on Sutter and I want complete work-up on this woman Grant called. Destiny Mitchell, is it? And I want dailies on the investigation over there. If this thing's fuckin gotten out of the prison, we might have to get our hands dirty, maybe bloody, maybe break a few laws, but we have to shut it down."

Agent Jake Martinez shifted to shallow breathing as he entered the dank, musty cell, the top two buttons of his dress shirt undone and his suit jacket and tie folded over his forearm. He turned back to the prison's health care manager.

"So this was his cell?"

"He was in this cell for the last eight years," the woman answered. "He was over on the other side before."

Jake's eyes scanned the perimeter of the small enclosure, the damage along the bottom of the wall in the far corner, the bubbled surface along the ceiling, the dust encrusted vent.

"When were these cells painted last?"

"According to our records, four years ago," she answered, her voice becoming annoyed.

Jake nodded as he, tweezers extended, reached for a flake of peeling paint.

"So I imagine you have records on the actual paint that was used?"

Dr. Irene Spagnola, the facility's health care manager, was quick to address the insinuation.

"We've already had it checked," she sighed. "This year's been a rare one. You could say extraordinary, but I don't believe there's anything sinister going on here. Even if there is and it's something environmental, it wouldn't be the paint. And it isn't anything related to the ventilation either. We've had the paint, air, food and water tested for toxins, possible carcinogens, and even for radioactivity. We tend to believe it wouldn't be something environmental."

Agent Martinez spoke as he scraped a layer of caked dust from the ventilation opening.

"Nothing *sinister*?" he interrupted, sarcasm evident in his voice. "So how would you explain forty-one dead inmates in one year? And all from either heart attacks or multiple organ failure? Somehow I don't think as health care manager you can rule environmental factors out."

"We've had the entire facility checked, twice."

Irritated by the doctor's impatience and attitude, Jake closed on her.

"Forty-one of your inmates are dead, Doctor. You obviously missed something, *twice*."

Martinez had been with the FBI for sixteen years, starting in the El Paso field office, moving to a bureau in Phoenix before finally landing at the San Francisco office on Golden Gate Avenue. He never married, but he had a son who visited him twice a year in the Bernal Heights home he purchased six years earlier.

Jake was stocky with a cheeky face, dark skin, Indian features and short black hair, styled up and tight, owing to his time as a Marine. He was still in shape at forty, though he had developed a bit of a potbelly over the last few years. He spoke good English, but there were traces of his native Spanish in occasional words and phrases.

"Doctor," Martinez warned, "you *must* realize I'm the last step in a process to save yours and your bosses' asses. You have a problem at this prison. Inmates are dying, and it's just a matter of time before it becomes a news story or worse, a national conspiracy theory."

"We've checked and double-checked. The Inspector General's been over here. They've checked. These inmates are dying due to natural causes. Autopsies are showing evidence of congenital heart disease and coronary problems that appear to have been hereditary, not attributable to any environmental factors. I admit it's odd. It's shocking, even for me, but there's nothing unnatural going on here, no foul play. There is no conspiracy."

"Forty-one inmates, dead in the last year?"

"Forty-two, actually," she answered. "But if something here is killing them, something we don't know about, it's beyond medical science as we know it."

Martinez nodded.

"Then we have to go beyond medical science, Doctor, as *you* know it."

He exited the cell.

"I'm going to need copies of medical records from all the inmates who've died in the last two years, and from the ones who've been sick. Obviously, there's something you missed."

"And *you're* going to find it? You're an ordinary FBI field agent, not a medical researcher."

"I'm an experienced investigator, and I'm not convinced that there *isn't* something sinister going on here. If there is, maybe you're a *part* of it. But then of course, you'd be part of the cover up. You'd be telling me exactly what you're telling me now."

The doctor gasped, insulted.

"From a self-proclaimed experienced investigator, that was unprofessional and out-of-line!"

She removed her glasses, staring into the agent's eyes.

"I'll provide the records *this* time, Agent Martinez, but I'm going to complain about you to your superiors, and to U.S. Senator Bernstein, who happens to be a friend of mine. And just so you know, the next time you need access to my records and these cells, I won't be so helpful. You'll have to take it up with the warden. Now, if you'll excuse me."

Doctor gone, Jake lingered in the cell. He knelt, examining every irregularity in the floor. He checked the walls and toilet, the ceiling and the cell door. Ten minutes passed before he removed the thin, lumpy mattress from the bed. Squeezing a tiny flashlight between his fingers, he traced the grease and dirt mattress line along the wall until he came to what appeared to be a damaged area.

Upon closer inspection with the flashlight and a magnifying glass, he could barely make out seven numbers, scrawled into the cement wall with a fine-tipped metal instrument, *7,5,2,3,4,0 and 4*, though there was an eighth number between the 2 and 3 that had been scratched out. And beneath the numbers, there appeared to be two words, separated by about a half inch, the words *Viral Vector*.

Bryan Osaka loved Destiny Mitchell. Their first year of marriage had been perhaps too idyllic, complete with adventures in Tokyo, Yokohama, Hong Kong, Cairo, São Paulo and Rio de Janeiro, but then reality set in. While Allegra Benson's ambition for the *Aegis Foundation* was humble and localized in San Francisco and Los Angeles, Destiny had taken the charter national. So what started as a modest Mission Street San Francisco shelter for battered women had become a national icon for female independence and empowerment.

After that first year of marriage, Destiny transcended her job as director, conferring many of her day to day, operational duties upon Lyndsey, Allegra's granddaughter. Destiny had taken Lyndsey in after her father's suicide and had adopted Lynette Alexander's daughter as her own. After a shaky start, this reassignment of duties freed Destiny to hire a lobbying firm and to pursue the political and financial needs of the foundation on a national level. *Aegis* had become an influential force in America, making Destiny a powerful woman.

Despite the separation, Bryan and Destiny talked on the phone a few nights a week. He complained he always felt rushed, as if she had him on a timer, and he said she used too many "summation" words. Recognizing her transgressions and the continuous slights, she apologized and swore to her husband she would leave the foundation once it became active in all fifty states and in Puerto Rico. Notwithstanding, he was less than optimistic.

They had just sat to dinner at a cozy, neighborhood French bakery and cafe on O'Farrell, near Union Square Park. It wasn't as fancy as some of the other restaurants in the neighborhood, but it was one of her favorites. They sampled a newly released Zinfandel on the rooftop patio on that cool summer night, looking down on the Square. He sipped, analyzing flavors.

"Blackberry?"

"It's off!" she insisted. "I'm totally unplugged. I said I wanted to spend this time with you. I meant it."

"How much time do I have?" he laughed.

Destiny sipped from the wineglass and smiled acknowledging his assessment of the wine.

"Oh, *blackberry!*" she laughed. "No, I'm yours for the night. I submit. I'm at your pleasure and command."

He leaned toward her, innuendo unmistakable.

"I'm going to hold you to that."

After dinner settings were cleared and coffee was served, Bryan plopped a manila file on the table and opened it, pen at the ready.

"Okay, Perseus Grant and that four o'clock phone call. Probably the best starting point. Do you want to tell me about it?"

She turned her chair and body away from his.

"I thought I wanted to earlier, but I've decided against it."

"Why's that?"

"Because it's too dangerous. I told you about the second call. Whoever it was said Grant got me involved in something serious enough to put my life in danger. But Kiyomi, you know her, she was at the prison the next day. That's bad enough. If there really is something diabolical behind all the deaths over there this year, the less you know the better."

Bryan was laconic by nature. He was tall for a *Nisei*, or second-generation Japanese, and dark, his hair half gray. His handsome face rarely smiled or showed emotion in public, but he was becoming angry.

"You're my wife and I'm a detective. There's no way in Hell I'm going to sit on the sidelines and let you and Kiyomi deal with this by yourselves. You have no idea what you're up against."

"And *you* do?"

"I know people inside. The prison guards' union, the CCPOA— I know their vice president. Not exactly a friend, but we have history. If there's something going on over there, he'll know. I'm sure he's already dealing with it."

Destiny sighed.

"Or maybe he's *part* of it?"

"I'm not ruling that out, but I'm not letting you and Kiyomi do this."

"Why? Because we're *girls*?"

Bryan exhaled, shaking his head.

"No, it's because you're my wife! This isn't about girl power. Anyone who could murder forty-one inmates at San Quentin Prison in one year won't care about that. They wouldn't hesitate killing both of you if you threaten to expose whatever details they don't want out there."

He leaned in, his voice taking on a menacing tone.

"Have you thought about what would have to be involved over there? Someone, we have no idea who, but someone is killing these inmates. This is bigger than you could ever imagine! So the sooner I reel in Kiyomi, the better."

She sat back, crossing her arms.

"*You're* going to reel in Kiyomi? What does that mean? You're taking over?"

"You two are way out of your league here. I'm saving your lives."

Destiny bristled, her nostrils flaring.

"Maybe *you* don't have a choice, Bryan. If whoever it is comes after me, I'm not sitting here like some damsel in distress depending on *you* to save me. I have to take the offensive."

"You don't even know what you're up against."

"That's what I have to find out. Look, I won't live in fear. I've done that before, and it's no way to live. I have to assume whoever it is knows about me, and they're watching me. I need to get some kind of leverage here, something to protect me."

Bryan paused a moment, thinking.

"I can see there's no reasoning with you, so I'll be moving back in with you until we get some answers."

She smiled. She had been waiting to hear him say those words for at least two years. And yet the actual thought of him moving back in did not live up to its anticipation. It was instead an awkward thought. She had grown comfortable living alone, again.

"Are you sure you want to do that?"

"Of *course*. Why? You seem disappointed. Do you *not* want me to move back in?"

She reached over, placing her hand on his.

"Of course I do. Like I said before dinner, I submit to you."

"I could possibly believe that if I didn't know you," he laughed. "Isn't your name Destiny Mitchell? Aren't you the person who said on Oprah that a strong man with a successful career represents the greatest threat to an independent woman?"

She grimaced.

"Did I say that?"

"If you would rather I rent an apartment up here, I will, but independent woman or not, I'm not going to let you and Kiyomi try to take on whoever is behind these prison murders, because that's what they are, murders. And if I let you two go at it your way, it would be *my* fault when one or both of you ended up dead."

Chapter 3

The warden's office was more austere than comfortable. In it were a large wooden desk, a row of black metal file cabinets, a computer station and old hung photos of the prison from varying perspectives of viewpoint and time. Behind the desk was a large wood lacquered placard bearing the expression: *In my country we go to prison first, and then become President.*

Paul McGinnis wasn't the sort of man most expected to see when they met him. He seemed more a professor than a warden. Tall and lean, his narrow face and features seemed more European than American. His thinning hair was mostly gray, with subtle hints it had once been red. He wore black, thick-rimmed glasses on the bridge of his slender nose.

The man in the chair across from him was shorter, stockier. His aggression and aplomb were evident by the way he sat and in his every movement, in stark contrast to the warden's cautious and often indecisive bearing. James Cassie was Executive Vice President of the California Correctional Peace Officers Association, or the CCPOA.

Over the previous twenty years, the CCPOA grew into California's most formidable labor union, with 31,000 members, mostly prison guards. The union's growth was due in part to a crime surge in the state during the 1980s, coupled with intelligent leadership that consolidated Youth Authority Supervisors, parole officers and prison guards under one umbrella.

With membership soaring, the new director spent a half million dollars a year during that time to boost the union's public profile. Meanwhile, California citizens and politicians were calling for tougher laws with longer, more severe sentences. It was a perfect storm that swelled the number of California prisons from ten in 1984 to thirty-one by the early 2000s. Collecting 1.8 million dollars in dues per month, the union became a powerhouse in state politics.

While the problem at San Quentin did not directly affect the CCPOA, it hadn't gone unnoticed or uninvestigated. Cassie had been to the prison five or six times in the previous three months interviewing guards, medical staff and administration personnel, ostensibly seeking to find a cause for the glaring anomaly. A scandal at San Quentin Prison was the last thing the CCPOA or the state needed.

Cassie glanced up from a notebook.

"So Mac, who's all been over here? Office of the Inspector General? State health officials? Department of Corrections brass? The FBI?"

The warden scoffed.

"All of them. Lately, there's been someone here every day. I put a call in to the governor yesterday. All these visitors are starting to present security concerns and raise suspicions. And they're insisting they want to interview inmates. Not going to happen."

"Any more dead?"

McGinnis pursed his thin lips and took a deep breath.

"None, but we've got one sick, dying. Doctors say congestive heart failure, natural causes."

He shrugged.

"I know what it looks like, but how can I argue with science? They've tested water, food and air and they've tested for anthrax. They've even checked the drugs that slip in and out of the block. There's nothing out of the ordinary over there that could be causing this."

"What about the rest of the population in the prison? Are any of them dying of heart disease or is it just East Block?"

McGinnis shrugged again.

"It's more than just East Block. East Block houses only about 415. They've also been dying over at the Adjustment Center. But so far this year, we haven't had any cases outside Death Row. My doctors—"

Cassie raised his hand to halt the warden.

"Forty-two dead in one year when you've averaged three or four a year over the last fifty? Come on, Mac! I'm on your side, but you've got to admit something strange is going on over there at Death Row. The only question is, who's doing it? Is it the state? The feds? Do you know?"

Nervous and frustrated, McGinnis stood, rushed to the window and yanked the cord, snapping shut the wooden window blinds. Flustered, he whispered.

"Maybe there *is* something going on over there, but I know nothing about it! It doesn't even make sense! If someone's found out how to commit murder by causing heart and organ failure, and make it seem like natural causes, why here? Why San Quentin? What does it mean? We've had autopsies performed by the best experts in the country. The OIG's investigated it. They can't find anything. The only red flag is the number of deaths this year."

Cassie tapped his fingers on the table, thinking.

"What if that was their intention, to baffle everybody? What if they were primarily after one or two of your inmates and they knocked off the other forty or so to throw everyone off? Plenty of people would say whoever's behind it did the state and the taxpayers a favor."

Seated again at the desk, McGinnis frowned.

"Already considered that. We've scrubbed the list of those who died this year. It's everybody—gang members, loners, black, brown, Aryans, Asian, everyone from child killers to mass murderers. Impossible to tell if they were after anyone specific. Good question, though."

Cassie sat in silence for a moment.

"It's only a matter of time before all this becomes public, and then what are you going to do?"

"No one's talking. I'll see to that. Eventually, if it gets out there, it'll blow over. Even if they *are* being murdered, who's really going to care? They're Death Row inmates. You know that Springsteen song. 'Dead men walkin.'"

"What?" Cassie mocked. "You can't think this is just an off year? Forty-one dead, as opposed to four? You don't want to know what's *happening* here?"

"Whatever it is, it's bigger than both of us," the warden answered. "I hope whoever it is accomplishes whatever their goal is here. If I knew who they were and I could help them, I would. I just want them to finish whatever they're doing and move on."

Cassie sighed.

"I just don't get it. Aren't you at least curious? Don't you want to know who's behind this and what they're *really* up to? Let alone the injustice?"

The warden seemed confused.

"Injustice?"

"Due process. These guys aren't being given due process. They still have rights. They're still entitled to appeals. Someone's murdering these guys and you don't care?"

McGinnis thought a moment and smiled.

"Oh, I get it. With you, Cassie, there's always an angle. Your primary concern is always about how whatever happens might affect your prison guards and your parole officers."

"Not true."

"And if someone's killing inmates here, maybe they'll do it on a larger scale in the state. And fewer inmates translates to fewer jobs, right? And fewer jobs means fewer union members and less money in dues for you? You're worried about *due* process, all right."

Cassie crossed his arms.

"I just don't want this thing to get out of hand. Whoever it is, who knows where they're going with it?"

"What do you mean?"

"I mean, once they get their methods better perfected, what if they don't stop at Death Row inmates? What if they start targeting those they believe are corrupt guards?"

McGinnis smiled.

"I thought there were no corrupt guards?"

Cassie couldn't help laughing.

"I'm serious. And what if they start targeting other people in the system? What if they don't like the warden and target you? How's your heart, Mac?"

"I get your point. So what are you suggesting?"

"Well, at least a dozen investigators, yours, the state's and the feds, have been at this for a year now, and you're still baffled about what's going on here. You're not any closer to figuring this thing out than you were a year ago."

McGinnis nodded.

"I concede that. So you have a plan?"

"I have resources. I can put together a team that can come in here and figure it out. All we would need is a little time and access. In a month, it'll be over."

Sitting back, Cassie resigned.

"I'll even pay for it. Come on, Mac, what do you got to lose?"

"Thanks for taking the time to meet with us, Agent Martinez. As you no doubt understand from our earlier conversation, name is Destiny Mitchell, and the woman over there is my friend, Kiyomi Yamakita."

Destiny was seated at the desk in her large office at the headquarters of *Aegis*, located on the forty-eighth floor in the Transamerica building, at the intersection of Montgomery and Washington Street at Columbus. Kiyomi sat in a brown leather chair across the room, far enough away so she was not necessarily a participant in the meeting, but close enough to monitor the conversation. She smiled and nodded toward the federal agent before her attention returned to her laptop screen.

"You said you got my phone number from somewhere *inside* the prison?" Destiny continued.

Agent Martinez glanced toward Kiyomi and leaned forward.

"I said I discovered what I thought might have been a phone number in one of the inmate's cells at the prison, San Quentin, that is. So I called it."

"I see. And that was the *first* time you called my number?"

Martinez seemed suspicious.

"Of course it was. Why do you ask?"

She ignored the question.

"Agent Martinez, would you mind telling me what you were doing at the prison when you found the number. Are you at liberty to say why you were there?"

"Afraid not. Is there a particular reason why you ask?"

"Professional curiosity, I guess. When I prosecuted cases for the district attorney's office, I sent a few people there, a few very bad people."

"Already checked that out. I know you did. And I already know what you're about to ask me?"

"Oh?"

"You want to know if the location of the number I found is related to any of the convicts you sent there."

"Not specifically, but yes," she smiled, nervous. "That is something I'd like to know."

Martinez opened a folder.

"How about if we do it this way? I tell you who it was and you share what you know about him. We can agree to share back and forth on this specific matter."

"But what if I tell *you* where you found the number?" she suggested. "Would you then be willing to share more significant information?"

He sat back.

"If you tell me where I found the number, I think a fairly involved conversation is in order."

"Okay," she nodded in agreement. "You found it in a cell, and that cell belonged to Perseus Grant."

He dragged his fingers through his hair and blew a sigh, eyebrows raised.

"You're obviously involved in this somehow. What do you need me to tell you?"

"Well, you're at the prison, and you're there because forty-one inmates have died in the last twelve months. What have you found out?"

"Nothing so far, and I mean nothing. If you look at each individual death, each case, there's nothing abnormal going on. These men are dying of natural causes. Textbook examples. But if you step back and realize forty-two men in that small, specific area of the prison have died of natural causes in one year, you have to wonder."

Destiny narrowed her eyes, contemplating.

"Obviously someone's wondering, since they have you over there. You're FBI, after all. Do you know how widespread this is? Is the same thing happening anywhere else?"

"No. So far it's unique to San Quentin Death Row."

"Something like this, everyone first guess—the government's got to be involved. No one could pull something like this off if it wasn't the federal government or someone working with the cooperation of the federal government."

Martinez sighed to himself and shook his head.

"Are you serious? You think you can rule out the *state* government? Someone or some entity here in California? Come on, it would be a lot easier to pull this off if you were taking your orders from Sacramento rather than Washington."

He glanced over at Kiyomi, who seemed to be taking notes, and whispered to Destiny.

"She's *so* hot!"

When Kiyomi looked up, Martinez grew embarrassed and continued.

"Besides that, the federal government doesn't have anyone within the state's prison system who could pull it off," he said. "We're non-existent in there. If whoever's behind this requires someone to, let's say, inject these inmates with something or introduce some experimental drug or agent, we don't have resources on the inside."

He paused to make sure Destiny understood the intimation.

"With the state it's another matter. State's got the CCPOA, the Department of Corrections, the Prisons Board and all kinds of other personnel inside there. Whoever it is could easily be working with or through the state Department of Health, which actually makes sense. Somewhere in all this, the state's got to be involved."

She nodded.

"So you think it's someone working with or through the state?"

"Or it *is* the state. The death penalty has already cost the state four billion dollars. If these prisoners are dying, the State is definitely going to save money—fewer inmates and guards to pay for, not to mention the cost of killing these guys. What's the cost now to kill one, almost three hundred million each, in legal fees and death row security costs?"

Kiyomi looked up, breaking in.

"It's actually *over* three hundred million now. And with all the tougher laws, the number of death row inmates is growing by at least twenty a year, while the state's executing less than one a year. Seven hundred death row inmates and growing," she shrugged. "Simple math—the state can't keep up. Something's got to give. Right now, the death penalty system in this state is on the verge of collapsing. California has *been* out of money!"

The office was silent for a moment as all three considered the implication of Kiyomi's last statement. Finally, Destiny began.

"So you think?" She was overwhelmed. "God, this really could be that big!"

"No shit," Martinez mumbled to himself. "I'm watching *my* back. Okay, I shared." He cleared his throat. Now it's your turn. How did you know I found your number in Perseus Grant's cell?"

"You sure you want to know?"

"Of course I'm sure."

She looked toward Kiyomi, who shrugged, contemplated for a moment and nodded. Destiny tightened her lips, building resolve, and answered.

"Well, I knew where you found the number because Perseus Grant *called* me two nights before he died. In the middle of the night."

"He *called* you?" Martinez asked, astonished.

"Yes, and he said someone was killing the inmates. He wanted me to help. And he was going to tell me something, but we got disconnected."

Martinez seemed worried.

"And then he died two days later? But if he called you, then someone inside, a guard or maybe someone in administration must have provided him with the phone. That means someone else knows about this. Grant wasn't acting alone. Is that it?"

Destiny looked away.

"No."

She drew a deep breath.

"Six days later, I got another call in the middle of the night. It was a male with a deep voice, and he asked me what Grant had told me. I hesitated at first, but I told him Grant was raving on about someone killing the inmates."

"And what did he say after you told him that?"

"He thanked me and said if I didn't hear from him again, it would be because he had resolved the matter, and he suggested he and I might both be in danger."

Kiyomi put the folder in her hands down, turning toward Martinez.

"The caller told Destiny that anyone she told about Grant and his phone call would also be in danger, so welcome to the club."

Martinez laughed.

"Are you kidding me? From the first time I went into that prison and started asking questions, I could feel the imprint of a target on my back."

Chapter 4

They hadn't spoken to each other for years. Bryan Osaka and James Cassie were best friends at one time. They worked together as inspectors for the San Francisco police, but they ended up on separate sides of an internal power struggle at the department. Bryan closely aligned himself with Commander Dennis Webber and a coup to weaken and supplant the power structure of long-time Chief Bill McGuire, while Cassie and most of the officers supported their appointed city boss.

In the battle, Webber and friends were routed and the commander was ruined. After being fired, he was forced to defend himself against criminal charges involving planting evidence, coercion and improper conduct with a prostitute. With Webber gone, his most visible supporters were left exposed and unprotected as McGuire conducted a purge of the department. Bryan became a primary target.

In order to prove his loyalty to the chief, Cassie was compelled to provide the department with the ammunition required to destroy his friend. He even testified against Bryan during the Internal Affairs hearing that led to Bryan's forced resignation. It was never personal. At the San Francisco Police Department, politics always trumped the personal.

Disheartened by the acrimony and ruthlessness, Cassie left the department and signed on with the state as a prison guard. He became a guard during the CCPOA's transition from a disregarded, innocuous labor union to a supreme power in California politics. Cassie, a natural political operator, moved from the guard position to a leadership role within a few years. And when the union became auto-percipient, when it became clear the union needed an intrepid, forward thinker to help take the CCPOA into the twenty-first century and beyond, James Cassie was one of the guards' overwhelming choices.

Over the years, Cassie reached out to Bryan. He felt terrible about what he had done. After the Internal Affairs hearing, he sent a long letter of apology that Bryan never answered. His daughters missed Bryan, his wife missed Bryan, but most of all, he missed the old friend he wronged. So when Bryan called and said he wanted to meet for dinner, Cassie and his family were filled with guarded excitement at the prospect of reconciliation.

The two men met at one of their old haunts in North Beach. It had been over twenty years since they had visited the place together. The bar had been modernized, but the layout remained unchanged, and the place still smelled of Italian spices, crab boil and steamed mussels. Seated at their usual corner table, each sipped a dark beer from a pilsner, avoiding eye contact.

Bryan glanced sidelong at Cassie, amazed at how much the man had aged in twenty years.

"How's Marybeth?"

Cassie smiled.

"She's fine. Marybeth and the girls are fine. Girls are grown. I've got grandkids."

He turned toward Bryan.

"Hey look, let's just get this out of the way. I'm sorry—"

Bryan raised a halting gesture.

"The past. It's in the past. It is what it is."

"I was forced to do it. I resigned right after that."

"I know. And it seems you haven't done too bad for yourself. Executive Vice president of the CCPOA? Pretty impressive!"

"Always been a team player kind of a guy. Finally found a team I could believe in. Great place to be. Know what I mean?"

He motioned toward Bryan.

"And I read that you're some super high-priced, super-secret investigator. Thousand dollars an hour, they tell me! Only the big corporations and billionaires can afford you!"

"Oh, I do my share of *pro bono* work."

Cassie leaned in.

"And is that why you called me after twenty long years? To offer your elite services, *pro bono*?"

Bryan leaned back.

"Well, I heard you were looking to put together a crack team to investigate a little problem over at San Quentin. I thought I might help."

Cassie laughed.

"Let me get this straight. You want to *help* me? For free? After twenty years of not even acknowledging me?"

"Yes."

"And you don't see where I might be a little skeptical? I mean, what's your angle, Osaka? Are you working for someone who needs to get you in there? Do you know who's behind these killings, if they are killings?"

Bryan sipped from the glass and shrugged.

"For the moment, I know less than you know, but I'm certain I could be of service to you."

"So tell me who you're working for. Tell me that and we can do this, together, like old times."

Cassie had extended his hand, which Bryan grasped firmly.

"I'm not working for anyone. This is personal. I can't tell you my angle, so you'll just have to trust me."

Bryan raised his eyebrows.

"Like I trusted *you?* You owe me one, Cassie."

Cassie took a deep breath and sighed.

"I suppose I do, and I'd like to think I know you well enough to know that when the smoke clears, you'll end up on the right side of this thing. Right?"

"You could bet your life on it."

Cassie paused, studying his old friend's face for reassurance.

"If it's all the same to you, Osaka, old buddy, I sure as hell hope I won't *have* to."

Kiyomi managed to get inside the prison on her press credentials, but as soon as she started asking questions about the recent mortality rate on Death Row, the warden took notice and had guards escort her to his office. There, he asked Kiyomi if the editor at the *Chronicle* sent her in to do the story or if she was acting independently. Kiyomi suggested the paper had sent her, but after further questioning, she admitted she was there on her own.

After excusing the guards standing by, Warden McGinnis closed the door and encouraged Kiyomi to sit.

"I don't know what you think you know, Ms. Yamakita, and I don't know what Nancy Drew fantasy you're trying to indulge as a part-time mom slash middle-aged reporter, but you won't be doing it here."

Kiyomi took a breath, wishing she had her notepad or voice recorder.

"It's your prison, so that's your call. But there *is* a story here, and while you can keep me from investigating your prison from the inside, you can't keep me from pursuing the story from other angles. I'll write this story, one way or another, with or without your help, Warden McGinnis."

He smiled as he poured himself a glass of water from a pitcher on the table.

"Oh, I'm certain you will, and I never said I had a problem with you *writing* the story. I just don't want you coming in here, asking provocative questions, making wild suggestions and stirring things up. You get me? I have a prison to run."

"I understand. But off the record: aren't you at least a little curious about why forty-two of your inmates have died, and all in such a confined area of the prison?"

McGinnis sat back.

"Of course I am," he answered, looking away. "But suffice it to say, I was dealing with 'this problem' literally twelve months before it came to your attention. I've had an investigative team look into it, the state's had its Office of the Inspector General's team in here and even the feds came in. No one's found a problem."

"Except the fact forty-two men have died in the last twelve months. Do you really think there isn't something going on in here?"

"Off the record? There may have *been* something going on, but I think it's pretty much over. If you've done your homework, which I encourage you to do if you haven't done it already, most of the deaths occurred between months two and ten of the last twelve months, at a rate of almost one a week."

He rested his hip on the desk, crossing his arms.

"But in the few weeks leading up to the Perseus Grant heart attack, whatever might have been happening had basically stopped. Doctors said Grant legitimately had heart disease, probably for years. Ticking time bomb. No mystery there. Whatever it was, if it *was* anything, it's over."

"And the man who died after Grant? What was his name, Aaron Popovich?"

"Yes, of organ failure. Meth addict all his life. Ruined his heart and lungs. And he smoked on top of that."

He sighed, rising and returning to his seat.

"Come on, not every prison death is a damn mystery or conspiracy! It's not like these guys are being poisoned or shot in the head. You gotta understand that a lot of the guys who go on Death Row have been exhibiting risky behaviors and lifestyles for years. Most of the time what kills them is something they literally brought on themselves, over time."

"It's very convenient to rationalize something like that, especially for a man in your position."

The warden folded his hands, steepling his index fingers.

"When you're a man in my position, Ms. Yamakita, you learn there are things bigger than you are, things way beyond your scope, things you have no control over, no matter what you do. And when you realize you're in a situation like that, you accept it. You don't question it. Otherwise, you find yourself in, as they say, *a whole heap of trouble.*"

Kiyomi had never been a person to back down from a fight or to wither at the prospect of danger. Despite her diminutive stature, 5'4" in high heels and 110 pounds on bloated days, she had bulldog determination and a lifetime of experience of kicking off those shoes, raising her fists, and scrapping it out.

Her father, Hank, like his father, refused to move from the family home in San Francisco's Western Addition on Divisadero between Geary Boulevard and Fulton Street. And while, in 1945, many Japanese families returned from internment camps to their neighborhoods to find them overrun by the *kokujin*, or Negroes, Hank and his father were able to retain their home by paying the mortgage through a proxy, a young Negro, who was Hank's friend.

Many Japanese felt the blacks had ruined their neighborhood and found other areas to live, while others, like Hank, were comfortable living among them. Hank was fascinated with the culture. He liked the fried catfish, the black-eye peas, the chitlins, the sweet potato pies, the ham hocks and collard greens, the backyard barbecues, the gambling, the drinking and the *big butt black girls*. He liked it all.

The junior high school his daughter, Kiyomi, attended was mostly black. Small for her age, she picked fights with the biggest girls at the school to prove her toughness. In the beginning, Hank got a phone call every week from the principal, telling him his daughter was initiating violence on campus, again.

The last fight Kiyomi got into during seventh grade was the worst. There she was, a short, little Japanese girl starting a fight with a stuck-up and uppity black girl who nobody liked. The mousy girl seemed like a pushover, but under her sweater, she was pretty muscular. So when she fired back with a hard right to Kiyomi's jaw, Kiyomi gained an instant respect for Destiny Mitchell.

Over time, the two became best friends. During summers, Kiyomi sometimes spent weeks at a time over at the Mitchell's, while Destiny was at the Yamakita's so often that she had a toothbrush, a set of ivory chopsticks and a cot over there. During the summer of the girls' sophomore year, they traveled to Gifu, Japan, and stayed with Kiyomi's grandmother, *Obasan*, for three months.

It had been years since Kiyomi had gotten into a physical altercation, but she remained quick to pick fights on matters of principle and respect. She had mellowed over the years, especially after having Natsumi, her daughter. However, when she sensed that someone, through action or inaction, might represent a threat or danger to someone she loved, she was unrelenting.

She studied Warden McGinnis as he sat there, her eyes filled with equal parts contempt and suspicion.

"You have an office here full of books, Warden, so I imagine you read?"

The warden nodded as she continued.

"And you've read Burke?"

"Enough of Burke to know Burke never actually wrote or spoke the line you're probably going to quote to me."

"All that is necessary for the triumph of evil is that good men do nothing."

McGinnis nodded.

"Ah, that's the one. Burke never said it."

"That's not the point. You know what I'm saying."

"I do. But your statement presupposes I'm a good man. You've no doubt read Shaw? In this place, that might be presupposing too much."

Kiyomi stood.

"Perhaps. Maybe you're *not* a good man, Warden. But let me make you this promise."

Her anger and resolve were evident in her breathing.

"Maybe you do feel you are as much a victim of this place as your prisoners. Maybe prisons really *do* claim the souls of inmates, guards and people like you, but there's something very wrong going on in here. And now, whatever that is has put someone I care about in jeopardy."

"How? Who is this someone?"

"I won't play games with you. Either you know about her, or you don't."

She approached, not intimidated by the considerable height difference.

"It's your prison. You can physically bar me from this place if that's what you want to do. I'm not here trying to reform the prison system. I'm trying to protect my friend, and I am a very resourceful woman. If anything happens to her, whether you're directly involved or not, I swear to you, Warden McGinnis—if anything happens to her, I will cut off your shriveled up balls and fish with them in the Bay."

Chapter 5

The startling sound of a single gunshot rang in the nighttime darkness of the cell block, loud and unmistakable. Shouting, murmuring and discussion among the inmates began immediately, as the men, on their feet and calling from the cells, tried to determine the location of the sound that still seemed to echo throughout the enclosure. Within a half minute, the alarm rang, and the lights began to come up, but guards outside were cautious, reluctant to enter the block.

By the time distinct features in the cell block became visible, the prisoners believed they had identified the source of the gunshot and pointed in the direction of a body slumped on the floor, in front of a cell. Some suggested it was a guard.

When a phalanx of correctional officers, rifles drawn, slammed open the door and rushed into the room, they shouted orders for all prisoners to retreat to the rear portions of their cells and threatened to shoot anyone who did not comply. Their movements were nervous, edgy, as they approached the body in uniform, obviously one of their own.

The man's eyes were still open, though no flicker of life stirred within them. Gore trailed from his mouth and right nostril. An area on the left side of his skull had been blown open, spraying bits of bone and brain over his brown hair, on the floor and along the bars behind him. His right hand, fingers still twitching, held his Ruger pistol.

"What the fuck? It's Sutter!"

The leader knelt, placing his fingers on the side of the man's throat, checking for a pulse.

"He's gone. Call it in."

The guards remained until the photographer finished his work and the prison paramedics carried the body away on a gurney. By this time, one of the warden's representatives arrived. Taking a place at the center of the enclosure, he shouted in a thunderous tone, calling to the inmates.

"This is a prison matter that, beginning now, is under investigation. No one talks! Hear? I shouldn't have to tell you that, but I mean to be clear. There will be absolutely no discussion, not among yourselves, not with the guards and *especially* not with those from the outside."

He eyed the guards, speaking in an undertone.

"The same goes for you."

He continued, shouting to the prisoners again.

"When our investigation is complete, we will inform you about what has happened, and we will let you know then what you will be able to talk about. Any prisoner who, by discussing this matter, interferes with our investigation, will be dealt with accordingly. So I'll say it one more time for the slow and ignorant. No one talks. No discussion. As far as you're concerned, nothing happened here tonight."

The cold and flu medicine Agent Jake Martinez had taken hours before made his hands unsteady and shaky. He sat back in a huge recliner in the living room, computer in his lap, a box of medicated tissue to the left on a table. It was a rare summer cold, a *rhinovirus* of some kind, he thought.

On the screen, the search engine he used featured a dog, eager to fetch the information he typed in the search bar, "*viral vector murder heart organ failure.*" He scanned the page of articles that came up. Nothing really made sense. Scrolling down the page, he came to an item by the Center for Disease Control that caught his attention, "*Epiornitic of West Nile virus in North America: a murder of crows.*" More interesting to Martinez was the onscreen reference to a footnoted source, "Center for Vector-borne Diseases."

His next search took him to a University of California Davis site, whose researchers study "arthropod vectors and the pathogens transmitted by vectors causing diseases of humans and animals worldwide." It seemed the site was put up by the UC Davis School of Vet Med and mainly focused on disease in birds and large animals. He could not conceive of a connection between vector-borne diseases in this context related to the deaths at the prison.

According to Wikipedia, viral vectors were *a tool commonly used by molecular biologists to deliver genetic material into cells. This process can be performed inside a living organism (in vivo) or in cell culture (in vitro). Viruses have evolved specialized molecular mechanisms to efficiently transport their genomes inside the cells they infect.* Martinez re-read the definition three times before copying it and pasting it in his research file. It still did not make sense.

Further down the page, there was a detailed discussion of viral vector applications relating to molecular genetics and xenotransplantation in very technical language. Becoming drowsy, Martinez reached for the box on a shelf of his computer desk, reading the side listing active ingredients. One of those long "dextromethorph" words must have been the culprit. He felt dizzy. The room seemed to be rotating slowly around him.

Saving his work, Martinez turned off the computer, rose from his chair and fell back onto the cool leather couch. He reached for the remote, turned on the television and brought up the guide, but he fell asleep even before he could make a selection.

It had been a long day for Jake Martinez. He arrived at the prison a little after six a.m. and had spent the majority of the day fighting red tape to get access to the cell that once belonged to Perseus Grant. It seemed there had been an incident in the area in front of the cell, but the entire cell block had been sequestered, inaccessible to Jake and other investigators for most the day.

At around five p.m., Jake heard a rumor that a prison guard committed suicide in front of the cell of Perseus Grant. According to bits and pieces Jake was hearing, the guard and Grant spent time privately discussing the prison deaths in the weeks prior to Grant himself dying from a heart attack. Some of the information had come in the form of a note from an unidentified inmate, so it could not be verified.

However, at six p.m., when Martinez was finally allowed access to the cell, a guard stationed at the entrance watched his every move. Martinez had been trying to regain access for almost a week, but he had been put off over and again so that six days had passed. Once inside the cell, he checked the vents and the paint to disguise the true purpose of his visit.

Martinez was convinced Perseus Grant was working with a guard or someone else inside the prison to discover who was behind the killings and to determine how whoever it was could murder forty-two inmates without raising suspicion or leaving clues.

Before incarceration, Grant was an incorrigible, cold-blooded killer without a conscience, but according to a clandestine interview with one of the guards, Grant had found religion on Death Row. Away from the temptation of prey, he had undergone a transformation. The guard said Grant often described the actual moment he had been "slapped down" by the very hand of God while taking a shower. He saw a bright light when he awoke, and then he felt arms and hands helping him to his feet, and these arms and hands belonged to Jesus Christ himself.

For more than a dozen years, Grant had told the story of how Jesus personally called him to the ministry and had directed that ministry. In his passion, the reformed murderer and rapist sometimes came across as fanatical, if not delusional, especially in the weeks before he died.

Three weeks earlier, Perseus Grant ranted to the other inmates about a group of evil, satanic men who had set out to kill half the inmates on Death Row at San Quentin. He said these men had corrupted "the power of God," to accomplish their immoral aims. Only after his death did many in the block begin to seriously consider his claims.

The suicide in front of Grant's cell served to further raise the suspicions of inmates and guards who struggled to convince themselves the rash of deaths in the block were coincidental and unrelated. Many were nervous, but few were willing to speak on the matter.

Inside Grant's cell, Martinez glanced sidelong at the guard as he lifted the lumpy mattress. To his surprise, the scrawled numbers and words were gone! The wall had be ground down so that the place, just under the mattress line, was smooth, wiped clean. It was as if the numbers and words had never been there!

Now more than ever, Martinez believed Perseus Grant was onto something. Grant had left two clues—one that led to Destiny Mitchell and the other to a tool used by molecular biologists. The cause of Grant's death was a heart attack, but perhaps some agency or group had found a way to cause that heart attack, and heart attacks or multiple organ failure in forty-one other inmates. Whatever methods were used, perhaps they were beyond contemporary medical science, something cutting edge. *Viral Vector*—the words were there before, but now they were gone.

Destiny Mitchell was another matter. Her phone number had been there as well. Whoever had the seven numbers erased from the wall, if they had half a brain, they knew who she was. Whatever person or group this was, he or they had already committed forty-two murders, so Martinez assumed that if Destiny's life might have been merely at risk before, it was definitely in danger now. She had to be warned.

"Warden McGinnis, I'd like you to meet an old friend of mine. This is Bryan Osaka. Bryan—Warden Paul McGinnis."

James Cassie stepped back as the two men shook hands. McGinnis smiled, his mien formal, professional, as he motioned for Bryan to sit. Cassie sat before he began.

"Osaka and I worked together as inspectors with the San Francisco police. He's a private dick now down in San Diego, best on the West Coast."

McGinnis examined Osaka and smiled.

"I'll have to take your word for that. But if he's on this crack team of yours and you're paying him, who am I to argue? Water?"

Guests having refused, he poured a glass for himself, glancing over at Cassie.

"I hear you've been here all day. Any news?"

"I lost a guard today, a good man. Robert Sutter."

"*We* lost a guard. That's too bad. And I'm not trying to sound insensitive, but if he felt the need to commit suicide, I just wish he had done it at home. We don't need the bad press. Not now."

Cassie clenched his jaw, resentful.

"Sutter was a guard for sixteen years, and he had a family. Not that you would care."

He took a breath to calm himself.

"The one thing you're right about? He could have done it at home, so we have to assume he did it here for a reason."

McGinnis sighed.

"And that reason just might be that he didn't want his wife and kids to wake up to find him with his head blown apart. Let's not assume too much here, Mr. Cassie."

"He committed suicide directly in front of Perseus Grant's cell."

"Because it was *empty*. All the other cells had inmates in them. He was at least conscientious enough not to let a crazy get his gun after he was gone. Like you said, he was a good guard."

Cassie looked over at Osaka and then back to the warden, his anger mounting.

"Get your head outa your ass, Mac, or out of that hole in the sand! You can't keep playing this off. It's coming right at you, at all of us."

McGinnis was offended by the coarse language and Cassie's attitude. His face turned red, and the water jiggled in the glass as he tried to steady his hand.

"I've had three groups of investigators in here over the past year, Mr. Cassie. They've turned over every stone, examined every brick and peeked up every asshole in the joint. They found nothing. What makes you think you and your dick can come in here in one day and find something they all missed?"

Cassie ignored the emotion.

"Mac, word's out there and you know it. Grant and Sutter had their heads together on something. They were onto whatever's going on. You think people aren't talking? The inmates *and* the guards! To people, to each other! And from what I'm hearing, Grant and Sutter weren't the only ones. Others know what's going on. You're not giving them enough credit for brains."

McGinnis studied Cassie's face and shrugged.

"You're wrong. I *know* what my prisoners are capable of. They know how hard it is to execute a con in California. They want to wreak havoc on the system. So if they get some controversy started up here, some conspiracy theory going on, the state will never be able to execute another killer, no matter what kind of sick son-of-a-bitch he is. And it'll spread to other states."

"I don't get it," Cassie sighed. "Does all this stuff come from a script they've given you? This is not about inmates killing inmates to save themselves. Come on! If we're going to talk, let's talk. No more bullshit."

"What do you want to talk about?"

"Forty-two of your inmates dead? And now a dead guard! They're figuring this out. And that means you're going to lose more inmates and I'm going to lose more guards. If you know anything about who's behind this, you have to talk to me."

McGinnis sipped from the glass.

"And all this because one of your troubled guards committed suicide? You can call me cynical, but you have to understand—I run a prison. These guys are always running one game or another, the prisoners *and* the guards. If I knew something, I'd tell you. But I think you're making too much of this. You're buying into whatever they're trying to sell."

He put the water down and pushed his glasses up the bridge of his nose.

"Come on, Cassie, I thought you were smarter than that."

Bryan, who had struggled to remain silent, finally broke in.

"Sutter, the guard—he shot himself in his right temple with the gun in his right hand."

McGinnis chuckled, nervous.

"Okay?"

"He was left-handed. I talked to the supervisor over at the range he always went for shooting practice. He never shot with his right hand."

"And that means?"

Bryan thought the explanation was unnecessary, but he continued.

"Sutter was awkward right-handed—clumsy according to the guy at the range. It must have been unnatural for him to use his right. This was a conscious action. He shot himself with the gun in his right hand to send a message to someone."

"What message? To who?"

"Don't know yet. Maybe to us?"

McGinnis thought for a moment, crossing his arms.

"Sounds a little far-fetched, but I admit it's possible."

Resigning, he looked toward Cassie.

"Before you start thinking I know more about this than I do, let me tell you, I simply don't."

He lowered the volume of his voice.

"Do you think this is the first time I've suspected there was something unusual going on at this prison, something coming at me from the outside?"

Backing, he wagged his head.

"No. Every few years, there's always some strange happening here. This is, after all, the only place in California where the state has a legal right to kill, and an obligation to the people. This is the killing place, and the criminals on Death Row not only deserve to die, but the people are counting on the state to execute them. And the State's broke. Forty-two death row inmates dying in one year represents a significant savings for the state."

Cassie narrowed his eyes.

"So you think the state's behind this?"

"Who knows? For my own survival, I can't question what I've seen and heard. It would be unwise for me to involve myself. Of course, you understand that. I'm here to *watch* the pot, not to stir it."

Cassie rolled his eyes in disgust and sighed.

"But you *will* let us investigate this? You won't get in our way? Won't threaten inmates with sanctions for talking to us?"

"That'll be up to the inmates. If you can get them to talk to you, have at it, but I'd be careful. You guys have no idea what you're dealing with."

"And you do?"

McGinnis stood.

"I know better than standing out in the open picking a fight with an enemy I can't see. You have to know it's a fight you can't win."

He checked his watch.

"I'll cooperate with your investigation. Where would you like to start?"

Bryan spoke up.

"Guard who killed himself today, Sutter—I'd like to see an autopsy."

McGinnis and Cassie exchanged confused looks. The warden laughed.

"He said you're the best in the West? And you're confused about what killed Sergeant Sutter?"

Bryan rose, staring straight ahead.

"I'm way beyond that. I'm looking for proof that Sutter committed suicide not because he wanted to die, but because he knew he was already dead."

Chapter 6

Jett Turner sat alone on one side of the table in the board room, while five men and a woman peered at him from the other side, all wearing masks. The Justice asked the questions.

"Mr. Turner, according to Mr. X here, the testing phase at the prison was completed and suspended two months ago. However, from intelligence we're getting, I understand there are lingering and perhaps very troubling problems still existing over there."

Jett was always more ballsy when dealing with men of power.

"That's right. A fuckin guard gave a cell phone to a fuckin inmate, and he called outside the fuckin prison. We had no control over that. They're both dead now. Dead as fuck."

Uncomfortable with the coarse language, the Justice shook his head.

"That's fine, but given the amount of planning and expense we've invested in this undertaking, I think I can speak for Mr. X and everyone else in this room in saying we are very disappointed with that result."

"Well, then be disappointed with that fuckin result, but that has nothing to do with me. That problem came from *inside* the prison. Whoever you had in there handling containment—they didn't get to Grant soon enough. Besides that, there are other guards in there like Sutter who know little things, and there's no way of containing them, unless you start killing them, and that's fuckin a whole new ball game."

Justice Greene smiled, nodding.

"Very well, containment wasn't accomplished inside the prison, so now we have problems *outside* the prison, and those, Mr. Turner, *are* your problems. Are you aware of the fact that a reporter, a Kiyomi Yamakita with the *Chronicle*, recently visited the prison, asking questions about the unfortunate string of deaths over there?"

His aside was directed toward others at the table.

"This reporter is a close friend of Destiny Mitchell, the woman whom inmate Grant called from the prison. Some of you might recognize her name."

Jett scoffed.

"With all due respect, Justice, I was the *source* of that intelligence."

The Justice assented.

"Well, then perhaps you will let us know how you intend to resolve the obvious liabilities lingering in California?"

"All the guards who know anything are taken care of. At least that's what your fuckin doctors who were inside are sayin. Said that would happen over the next twenty days. Me, I'll up the intimidation factor so no guards talk over the next few weeks."

"And the reporter?"

"Intimidation and debriefing. It's what I do. I've already got a plan, both for the reporter and for Destiny Mitchell. They'll never come close to causing a problem. But I have to tell you, if my plan doesn't work, if they get around me and you think they need to be put down for good, you'll have to find someone else for that job. Cuz that's not my fuckin tea."

"Just to be clear, these are things I've only heard. I don't have any proof."

Guard Joseph Villaflor fidgeted with the pen in his damp fingers, his nervous eyes staring down at Kiyomi's voice recorder.

"I realize that, Joseph. I just appreciate you coming forward to speak with me. I know how difficult this must have been."

They agreed to meet in a small restaurant near Manilatown Center on Kearny. Joseph's mother lived in a nearby apartment in the International Hotel, so to him, the environment felt safe, familiar. The reporter guaranteed anonymity and had agreed to pay him seven hundred fifty dollars for fifteen minutes of his time.

He never wore his guard uniform outside the prison and never told friends and family where he worked. It was just something he never talked about. At five feet eight inches, he was tall for the neighborhood, and he was in good shape, his form Americanized. His hair was dark, though thinning and receding. He wore khaki shorts, sandals, a white pullover shirt and dark sunglasses atop his head.

Kiyomi, sitting across the table, sipped her chrysanthemum tea.

"What have you heard?"

He turned his head, glancing around to make certain no one was listening.

"There was a doctor, in the infirmary. I heard he was somehow involved in this."

"Do you have his name?"

"No. He's gone now. He disappeared, but I think I could get his name."

Kiyomi looked up from her notes.

"Great, if you can. Did you hear *how* he was involved?"

Joseph leaned forward.

"These are all rumors, of course, but I heard they were doin some kinda government experiment, givin diseases to inmates who came in there."

She nodded, urging him as he continued.

"That's what the cons figured out. They're sayin all of them that died in this past year had been to the infirmary a month or two before. Can't get any of them to go near there now. Rather take their chances, you know, without the government's help."

"Do you think the government's behind it?"

"I think there's somethin up over there. And when that doctor disappeared two months ago, the dyin stopped—at least till they got Grant. He was onto them. They had to shut him up."

She finished scribbling something down before continuing.

"Did you ever talk to Grant?"

"Months ago, I used to talk to him. He was a smart dude. Some of the older guys say he was part of a government brain experiment in the sixties. Anyway, over the last year, Grant started sayin things that, if they were true, were pretty scary. So I figured if the government really *was* in there killin people and he was *talkin* about it, they'd be wantin to shut him up. I had to distance myself. I didn't want anyone wonderin about me—you know, about what *I* might know."

"And the guard who just committed suicide over there? Sutter? Did *he* talk to Grant?"

Joseph sat back and sighed, nodding.

"Yeah, they talked, both Christians. Sutter was the first guard to start believin Grant's claims. Sometimes he would go up to

Grant's cell, and they'd stand there talking for twenty minutes at a time, whisperin. Sutter even got some of the other guards to start believin Grant. I mean, we all started getting worried over there."

"Why's that?"

He sighed.

"Because if they're givin some kinda experimental disease to the inmates, and we're over there with them, then it's only a matter of time before *we* start dyin? And who can trust the government? If they're doin something to the prisoners over there, they're doin it to us too. They could give a damn about us."

He shook his head.

"I put in for a transfer out of there, but they won't move me. A lotta the guards are tryin to get out of there."

He picked up the menu and examined it, though cursorily. He already knew what he wanted. Kiyomi however, wasn't finished.

"Has anyone made a suggestion about *why* the government would want to test giving diseases to the inmates?"

"Well, they're on Death Row. Cheaper to give em diseases and kill em than takin em through the legal process. Look at it that way, and California's killed more people on Death Row this year than any other state."

Kiyomi considered his words for a moment and sat back.

"Well, do you think the killing's stopped? Do you think it's over?"

"Not by a long shot. There are a lot of folks over there who know things, secret shit, inmates *and* guards. If Grant and Sutter dyin means the government is tryin to clean up things, if it means they wanna leave no clues behind, then there's gonna be a hellava lot more dyin over there before it's all done."

He checked his watch and flagged the food server.

"Time's up. I'm hungry. I'm ready to order."

Bryan had been to Menlo Park on more than a few occasions. Years before, he had a friend who lived in Stanford Hills, so he knew the neighborhood well. In fact, this friend had lived one block over. As he paced up the walkway, he noticed the well-manicured lawn and a recently detailed, silver Lexus in the driveway. The front door seemed freshly painted. Leaning in, he could hear the faint sound of a television on the other side. Identification in hand, he rang the bell.

"Mrs. Sutter, thank you for taking the time to meet with me. I'm Bryan Osaka. I spoke with you earlier?"

Her eyes were swollen from crying.

"Yes. Come on in."

At a table in the dining room, she held a framed 8x10 color portrait of her husband, forcing a weak smile.

"You didn't say on the phone. But did you know Bob?"

"No."

"He was a good man. He was just in a bad place."

Bryan nodded, reverent.

"I'm very sorry for your loss, Mrs. Sutter."

He paused, uncomfortable.

"As I was telling you on the phone, I have reasons to believe that your husband's death wasn't a matter of a simple suicide. There was something else going on."

"Please explain," she insisted, seeming startled.

"When he shot himself with the gun in his right hand, I think he was trying to send a message."

"What message?"

"I don't know yet," Bryan shrugged, "but I think he was involved in investigating some unusual occurrences at the prison."

She stopped crying.

"Do you work for the prison?"

"No."

"The government?"

"No."

She blotted her eyes and looked away.

"So how are *you* involved in this?"

"I'm a private detective working on an independent investigative team."

Her voice began to take on an irritated edge.

"Who are you working for?"

"The guards, CCPOA."

She sighed.

"What difference does it make? You're *all* in on it."

Eyebrows raised, he responded.

"What do you think we're all *in* on, Mrs. Sutter? Please tell me."

She stood, turning away.

"It doesn't matter to me anymore. Bob's dead. It, it was a mistake to let you come. I'm sorry, but I would like you to leave now."

Bryan stood, unwavering.

"I believe your husband was a good man, a man who was trying to do the right thing. If he was trying to send a message, then perhaps you could help us figure it out. At least then he won't have died in vain."

She glanced back, allowing him to continue.

"I'm on your side. I'm on Bob's side. He obviously talked to you. He was investigating a series of deaths in the prison. He told you that, right?"

She nodded, conceding.

"Yes, beyond his duties as a guard, he believed he had more important duties as a moral human being, and a Christian."

Her eyes swelled with tears.

"That's what doesn't make sense."

"What's that?"

"He was a Christian. He *wouldn't* have committed suicide. That's a sin against God. I know he wouldn't have done it on his own. Someone must have *made* him do it."

Bryan took a step into her field of vision.

"Mrs. Sutter, you have no reason to trust me, but I think you're right. I believe he was forced to shoot himself, and that's what I'm trying to figure out here, why he did it."

She turned toward the detective, her speech a little slurred and slow, jiggling martini glass in her hand.

"Just call me Bev. You're right. I don't trust you, but I trust you slightly more than I trust the rest of them. You obviously know about all the deaths over there this past year?"

"I do. I just don't know how they're pulling it off. So far, no one's been able to find anything unusual about any individual death. The sheer number and the high incidence of heart disease is another matter. We all know there's something going on."

He paused, watching her finish the martini.

"Did your husband ever say anything to you about it?"

She looked up as she refilled the shaker.

"Osaka, is it? My husband was *killed* for what he knew. You obviously didn't know him then. He would never share anything with me that might put me in jeopardy. He said nothing specific about what he was doing."

"Of course. But as I understand, your husband was pretty smart. If he knew something, I imagine he left some clue as insurance either here or at the prison, something that would help us."

"Well if he did, I sure haven't seen it."

She stopped, dumbstruck.

"You know, just this morning, I got a call from some administrator at San Quentin. He said Bob had been using one of their laptops and wanted it back. I said I never saw it. He acted like he didn't believe me, but I insisted Bob never had a laptop."

She sipped from the fresh martini.

"And now I'm thinking he *did* have a laptop, or at least I think I saw him with one."

"Do you know where he kept it?"

"Haven't a clue. I'll look for it. What should I do if I find it?"

Bryan handed her a business card.

"I wouldn't tell anyone about it. If it's here, make sure it doesn't stay here. You wouldn't want anyone to come looking for it. Call me if you find it or if you think you know where it is."

She closed her eyes, nodding.

"I will. Now if you'll excuse me, Mr. Osaka, I really *am* tired. I'm wiped out. Can you please just leave so I can rest?"

He did not move.

"Call me Bryan. The reason I came over here, Bev, is to ask you to order an autopsy on your husband's body."

She became strangled as she sipped.

"For the love of God! Have you lost your mind?"

"The suicide makes no sense to either of us. He sacrificed himself to expose whatever's going on, and I have reasons to believe an autopsy will explain some of things we're not understanding here."

She crossed her arms, shivering a little.

"An autopsy?"

"Unless you find that laptop and there's something on it, he left us nothing else. An autopsy is the only way to get what he wanted us to know. I've got the medical examiner standing by. I'll even pay for it."

"I don't know. They'd cut him into pieces like a lab animal. I wouldn't be able to live with the thought of that."

Bryan bowed his head.

"I understand. I plan to be there. I'm looking for something very specific. I promise you I won't let anyone disrespect his remains. I'll be right there."

She took a big swig from the glass and stood for almost a minute without speaking.

"Okay. I'll do it because I'm too drunk to think any better about it. If you have the papers now, I'll sign them."

It required major adjustments in her daily routine, but she was getting used to the new arrangement. Bryan was back in the loft after three years of separation. That meant giving up closet space, having to wait for the bathroom, not being able to toss the bra and panties around after a long day of work and putting up with his snoring and other occasional body sounds in bed. But it also meant convenient sex, someone to share with at day's end and a reassuring sense of security.

Bryan was a detective, after all. He always carried a gun. With him in the loft, she didn't have to worry about some scary person coming in on her or late-night phone calls. He upgraded the security system and was working to find the identity of the man who had threatened her. In the balance she had to put up with his constant interrogation, his demands to know where she was going and when she was returning, his unsolicited suggestions and advice, and that illogical male desire to control her and the people close to her. Overall, she figured she was better off with him there.

Earlier in the day, when she received a call from FBI Agent Martinez requesting a meeting at nine that evening, she noted a sense of urgency in his voice. He wanted her to come to the field office on Golden Gate and he asked her if she would bring Kiyomi along, but he refused to tell her the subject of discussion. Curious, she watched the hours pass during the drawn-out day, hoping Martinez would share something new.

His desk was small and its surface disorganized. Nervous, he stood as the women came in, stacking and sorting piles of paper before getting a seat for Kiyomi from a nearby adjacent desk. Destiny hardly knew the man, but he seemed different than before. His eyes seemed puffy and watery. His voice was higher, his vocal cords stressed.

"Are you all right, Agent Martinez?"

He blew his nose, motioning for her to sit.

"I'm fine," he insisted. "I'm just fine. Dealing with this damn summer cold, though! Don't worry."

He held up antiseptic wipes.

"I try to keep my germs to myself."

His eyes smiled as he turned toward Kiyomi.

"It's very nice to see you again, Kiyomi."

Destiny glanced at Kiyomi, who seemed a bit embarrassed. Martinez was not subtle.

"I asked Destiny to bring you because I wanted to see you again."

It was at such times she wished she wore her wedding ring. She put a hand on her hip.

"Excuse me, Agent Martinez, or Jake, since you want to step up like that—do you really think you could *handle* me? I'm petite, but I would break you in two!"

"And I'd be two happy to let you!"

She laughed, sighing.

"We *are* here for a meeting, right?"

Martinez nodded as he sat.

"Yes, yes, we are! I called you here because I think we have reason for concern, and specifically, I wanted to put Destiny on notice."

Destiny held her breath, uncertain if she wanted him to go on. Kiyomi's response, however, was immediate.

"On notice about what?"

"Last time we met, I told you I found Destiny's phone number in Grant's cell? Well, when I went back in yesterday, it was gone. Someone else obviously saw it there and wiped it clean, with a grinder. I figure whoever did that or ordered that knows who you are."

Destiny nodded.

"Okay?"

"I think we can safely assume that if someone murdered Grant for what he knew, they might be coming after you, especially if they think Grant told you something."

She sat rigid in the chair, her face grim.

"He didn't tell me anything, but I'll have to expect they don't know that."

"If you say so. But it also happens that yesterday, when I went back, I found out a guard had committed suicide in the cell block."

Kiyomi shrugged, playing down her fears for her friend.

"That's not news. I already heard about that."

"I imagine you did," he said, "but did you hear he shot himself directly in front of Grant's cell? Maybe to make a point?"

"No, I didn't hear that," she answered, sitting back.

He looked toward Destiny.

"And there's something else."

"What?" she demanded.

"I wasn't going to tell you this because I'm in the process of investigating it. I understand from your background that you're a smart woman, scientifically speaking. Chemistry major, law school? So I'm thinking it's something you might know. Maybe you'll understand it."

Destiny's eyes narrowed to intense beams on his face.

"What is it?"

"When I originally went into Grant's cell, and I told you I found your phone number, I didn't tell you there was something else scratched on the wall."

"No you didn't. What else was there?"

He paused.

"Do the words 'Viral Vector' mean anything to you?"

Chapter 7

Dr. Singh began with the scalpel behind the corpse's left ear, below the wound, cutting downward deep into the flesh of the neck, across the chest and stopping just below the sternum. Then she repeated the process from the right ear. At the point the former cut joined the latter at the base of the sternum, she continued the Y-shape incision, deviating left of the navel, to the pubis.

Bryan stood on the other side of the table, his arms folded, detached, watching without expression. When he entered ten minutes earlier, the doctor was placing a rubber brick, or body block, under the corpse's back, causing the arms and neck to fall backward whilst stretching and pushing the chest upward.

He had watched many autopsies, but he had never grown accustomed to the initial waft of odor at the moment that the body cavity was opened. It came from the yellow liquid that was viscous, like popcorn butter. It was a sick, mortal smell, heavier than air, which reacted with the saliva in his mouth and threatened to drag his throat and lungs to the pit of his stomach. He swallowed the odor-tainted spit and fought an involuntary urge to heave. Closing his eyes, he focused, calming himself.

When he looked up again, Dr. Singh held a motorized Stryker saw above the chest cavity, cutting through the ribs on the lateral side of the chest cavity. Add the stench of burning flesh. Working deftly, she lifted the sternum and the ribs attached to it in one chest plate, exposing the organs beneath it.

With a scalpel, she opened the pericardial sac in order to examine the heart. Inserting a needle into the inferior vena cava, she removed two vials of blood for analysis. Then she cut through that vein, the pulmonary veins, the aorta, the pulmonary artery and the superior vena cava in order to remove the organ.

Looking up, she winked at Bryan, heart in hand.

"You all right? Whatever you do, don't puke in the cavity. Had it happen once."

He raised his right hand and nodded, his left hand on the paper mask, cupping his nose.

"I'm fine. I've done this a hundred times, so you'd think I'd be over it, but I'll never get used to that smell!"

She smiled, drawing a deep breath.

"Oh, the smell of *cadaverine* in the morning!"

Hands back at work, she cut the bronchus and the artery and vein at the hilum in order to remove the left lung, and then she repeated the procedure for the right lung.

"That's all you wanted to check, right? The heart, liver, kidneys and lungs? Anything else?"

"No, that'll be fine."

"You sure?"

He nodded, his face lacking color, as he headed toward the door.

"That's it. Call me when you get to the lab."

Three hours later, Bryan Osaka watched Dr. Medha Singh as she worked at the metal table, examining the heart.

"You asked me to speak in layman's terms? Okay, weight's fine, left ventricle seems a bit enlarged, but that's not uncommon for a man his age."

She returned the scalpel to the table.

"I could go on. I could spend hours dissecting this heart and the lungs, running any number of tests, but I really don't have to."

"Why? What do you mean?"

"I figured you were resourceful, being the high-priced detective you are. I didn't check because I thought you somehow had access. Would have saved us both the guessing."

"Access to what?"

"His recent *medical* records. It was strange, because they were buried, hidden, possibly deleted. This morning I had the hospital IT person run a special search on the computer mainframe using the name 'Robert Sutter.' She found one copy of previously unavailable records in an email attachment that you and everyone else apparently missed. She read it to me a few minutes ago, when you were meeting with *Dom Corleone* out there."

Bryan closed his eyes, trying to imagine what he could have missed.

"No. I *checked* his medical history. I went over his records. I didn't see anything."

"IT person—" Dr. Singh insisted, "she didn't send me a copy because she didn't want to get involved in something that might be illegal or dangerous. But she told me Robert Sutter had been seeing a heart specialist in Sacramento. Said the sergeant was a very sick man."

"Heart disease—that's what I wanted to confirm."

"CAD, coronary artery disease. He was at an advanced stage of atherosclerosis. Heart was clogged with fat and plaque. According to the records, he was going to need a quadruple bypass just for starts, but it probably wouldn't have saved him. Specialist said it was only a matter of time."

Bryan looked at the organ on the table.

"And you can document those facts in your examination of the heart?"

"An MRI will show the plaque and the fat. I'll be issuing a complete report when I'm done. Of course it can be documented."

She paused.

"But there's something else at work here, right Osaka? An autopsy on a *suicide* victim? Deleted medical records? Is there something I should be worried about?"

"I don't think you have anything to worry about for completing the autopsy. You're just doing your job."

"And you want me to examine the lungs, liver and kidneys?"

He nodded, notepad in his hand.

"Yes. I have a question. From your perspective, would you be able to tell if this coronary artery disease was induced?"

"Of course. People do it to themselves. Sometimes it's diet related, bad eating habits, but other things factor in: diabetes, smoking, high cholesterol, high blood pressure, genetics—gender makes a difference. Men are more susceptible."

Bryan thought for a moment, scribbling and flipping the page.

"Okay, but is it possible for a doctor or someone like you to do something that would *cause* coronary artery disease in a person? Is there a drug?"

"Not to my knowledge. I'm sure the specialist he was seeing did blood work. I can ask my IT person if there was anything unusual in the blood work records."

"Can you put me in contact with that person?"

She shook her head.

"Not a chance, and don't insult me by trying to bribe me. I make a good living doing what I do. I'll ask about what's in the record, and I'll do toxicology on the blood I collected. If I find anything unusual, I'll let you know."

He shrugged.

"Fair enough."

"You know," she began, "I became a pathologist because I'm naturally curious. I know this man was a prison guard, and I've heard from a doctor friend at the prison they've had a pretty good number of deaths over there lately, most of them from coronary complications. Are you suggesting someone's doing something to *create* heart disease over there?"

"It's the only conclusion I could reach," he answered. "As a pathologist, is it possible?"

She looked at the heart on the table and sighed.

"Not in any way I would understand, but I don't know everything. Have you checked what they were feeding the prisoners who died?"

"They were fed the same diet as the rest of the inmates at the prison, but this problem has been specific to the Death Row prisoners. The attrition rate in the other cell blocks has been consistent over the last thirty years, and I think only one person outside Death Row died from a heart attack in the last year, but he was seventy-two years old."

"What exactly *is* Death Row? A sequestered off section of the prison?"

"Yes. It's actually two sections. There's East Block and there's the Adjustment Center. Inmates were dying in both."

"And you checked ventilation, water, environmental factors?"

"Warden's had three teams in there over a nine month period. Exactly the same as the rest of the prison, but it's only the Death Row inmates who are dying."

She raised her eyebrows.

"And now a guard. Let me guess. He worked in the Death Row section of the prison?"

"Yes."

"Nice little mystery you've got going on over there, Osaka. You obviously think there's someone doing this to the prisoners. Who do you think it is?"

Bryan sat in the chair across from her.

"I think I know, but I can't say because I'm not certain. I'm more concerned with the more significant question."

"More significant question? What's that?"

He took a deep breath.

"The 'why' of it all. Whoever it is! *Why* are they killing Death Row inmates? What do they really want to do, and where are they going with this?"

"I don't get it, Mom. Why would you let him move back in?"

Lyndsey Alexander-Mitchell sat at the dining table across from Destiny, her finger tracing the rim of an empty champagne glass. A steaming cup of coffee sat before her.

"I mean, you were *free* of him. You don't need a man. You're an *Oprah*! It's ridiculous for you to let someone come in here and start trying to tell you what to do. Men will be men, plain and simple."

"It's *temporary*. He's only here for a few weeks, and then he'll go back to San Diego. For now, I need him here."

Lyndsey did not resemble Destiny because she was not blood related. Destiny became her surrogate mother after her father murdered her mother and in remorse, committed suicide, after which Destiny adopted her. And Lyndsey was the granddaughter of Allegra Benson, the woman who had started the *Aegis Foundation*.

Unlike her blond birth mother and sisters, Lyndsey's hair, eyes and skin were tinted with color. During summers when she would lay out, her skin browned. She kept her dark hair and fingernails cropped short and wore little make-up. She had full lips, high cheek bones and a pretty face with a diamond stud in her left nostril. At twenty-six, her waist was still slim, though her shapely butt stood out in everything she wore.

As assistant director at the foundation, she had to attend many social and political functions, but she hated wearing skirts or dresses, anything demonstrably feminine. She preferred stylish pantsuits instead. However, when she was at Destiny's, it was usually jeans and a t-shirt. Her voice held a slight lisp, owing to the platinum barbell in her tongue.

"I never liked him. I never thought he was right for you."

"I know. How many times have you told me that?"

"Apparently not enough times."

Lyndsey looked over, trying to gauge Destiny's reaction.

"Mom, it's just that I don't trust him. I read the transcripts from the trial. He wanted to do the right thing, but he lied. We both know it! With him, the end has always justified the means. You can't *trust* a person like that."

Destiny sighed.

"At this point, I don't have a choice. Whether you like him or not, he's a very good detective, and he's got connections."

"Auntie Kiyo's got connections."

Destiny shook her head as she rose.

"She does, but you're just going to have to trust me on this one, Lynse. I need all the help I can get. More coffee?"

"Thanks. Can *I* help?"

Returning to the table, Destiny sat.

"Yes. For the next few weeks, you can get over whatever bad feelings you have about Bryan, because he's here trying to help me."

"What? Are you in some kind of trouble?"

"I don't know, but I can't afford to take any chances."

Lyndsey's eyes widened.

"You *are* in trouble? What kind? Legal?"

"No."

"Financial?"

Destiny paused, taking a breath.

"No, I think someone might be trying to kill me."

"Really! You're kidding me, right? Why?"

"Because of something they think I know."

Lyndsey reached across the table, placing her hand on Destiny's.

"Why? Mom, you have to *tell* me!"

"Lyndsey, let's be real here. If someone was trying to kill me for something I knew, why on earth would I tell you and put your life in jeopardy?"

"Because I'm your daughter, and anyone who goes after you is going to have to come through me! Who is it?"

Destiny sipped her coffee.

"I don't know, but if I did, I wouldn't tell you. I've already said too much."

"And you think Bryan can help you?"

"If anyone can, he can."

Lyndsey raised her hands in symbolic surrender.

"Okay, I'll suspend my feelings about the man for the time he's here. You just stay alive."

"I will."

Destiny reached over, taking her daughter's hand.

"You know, Lynse, I've been thinking it's time for me to leave the foundation. You're completely up to speed and you're a good administrator. *Obasan* always said, *time for the old to get out of the way to make room for the new*."

Lyndsey smiled.

"So *now* you're admitting you're old?"

"You know what I mean."

"Bullshit! I know you love what you do. And you're at the top of your game, ready to take *Aegis* international. You've worked hard to make Gram's dream a reality, and it's your dream too. Why would you quit now?"

Destiny bowed her head.

"I don't know. Because I'm scared, okay? I'm involved in something here I don't understand, but I know it's dangerous. If you want to help me, step up. Give me some time. There's no way I can deal with the threat I'm under and still run the foundation."

"So what do we tell Gram? What do we tell Mrs. Allegra Benson?"

"I've always told her the truth, so I see no reason to change that. We'll tell her one of the men I convicted as a DA got me mixed up in something I have to deal with directly— that I'm taking some time off. We'll tell her I'm trying to protect the foundation. It's a temporary adjustment."

Lyndsey hesitated.

"She's gonna ask—"

"No she won't. Believe me. I know your grandmother."

It was a tell-tale sign of his arrival. Bryan always tried to open the door by twisting the knob before using his key in the deadbolts. Once inside he, fumbled, reengaging the locks, and recoiled as he turned the corner, his eyes resting on Lyndsey.

"Hello?"

Rising from the seat, Lyndsey seemed stiff, uncomfortable.

"Bryan—hello, it's been a while. You look, thinner?"

He smiled.

"What do you expect? I've been cooking for myself these past three years."

She smiled, remembering her promise.

"Good line, but I happen to know Mom *never* cooked for you. You'll have to sell that one to someone else."

She glanced around Destiny at the clock.

"Oh shit! Is it already after nine? I've gotta get home and go to bed. Gotta work in the morning. Mom—"

She leaned over and kissed Destiny. Moving toward the door, she lowered her head as she passed Bryan. His own head bowed, he waited for the door to close before looking up.

"The years go by and they grow up, but some things never change. Tell me, *what* exactly does she have against me?"

"Your Machiavellian nature. Funny, I've always thought it was one of your more endearing attributes."

"She looks like she wants to *throw up* whenever she looks at me. Am I that bad?"

Destiny laughed.

"I'm sure it's a generational thing. She's young, you're old. But then she's always been protective of me. She was in therapy for all those years feeling she failed to protect her own mother."

She bowed her head, reflecting.

"She seems a little frosty on the outside, but inside, she's still fragile, still afraid. Albeit from a distance, but she stood out in the hallway at eight years old, listening as her father murdered her mother, and then he told her it was her fault. *Sick bastard!*"

"I know. I was there."

"So don't take it personal if she doesn't trust you. Give it time. She'll warm up to you."

Bryan removed his jacket and gun holster, hanging them on the rack.

"It's been over five years, but I've got more important things to worry about."

He leaned over the table, kissing her.

"How was your day?"

"Frustrating. Waited all day to talk to Agent Martinez, go to his office, and he basically gives me nothing."

Her experience as a trial attorney served her well. She studied his face as she posed the question.

"Did you hear about the prison guard, Robert Sutter, who committed suicide in front of Grant's cell?"

"I heard something about that. Heard he was a friend of Grant's."

"Did you hear someone ordered an autopsy?"

He hesitated, uncertain if he was being set up.

"I heard something about that too. I think his wife ordered it."

"Really? *I* heard a guy named James Cassie was the one pushing for it. Isn't that the friend you told me about? The CCPOA guy? The old friend you're working with?"

Bryan feigned nonchalance as he sat at the table, scanning the newspaper.

"Yes, I work with Cassie and he is an old friend, but as I understand, the *wife* ordered it."

He looked up at Destiny.

"See, that's the problem with trusting Kiyomi's sources. Sometimes they get it wrong."

"And you trust your friend with the CCPOA? How can you trust anyone working for an organization with that much money and power? They could be feeding him anything. They could be using you to cover this thing up."

He laughed.

"You can't be serious. Why would the guards' union want to kill the prisoners? Less prisoners mean less jobs for them."

She did not smile.

"You and I both know things aren't always what they seem, especially when there's a cover-up. On some odd angle, in some screwball way, they might be benefiting from this, depending on where it's going."

Bryan yawned, his left elbow on the table and his hand covering his mouth.

"It's possible."

"You're the detective. You mean to tell me you've never considered it?"

"I haven't ruled anything out. And you're right—I am the detective. So why don't you cool your heels a little and let me finish figuring this thing out. Give me a couple of weeks."

She rolled her eyes.

"Cool my heels? I'm just getting my heels heated up. And just so you know, I'm taking a break from the foundation to deal with this."

He looked up, eyes glowering.

"You what?"

"I'm taking a break from the foundation. I'm not waiting for you or anyone else to figure this thing out for me. I won't stand around feeling helpless."

He sighed.

"Is that what this is about? Your need to control everything and everyone around you? When our marriage was on the line, you never once considered taking a break from the foundation."

She gasped, rising from the chair.

"What? I can't believe you just said that! When you married me, Bryan, I had a career. But this isn't about our marriage. Whoever's killing those inmates at San Quentin, now they're coming after me!"

"What do you mean? How do you know that?"

"It doesn't matter! I just know."

She crossed her arms, uneasy.

"I have to protect myself."

Bryan stood and approached his wife, grasping her shoulders in his hands.

"Listen Destee, I understand you're afraid, but you have to tell me everything you know. You have to let me do what I can do for you."

She closed her eyes and took a deep breath.

"Okay, but does that mean you're going to share everything you've discovered with me?"

He released her, backing.

"I can try, but you have to understand I'm *working* for someone. Some information might be proprietary in nature. That information I can't share."

"Not even with your wife whose life is being threatened?"

"I didn't say that. But for starts, what makes you think your life is being threatened? You have evidence?"

She paused, contemplating.

"Well, I have a source, and this source told me my cell phone number was etched on a wall in Grant's cell. That's how Grant had my number to call me."

"Let me guess. Your source is FBI agent Jake Martinez. He made the same claim to the warden yesterday afternoon. The funny thing about it is he's the only one who saw it. When the warden had it checked out, there was nothing on that cell wall."

"Because someone had it ground down."

Bryan raised his eyebrows.

"That's also what Martinez said, but I saw a photo of that wall. The aging of the concrete and the staining were consistent along its entire length. There was no *evidence* of it being ground down."

"So your team and the warden think agent Martinez is making it all up? He's lying?"

"No, not necessarily, but his assertion is not consistent with the evidence. Maybe he was mistaken."

Her voice began to take on a frustrated tone.

"Bullshit! Martinez called me, on my cell phone, from a number he said he found in Grant's cell after Grant *himself* called me! Is the warden in on this? Are you in on it?"

Bryan sighed, wagging his head.

"Come on, I'm not saying Martinez made it up. He obviously called you, so there are three possibilities here. One, the warden and the prison *are* in on it, and maybe the prison guards as well. Two, Martinez and the federal government are somehow behind these killings, and he's basically been assigned to debrief you after they found out Grant called you. And three, Martinez made a mistake, maybe he got confused about where exactly he came across your number. He was in a lot of those cells."

He shrugged.

"Me, I favor number three. He's been taking all that flu medicine lately. It's understandable he could have been mistaken about where he found your number, if he even found it in the prison at all. Or two, if the government's behind it, he was assigned to debrief you. That's why he had your number."

She thought for a moment and answered.

"Me, I don't exactly trust *you* or anything I'm hearing. Maybe someone hired *you* to debrief me? How would I know any differently? You want me to share everything with you, but you won't share with me. And *that's* going to make me trust you?"

"What about me being your husband?"

"What about it, Bryan? My life might be in jeopardy here, and you're feeding me a line about proprietary rights to information? What about my life? That's as proprietary as it gets for me."

He held his hands up as if to halt her advance.

"I won't even try to out-argue a lawyer. What do you want me to do?"

"Share everything with me. Let's be partners in this. Let's get through it together. Can you do that?"

He took a deep breath, blowing out.

"You know what I do. I wouldn't go to your foundation and try to shake up the way you do things over there. I'm working for CCPOA. It would be unethical for me to share some of their more confidential discovery with you."

"I am your wife, and whoever's behind this thinks I know something!"

"I know, and that's why I'm trying to help you."

"I'm open if you're open. Are we going to do this together? No secrets? Nothing held back?"

He turned away to hide his frustration.

"I'm a professional, Destiny. You know I can't agree to something like that. I'm trying to help you here. Will you please just tell me what you know?"

"Again, I'm not some helpless damsel in distress. I won't accept anything less than full disclosure from both sides. Otherwise, we can trade information on a *need-to-know* basis."

He lost his temper.

"God, that's what I always hated about you! You're so goddamned stubborn!"

He stopped, rueful.

"I didn't mean that. It's just I'm your husband and I want to help you, but you have to fight me on everything I'm trying to do! I'm sorry. I'm just frustrated."

"Imagine that! It's *me* they're coming after, Bryan."

He nodded.

"You're right. I give up. There's no winning with you. We'll share things on a *need-to-know* basis."

"And I can trust that?" She shrugged. "Well, since you're being so magnanimous now, you first."

"First thing in the morning, or better yet, we'll do it tomorrow night. First, I'll need to figure out if there's even anything I can share and exactly what that might be. I'll figure it out and we'll plan on meeting tomorrow night, you and me."

She put on her practiced courtroom smile.

"That's right, you and me. And Kiyomi."

Chapter 8

The drive to West Sacramento was relaxing. Every other week, it was good to get away from the city. The mandatory trip offered contrast and perspective. West Sacramento, after all, wasn't even Sacramento. With a population of about 45,000, it was the quarter the size of the Chinatown neighborhood. Directly across the river from Sacramento, it offered convenient access to the State Capitol and to the business of government in California.

James Cassie always took the Reed Avenue exit to CCPOA headquarters on Riverpoint Drive. The meeting's agenda, mailed to him two weeks earlier, suggested little departure from the status quo. There would be remarks from the president, a financial report, a governmental relations report, several items up for committee vote and an opportunity to present new business.

A week earlier, when he phoned the president with a progress report on the investigation at San Quentin, Cassie suggested bringing the problem at the prison to the attention of board members, off the record. CCPOA President Donovan Baker however, thought the vetting of news with such lurid implications was premature and reckless.

Baker was a bottom-line, cold-natured, impatient man who behaved as if he was always five minutes behind schedule. Months earlier, he resisted any inquiry into the problem at the prison, but he relented under pressure from union leaders at the facility. When the investigation was complete, he insisted findings would be minimized, if ever brought before the board at all.

During baseball season, Cassie and Baker went over to the local baseball stadium to take in an afternoon minor league game, have a couple of drinks and talk union business. They seldom ever noticed what was happening on the field as they sat at the bar. Cassie liked the locally brewed pale ale, while Baker always had martinis made with Sapphire gin. While both men wore suits, the shorter, thinner Baker seemed more at home in his. Baker, in his sixties, looked more like a businessman, graying at the temples, tanned and in shape. His iPad was rarely more than inches from his fidgety fingertips.

"And just so you know, the autopsy findings came back on Sergeant Sutter."

Baker furrowed his brow in disgust.

"Autopsy? The man shot himself! Who ordered an autopsy?"

"The wife. Anyway, medical examiner said if he hadn't shot himself, he would have been dead in a month anyway. Two months max. His heart was all clogged up, just like Grant's and most of the other inmates that died."

Baker sat thinking for a moment and turned away to light a cigarette.

"Well, according to the American Heart Association, heart disease is *still* the number one killer in America."

He took a drag and blew it out, shrugging.

"It'll probably kill me."

He paused, massaging his closed eyes with his fingertips.

"It's the lives we lead: fast food, medications, pollution, lack of exercise, stress, and for me, three marriages. I'm not surprised about Sutter. Just look at the rest of the population. It's happening all over."

"It's different with Sutter. His wife gave us a copy of a medical examination done last August when he took out an additional insurance policy. His heart tested healthy, no indication or any concern about plaque or atherosclerosis."

He answered the interrogatory expression on Baker's face.

"Clogged arteries. Sutter's heart was in perfect health last summer, and ten months later, it was full of so much plaque and fat that it could barely function. Something happened."

"He shot himself."

"No. I talked to the doctor he went to in Sacramento. Doctor said based on the degree of blockage in Sutter's heart, the problem would have had to have been building up over ten, twenty years."

He paused to order another beer.

"I asked the doctor if the blockages could have built up over one year, or to stretch it, two years or five years. He said it was impossible. He said Sutter was a rare case, very advanced heart disease. He said unless there was something fishy going on, Sutter would have never passed a medical examination for insurance, not for the last ten years."

Baker mashed out his cigarette in the ashtray.

"*You* talked to this doctor? You personally?"

"Yes."

"Listen Cassie, from my understanding when you started this, you were to put together a team of outsiders, and this objective team was going into the Arena to bring back a report in two weeks. Am I right?"

Cassie bit his bottom lip in anger. He could feel it coming.

"Right."

"Then what the fuck are you doing interviewing the doctor? This was supposed to be an unbiased investigation, wasn't it? But you're on a mission to uncover something, to implicate the prison. Or maybe the warden? I see a conflict of interest."

Baker leaned in toward Cassie, speaking in an undertone.

"You're Executive Vice President of CCPOA, the most powerful lobby in this state. Your duty is to the union, not to the prisoners. Do your job or you won't have one—and that's not coming only from me. The State Board of Directors and the OIG are on my back. You're pissing people off."

He backed.

"Let the team finish their work without you. And keep your suspicions to yourself. You're making people nervous."

"Who?"

"The guards. You've got them talking, especially after that Sutter incident. They think this thing is going to spread from the inmates to the guards and from San Quentin to other prisons."

Cassie glanced over.

"What thing?"

"Whatever killed those inmates."

Baker sipped his drink and picked up the iPad.

"I'm not saying there's nothing strange going on. But no matter what, we have to do our jobs."

He selected a contact and began typing without looking

"Can you imagine what would happen if this got out there and it created some big panic with the guards? If they thought that there was some disease going around the prison that could kill them? That was *already* killing guards?"

He sent the message on the device.

"You'd have pandemonium. There'd be wild accusations, all kinds of investigations from the state and the feds. There'd be paranoia from guards at all the prisons, everyone looking for someone to blame. With all that going on, security would be compromised. In the end the guards would lose. We would lose. I could give a fuck about inmates dying. Right now, it comes down to containment. We're going to have a real big problem if guards start dying."

Baker read an incoming message on the device.

"Who's your lead man on this team of yours?"

"Osaka. Bryan Osaka. Very smart, good man, I trust him."

"I'm sure you do. What's Osaka come up with?"

Cassie was becoming irritated by Baker's attention to his handheld distraction. He shook his head.

"Osaka found the doctor in Sacramento. From the look of things, Sutter's recent medical records had been lost or erased from everywhere. Osaka was able to trace down an email attachment and retrieve them. They were even missing from the doctor's computer."

"Okay, anything on what's killing the inmates?"

"Nothing yet. The only consistency so far is they're all inmates and they're all on Death Row."

"And Sutter?"

"Sutter had heart disease symptoms consistent with the inmates who died, and he worked on Death Row. Osaka says guards he interviewed indicated Sutter was close to one of the inmates, Perseus Grant, who died of a heart attack a few weeks ago."

Baker looked up.

"Close? As in intimate? Inappropriate?"

"No, Sutter was married and a Christian. According to inmates and guards, Grant suspected months ago the inmate deaths were part of a more ambitious scheme, something sinister, and he talked about it to anyone who'd listen. Apparently, he convinced Sutter at some point, and they were trying to investigate things together."

"So why the suicide in front of Grant's cell?"

"To shake things up, to make fellow guards realize they weren't safe either. If Sutter had died in his bed or anywhere else, no one would have known a guard had been affected by whatever was killing the inmates."

Baker thought for a moment.

"What's our warden McGinnis saying?"

"Nothing. He just wants this all to go away. But I've talked to him, and I'm sure he knows more than he's admitting to."

"And your team's going to be done in a week?"

Cassie answered as he signed his credit card receipt.

"With the investigation, yes. I'm not saying we'll have this whole thing solved by then. Solution might take a few weeks after that, but it's coming."

Baker nodded.

"Okay, the medical records on Sutter that you say your man Osaka found—I'll need you to forward those to my email and then personally make sure they're deleted from his computer. And all discussions with Sutter's doctor and any other information that might be, well, provocative in nature. I don't want it out there. Zero discussion, zero leaks. If there's a panic, the Board will hold your ass responsible. I'll hold you personally responsible. We'll wait for your report."

He stood, leaning on the table as he signed his receipt.

"Is there anything unclear about what I just said, Team Player?"

Angry, Cassie sighed and forced an ambivalent smile.

"No, that's fine. I'll play, but I don't like the game."

She checked the house address against the address listed in the file in her hand. Four times she had been wrong. It was her last chance. She knocked. Seconds later, the door opened, though only about three inches, to the length of the brass door chain guard. The accent was evident in his voice.

"Can I help you?"

"Dr. Hussein Rashid? From California?"

He shut the door at once and turned off the porch light. Convinced she had found him, she pounded the door with her fist.

"Dr. Rashid! I'm not going away! Dr. Rashid!"

She continued to pound, shouting.

"Dr. Rashid, I work for the *San Francisco Chronicle* newspaper! And I'm going to stay right here beating on your door until you open it."

Nothing stirred within.

"Doctor, I'm not going away! In fact, I'm going to call the *Herald* and tell them what you've done. I'll get them out here, and I'm calling the *Channel 7 News*! Doctor Rashid!"

Kiyomi's shrill voice carried through the quiet neighborhood where most residents were sleeping. It was one-thirty in the morning. The bedroom light at the house next door came on.

"Dr. Rashid. People are dying because of you! Dr. Rashid! And your neighbors can hear me."

After a minute the porch light came back on, the chain guard disengaged, and the door opened. A bearded man's face appeared, his expression pained, troubled. He was probably in his late fifties, graying and slight of build.

"Who are you?"

"Kiyomi Yamakita with the *Chronicle*. I just want information. Can I come in?"

"You are just a small woman. How do you know I will not take you in here and kill you?"

She pushed the door open.

"Cuz I've got your balls in my hand, Doctor. Besides that, yes I'm tiny, but I know I could still kick your old ass."

She stared into his eyes.

"You going to let me in?"

They sat at his dining room table, chandelier lights dim.

"How did you find me?"

"It wasn't easy. I wouldn't have known it, but 'Rashid' is a common last name. I paid off a records clerk at the prison infirmary. Someone had pulled your file and erased all traces of you being there. But I have a friend who knew how to get back to your information through a federal government computer system, Patriot Act files."

"What do you want with me?"

She turned on the recording device and placed it on the table.

"What do you know about forty-two Death Row inmates dying at San Quentin over the last eleven months?"

"Nothing, I did not know so many had died."

"Why did you leave there? And why are you hiding in Florida?"

He hesitated.

"When I was there, at the San Quentin, I had several threats to my life. A man with a medical research firm that contracted with the prison, he told me the threats were very real. He made arrangements for me to get privately away from there and to start a new life here."

"This man from the research firm, what was his name?"

"Mr. Hancock. That was his name. I never knew his first name."

Rashid's hand was shaking as he wiped his brow with a white handkerchief. Kiyomi spoke, pen in her fingers, still writing.

"What was the name of the medical research firm Mr. Hancock worked for?"

Dr. Rashid took the recording device from the table, turning it off.

"How are you going to use this information? You will cause trouble to me and my family."

"Anything you say will not go beyond me. I promise. This is just a background interview."

"Then it does not have to be on this tape recorder."

She smiled.

"Fine. We'll leave the tape off. What was the name of the company?"

"Are you writing a newspaper story?"

"No, I'm trying to save my best friend's life. Please answer my question."

He sat silent, contemplating.

"Rosetta Biotech."

"Out of where? What city? What state?"

"I don't know."

Her eyes narrowed.

"What did you do for them?"

"I took blood and the oral swabs. Sometimes I took hair."

"You had to send it to them? Do you have the address?"

He took a breath to calm himself.

"No, always a courier service. Their information was on the bar code that went on the samples."

"I see. Did you ever administer medication to the inmates you saw? Did you give any injections? Any pills? Any elixirs?"

"No, not me. When they had a cold or the flu, they would go to the main doctor to get medicine. I worked mostly in the lab, and I assisted in the dental office."

She paused, thinking.

"Dr. Rashid, doesn't it seem a little strange to you that you're in all this trouble, having to move and change your name, all this over working in a lab, drawing blood and taking oral swabs?"

"I do not know."

"Either you're incredibly stupid or you're not telling me everything. But you're not just a lab doctor. Records indicate you were trained as a genetic specialist at Tel Aviv University. What else did you do for Rosetta Biotech?"

"I told you everything."

Kiyomi looked up from her notes.

"I'm a reporter, and my gut is almost never wrong. You're lying to me. There's something you're not telling me, something you really *need* to tell me."

"No! I have told you everything. There is nothing else to tell."

Kiyomi stood, her voice ominous.

"Doctor, I don't believe in making idle threats, but there are lives at stake here. If I find out you were doing something else and you didn't bother to tell me, I swear I'll find you again, and if there really is someone out there who wants you dead or sees you as a liability, I'll find them and bring them with me."

The mistrust and frustration had been smoldering for months. Inmates, trapped in hot cells day after day, lashed out at the guards every chance they got. Successful attacks at the Adjustment Center were up. They usually happened in the morning, at mealtime, a time when correctional officers were arriving to start their shifts.

Breakfast that morning was two pancakes and grits, along with a bagged lunch. Unlike the more modern prisons in the state, San Quentin's Adjustment Center and the other blocks were comprised of cells stacked on tiers, five high. Lacking the solid doors of modern prisons, the prison's cell fronts were open, providing inmates the opportunity to assault guards directly at mealtime.

In order to serve breakfast, guards would place the food in containers, on trays. Mindful of the danger involved, guards then had to pop open the food port in order to insert the trays, exposing themselves to attack from often vicious inmates awaiting opportunity on the other side.

Over time and thousands of attacks, the guards had developed safety measures during mealtime that involved donning full riot gear and a plexi-glass shield on rollers to protect them from projectiles and slashing weapons whipping out from the food port. For the last two days, there had been no successful attacks.

Raymond Gutierrez lived with his two sons in one of the eighty-seven family homes located within the gates of San Quentin prison. His neighborhood looked similar to any other suburban neighborhood, with beautiful trees and well-manicured lawns, but it was less than one hundred yards from the penitentiary building. Single parent Raymond chose the home for the easy commute and the cost versus living in San Francisco.

Raymond had little time for exercise, so he was overweight, with budding man-boobs, a pudgy stomach and a bulging butt. Guarding Death Row over the last twelve years, he had seen inmates pull just about every attack tactic imaginable. He knew which inmates were safe enough and which had to be handled with extreme caution.

Recently however, Gutierrez hadn't been feeling well. He wasn't sure if he was coming down with something, but over the last few weeks, he began to have difficulty breathing and he noticed he was becoming drenched in sweat while performing even low-stress tasks. He took two days off in the previous week because he could barely rise in the morning, and the bed rest seemed to help. He felt much better, though his sluggish physical state had a resultant effect on his mental alertness.

He smelled it before he realized what it was. The inmates called it "gassing," and it was the most disgusting assault a prisoner could ever deliver. The practice involved the inmate filling an empty can with his own feces and urine and letting it ferment for a few days, the heat of the cell stewing it to a bubbling state of putrefaction. The prisoner would then wait at mealtime, can poised, until the guard opened the food port. With a quick flick of his wrist, the inmate would let fly the contents of the can, which if it hit its mark, would drench the guard with the vile mixture.

Normally, Gutierrez would have seen it coming and stepped out of the way, but he just didn't have the energy to react that day. And normally, he would have had the visor on his helmet down, but it was up because he was having difficulty breathing.

The shock and the smell were hideous. The muddy liquid splashed on his chest and into his face, while his mouth was partially open. He stumbled backward, gasping, and fell, clutching his chest. By the time the two other guards near him sprayed the prisoner with pepper-spray and reached Gutierrez on the floor, he was blue in the face. One of the guards administered CPR until paramedics arrived.

Within minutes, a rumor went through the cell block, circulated through whispers and notes attached to fish lines: Raymond Gutierrez had died of a heart attack on the way to the infirmary, and Reuben Trejo, the inmate who gassed him and laughed about it, was headed there also, where he would be "evaluated." Smart money said Trejo would be the next to die, and in short order.

Chapter 9

Destiny was in Atlanta when Kiyomi phoned her with the news. San Quentin guard Raymond Gutierrez had died of massive heart failure on the way to the prison infirmary after an inmate attack. Kiyomi said she would be writing a human-interest story about Gutierrez for the paper, an in-depth perspective on the life of an ordinary California prison guard. Of course, the underlying intention of the article was to pressure the prison to keep a communication line open with the paper and to provide a channel for anxious guards and inmates to share information.

Destiny traveled to Atlanta to meet FBI Agent Martinez at the U.S. Department of Health and Human Services' CDC, or Centers for Disease Control, in the northeastern part of the city. He had set up an interview with a Dr. Aaron Wexler, an infectious disease specialist. Martinez believed the prison deaths were the result of someone targeting inmates and infecting them with an erstwhile unknown agent that induced heart disease.

They met in Dr. Wexler's office deep within the gut of the massive complex. Rarely impressed, Destiny was in awe. It was bureaucracy at its finest. The place possessed its own language of acronyms. Dr. Wexler worked for a division of the NCPDCID, or the National Center for Preparedness, Detection and Control of Infectious Diseases, as part of the DEISS, or the Division of Emerging Infections and Surveillance Services.

Agent Martinez was referred to Dr. Wexler by a doctor at the University of Berkeley School of Public Health, as part of the CEIP, or California Emerging Infections Program, a federal partner of the CDC. At the university, Martinez worked with doctors in the Surveillance for Unexplained Deaths, or the SUD project. Doctors there were interested in *any previously healthy patients less than fifty years of age who had died from an unexplained illness that may have appeared to have been caused by an infectious agent.*

After more than three months of studying data from forty dead inmates, CEIP doctors were stumped. They tested the heart, organs and blood for the presence of antibodies in order to identify any inducible disease that might have increased chances of atherosclerosis, the probable course of illness in such cases and the pathology involved.

Unfortunately, with most of the inmates, medical records provided little insight. According to doctors working with Martinez, the overcrowded state prison system, with nearly 160,000 prisoners, provided substandard and intermittent healthcare to the inmates. Inmates with diabetes, in particular, were often much worse off after spending time in the system. Inconsistent glucose monitoring, untimely insulin injections and the lack of diet-management led to strokes in some cases, blindness and amputations in others and even premature death.

The prisons provided no automatic testing for deadly and infectious hepatitis C, and while the state estimated 15,000 inmates were affected, the CDC put the number closer to 50,000, or about one in three inmates. HIV/AIDS also ran rampant, though most of the prisons made efforts to identify infected prisoners. There was no infectious disease specialist, no special dietary considerations for inmates who were HIV positive and no access to clinical trials.

Doctors at the UC Berkeley School of Health however, established that thirty-seven of the forty-two inmates who had died in the last year had at least some form of advanced heart disease, a fact pattern that skewed statistics. After hundreds of tests involving tissue, blood and body fluids, frustrated doctors and researchers were unable to identify or isolate an infectious agent involved in the San Quentin Death Row Deaths anomaly.

Dr. Wexler's CDC office in Atlanta was small in relation to the building, but it was huge compared to doctor's quarters at the Berkeley School of Health. Wexler shared the clean, organized space with a receptionist, an assistant, an integrated technology specialist and four full-time researchers. Most impressive, it was a paperless office.

There were no books, no letters, and no bulletins to be seen, and only one visible phone. The researchers used laptops, but there was a computer at each dust free workstation. Six employees were hard at work around the space, and yet, save the constant clicking of computer keyboards, the room was silent.

Wexler sat behind a walnut desk in his private office, Destiny and Martinez across from him. While his face seemed smooth and young, his hair was completely white. Gauging the level of his schooling, accomplishments and experience, Destiny guessed he was in his early fifties. She thought he was handsome, interesting.

"If my daughter knew I would be meeting Destiny Mitchell this morning, she'd have begged to come with me to work. She's a big fan."

Destiny smiled as she removed a business card from the shiny golden holder.

"How old is your daughter?"

"Twenty-two. She's over at Georgia in Athens. Public Administration."

Destiny reached across the desk.

"Tell her she's at the perfect age to volunteer service. That's my direct number. She can call me if she's interested in helping less fortunate women."

Agent Martinez was anxious to begin.

"Thank you for meeting with us, Dr. Wexler. I asked the team over at Berkeley to forward all the electronic research and medical records from this investigation. In our phone call yesterday, you said you received them and got a chance to look over them?"

Wexler hesitated, sitting back.

"I did. I took some time to examine them in careful detail. In my opinion, there's definitely something peculiar going on at the prison. It doesn't take a specialist to realize that, but I regret to say nothing I saw in any of those cases would lead me to believe an *infectious disease* is responsible for the deaths over there."

Disappointment showed in Martinez's face and voice.

"But if it isn't an infectious disease, what else could it be? The Berkeley doctors concluded a definite pathology was involved, and that pathology was consistent in most of the cases, and all in one year, and all in one place."

"Heart disease pathology present, yes, but evidence of an infectious agent, viral or bacterial? Inconclusive. There's just nothing in the record to indicate these men died from anything other than the same heart condition that kills millions of people all over the world on a regular basis. Why so many in such close proximity? I'm sure there's an answer, and maybe there *is* something creepy going on, but there is no evidence whatsoever that an infectious agent was involved."

He sat back in the chair and shrugged.

"Of course, I'm not ruling *out* the possibility of an infectious agent. I just didn't see any evidence in the record. And it could be we're dealing with something more sophisticated than a mere virus."

Destiny glanced over at Martinez and back at the doctor.

"Something like what?"

"Perhaps a chemical agent designed to trigger heart disease, something that might alter the physical make-up of cardiac tissue, veins and arteries on a cellular or chemical level, thus giving the heart a greater propensity for building-up plaque or fat."

Martinez bit his thumb, thinking.

"But if they were killing these inmates by administering some designer drug, wouldn't it have shown up in the blood and tissue tests they performed?"

"It depends. It might be something that had already dissipated or flew beneath the threshold when they were testing, or something so unique they didn't know how to test for it. But then, we're getting away from my area of specialization."

Destiny looked up from her notepad.

"Bear with us for a moment please, Doctor. Not my area of specialization either, but a chemical that would eventually alter the cellular structure of the heart—wouldn't it have to have been administered over time, and over several or more doses?"

The doctor nodded.

"Generally speaking, I would suppose it would, but I see what you're getting at. How would someone administer multiple doses without it being obvious to the prisoners, especially after people started dying?"

Martinez continued in the doctor's line of thought.

"We have records of all official inmate trips to the infirmary. Some of the victims visited in the last eleven months, but some of the others hadn't been over there for years."

Wexler put on his glasses and reexamined the computer screen.

"Which means, whatever this is, it wasn't introduced in the infirmary. That leaves food or water or some other environmental factor. And it could be something so advanced that it's beyond our understanding. This whole thing would be intriguing if the implications weren't so disturbing."

The doctor spoke while reading.

"There was something I found a little odd though, and I'm looking at it now."

Martinez leaned forward, trying to see the screen.

"What's that?"

"In the late going, when doctors had an idea that these prisoners were in fact coming in with advanced heart disease, they were helpless to save any of them or slow the progression. Changes to diet, cholesterol reduction, stent surgeries and bypasses, they made zero difference. In that sense, this seems more like a disease."

Martinez sighed.

"Really? That's what I was hoping to hear you say. If it's a disease, then there's possibly a cure, right?"

"Theoretically yes, if it's a disease."

"So if it's a disease, then a specialist like you could possibly find the cure? Am I right, Doctor?"

Wexler nodded.

"Yes. I said yes. Why are you so anxious?"

Martinez opened the top of the accordion file next to his chair, withdrew a file and slid it across the desk.

"I had a physical performed last week. I hadn't been feeling well, so I had the Berkeley doctors check out my *own* heart. Open the file and look at it. Last physical, it was fine, but now it's full of plaque, they say. If you can't find a cure for me, Dr. Wexler, I'll be dead in a month, maybe two. I don't know how they did it, but they *got* me."

It was not the first time Bryan had taken a case involving such intrigue and so many layers of complexity, but never one involving his wife. It was inescapable. Perseus Grant's communication from the prison, a two-minute call to her cell phone weeks earlier, made her a central character in the developing drama. He had been a detective too long to consider such an unlikely connection as coincidence.

They had been separated for over three years, but fate brought them together again. He knew all along, even after he left, there was unfinished business between them. There had always been a deeper bond, along a spiritual plane, that assured him time and space notwithstanding, she would be with him in the end.

Yet the case was unusual for other reasons. While Destiny, prison officials and the prison guards' union believed Bryan was working for the CCPOA to solve the mystery of unprecedented Death Row fatalities at San Quentin, he was actually retained by a well-financed private citizen for an undefined purpose. A month earlier, an operative claiming to represent former Massachusetts governor Hugh Gordon hired him to investigate and report on state and federal investigations into the prison deaths.

Ego aside, Bryan understood he was chosen after the agency or group responsible for the deaths realized he was a detective with a connection to Destiny Mitchell. Concerned about what information Perseus Grant may have shared in the short phone call, the operative asked Bryan to debrief his wife, for her own safety, before beginning work at the prison. He also expressed concerns about Destiny's relationship to a high-profile *Chronicle* reporter.

Bryan suspected the prison deaths were the result of some shadowy agency or confederate group employing experimental methods to induce heart disease in a specific segment the prison population. He believed someone was using San Quentin's Death Row as a testing ground for an undetectable new technology for killing. Most Americans viewed former Governor Gordon as a man of high moral character, but the inferences from the investigation were disturbing.

If an agency eventually acquired the technology to target individuals *outside* San Quentin to produce similar results, it would have a reality changing, nefarious weapon at its disposal. Even more troubling, there was growing circumstantial evidence that guard Robert Sutter was selected to be murdered employing this experimental method. His suicide before Perseus Grant's cell was a desperate flare fired at the dusking of a dark night. If an agency could use the technique for personal or political reasons, the global implications would be profound.

Bryan sat in a dimly lit bar at San Francisco International Airport, awaiting billionaire Nate Driscoll, who would be laying over for an hour and a half before heading down to Los Angeles. Nate was a huge political donor who supported conservative causes and who had publically supported Governor Hugh Gordon in the December through March primary leading up to the general election. It was only the second time Bryan had met him face-to-face, and he recognized the portly, squinting man from a distance.

Driscoll was a large white man. At six-feet-three-inches and three hundred pounds, he was larger and whiter than most. He looked like an east coaster: dark suit, white shirt, conservative tie and wide, black shiny wingtip shoes, but he lived in southern California. He smelled of *Old Spice* or some other Walgreens gift box cologne. His hair was brown and thin, parted on the left and combed over his balding dome. He was late fifty-something, maybe even sixty. His eyes searched for "the Asian guy" in the room, but in that San Francisco bar, *it seemed there was an Asian at every other table!* Bryan stood and waited for Driscoll to settle into his seat.

"You had to know I'd check. You're not involved in this because you own shares in a prison construction company, and you didn't hire me on behalf of an old friend at the Office of the Inspector General. Your project this spring and summer has been Hugh Gordon, who's a long shot to win, despite the fact you've always said you only bet on sure things."

Driscoll yanked down his tie, unfastening the top button of his shirt, chuckling.

"If you really checked, I'm sure you know by now that I'm a major *benefactor* to both political parties. But yes, my Super PAC got him through the primary. I've made a lot of money over the years, and I'm willing to spend it on worthy causes. *All* of it if I have to."

Bryan was mindful of his word choice.

"About my assignment, I'm sure you already know, but it seems someone was perfecting a sort of case-specific biological or genetic weapon over at the prison. Exactly *how* are you involved in that?"

Driscoll reared back.

"How about this? I'm paying *you*. Why don't you let me ask the questions?"

The detective took a deep breath, resolving himself to redefine his position.

"You can keep your money. I told you when we talked the first time. For me, this isn't about money."

Driscoll placed a large, sealed envelope before Bryan.

"You got *in* there, the prison. You're investigating. You earned it. What have you found out so far?'

"FBI's involved, agent by the name of Jake Martinez."

"I know. Have you met him?"

Bryan shook his head.

"We've talked. He's spent the last two months working with the Berkeley School of Public Health and the CDC. He's convinced inmate Perseus Grant and Sergeant Sutter unearthed a bombshell before they were murdered, that there's something dangerous going on over there."

Driscoll furrowed his brow, irritated.

"Sutter wasn't murdered—he committed suicide. Martinez is an idiot."

"An idiot who has somehow contracted the same disease that killed all those inmates and would have killed Sutter? No question about it, Grant and Sutter were onto something. They were a threat and someone felt they had to be eliminated. And whoever that is must think Martinez is onto something as well. Where there's smoke, there's fire."

Driscoll thought a moment and smiled.

"It's possible, but we all know this mysterious 'someone' can't kill everybody at the FBI, at the prison and over at the *Chronicle* where that Yamakita woman works. I'm sure this 'someone' you're talking about would prefer *containment* to killing people."

He tilted his head, staring into Bryan's eyes.

"Have you found out what your *wife* knows and who she's talked to?"

"She knows more than she's telling me. Doesn't *trust* me. She thinks I could be working for someone who's asked me to debrief her. Are you married?"

Driscoll undid a second button, sipped from the club soda and nodded.

"Thirty years."

"Think about how hard it would be to debrief your wife."

Driscoll's mouth wanted to smile, but the weight of his full-jawed countenance suppressed any indication of levity.

"Did she tell you what Grant said to her on that cell phone call? She was on with him for more than two minutes."

"No. She's a smart woman. Claims it's the only leverage she has."

"You think she's told it to the reporter?"

Bryan nodded.

"I think she and the reporter have taken serious measures to protect themselves. Whatever Grant told her is their insurance policy. And believe me, they know how to execute. My wife is a former prosecutor, and Kiyomi Yamakita would know how to put it out there."

"As her husband, do you think she and the reporter will go public with this?"

"Not unless they're absolutely forced to. Look, she didn't ask for any of this. Grant called *her*, and she believes that call and the nature of the information he shared make her a liability to whoever's behind these murders. She thinks the threat of going public is her only protection."

Driscoll's private flight from Washington DC took five and a half hours, but the grilled sea bass served onboard was dry and unpalatable. Stomach growling, he raised the small, laminated menu to study the bar's offerings, opting instead for the complimentary cracker snacks in a dish on the table.

"Do you think you could assure her she has nothing to worry about? That there are well-financed people who would show their profound gratitude for her cooperation? Who would make substantial donations to her foundation on an ongoing basis?"

"She wouldn't trust you."

"You're her husband. Can you *persuade* her to trust me, or better yet, to trust you?"

Bryan sighed, wagging his head.

"Your wife is white, right? You think just by talking I'm going to change that black woman's mind?"

"We'll donate money to her foundation."

"You don't know her. She won't want money. She'll want proof."

Driscoll tilted the dish, pouring the remaining cracker snacks into his hand.

"Proof of what?"

"Proof that her life and Yamakita's life will not be in danger, not now or in the future. Proof that this killing method will no longer be used on inmates or anyone else for any reason."

The portly man shut his eyes, contemplating for a moment.

"If she agrees to a debriefing and is willing to sign some form of a non-disclosure agreement, I can unequivocally guarantee she and the reporter will have nothing to worry about. And as for the other matter, I'm not aware of any so-called murders occurring at the prison. I understand an unusual number of the inmates have died of natural causes, and that's disconcerting, but murder? Now that's a stretch."

He fixed his eyes on Bryan's own.

"Unless of course you know something you're not sharing. I hired you because you're a great detective, one of the best. And you've been at this for two, three weeks? If these prisoners are being murdered and you *know* something, I need you to tell me how, right now."

"I don't know how. Not yet."

"But you're certain they're being murdered? What have you discovered?"

Bryan hesitated in his answer, uncertain of what Driscoll was really asking. Nate Driscoll was a smart man, a former Army colonel turned defense contractor and CEO of the firm WPNS, Inc., a strategic defense research and weapons company. When Driscoll hired Bryan to investigate the investigations at the prison, it wasn't because he didn't already know what was going on there. It was because he wanted to monitor and to influence the output of the investigations. It was because he was intimately *involved*.

"As for the 'what': whoever's killing them, they're using something cutting edge, which would make me think it's on a DNA or genome level. *How* they're doing it is beyond me for now."

He shrugged.

"Who? It's got to be someone capable of financing the research into whatever technology they're pioneering. Probably not the government, but someone closely aligned—someone who can acquire government access and influence by manipulating elected officials, appointees or the process. Someone a lot like you, Mr. Driscoll."

Driscoll smiled as he assaulted a new dish of snacks, urging Bryan to continue.

"Someone like me?"

"Yes, but all the foregoing is not surprising to me. I've seen my share of shadow reality. What troubles me is the objective, the *why*. Someone's obviously gone through a lot of trouble and expense to murder dead men walking, a bunch of Death Row inmates. And it's not for revenge or a sense of justice. There's something more to it."

"Is that what you think? Something like what?"

Bryan glanced sidelong at the older man.

"What was happening at San Quentin is an *experiment*. Whatever high tech murder weapon they've devised and are developing, they were testing it on human subjects at the prison. They might be trying it in other places, but it was definitely being tested there. At significant risk and expense. What they want to do with it when they perfect it, now *that's* what scares me."

Chapter 10

James Cassie learned about the secret assembly from his wife. On Wednesdays, Marybeth played *Canasta* with two of her best friends whose husbands were still guards at San Quentin. The wives didn't know the full import of the meeting, but they knew their husbands had become anxious about the recent series of deaths at the prison. The clandestine gathering would convene in a conference room at a hotel in Sausalito on the following Monday.

Warden McGinnis and lieutenants prohibited any discussion of the deaths among the guards, but details about Raymond Gutierrez' sudden heart attack created a quiet panic throughout the prison. Guard Gutierrez after all, suffered the attack after being doused with a can of an *inmate's* putrefied feces and urine. The connection? Like most of the Death Row prisoners who died over the last year, Gutierrez' autopsy indicated his heart was clogged with plaque and fat. Guards surmised that whatever killed the inmates, whether it was a disease or a government experiment, had somehow crossed over from the inmates to their ranks.

A week later, rumors circulated about an autopsy performed on Sergeant Robert Sutter. Sutter had befriended inmate Grant, who died from heart disease, and Sutter himself committed suicide in front of Grant's cell. The medical examiner's report revealed the same—advanced atherosclerosis in the Sutter case, identical to that of Gutierrez and the dead inmates. Over the course of that week, over one hundred guards, more than forty from Death Row, put in for transfers to other prisons. All but one, who had a family connection to a congressional representative, were denied.

Desperate, the guards turned to Cassie, whom they saw as their most staunch advocate and supporter in the system, but he was evasive. Unresponsive for two days, he finally instructed an aide tell the distraught men and women to redirect their requests, questions and concerns to CCPOA President Donovan Baker's office.

But rather than hearing a single complaint, Baker's office issued a terse statement assuring guards that conditions at the prison posed no immediate health threat to anyone. Baker predicted results from the onsite investigation being conducted would corroborate his assertion. He asked guards to show courage, exercise patience and refrain from all discussion with media sources.

Unsatisfied, several groups of guards returned to Cassie and begged him to intercede, but their union vice president was in a difficult place. Baker had visited Cassie's office a day earlier to make his threat clear: if Cassie involved himself in any way, he would be fired, with extreme prejudice. His close friends understood his predicament, but many of the other guards felt betrayed. Cassie was their last hope, and yet he was unwilling to help.

He should have known better. When he slipped into the conference room late and took a place in a darkened corner, he was hoping to attend the meeting as an objective though interested observer. Instead, all discussion in the room came to an abrupt halt when the moderator and then the other guards recognized him. In the silence that followed, the older, stocky man at the dais faltered, unsure about how to proceed, but the woman standing next to him, a short, thick black woman in her mid-forties, moved over, almost nudging the man aside. Adjusting the microphone, she called out.

"Nice to see you here back there, Mr. Cassie, but before we go on, I think you better tell us: in what capacity are you here?"

He bowed his head, clenching his jaw. He thought to stand, about face and head for the door, but when he stood, he couldn't turn away. It went against everything he believed.

"I'm here as an objective observer."

"No such thing. Either you're here to help us, or you're here because Baker sent you, or worse, the warden. No one here wants to lose their job."

Cassie walked down the aisle, closing on the stage.

"My ass is on the line just like all of yours. I'm risking everything. If Baker finds out I'm here, I'm done, just like that."

"So I ask again, why are you here?"

Arriving at the front of the room, he turned to face the crowd.

"Because I worked as a guard at San Quentin, on Death Row. I'm one of you. And I can't sit back and do nothing if there's something going on over there that might threaten any of you, even if it costs me my job."

A man in the front row spoke out, unprompted.

"I thank you for that. So what is it? You *know* something, Cassie? Tell us."

"Nothing more than any of you individually, but I do know if anyone's going to get to the bottom of this thing, it won't be the team that's investigating over there now. It'll be the guards, if we all put our heads and our stories together, if we're brave and together enough to do that."

He studied the faces in the group, confident he was winning over a few hearts.

"Don't you get it? They don't want you to figure it out. That's why this meeting had to be such a secret. It's why they don't want you talking to each other. Think about it. They don't even want you talking to their own investigators."

He recognized a face in the third row, a guard he knew was an informant for the warden, and next to him, a second informant. Cassie's eyes lingered in the gaze, making certain the man knew he'd been made.

"I don't know what's going on over there, but I know inmates have been dying. And now guards are dying. Sergeant Sutter was trying to tell us something— that we have to take matters into our own hands. We have to conduct our *own* investigation. Whatever the cost, whatever we lose is nothing compared to the lives that might be lost if we do nothing, and for some of us, our own lives."

There was vigorous nodding and verbal affirmation from the crowd. The older man standing next to the dais motioned for the microphone, clearing his throat to make sure he could be heard.

"That all sounds fine, but how do we conduct this investigation?"

Cassie turned toward the two standing beside him.

"You're in charge, right? And you?"

There was reluctant acknowledgement.

"We just all share what we know, our suspicions, things we've seen and heard over there in this past year. We share everything, we put it all together, and we figure this out."

He looked out to the crowd.

"Anyone out there want to start with something?"

After a lengthy silence, a man in the back rose and began.

"Well, I've been in and out of the infirmary working, and I've looked at the records. I compared them to the inmates that died. Most of em had been to the infirmary in the last twenty-four months, but about seven or eight of em never been there at all."

Cassie shrugged.

"Okay, that's important to note. Write that down. Anything else?"

The man crossed his arms.

"Not from me, but I'm wonderin if anyone knows anything about that Arab doctor that used to be over there."

A man in the front row turned to answer.

"Who, Rashid? That geek? He wasn't a doctor. He was some kind of lab technician."

"No, he was a doctor, a specialist. I saw his records."

A thin man in the back spoke in a nervous voice.

"That Rashid, wasn't he some kind of foreign national? Maybe there's an Arab country behind this, and they're testing out some new biological warfare weapon over here?"

Cassie's face showed disappointment.

"Let's just try to focus on the facts we *know*, things we've seen and heard at the prison. Anyone?"

A man standing on the far right in the back called out.

"Well, we all know they're coming in Death Row twenty or thirty a year, and the state barely kills one a year. Something's gotta give. Maybe they're created a disease to cut down on the Death Row rosters across the country. It's the state. They're out of money in Sacramento and they're killin cons to balance the budget."

"Who knows? But whenever you got something this hush-hush and shady, the government's mixed up in it somewhere."

A petite brown woman in the second row nodded.

"Sergeant Sutter was definitely onto something. He was close to figuring out what it was and who was behind it. He just ran out of time."

"And how do you know this?"

She was stiff in the chair, nervous.

"I have a very good friend who was *his* very good friend, Sutter's that is, who insisted he wasn't coming anywhere near here tonight. He doesn't think we're going to be able to figure this thing out. Says they can get to every last one of us before we do, told me I was risking my life by coming here. He told me to warn you you're all risking *your* lives."

"He was a friend of Sutter? And he knows something?"

"He knows more than he ever wanted to know. It scared him. Right after Sutter shot himself, the man put his ex back in his house and moved out of the city."

The room erupted in chatter. Questions came from all quarters.

"Was this guy a guard?"

"Did he work in the pogey? What does he know?"

"Did he put you up to this? To *scare* us?"

She shook her head.

"No. I came here cuz I'd rather stand and fight than run."

"Will you tell us who he is?"

"Not gonna happen."

The older moderator at the dais pleaded.

"Is there anything at all you *can* tell us?"

"Only that the people behind these killings are scary powerful, that they probably have spies sitting right in this room tonight."

Once again, Cassie found the eyes of the McGinnis informants.

"That would be unfortunate. But what sticks in my mind is Gutierrez. I mean, why Gutierrez? Like you said, Sutter was onto something, but Gutierrez was just a regular guy!"

A medium-built man with a paunch stood at the center of the crowd.

"Grant scratched a phone number on the wall of his cell, and he wrote two words, some kinda clue, in a place no one saw till we moved the mattress. Then someone else came back in and erased the wall clean."

"Do you know the number and the words? Did someone write them down?"

"Yeah, we got em. I got em right here."

Cassie interrupted.

"Good. We all have little pieces of a bigger puzzle, and the only way someone's going to be able to put them together is if we all write down what we know, everything we can remember. And we need to do that right now."

Within minutes, most of the guards had moved to tables in the back, scribbling into college examination blue books with borrowed hotel pens. A half hour passed before the majority returned to their seats. The moderator remained in the back of the room, collecting books as they were completed, while his counterpart and Cassie continued to explain the process in the front.

"I'm not sure how involved Mr. Cassie can or will be, but Hartog and me, we're gonna pore over everything you've written down, and we're gonna try to make some sense of it. We'll put it together and we'll meet in exactly one week so we can talk about it. That work for you?"

Even as the group signaled agreement, Cassie added a comment.

"During the week, if you think of anything you forgot to write down tonight, jot it down and bring it with you. And if anyone runs across a story about a missing laptop computer belonging to the prison, find out what you can and share that."

The petite woman, already returned to her second-row seat, sighed aloud.

"You mean *Sutter's* laptop computer? That friend I told you about? He's got it, but it's his insurance policy and I don't think it'll be easy to get him to part with it."

Cassie smelled a set-up. He took a deep breath and began.

"So is *that* why you're here? To extort money from us? To broker a deal for this guy?"

She sighed, rolling her eyes.

"Look, by the time you've gone through all those books back there, you'll probably know who he is. I'm a guard. I'm here to fight like everyone else. But he's not that stupid or loyal. He's not going to just give you that laptop for *nothing*! We're not naïve here. We all know the relationship between risk and money."

The woman at the dais wagged her head.

"So how much is it gonna cost us, Lopez? Do you know?"

"More than the people in this room can afford. He wants to deal with the union, and that means *you*, Mr. Cassie."

"Well, I'm honored. It isn't often that I get a personal visit from the president of the prison guards union. Please sit down, sit down."

Warden McGinnis unbuttoned his jacket and settled into his own seat behind the desk, adjusting his tie.

"I've gotten quite used to dealing with Mr. Cassie. He's a good man, cares profoundly about the guards and all."

A visit to a warden by CCPOA president Donovan Baker was extremely rare. In fact, McGinnis had never met him in the six years since Baker became the union boss, though they talked twice on the phone, once just that morning. Baker wanted to meet at a restaurant, but the warden said he was busy and insisted having the meeting in his office. McGinnis and his counterparts in the state had never been fond of Baker, who seemed to go out of his way to be critical of the wardens at every opportunity.

Not that he cared anything about the guards. For Baker, it was more about business, more about asserting and maintaining power. There was a story about him having a secret scorecard on each of the wardens and their prisons. This scorecard contained dirty little secrets, ethics violations, conflicts of interest and other sensitive personal information acquired through investigators and operatives. He used the information when necessary for coercion in dealing with the prisons and the correctional system.

Rather than being intimidated by the visit, McGinnis was intrigued. He respected Baker's intellect and saw the meeting as a challenge, as something of a cerebral chess match. For many years, McGinnis regretted his erudite inclination was wasted in his bullshit job as a mere prison warden, so Baker's call that morning excited him, though he suppressed showing it. McGinnis had Baker pegged. He was smart, but he was not a wit, an interesting adversary, though not a formidable opponent. Nonetheless, it had been years since the warden felt so engaged, so energized.

"Water?"

Distracted by the iPhone in his hands, Baker hardly heard the offer.

"No thanks, I'm fine."

McGinnis began while pouring himself a glass.

"I realize how valuable your time is, but so is mine. I have a longstanding rule in my office: no electronic devices. Would you mind?"

"Excuse me?"

"Would you mind turning it off? Your little computer device or whatever."

Awkward and insulted, Baker hesitated and then slid the iPhone into the inside pocket of his jacket, reflecting on the earlier conversation.

"Very well. It is your office."

McGinnis smiled, pleased with himself.

"You said you had a matter to discuss with me."

"Yes. I want to know what's *really* going on here, at the prison."

The warden shrugged.

"Certainly you know what goes on at a prison, but that's not what you're asking me."

"You know what I'm asking. Forty-two dead inmates, and now two of my guards."

McGinnis sipped from the glass, nodding.

"Outside the ongoing investigations, I have no special insight or knowledge. *You* probably know more than I do."

Baker's face showed disappointment.

"Warden McGinnis, last year you bought a new home in Livermore, acre of property, cul-de-sac, six bedrooms, five bathrooms, almost five thousand square feet. You paid six hundred thousand for it, but it was worth more than a million and a half."

"Is that the best you've got? I bought the house on a short sale, pretty common in California these days. I'll admit it was an incredible deal."

"The loan you secured was at a five-and-an-eighth percent interest. *Lenders* couldn't even get that rate at the time you did, and you didn't buy it down."

McGinnis pursed his lips, perturbed.

"I have a banker friend."

"Yes you do, and I'm sure your banker friend is impressed with how well you've done in the stock market this year. Seasoned traders lost their shorts and you somehow made over a million dollars."

"And that means?"

Baker lowered his voice.

"Someone out there, someone powerful is paying you off to let things happen at this prison. I'm not sure if it's because you're in on it or if you're being paid to look the other way, but I've got guards dying now and I'm sitting on the verge of a major panic. I need you to tell me what's going on."

McGinnis sat back in the chair.

"You're right. There *was* indeed something going on over there with the inmates at Death Row. I'm not sure who was involved, but I'm appointed state employee. They don't pay me enough to take on anyone capable of doing what was done there. So yes, call me guilty of looking the other way, but no one's paying me to exercise good common sense. Besides, the killing was over before we even realized it was going on."

"And the guards? Sutter and Gutierrez?"

"*Exactly* my reason for staying out of it. Sutter tried to take on these guys and he got snuffed out, Gutierrez too. Whoever's behind it was cleaning up loose ends. As far as I'm concerned, this thing is done. Whoever was here has moved on."

Baker raised his eyebrows.

"You really think so?"

McGinnis nodded.

"Situation is contained on this end, unless more of your guards somehow decide they want to take on these guys."

Baker sensed the insinuation in the comment.

"Is that the case? *Are* some of the guards going after whoever's behind this?"

McGinnis shrugged.

"I heard they went to you, and you turned them away. You wouldn't even let *Cassie* talk to them."

"You didn't answer my question."

"Desperate men resort to desperate measures."

Frustrated, Baker narrowed his eyes.

"What are they doing? How many are involved?"

The warden smiled and wagged his head.

"You are in a position unsuitable to make demands, and I'm not feeling especially generous owing to the fact you tried to come in here and threaten me. Unfortunately, however, our destinies are conjoined. If more guards die, we both suffer the risk of a prison-wide panic, with guards refusing to work here, and that's just for starts. As I said earlier, the situation is contained on this end."

"So, you're saying it's not contained on *my* end?"

McGinnis paused for dramatic effect.

"Some of your guards have decided to take up where Sutter left off. They're conducting their own investigation. They feel they have to protect themselves, since you've already demonstrated you *won't* do it."

Baker sat a moment in silence, thinking.

"It's, it's like you said earlier. We're in this together. If guards start dying, it'll be bad for both of us, and for the state. You have to help me stop them."

"I'm already acting on my end. On your end, you have to do something more for them than just putting them off."

"I will."

Baker retrieved the buzzing iPhone from his jacket pocket and scanned the message.

"Warden McGinnis, you're obviously more on top of this thing than I am, and I realize you don't owe me any answers. But in order for me to take appropriate action, I have to know: is Cassie involved? Is he helping the guards?"

McGinnis shook his head.

"I talked to Cassie. He cares about the guards, but he told me you threatened to fire him if he got involved. So, of *course* he's not involved."

Chapter 11

She was beginning to believe she was not a good fit for the job. When Lyndsey Alexander-Mitchell first took over for Destiny at the *Aegis Foundation*, she was excited at the prospect of getting some of her ideas implemented, but the politics involved were frustrating. First of all, she wasn't Destiny. Destiny had a way of intimidating people with her intellect and her certainty about things. As a lawyer, she was usually the smartest person in the room. However, what worked for her wasn't working for Lyndsey.

Lyndsey had earned an MBA from the Stanford School of Business, but most of the directors and upper-level management staff had equivalent educations. Many believed she was too young and too inexperienced to assume the reins of power at the foundation, especially while in an expansion phase. And while she wanted to project confidence and competence in meetings and conferences, at least once or twice a week, she would lock the door to her office, turn up the music and succumb to tears.

She called Destiny every evening, frustrated and spent, and Destiny always encouraged her, telling Lyndsey about her first days with the San Francisco prosecutor's office. Like Lyndsey, Destiny was discouraged and wanted to quit. She felt no one respected her, not only for her youth and inexperience, but also for her gender and race. She pushed Lyndsey to step up to the opportunity and character-building challenge presented her. It would make her stronger and better in the end.

Besides Destiny, Lyndsey relied on constant encouragement from her spouse, Carla Ettinger. The couple got married eighteen months earlier, on the second-year anniversary of their first date. Carla was twenty-three years older and well-established. She was a realtor who specialized in multi-million-dollar properties, though she inherited her fortune from her parents. Carla was smart and supportive and sometimes reminded Lyndsey of Destiny, but the two did not get along.

Early on, Destiny thought Carla was too old for Lyndsey, being almost twice her age. She later insisted Carla was using money and glitzy social affairs to manipulate the impressionable girl. She insisted Carla was like Lyndsey's father, an insecure, incomplete person whose goal was to create dependency. Carla countered that Destiny was jealous, and that on some level, Destiny harbored a secret love for Lyndsey, suggesting Destiny resented seeing Lyndsey with another woman.

To Lyndsey, Destiny was just "Mom." When her own mother, Lynette, was murdered, Destiny became Lynette's surrogate voice, telling her tragic story to the world and demanding justice. Destiny fought for Lynette, at great personal sacrifice. With the money won from Lyndsey's father, Jordan Alexander, and his estate, Destiny helped Grandmother Allegra create the *Aegis Foundation* and took it to heights her grandmother never imagined. Through the foundation, Destiny helped tens of thousands of women escape violence and degradation, empowered them to self-reliance.

And now the foundation Destiny spent ten years defining, building and expanding was Lyndsey's to control. Sometimes the idea of it was too much. Attempting to get up to speed, Lyndsey went to work at seven a.m. and often stayed later than ten at night. Because security in the building was strict and reliable, she never worried about being at the office late.

However, as she sat alone in the suite that night, she was caught completely off-guard.

"How did you guys get in here? Can I help you?"

The men, dressed in black suits and white shirts, sporting dark glasses, said nothing. They stood next to the chairs on the other side of her desk. When she reached for the phone to call security, one of the men gripped and twisted her wrist, removing the phone.

Her voice trembled, though she tried to project confidence.

"What do you *want*?"

"The money in your purse and your car keys. This is a robbery gone wrong."

Hand fidgeting under the table, she reached for the silent alarm and pushed the red button. Suspicious about what her hand had done, out of sight, one of the men reached over, taking her purse from the desk. The other reacted as well, reaching into his jacket.

"When you're recovering in the hospital, we have a message for you to deliver to Destiny Mitchell, your mother. She doesn't know who she's dealing with. Tell her to tell us everything she knows and back off. That way, no one else will get hurt."

By the time she saw the gun and flinched, the shot had already been fired. The bullet struck her abdomen, burning like fire, weighing her down, causing her to double over. A second bullet burned into her right shoulder. She screamed as she fell, certain she was going to die.

"Please don't kill me! I don't *know* anything!"

She cried as she bled onto the carpet, anticipating another shot, but through a gap at the bottom of the desk, she could see the men's shiny black shoes turn and exit the room.

It seemed to take forever for the police to arrive, followed in by the guards. One guard called for an ambulance, while the other turned her over to examine the wounds.

"Now you hang in there. You'll be all right."

When she coughed up a mouthful of blood, she knew the wound to her abdomen might be serious. Feeling nauseated, she sensed the bullet had pierced her stomach, causing internal bleeding. By the time paramedics arrived and began working on her, she could not feel anything in her extremities. Her body was numb, unresponsive and freezing cold.

"Call Destiny!"

A fuzzy darkness crept up around her, closing in from the outside edges of her vision, threatening to suffocate her. Struggling to breathe, her eyes fluttered once, and she spewed another mouthful of blood before her body tensed and fell limp.

Kiyomi was the first to arrive at the waiting area outside the recovery room. She was headed south on the 101 when Destiny called to tell her about Lyndsey. From the sound of things, three gang-related Asian teenagers had somehow managed to slip past the guards and into the director's office. During the robbery, one of the kids shot Lyndsey twice, at close range. She was in surgery for three hours as doctors removed a bullet from her abdomen and repaired the wound to her shoulder. While she was seriously injured, the hospital expected her to make a full recovery.

Kiyomi was speaking with the attending physician when Carla Ettinger arrived, approaching the two.

"Excuse me, who are *you*?"

Kiyomi sighed.

"You know who I am, Carla."

"Yes, I know who you are, but who are *you* to talk to Lyndsey's doctor concerning her condition?"

Carla turned on the doctor.

"I'm Carla Ettinger—Lyndsey Alexander-Mitchell's *spouse*. From this point on, I don't want you to discuss her condition, the nature of her injuries or any details about treatment with anyone but me. I have a legal right, and I'm insisting on it."

Uncomfortable, the doctor nodded, extending her hand.

"Very well. Nice to meet you, Ms. Ettinger."

The doctor gone, Kiyomi reeled.

"Lyndsey's conscious and coherent. She can make her own decisions, and she's asking for Destiny."

Carla turned her back on the reporter, raising her arms in frustration, and then crossing them.

"She's just been shot! She's in shock. She doesn't know what the hell she wants! Until *I* think she's mentally and emotionally stable enough to make decisions, I'm making the calls. So, you might as well get Destiny on the phone and tell her it'll be a waste of her time for her to come down here. Lyndsey won't be seeing or talking to anyone today. She needs her rest."

On the way out, Kiyomi interviewed the detective in charge of the investigation into Lyndsey's shooting. He told Kiyomi circumstances surrounding the crime were unusual. He had spoken with the guards and reviewed the surveillance tape. Both guards, who were at the post the entire night, suggested there was an error with the tape. Scrutinizing the still images of the bald teenagers, all dressed in white t-shirts and baggy black jeans, they insisted the kids' appearance alone would have been a red flag. In order to get to the elevator, they would have had to walk right past the station. The staircase door was locked from the outside. One guard swore the teenagers from the tape were never in the building, at least not on that night.

The inspector also found it odd that Lyndsey was shot with a .22 caliber weapon, "not exactly the choice piece carried around by gang members. If she had been shot point-blank like that by one of the typical guns these guys carry, we'd be having this discussion at the morgue." He said the whole situation smelled like some kind of set-up, though he admitted he couldn't imagine a practical motive for it. Her purse and car keys were taken, and yet the car wasn't stolen.

As a reporter, Kiyomi felt up to her professional duty only when she was pushing the envelope, creating chaos and making people uncomfortable. This time, however, duty gave her personal satisfaction. She was careful not the break the law, but institutional rules and guidelines were another matter. Pushing open the door, she glanced over at Carla and walked toward the bed.

"How do you feel, Lyndsey? What happened?"

Surprised and angry, Carla stood.

"You, you're *not* allowed in here! Get out!"

Kiyomi held an open palm in Carla's direction and continued.

"Do you remember, Lyndsey? Detective said it was three Asian gang members. Is that true?"

Lyndsey wagged her head, indicating it was not true. Carla went for the door, making a commotion, screaming for a nurse.

"Did you see them? What did they look like?"

"Two men, suits, dark glasses, like in the movies."

"Did they say anything to you?"

By this time, a nurse arrived and took up a position between Kiyomi and the patient.

"Ma'am! You have to leave! Now!"

Kiyomi looked past the stout woman.

"What did they say?"

Lyndsey bowed her head, elbows forward, her palms covering her eyes, crying.

"Where's Destee? Get Destiny! I just need to talk to my mom!"

The mood at the table was somber. Destiny's eyes seemed sunken and the lines around them more pronounced. Her complexion was different, lacking color. Though she tried to smile, her expression showed strain. She sipped the steaming *Genmaicha* from a ceramic flowervine teacup.

"They were trying to accomplish exactly this! They're attacking me where they know I'm vulnerable. Bastards! I don't even know who I'm up against!"

The small, family-owned restaurant on Webster in Japantown was one of her favorites, especially when she wanted to get away from the typical San Francisco social circles. She and Kiyomi were friends with the owner, Kimiko, who always provided a table in a corner of the little used private dining room. The trio had traveled together to Tokyo and Gifu earlier in the year.

Kiyomi had come over from the hospital after checking on Lyndsey. The police assured her that until the perpetrators were apprehended, they would station a guard near the room. When Kiyomi phoned Destiny to warn her about Carla's opposition to any visitation, Destiny suggested they meet at the restaurant instead.

Seated across the table, Kiyomi nodded.

"You're right. They could have killed her if they wanted to. They wanted to shake you up, something they've apparently accomplished. You look wasted."

"I thought to go over there anyway, but Carla was gonna make me lose my religion!"

Destiny exhaled aloud.

"Two martinis before you got here. I swear if they do anything else to her, I'll *kill* someone! Or I'll blow this whole thing out of the water! I just wish I had more to go on, a name, a piece of evidence, anything!"

"Maybe after this, Bryan'll come around and share what he knows?"

"I can't count on that. He's somehow mixed up in this whole thing and he won't tell me what he's doing. He says he's trying to protect me, and you."

Kiyomi raised her eyebrows as she sipped.

"Too bad he didn't include Lyndsey there."

She sat back in the chair.

"I heard the guards had a secret meeting a few days ago, and at that meeting someone said there's a laptop out there, Sergeant Sutter's laptop. The guards, the prison, everyone's looking for it. It's supposed to have something on it, some kind of proof."

"Proof? When Bryan gets here, we'll ask him about it and see what he says."

When he arrived ten minutes later, Destiny and Kiyomi were already having soup. Destiny shoved a bowl his way.

"We already ordered for you."

He had barely finished his first sip when Kiyomi began.

"You know, Bryan, Lyndsey could be dead today. You couldn't protect her, and you can't protect us. Will you admit *now* we're going to have to work at this together?"

He smiled.

"I never said we *couldn't* work together at this."

"No, but Destee tells me it's *need to know*. That's not the same thing."

Setting the bowl on the table, Bryan sighed and began.

"Look, I'm sorry about Lyndsey, but she's sitting in that hospital right now because you two wouldn't listen. I told you from the beginning to let me handle this! I can still get you out of this thing, if you'd only let me."

Destiny slammed her bowl down.

"And how are you going to do that, Bryan? What? You know something? You know who did it?"

He sighed.

"You've been drinking. I know someone who might know who's behind it, but I won't be able to get him to work with me unless I can guarantee you two are going to let this thing go. It has nothing to do with you. Stop your meddling!"

"And then what?"

"Then you can get back to your lives. Call it a stalemate. No one wins, no one loses."

Destiny shook her head.

"No. They already know who I am, while I'm sitting here with no clue about who they are. And they've proven today they're willing to shoot innocent, uninvolved people. How do you expect me to trust anyone who would shoot my daughter?"

"You two have no idea what you're up against."

"And you do?"

He nodded.

"Yes, I do. It's bigger than you. You can't win. Look, you both have great careers. Share what you know and walk away from this thing so you can get back to your lives. Let me finish this. I promise you'll be safe."

Kiyomi bowed toward the server as she passed off her bowl.

"What is it, Bryan? You think you're *that* much smarter than we are? We're supposed to just put our lives in your hands because you're a man and you know better? Are you working for the people who had Lyndsey shot?"

Anger showed in his expression.

"No! I just know they mean business and they wouldn't think twice about taking out a suburban mom slash newspaper reporter and a former attorney who no longer runs a big foundation."

Destiny sighed, shaking her head.

"And *you're* going to save us? These are the same people who murdered all those inmates, the same people who murdered Shaw and Gutierrez and who are presently murdering FBI Agent Martinez. And they're going to just forget about us because *you* say so? You hold that much sway? What exactly *is* your involvement in this, Bryan?"

Kiyomi did not let him answer.

"Why don't we just *all* share everything we know? Do you have a problem with that, Bryan?"

He contemplated for a moment and sat back in the seat.

"I can do that, to an extent. What do you want to know?"

Destiny was quick to begin.

"Who shot my daughter?"

"I don't know, but it wasn't the Asian kids in the surveillance tape. That segment was spliced from a remote computer. Professional job."

"Who are you working for?"

He lowered his voice.

"Relevantly? A powerful man whose name I can't share. Washington player. Right now, I'm still trying to figure out if he's a good guy or a bad guy, but he's involved in the prison murders. He's paying me to investigate and report on all the investigations going on over there."

Destiny stared at him.

"Are you losing all your objectivity? How can he be a good guy if he's involved in the murders?"

She took a breath, attempting to control the emotion.

"Did you know in advance they were going after Lyndsey?"

"How could you ask me that? I care about Lyndsey! She's our daughter. I do! You know me better than that."

She closed her eyes, bowing her head.

"I believe you do, but after this, you have to share with us or get the fuck out of our way, because we're going to get to the bottom of this one way or another."

"No, now just stop! Both of you! You'll die! They'll *kill* you."

"Again, who? Who is *they*?"

Kiyomi sighed.

"If they're as powerful and dangerous as you say, and they want us out of the way, *you* can't protect us, that is, unless you have leverage, something on them."

She stopped, her mouth dropping open.

"Wait! What do you have on them, Bryan?"

He looked toward Destiny, sat back and took a hesitant breath.

"I have the game changer. I have the back-up copy disk from Sutter's laptop computer."

Chapter 12

"So, are we to infer from the foregoing, Governor Gordon, that you're tossing your hat into the ring for the next election? Can we say we heard it here first?"

Over recent weeks, former New Jersey governor Hugh Gordon had made several appearances on the Sunday morning political talk show circuit. Handsome and well-informed, the governor was a popular guest on cable news broadcasts, though he was preferred by the more conservative hosts. A governor for four years and successful CEO of a Fortune 400 company, he looked presidential, though he was careful by nature.

"Let's just say I'm keeping all my options open. It's still a little early to apply for the job, but somehow I get the impression you guys won't stop until we're doing four-year campaigns."

The commentator laughed.

"Believe me, Governor, we're working on that!"

Since the end of the last election, rhetoric in the media and in communities across the country had become increasingly desperate and dangerous. Militia groups and rural Americans, mired in recession and high unemployment and frightened by change, clung to their second amendment's right to bear arms and looked to an agent, or martyr, with the courage and patriotism to "do whatever was necessary" to restore America to its true nature.

For conservatives and right-wing extremists who saw the Republican Party and the Tea Party as the last hope for a political solution, the real battle for "America," or America's real war was being lost to socialist liberals, women politicians, homosexuals, ungodly people and minorities. Many were ready and willing to "refresh the tree of liberty with the blood of patriots and tyrants," and with their own blood, if necessary. Whether by violent revolution across the country or political assassination, something had to be done.

And yet, before dismissing the call for political assassination as the ranting of ignorant, frightened, uneducated rural racists and southerners, it became apparent the idea had originated with, and was propagated by many other, well-educated, well-moneyed groups, by lobbies, special interests, media moguls, personalities and radio hosts.

To those groups, this president posed the biggest threat to traditional American institutions, and by extension, to the country. They compared the president's charisma to that of Adolf Hitler, with the ability to lead the ignorant and hope-filled masses to destruction. A master manipulator and skilled orator, he was able to move his initiatives forward on almost every front, despite the protests of angry and motivated resistance.

If there was to be a political solution, many saw former Governor Hugh Gordon as the instrument of God's restitution. He had the solid support of the conservative base. He believed in God and Jesus Christ, he was a creationist, pro-life, against stem cell research, against quotas and affirmative action, anti-gay marriage, anti-immigration, pro-gun, pro-law enforcement, he opposed the president on just about everything, and he favored a stronger display of American power and "swagger" abroad.

The conflict within Governor Gordon, however, was reconciliation. Unlike some of his colleagues and co-patriots, he was a pious man, meaning that for him, if political expediency came into conflict with his biblical and religious principles, his first inclination was to choose the moral course. So while his thoughts and motivations usually came from no discernable bias or hate, he was never comfortable working with many of the overt racists and sexists, men and women, who operated at the highest levels in his party.

In the weeks prior to being offered a role in the clandestine *Secure America* group's inner circle and agenda, he recognized an indirect vetting process at work. Former Associate Supreme Court Justice Wendell Greene asked most of the questions, occasionally joined by another member, and Gordon answered honestly. Greene had asked Gordon to read Plutarch's *Life of Brutus* and the writings of Thomas Jefferson, and the two discussed the material at length.

It was one thing to join an activist right-wing group to advance a conservative agenda and quite another to become involved in a plot involving high-tech political assassination. And yet, while Gordon struggled with moral imperatives which pitted his sense of country against his innate sense of rectitude, others in the country sought a more immediate and bloody solution.

The plan, *Operation Firepower*, originated in an executive committee meeting of the New Order Militias of the American Southwest. A loose band of militias ranging from Arizona, Utah, Wyoming, Colorado, Kansas, Oklahoma and Texas, *NO MAS* boasted over 200,000 gun-toting members. *NO MAS* leadership was aware the government had operatives within their ranks, so they created two plans. The first was to be a distraction to advance the success of the second.

The seething pot of hatred and anger in America had bubbled and boiled for over eighteen months and was threatening to explode. The conservative state of Arizona, with the most liberal gun laws in America and one of the country's most heavily armed populations, was to be the staging area. The President was scheduled for a speaking engagement and meeting in Phoenix during late August at a venue where secret service indicated security was a concern.

The goal of the militias was to "just show up armed," literally outgunning the President's security detail and local law enforcement, pick a fight and amid the distraction, give a sniper a clear shot. The militias expected to suffer massive casualties, but many of their young men had been briefed, convinced to take part in a heroic effort that would liberate America from tyranny.

The leadership of the militias however, underestimated the degree the government had infiltrated their ranks, right up to their executive committees. The President's speaking engagement was cancelled without prior announcement and the arrests of militia leaders began. The two designated snipers were arrested upon arrival. One group of young men retreated to a local self-storage facility and set up a base, vowing to fight the government to the death. In the brief firefight that ensued, nineteen of the

teenaged militiamen were killed, and the balance surrendered to
the FBI and law enforcement after it became obvious the feds
would not negotiate terms.

Sobered by events in Arizona, militia groups became even
more paranoid about the federal government and went about
purging their ranks, sometimes turning on themselves and on
each other, leading to more killings and arrests. The assassination
attempt was repudiated by congressional members of both
parties, by the American public and by most of the media.

For conservatives, this repudiation unified the party and other
disaffected Americans around a leader who offered a viable
political solution, and that was Governor Hugh Gordon. There
were other aspirants, but Gordon possessed the right qualities,
disposition, combination of values and genuine morality to
challenge the other party's candidate on all fronts.

The Sunday morning commentator was not going to let
Governor Gordon off without eliciting a comment about the plot
against the President.

"Governor, you were one of the first to come forth and
condemn the New Order Militias of the American Southwest for
their actions and to call for more federal surveillance and tracking
of these militias and their members. If you somehow end up the
nominee, do you think you will be able to bring this extreme
faction of conservatives back into the fold, if you even *want* them
there? Or will they hate you even more than they hated the other
side for coming out and condemning them so forcefully?"

Gordon smiled.

"That's a good question. For the answer, I hearken to the words
of Founding Father Thomas Jefferson, who in the Declaration of
Independence said, 'Prudence, indeed, will dictate that
Governments long established should not be changed for light
and transient causes; and accordingly, all experience hath shown,
that mankind are more disposed to suffer, while evils are

sufferable, than to right themselves by abolishing the forms to which they are accustomed.'"

He looked toward the cameras.

"You see, our American system is so designed that the people have a right to revolt every four years, to bring about a *bloodless* revolution. If the people don't like who's running the country, they have a right and a responsibility to change that, every two years for congressional representatives, every four years for president and six for our senators. Anarchy doesn't work, not in the long run. As Americans, we *correct* what's wrong. That is the political solution I've been advocating for the people who've been listening, and that's what will continue to make America the model for freedom on Earth."

Cameras off, Gordon bowed his head and sighed, the resonance of his own words weighing heavily on his heart.

Destiny sat in the lobby, her legs crossed, skimming a magazine as she waited for Agent Martinez to arrive. She had visited Lyndsey at the hospital earlier. Because Lyndsey was healthy, her wounds were mending nicely. However, the surgery required to remove the bullet left a two-inch-long scar on her abdomen.

Lyndsey told Destiny she believed the men who shot her were professionals, and she was afraid they would come back and finish the job if Destiny did not comply with their demands. Crying, she begged Destiny to back off, warning she was up against overwhelming odds.

"Listen to me, Mom! If Bryan says he can make this all just go away, let him! I don't care if or how he's involved. Just let him do it if he can do it. Whatever it is, it's not worth it, not if we all are going to die!"

Destiny sighed, nodding.

"I wish it were that easy, Baby, but it isn't. And I don't doubt Bryan's abilities, but this isn't going to just go away, not for me. These people *know* who I am, and they know I know something. That makes me a loose end, a liability. The only reason I'm still alive is that they don't know what I know. And they don't know the details of whatever they think I'm using as an insurance policy. I don't trust them. As soon as they have their answers, they'll kill me."

Tears welled in her eyes.

"Even if I tell Bryan I'm going to walk away from this thing, they're still going to want to know what I know and what I have, and once they get it, they'll send in those same men in suits and dark glasses. My only hope is to keep on digging, to keep clawing and get some real leverage, and then I can turn the tables. I'm going to make someone pay for what they did to you."

She stroked Lyndsey's face and smiled.

"I did ask Bryan to find a place for you to *hide* until this thing is over. When I spoke with your doctor, she said you'd be cleared to leave this afternoon. So listen, Lynds—you have to leave this afternoon, while Carla is at work. She can't know where you are hiding, and you won't be able to call her, for her *own* protection. *I* don't even want to know where you'll be. You'll go with Bryan and stay hidden until the danger has passed. Do you understand that?"

Lyndsey seemed mortified.

"You want me to just *leave* without saying anything? Carla's my wife. I can't do that to her."

"You can if you want to live, and you want *her* to live."

Destiny softened.

"Look, it's only nine o'clock now. Why don't you spend the afternoon writing Carla a letter? You can explain everything to her and let her know you're safe, and you *will* be safe until you return to her."

She kissed her daughter's forehead.

"I'm sorry you're involved in this. I don't know exactly how I got involved. I just have to believe that I was *called* or chosen for whatever work lies ahead, however difficult or dangerous, and I've chosen to obey the call. Life's not a matter of chance. It's a matter of choice."

Eyes moist, Destiny left the poignant memory. Still seated in the lobby, she checked her watch. The space was empty, save a man and a little girl seated next to a play area. Hope Jefferson, Destiny's sister, was a genetic researcher who worked at this Emeryville office.

Two weeks earlier, Destiny asked Hope to look over Agent Martinez's medical files in order to determine if his sickness had been brought on by an agent that altered his DNA. Hope called earlier that morning to tell her sister confusing results had come back. Eager to see the findings, Destiny phoned Martinez and asked him to meet her at Hope's office at noon.

When Martinez arrived, it was obvious his heart condition had taken a toll on his overall health. He seemed thinner, wan and tired. His face was wet with perspiration, and he was out of breath by the time he approached her.

"How are you feeling, Jake?"

"Oh, like a semi just ran over my chest." He smiled, wheezing. "But other than that, I'm fine."

Hope Jefferson resembled her younger sister, though her hair was grayer, and she carried a little more weight in her hips. She sat across the desk, queuing up the oversized computer screen for her guests.

"Are you both going to be able to see that?"

Jake nodded, whispering to Destiny.

"We can sit closer. I don't bite, and it's not contagious."

Hope worked from her side of the desk, while Destiny and Jake followed on the screen.

"Okay Jake, on this screen is an isolated section of your DNA sequence from the first time you got tested over at Berkeley three months ago. Now, I'm going to split the screen. And there. The second screen is that same section as it exists now. Can you see that?"

Jake squinted at the computer screen. On one side, there was a rectangular sheet, or slide, and on that slide, there was a grid with a random series of horizontal bars, five columns across. Some of the bars were heavy, others were lighter or opaque and several appeared to be double bars. Hope sequestered a section in the chain and enlarged it.

"And now I'm going to zoom in on each and place them side by side."

Jake shrugged.

"Okay. So what am I looking at?"

"I'll try to make this short and simple. In humans, ninety-nine-point-nine percent of our DNA is identical, but what makes us unique as individuals are the isolated variable repetitive sequences that we call variable number tandem repeats. The process I used is called STR, for short tandem repeats."

He nodded as she continued.

"In that process, I examined thirteen polymorphic regions of your reference sample and compared them to the sample you provided recently. Because you are the same person as you were when they sampled your DNA over at Berkeley three months ago, there should have been no difference. But there you *see* it. It's slight, noticeable in only this one region here, but it's different. I don't know what it means, and I'm not sure if it explains your condition. It's the oddest thing!"

Martinez stared at the screen.

"So that's it. It got *changed* somehow. What I need to know is, can it be reversed?"

Hope paused, her voice softening.

"I'm sorry. I don't think that's possible. Science just isn't there yet."

"But if someone had the science to do this to me, shouldn't the science exist to undo it?"

Hope removed her glasses, wagging her head.

"No one could have *done* this to you. I'm a genetic researcher. I've worked with all the cutting-edge technologies over the last fifteen years, and I can't begin to understand this. This isn't science. What we're looking at is impossible, a freak of nature."

Destiny hesitated because she did not want to get Hope involved. She was careful not to say too much.

"Would something like that *be* possible through gene therapy, using a viral vector to introduce a defective or altered gene?"

On hearing the words, Martinez gasped, making the connection. Hope answered.

"It's like I said. Something like that would be at least ten, fifteen years away. Some doctors have been working with cell-based therapies to repair damaged hearts, but gene therapy is ineffective in its current stage of development for one main reason: it's too short lived. Any altered DNA introduced to the system has to remain functional and stable, and it's got to be long-lived if it is ever going to be integrated into the genome. No one's even close to solving that problem. This couldn't be gene therapy."

Destiny took a picture of the computer display with a small camera and looked toward her sister.

"But what if someone *did* solve it? What if someone did manage to get over that hurdle and make it functional and long-lived? Could gene therapy then be used to turn on a gene that could trigger heart disease?"

Hope was suspicious of the question and sat back in her seat before answering.

"Theoretically yes, but gene therapy is used for therapeutic purposes. No one would ever *do* that."

Excited, Jake interjected.

"But theoretically, if it could be used to turn a gene on, then theoretically it could be used to turn one off, right?"

Hope paused.

"Well yes, but someone would have to have the technology to do that, and that technology doesn't exist. All right, what's going on here? There's something you two aren't telling me."

Destiny stood.

"No, it's nothing. I was just wondering, that's all. You know how my mind works—the 'what if' questions never stop with me. And it's not often I get to talk science with my big sis. Jake?"

She tapped his shoulder.

"Jake, I think we've taken up enough of Hope's time. I'll walk you out."

Hope stood.

"Jake, why don't you wait for Destiny outside? I have a question to ask her in private."

She began the moment the door closed.

"Come on, Destee. You think I don't know he's FBI? *And* that he was over at Berkeley checking out a series of deaths at San Quentin prison? I have friends over at CEIP. And while all this is happening, someone up and shoots Lyndsey? What's going on?"

Destiny crossed her arms and took a deep breath.

"I can't tell you and you *don't* want to know, believe me."

"What's wrong? Are you in trouble?"

"All the records you got from Jake, destroy them. Anything you did here with his name on it, get rid of it. If anyone ever calls and asks you about him, say you never met him. If anyone asks you about me, tell them we're estranged. No, tell them you *hate* me."

Hope's eyes were wide and desperate.

"Destee?"

"Stop. I'm just trying to protect you and your family."

Destiny hugged her sister hard, crying.

"If I never see you again, look after Lyndsey for me. And please know that I love you. I've always loved you."

When Bryan arrived, Cassie was on the phone with one of the guards.

"So what happened? Last week you were all *gung-ho* to get started on this! You said you had a lead on one of the doctors. And now you're telling me you won't *do* it?"

Cassie motioned for Bryan to sit as he concluded the call.

"Danger factor? How has the danger factor changed?"

He sighed.

"Let's call it what it is, the *bullshit factor*, or the coward factor. What are you going to do? Not go to work? The only way we're going to protect ourselves is by sticking together here. Come on, you're a leader! If you don't show up, then Harris'll stay home, Rodriguez and his group won't come, Santangelo, Murphy and his brothers! That's about a quarter of everyone we started with."

He listened for a moment, resigning.

"Just think about what I said, okay. And if you change your mind, you know where we'll be. Later."

Bryan looked over, smiling.

"I take it things aren't going great with the guards?"

"They're spooked! We had that first meeting, and everyone agreed to write down what they had. We were going to put all our information together and maybe solve this thing."

"Sounds like a good idea. What happened?"

"A few days after that meeting, some of the guards reported they were being followed by goons in big cars. Others said they had cars rolling by their houses. One guy said a scary person knocked on his door when he was at work and started asking his wife personal, threatening questions."

Bryan shrugged.

"Typical scare tactics, but it seems they're working."

"Yeah, and I know who's behind it—that asshole Baker!"

"Baker?"

Cassie walked over and closed the door.

"You met him. Baker, my boss, the president of CCPOA. Mother fucker! He's more a politician than anything else. He threatened to get me fired if I got involved."

Bryan placed his laptop computer on the desk, prying it open.

"Don't lose your job. We'll lose access to the prison."

"Oh, thanks for caring so much about my *family*."

Bryan smiled, waiting for the disk to load.

"I've got something here that just might make up for that."

"What is it?"

"Well, what you're looking at on this screen are the names, email and office addresses for all the doctors who worked over at San Quentin over the last three years."

Cassie leaned in.

"My god! Where'd you get that?"

"It gets even better. Look at this, monthly records of all infirmary purchase orders, deliveries and accounts payable. Phone records are only partial, and so are the ones for outside lab records, fees and courier services, but there's enough here."

"Let me guess. You got Sutter's computer. You found the guy who had it and paid him off?"

Bryan wagged his head, scrolling down.

"No. Just dumb luck. Sutter's wife found these back-up disks hidden away in his high school yearbook. I picked them up this morning. I'm not sure how current his records were when he killed himself, but there's a trail somewhere in all this, and I'm going to follow where it leads."

"What can I do?"

"Well first of all, don't get fired. I still need access to the prison to verify some of the data. You know, fill in the blanks and connect the dots. And if any of your guards have additional evidence or information that's not here, you can make sure it gets to me."

Cassie returned to his chair and sat, raring back.

"My boss is putting the pressure on me to wrap up this investigation. When do you think you'll be done?"

"Another week in there and I think I'll have everything I need. I'll do the rest from my office."

Cassie nodded.

"You know, no one's died over there for over a month. Last inmate was Popovich, right after Grant, and before that it had been three weeks. So that's only two in the last three months as opposed to one a week at the height of this thing. McGinnis is sure whatever was going on over there has run its course and we all need to get back to business as usual. I don't think he'll let you go back *in* there."

Bryan looked up.

"I need a week. You have to get me another week."

"I'll see what I can do."

Cassie glanced over at Bryan and then stared straight ahead.

"Bryan, I need you to be honest with me. When you first came to me about the deaths at the prison, I asked if you had an angle, any hidden agenda, or if you were working for someone who needed an operative on the inside."

Bryan nodded.

"You did."

"And you denied it. In fact, you said you knew less than I knew. Remember that?"

"Yes. What are you getting at, Cassie?"

Cassie shut the laptop and placed a sheet of paper before Bryan.

"You *lied* to me. One of the guards saw a series of numbers and some words in Grant's cell before they got erased. We had the numbers checked out. Turned out it was the phone number belonging to the prosecutor who convicted Grant, and I think you know who that was. It was Destiny Mitchell, your *wife*! You lied."

Bryan held up a hand in a halting gesture.

"Grant called my wife two days before he died. So yes, I knew that, but that's *all* I knew."

"Why didn't you tell me that?"

Bryan sighed.

"I'm sorry, James. I hadn't talked to you in ten years. I was worried about her, and I didn't want to say or do anything that might jeopardize her life."

"Jeopardize her life? What are you talking about?"

"Listen to me. About a week after Grant called her, she got a scary call from some other person, and he was demanding to know what Grant told her. Naturally, she got all freaked out and called me, asking for help. I didn't have an 'in,' so I called you to volunteer my services. She's my wife. I wanted to investigate this thing further. That's *exactly* how it happened."

Cassie remained skeptical.

"You know, I appreciate you sharing this information of Sutter's. You didn't have to do that. And the story about your wife might be true, but I just have this feeling right at the pit of my gut that you're not telling me everything. I know you. I was your partner when we were police detectives. You've always been squirrelly. You're working some other angle in this thing, and no matter what you say, you can't convince me otherwise."

Chapter 13

Justice Wendell Greene tapped the gavel, calling the meeting to order.

"Once again, thank you all for coming. It has been two months since our last meeting, so we'll begin by briefing you on recent developments, and then we will proceed to our very necessary business. Mr. X?"

The boardroom was dimly lit so that none of the committee members were recognizable. For the protection of members, great efforts were undertaken to protect their individual identities. Each arrived at fifteen-minute intervals, had their cars parked by valet and were blindfolded and gloved before being escorted into the building up to the darkened boardroom. Before being seated, a mask was placed on the face of each. A cued-up laptop before members usually contained the agenda and the meeting script.

Billionaire Helmut Wolf, or Mr. X, stood before the group.

"Brave gentlemen and gentlewoman of *The Committee*, when last we met, I told you we were nearing the application phase of a process which would allow us to achieve the aims of our enterprise, covert political assassination, reserved for the narrow and extraordinary aims of our *Country First* agenda.

"Well tonight, I am pleased to inform you that we are fully operational. Beyond that, I am prepared to show you our process in action. Please direct your attention to the computer screens before you. The feed will begin shortly."

Governor Gordon adjusted the mask to get a clear view of the screen, which displayed the *Country First* logo for a few seconds before dissolving to a screen displaying, *Viral Vector Project... Shaping the World*.

Wolf smiled behind the mask, excitement in his voice.

"And we begin..."

When Gordon's eyes returned to the laptop, a CNN news anchor's stern expression tempered the mood of the moment. At the bottom of the screen were the words, *Supreme Leader Dead, Thousands Mourn*. The anchor took a breath and began.

Today, hundreds of thousands mourn the death of Supreme Leader [missing audio] *in the Islamic Republic of* [missing audio].

According to government sources, the Supreme Leader fell ill a little more than one month ago, and despite efforts by doctors, his condition deteriorated rapidly. While government officials have not yet disclosed the precise cause of death, unnamed sources indicate the Supreme Leader had a history of health problems. This news comes on the heels of the unexpected death his named successor, [missing audio], who died of heart complications earlier this month.

Although the broadcast had been redacted to obscure the leader and the country involved for purposes of the meeting, there was no question about who had died. When the story broke on the international news scene a week earlier, no one at the table perceived the connection. Was it possible? Governor Hugh Gordon almost voiced his bewilderment, but the sound stuck in his throat, and he changed his mind about speaking out. The anchor continued.

Many predict the death of the Supreme Leader, the highest ranking religious and political authority of the nation, will spell significant changes for the region. Had [missing audio] been alive to succeed him, the republic could have expected a smooth transition of power, as the Supreme Leader and his successor, his former student, shared nearly identical religious and political views.

The anchor paused for effect.

But the Leader died before naming another successor, leaving that responsibility to the Assembly of Authorities, who will appoint the next Supreme Leader. Almost immediately, experts on the region were quick to highlight the religious and political divisions among the Assembly of Authorities, including an indication that the current speaker, [missing audio], who, though he's taken a defiant stand against Israel, has been criticized among the ranks of the body for being too willing to accommodate the United States and some of its European allies. For more of this, let's hear from Siyyid Alí Muhammad, cleric and former professor of Islamic Studies at Kabul University...

The feed dissolved, cutting to another story involving the recent death of a political figure from one of the Balkan states, followed by an analyst speaking on its implications to the balance of the region. That story was followed by another report of a death with political ramifications that occurred in a Central American country, and then one from an African nation. The masked members listened to the reports in the silence of incredulity so that by the time the *Country First* seal returned to the screens, the air in the room weighed heavy, beckoning an explanation.

Helmut Wolf raised his arms wide from his sides in a gesture of victory.

"What we are looking at is the actualization of our plan. Over the past few months, we have all weighed in on trouble spots in the world and viable political solutions. In each of the situations you just saw, the sequel will favor making America and her interests more secure. I must admit, we have been a little ambitious early on, but I assure you: no one outside this room has any idea about what we are doing. Of course, the assassinations alone are no panacea. Beyond this room, we have operatives and officials who will work the political and military angles of our agenda, though they know nothing of our actual existence."

Wendell Greene spoke slow words.

"Just to be clear, Mr. X, what exactly *is* our involvement in the news stories we just now saw?"

"It is natural that you should ask, Mr. Chairman. And for that reason, I brought the good doctor with me today. He is waiting outside."

Wolf phoned an aide outside the room, asking him to bring the doctor in before the committee. Within a few minutes, Rosecrans stood beside him, head bowed as Wolf continued.

"What you just saw were the perfect results of covert political assassinations. In each of those cases, we were able to acquire necessary information from our targets and launch what the doctor calls a *DNA code specific viral vector*. I will let the doctor explain further. Doctor?"

Dr. Benjamin Rosecrans rose and stepped forward, standing in the shadows. In a ray of moonlight, the features of his mask were barely perceptible. It was the face of Thomas Jefferson. In fact, it seemed Mr. X was wearing the same face on his mask. The doctor, nervous, cleared his throat and began.

"Thank you. What you just saw, fellow Americans, my fellow Americans, were four deaths from natural causes, and no investigation or autopsy by any doctors or government, including ours, would yield a different result, or yield different results. And yet these men were assassinated, no less than Lincoln, Garfield, Kennedy, Sadat, Rabin and Bhutto were assassinated. Only in your operation, there is no smoking gun, no explosive residue and no trail leading back to you. Ironically, in each case, the only trail leads directly, um, directly back to the victim."

Mindful that he was rambling, the doctor came back to the point.

"The *DNA code specific viral vector* allows you to eliminate targets selectively and discreetly, minimizing collateral killing and utilizing phenomenal advances in gene therapy. We've had several incredible breakthroughs in gene therapy and viralgenetics, all made possible by a state-of-the art lab and unlimited research funds donated by Mr. X through his various companies. Never in my life have I worked in a lab so well organized and responsive to the needs of my researchers. I owe Mr. X a debt of gratitude for the opportunity to advance medical science forty to fifty years—"

Justice Greene was beginning to lose patience with Dr. Rosecrans, whose stuttering and halted speech belied his intelligence.

"Please come to the point, Doctor. What is this process?"

The doctor shook his head, embarrassed.

"Well, the uh, the short story is this. It begins with collection of a DNA sample from your target—it's usually oral fluid from the, the buccal cavity, but sometimes it will come to us through other methods, some still being developed. If it's properly preserved and comes to us intact, we have the target's code. In our labs, we sequence that code to identify the specific segments we want to alter. In most cases, we alter a gene associated with coronary disease... It will trigger arteriosclerosis in the heart—plaque buildup, a hardening of the arteries. After we've done that, we replicate the altered DNA and insert it into a viral vector. Then the altered code in the viral vector is reintroduced to the target."

He halted, hoping he was being understood.

"Of course, this code is target specific, and we've managed through hybridization to create a very aggressive vector. It could be introduced in a room full of people and only affect a single person, or a single targeted code. Anyway, once the vector is introduced and altered code with enhanced longevity begins replication in the body, the body will simply follow instructions to replace necessary DNA with the new code. If we've altered the code to induce heart disease, the target will ultimately die of a heart attack, and it won't just *seem* like natural causes. It *will* be natural causes. Only we've managed to alter nature."

This time, Governor Gordon could not help himself.

"No, that's not it. Call it what you want, Doctor, but you're trying to play God."

The doctor seemed flustered.

"You? I don't, don't believe you understand—"

The governor continued.

"I realize men like you don't believe in God, and I can see you're very proud of what you've managed to accomplish, but to play God is to mock God, and God will not be mocked."

In the uncomfortable silence that followed, Justice Greene cleared his throat and tried to spin the impromptu discussion into a more positive direction as security personnel escorted Dr. Rosecrans from the room.

"I'm encouraged by the passion you've shown, Governor, and I'm equally impressed by the excitement and creativity the doctor has shown. Like you, Governor, I am a Christian, the same as everyone in this room I think, save the doctor—Christians in an ungodly world. So, before we pronounce judgment on anyone, perhaps we should consider that we ourselves might be *doing* the work of God, sort of helping God along. Let's keep open minds on this matter."

The governor raised his hands outward, as if to defend himself.

"Listen, I'm not some religious quack preaching gloom and doom, but if any of you have ever really read the Bible, you'd realize God doesn't *need* our help. Don't get me wrong. I'm in. I'm in like all the rest of you, to the death, and I'll just have to make my own peace with God, if and when that time comes. The less I know about whatever that doctor is doing, and you, Mr. X, the less I know about what you're doing, all the better."

The Justice was quick to respond.

"Well said. However, the purpose of showing the relevant feed and bringing the doctor in was to make certain that everyone on this executive committee was aware of all aspects of our operation, including those more unsavory in nature. We agreed from the outset that assassination is, at times, the most effective way to bring about political change. The White House already sanctions it publicly, specifically using drone attacks and JSOC, who went in and killed bin Laden."

Justice Greene smoothed his hair back and continued.

"What we're doing is like a drone strike or JSOC attack, only neater, and with no unintended casualties, no collateral damage. It's the next front in America's war against her enemies. Now, we could argue and moralize about methods, but assassination is what it is. We knew from the beginning we'd be ordering men and women to their deaths."

The irritation in Mr. X's voice was obvious, though he tried to disguise it as he took up the narrative.

"Not unlike these same political leaders, some who are our targets, order men, women and children to *their* deaths. There are no innocents. Even I believe in the concept of God, Governor, but I respectfully disagree with the judge. God has no place in what we are doing. *Money is the barometer of a society's virtue.* This is the work of man in a world ruled by men..."

He nodded toward the former congresswoman.

"And women. I respectfully submit we keep God out of all future discussions. It only serves to distract and complicate what is already a risky and difficult work. Mr. Chairman?"

"I concur. It is imperative we keep our focus trained on our goals. Whatever personal feelings any of you may have, all of you, we encourage you to resolve them within yourselves. When we are here, we will focus specifically on the business before us."

One of the men at the table raised his hand.

"May I be heard?"

The chairman nodded.

"The gentleman from Virginia—certainly. Please, you have the floor."

The member paused and began.

"I have a source who has informed me that this *DNA code specific viral vector* was tested on Death Row inmates in a west coast prison. Is that true?"

Mr. X answered.

"That aspect of the operation is classified for your own protection. I can neither confirm nor deny that allegation. Who is your source and how did this source say he or she came by the intelligence?"

Ignoring the question, the member continued.

"I also have information that contradicts your statement earlier when you said that we are the only persons in the world who are aware of this new technology. According to the source, there has been an investigation at the prison, and as a result, there are *other* people who have knowledge about this process, whatever it is. True?"

Mr. X wagged his head.

"I stand by my earlier claim. No person beyond this room knows what we have done and what we purpose to do. And yet by virtue of the fact that you have even heard as much from this source, we have obviously had containment issues. Those, however, are being remedied even as we speak."

"I'd like to take your word for that, but I'm not convinced. We have gone through extreme methods to protect our identities and our connection in this. We're putting more than our careers and reputation at stake; we're putting our lives on the line here. If someone out there can link the murders at the prison and these political assassinations to us, even our closest allies will disavow any loyalty or connection to us. In fact, they'll have no choice. The world will come after us and we'll take the fall. We will all die."

Justice Greene answered with a sense of authority.

"Which is something we've been prepared to do since our first meeting—and yet, I see no purpose in taking unnecessary risks. Mr. X, I believe this committee is owed a better explanation about this obvious breach and its containment."

Mr. X held his ground.

"Very well. A significant part of that containment involves controlling what information we share. Obviously, I cannot share specific details about the breach without exposing the members of this committee to additional hazard or providing the opportunity for a more significant breach from within our own ranks. I can confirm there was an investigation at a prison where there was limited exposure. We have got our best team on detail there and elsewhere. I expect full containment within a few days."

He glanced through his mask toward the gentleman from Virginia.

"And that will almost certainly include silencing your *so-called* source."

Chapter 14

"How are you feeling, Jake?"

"Like I'm trying to breathe through a tiny crack in a wall, knowing there're gobs of air on the other side. Like I'm on another planet, with less air. I'm addicted to this thing."

Agent Martinez cupped the oxygen mask to his face and drew a deep breath as Destiny sat next to the bed, her gentle hand on his shoulder.

"Like one of those cons on Death Row—dead man walkin."

He struggled to smile,

"Or in my case, dead man lyin in a bed."

From the room, Jake could hear the fishing boats when they pulled out in the early morning and occasional conversations between customers and vendors on the pier during afternoons. On windy days, he could hear the surf pounding the rocks along the shore. When the window was open, briny air, with sort of a primordial essence, ebbed and flowed into the room, bringing him peace and rest. Jake felt a deep connection to the ocean and everything in it.

Lying there at the end of his life, his urge had been to return.

"You aren't dead yet. You didn't think you'd survive the stint surgery, but you're still here."

"Just a matter of time."

No one, save a couple of FBI contacts and Destiny knew where Jake had gone to die. He checked in the room using his grandfather's name, complete with a driver's license and credit cards, courtesy of the Bureau.

When his health issues became known at work, his supervisor retired him with full benefits and placed him and his son in an FBI agent protection program. Jake resisted initially, until he learned he could stay near the water at Bodega Bay. In the back of his mind, he was sure the people who were killing him would send someone to debrief him, especially after the break-in to his apartment.

"Too tired to run and too weak to fight," he admitted to Destiny when he told her he was going away. She had visited him in the room once before, earlier in the week, and though he was officially retired and off the case, he was determined to investigate the matter right down to his last breath.

"Where are *you* staying now?"

"The *blackest* neighborhood in Oakland, for now. They don't know what I have on them, so they won't outright kill me. I think they'll try to kidnap me if they can get their hands on me. Bryan gave me a gun to protect myself."

Jake took another oxygen hit.

"I'm a dying man who just wants an answer. What do you know? Really, what did Grant *tell* you?"

"I feel for you, Jake, but it's the only insurance I've got. Besides that, I swore to Kiyomi when she got involved that I would never tell anyone else. It's the only thing keeping her alive as well."

"What if they kill you both?"

Destiny smiled for the first time during the visit.

"Kiyomi's well-embedded with the media. She's documented everything we've learned so far, and she's constantly updating it. If anything happens to her, or me, the story's going out there, to all the newspapers, to broadcast and cable news and all over the Internet. You're in it."

"Only until Kiyomi comes to the part about me droppin dead with a heart attack! How do you think this is going to play out?"

"We're investigating, Bryan's investigating. At some point we'll figure out who's behind it and what they're really up to, and then we'll be able to negotiate. We used to have an 'in' at the FBI, but now you're retired."

Jake sat up, wheezing.

"Wait. You *still* do have an 'in' at the FBI. I've been meaning to tell you. My supervisor assigned another agent to replace me. I told him all about you when he was preparing to come on the case. He wants to work with you. His name's West. Easton West. He's good—and he's got juice over there."

She furrowed her brow, thinking.

"Well, okay. But how do I know if I can trust this agent West? This could all be a set-up. It's hard to trust anyone."

"Trust *me*. He's one of my best friends. He's like a brother. You'll like him. And same deal—you share both ways only what you want to share. No other expectations."

She nodded.

"What does he know?"

"All the things I haven't been able to tell you. That and more. If you and Kiyomi are trying to put a puzzle together, he'll have at least a few of your pieces. Believe me, he's on our side."

Destiny shut her eyes and bowed her head, placing her hand again on his shoulder, thanking him.

"You're such a good man, Jake. I'm sorry about all this. Really, how do you think they got to you?"

"I think they came in my house and took DNA off my toothbrush or dental floss, from my razor or something in there. Then they cooked it up in their lab and shot it back at me. You're lookin at the result. Is your apartment protected?"

She pursed her lips, nodding.

"Bryan and I, we went over the whole place with bleach and had a criminalist come in to remove anything else that might have traces of him or me. Kiyomi did the same before she sent her husband and daughter away. We're already at the next level."

Martinez took another drag from the oxygen mask and smiled.

"Well, I'm rooting for you. I just hope I'm still around to see the end of this thing."

"Are you sure this is a secure line?"

"State-of-the-art secure on this end."

Bryan launched the tracking software as he spoke in calm, reassuring speech.

"For all intents and purposes, this line does not exist."

"And this conversation between us never occurred."

"Believe me—I'm infinitely more interested in *what* you have to share than who you are."

The disguised male voice hesitated on the other end in seeming deliberation.

"I got shut down when I tried to access the file, but I managed to snap a few quick pictures of the screen. The image files are encrypted twice over, but a friend assured me you'll be able to access them if you know what you're doing. I sent them to the profile we set up earlier."

"And the images are there?"

"Pieces of the most important one I had access to. Obviously, the principals aren't sharing a lot of the fine details on this level."

The display indicated that the call tracking was near complete.

"Again, exactly *why* are you sharing this information with me?"

"I told you before—for personal reasons. Last week a friend at the NSA gave me your number and told me you would know what to do. I have to hang up now."

He was gone before Bryan could protest and certainly before the detective could determine his location beyond the general Northeastern seaboard region of the United States. Over the last few weeks, Bryan's investigation had narrowed and intensified. Early on, he was tasked to report on the activities of a genetic research company in industrial Massachusetts, so he figured there was a tie-in, especially when all indications suggested San Quentin Death Row inmates were being murdered through some manner of genetic manipulation.

But inmate Grant's unanticipated call to Destiny from his locked-down prison cell was too uncanny to dismiss as random coincidence. There were many layers of duality and deception. Nothing was as it seemed. This time however, events from his private life had struck too close to home. By all calculation, Destiny should have been dead weeks before.

His investigation revealed the players, rich and powerful men, mostly Americans, who had invested hundreds of millions of dollars in the innovative technology being tested at the prison at the risk of significant financial loss, criminal prosecution and government retaliation. There was too much at stake to spare her life, regardless of Grant's two-minute phone call... unless Grant had revealed something so damaging that Destiny held a temporary advantage. *But what information could he have possibly shared with her? Was it there, in front of him?*

Bryan had spent dozens of hours poring over the volumes of files, documents and note sheets amassed by Sutter and Grant over their three years of scrupulous investigation, obviously assisted by thirty or more inmates and at least eleven guards. He had shared most of it with CCPOA vice president James Cassie and some with Destiny, reserving only the most promising leads for himself.

He knew *Country First* was the name of the political Super PAC founded by Nathaniel Driscoll and supported by at least five other billionaires, but it was also a secret society of men and women with plutocratic-based international political agenda, purposed to increase personal wealth and consolidate power in an emergent global economy.

It was logical to assume the group would use the genetic weapon to advance their interests through clandestine murder and manipulation. *But there had to be something else to it!* Whatever it was, he could not find it in the notes or documents before him, but Grant told Destiny something that threatened to bring their great ambition to ruin, and worse—to expose the privileged principals as murderers and destroy empires.

The doctor kicked the front door closed and hurried to put the grocery bags on the table. Rushing back, he locked the bottom lock, the deadbolt and attached the chain before going to the window, ducking lower than the curtains, and peering down the walkway. He sighed, comfortable that he had not been followed.

Inside, all his possessions were in boxes, with the exception of a pot and skillet on the stovetop, a few plates and utensils on the counter. He pulled the black leather strap attached to a large satchel from around his neck, unzipping the bag it as he put it down. He pulled out an airline ticket, re-examining the departure time, and then he opened a passport, nodding. A thick bundle of cash had tumbled from the bag to the counter. He grabbed it, thumbed through the fifty-dollar bill wad, and tossed it back into the satchel.

Placing the cell phone on his ear, he issued the command.

"Call, Cotton."

He waited a moment and began.

"Mr. Cotton. Thank you. I have everything I need. I will be leaving in the morning. I will disappear, change identity and no one will ever hear from me. Thank you so very much."

He paused.

"I have been careful, watching. No one has come. In twelve hours, I will no longer be a liability in any way. I promise you."

He paused again.

"Yes, I will. I will be up all night. I will call you if there is a problem. Thank you. Good night."

He was staring into the refrigerator when he saw, from the corner of his eye, someone standing in the doorway leading down the hallway. He recoiled, slamming the door.

"You? How did you get in here?"

Kiyomi shook her head, entering the room, stopping so that the counter was between her and the doctor.

"I warned you, Dr. Rashid. I said I'd catch up with you if I found out you were lying to me, so here I am."

"How did you find me again?"

"I have a detective friend. He's kept tabs on you through all your moves and name changes. You lied. You are at least indirectly responsible for over forty deaths over at San Quentin, and for getting my niece shot. So you won't be going anywhere unless you give me some truthful answers, tonight."

Nervous, he nodded, edging toward her.

"What answers do you need to know?"

"Who were you working for? And who is Mr. Cotton?"

When he tried to come around the counter, she shouted.

"Stay where you are, Doctor! And we won't have to have a problem. Just answer the question. Who were you working for and what did you do?"

"Not so simple. I was working for another doctor who was working for another doctor. It was a government project, I think."

She turned on the tape.

"The doctor you were working for—what was his name."

"*Her* name. She was Dr. Spagnola over at the prison. She worked for the other doctor, and I worked for her."

"What did you do for her?"

His eyes seemed desperate.

"Oral swabs. Mostly oral swabs in the infirmary, in the dental facility and sometimes in the cells at East Block. Did you come alone?"

"Yes. Did Dr. Spagnola tell you *why* you were taking the swabs?"

"She told me to 'don't ask questions.'"

Kiyomi sighed.

"You're not telling me everything. I came alone, but I have someone standing by on speed dial, an FBI friend, who would be very interested in speaking with you about your fake passport and the money in that bag. Talk to me, Doctor."

Rashid sighed.

"I am a desperate man. I have family. You have family?"

"Yes, a niece who was *shot* by the people you worked for. And my FBI friend they're killing, he has a family too. Stay right where you are, Doctor!"

Her voice softened.

"Look, I'm not after you. You were just stupid. You let them use you. But I need you to give me something, something I can work with, to save my life and the life of my friend."

He nodded.

"Somewhere, I heard they were testing a process, a weapon or something, at the prison there, at San Quentin."

"Who?"

"I do not know who, maybe military, maybe someone else, but they want to use the weapon for political purposes. That is what I heard. Is it true? I do not know. I cannot say."

His voice pleaded.

"I said all I can tell you, but I just got home after a long day, long driving. I have to go in there, the bathroom. You will excuse me?"

Kiyomi backed away from the counter to give him a path.

"Go on, but we're not done. Leave your phone on the counter."

Rashid nodded, placing the phone down, and made his way to the door in the hallway, closing it behind him. Kiyomi heard the toilet flush a minute later, but the door did not open. Three minutes later, the door was still closed, and the bathroom was quiet. Kiyomi waited another five minutes before she approached the door with appropriate trepidation.

"Dr. Rashid?"

No response.

"Dr. Rashid, I'm not going to play games with you. You need to come out and we need to finish this."

Finally, he answered.

"I'm here."

"I can just make my phone call now. Come on out!"

The door opened and Rashid approached Kiyomi, his hands raised.

"I told you all I know, and now I need for you to go away. Leave me alone."

Kiyomi backed as he approached, warning him.

"Doctor! Stop! Back off. Don't fuck with me!"

In an instant, the doctor was on her, his left hand clutching the back of her neck. With his right hand, he snatched a wet towel from his back pocket and rushed it toward her face, holding it over her nose. He was certain he had overcome her before he realized what had happened. Cringing, his face horrified, he looked down toward the sudden pain in the area just below his rib cage and saw it. It was the hilt of a large knife buried in his abdomen.

His eyes returned to Kiyomi's face, her eyes glazed over, losing consciousness. He pressed the cold towel harder.

"You are just a woman!"

On hearing the words, her eyes widened. Summoning all the strength she had left in her two arms, she narrowed her eyes, and she turned the knife.

Chapter 15

Through the one-way window looking down on the lab, billionaire financier Helmut Wolf watched Dr. Rosecrans, who directed his team of researchers, doctors and technicians through the final steps of the process. No one, save Wolf, knew the identity of the person whose DNA was displayed on the screens, and no one knew the purpose of the innovative high-tech process employed to alter the genetic composition of the strand.

Utilizing zinc finger technology, Dr. Rosecrans was able to turn off a gene that encouraged the growth of new blood vessels in the heart, a change that would result in a significantly higher build-up of plaque and fat due to higher levels of cholesterol produced by the body. Over months, it would cause a thickening and chronic inflammation of arterial walls, leading to certain death. After performing a series of tests, the doctor confirmed for the twenty-person team that the DNA strand had indeed been altered to that effect.

He gave directives to another team of doctors who would be responsible for replicating the altered strand, along with protocols and conditions for inserting it into the newly developed VSV G-pseudotyped lentiviral vector that would be utilized in the procedure. Finally, he spoke to a third team of doctors who would create a distinctive delivery system adjusted to the specifications and vulnerabilities of the target.

Assured the task was moving forward, the doctor ascended the stairs, tapped his code into the keypad next to the door, turned the handle and entered, at once removing his gloves and mask. Wolf was still standing at the glass, arms crossed, watching the teams huddle as leaders assigned specific duties.

"At last, the wheels are in motion, Mr. Wolf. We'll have the vector loaded and ready for delivery in two weeks."

Wolf nodded.

"And this is how we shape the world. *The spark of a genius exists in the brain of the truly creative man from the hour of his birth. True genius is always inborn and never cultivated, let alone learned.*"

Rosecrans seemed confused.

"Excuse me?"

"Words, Doctor. Yet now *Country First* has the means to secure America and reshape the leadership of the world. Five years ago, I would have never believed this could be possible. Our achievement is the perfect marriage of genius and money. There are no limits to the possibilities now."

He smiled.

"I am certain I sound like some madman from a James Bond movie—evil genius out to take over the world. I never rooted for Bond. I do not know why, but I always preferred the villains to the effete Englishman."

Rosecrans seemed still uncertain as Wolf continued.

"United in purpose, Doctor, and that is why we have been successful, but our motives could not be further apart."

"What do you mean?"

Wolf, now seated at his desk, wagged his head.

"Why are you *doing* what you are doing, Benjamin? And do not tell me you are trying to make America more secure. Do you realize what we have done here? The good and wickedness we are now capable of?"

Rosecrans thought a moment and answered.

"I do. I'm afraid you're right. My motive *was* a selfish one. The security of America had nothing to do with it. For me it was ambition. You presented me with the possibility to do what no other doctor or scientist on this Earth would ever be able to do, not at least for another fifty or sixty years. Now that was irresistible to me."

He sat in the seat across from Wolf and continued.

"Maybe I should have been more the moralist. Maybe I should have considered what would happen beyond the lab, but how could I have said *no* to you? I was thinking of the possibilities! I was thinking of the good that could be done. This same process could be used to save or extend lives!"

"But you knew all along that you were developing a tool that could potentially be used for political assassination. You knew your process would be responsible for the deaths at San Quentin and at that other prison. And the instructions you gave now—you do not *know* who the high-profile target is, but you know that high profile target will die."

The doctor nodded.

"Yes, unfortunately I do. What are you getting at, Mr. Wolf?"

"Let us be honest about this. You tell me, Doctor. Are you suggesting history also should revisit the intentions of Dr. Josef Mengele? And Dr. Miklós Nyiszli—one of your own? Perhaps Mengele too, had some benevolent motivation beyond the gas chambers of Auschwitz?"

Rosecrans stood, angry.

"You insult me. You compare me to a monster and a traitor!"

"For that I apologize, Doctor. I did it only to make a point."

"And exactly what *is* your point, Mr. Wolf?"

Wolf stood and came around the desk.

"I just want you to remember, if news of this ever gets out and they start comparing *me* to a monster. As Coleridge pointed out, no man does *anything* from a single motive. I am willing to consider your better intentions if you are willing to consider mine."

The doctor sighed and nodded.

"That's only fair. May I ask about *your* better intentions?"

"My intentions are biblical. I want peace and security."

"Through political assassination?"

Wolf smiled.

"It is reliable, on the DNA level. It is expedient, and with what you have done, it is neat, an invisible hand. It is the perfect weapon for peace."

"But you're murdering people."

"I am becoming like *God*, shaping the destiny of man through selective killing—it is in your *Torah* and in your *Chronicles of the Kings*. And what is the White House doing now with all the drone attacks and Special Forces behind the lines? They are taking out cars full of people. They are taking out houses and complexes, murdering innocent people and families in order to neutralize their targets. But the President is a sloppy god. I will become more powerful than the President. I will become the *Godship Incarnate*."

He laughed to himself.

"Our weapon is precise on the genome level. Fewer lives will be lost, and the targets will die of natural causes, meaning there will be no lingering resentment as we reshape the governments of the world. How could anyone judge me without first condemning the President of the United States for what he is doing in Afghanistan,

Pakistan and Iran? They do worse! If we can control world leaders who we allow to be in place, there will be no more *need* for conventional weapons."

Wolf paused, bowed his head and continued.

"My only regret is that we have had to risk killing regular Americans, the takers that the government pretends to care about. Not the Death Row inmates, but the ones who foolishly got involved and who by even being alive threaten this entire operation. They are our only liability. They all have to die, the sooner, for the better."

Rosecrans reflected on a troubling rumor he heard that had resulted from the last meeting.

"And what if this apparent breach can't be contained? What if the U.S. government and the world find out about what we're doing?"

His face becoming red, billionaire Wolf's voice trembled, animated by anger.

"The breach *will* be contained! It will be contained even if I have to get teams out there who will kill every man, woman, parent, child, friend, husband, wife and acquaintance related to anyone who knows anything about our project. I have invested too much time and money to let some goddamned nigger *bitch* ruin this for me! The future of the world is at stake."

"So tell me, Kiyo, what exactly do you *remember* about the room when you woke up?"

Kiyomi closed her eyes, trying to recall something specific.

"That's just it. There was nothing, nothing left. Someone must have come in and cleaned out the whole place. The body, the blood on my hands, the knife, all the furniture—everything was gone. Refrigerator was empty, television was missing, closets cleaned out. No dust, not even on the vents."

Her daughter Lyndsey in hiding, Destiny had reclaimed her office for the interview, though she was nervous about meeting in such an obvious place. Despite the cameras and security guards stationed downstairs, two phantom goons had come up into that very office and shot Lyndsey. Bastards!

But no one would be interrupting this little conference. She and Kiyomi were scheduled to meet with federal agent Easton West with the FBI, who would be taking up where Agent Jake Martinez left off. Jake assured Destiny that she could trust Agent West, who was "closer than a brother," and Jake insisted on a meeting "before the final curtain" was drawn over his face where he lied in that stuffy motel room, the sticky air heavy with the mortal scent of his impending death.

Destiny looked up from her notes.

"When you first got here, you were saying something about a Cotton, a Mr. Cotton?"

Kiyomi nodded.

"That's the person Rashid called when he got home, probably the same person who cleaned the place out. Rashid was saying something about an identity change and leaving the country. He had a lot of money in his satchel, bundles of fifty-dollar bills. Wherever he was going, he was going to disappear."

"And he still *did* disappear, dead or alive. No one will ever see him again. So you got nothing?"

The reporter sighed.

"Please! You underestimate me. I got Rashid to tell me that Dr. Irene Spagnola, the health care manager at San Quentin— she was in on the whole thing. Rashid was working under her direction, and she was working for a bigger doctor, I think a Dr. Hancock, someone with powerful connections."

"Did he say what they were up to over there?

Kiyomi strained to remember.

"He told me they were testing a process, a process or a weapon over there. He thought it could have been the military or someone else associated with the government, but not the government directly. He said he thought it was a weapon that would be used for political purposes, a political weapon."

Destiny thought for a moment.

"A political weapon? But they're killing people. So we're talking about a weapon for political assassination?"

Kiyomi shrugged.

"I would think so."

"Who would they be trying to kill?"

Destiny shut her eyes, massaging them with her fingertips before continuing.

"And these are doctors, and they collected samples from the inmates they killed, and it has something to do with a viral vector?"

Destiny's glance indicated she knew more than she wanted to say.

"I don't completely trust this office. It might be bugged. We'll talk later, where we know for sure no one's listening."

Kiyomi narrowed her eyes, studying her friend's face.

"You know something, don't you? Was it something Grant told you that you're not sharing?"

"I'll tell you later. We'll meet somewhere private after Agent West leaves."

The security desk buzzed the phone fifteen minutes later, indicating a guest had arrived downstairs. Destiny asked the guard at the concierge desk to escort the visitor to the office.

FBI Agent Easton West's appearance was an anomaly. Superficially, he seemed African American, about five feet, eleven inches tall, and handsome. He was dark-skinned with a broad nose and heavy lips, but his voice indicated a choppy British accent, owing to an upbringing in England. He was formal in manner, succinct in speech, abruptly to the point.

"Ms. Mitchell, you were working with Agent Martinez, but obviously, I am not Agent Martinez. He told me you had information you were unwilling to share. However, if you are going to work with me, there will be *nothing* you won't share. I trust you understand that?"

Destiny bristled.

"Then I'm sorry you wasted your time. There's the door. You can go out the same way you came in."

West hesitated and grinned.

"I know, but I did not say that *I* was unwilling to share information I've discovered with you, and your reporter friend there. It's your lives on the line, not mine, so that is up to you."

Destiny sighed.

"Look, I don't know you. All I've got is Agent Martinez's possibly *misguided* assurance that you're somehow a good guy, but what I'm seeing is arrogance and insensitivity. Our lives *are* on the line. So, if you're not here to do us some good, *then go.* Don't let the door hit you."

West smiled again.

"Martinez told me you were ballsy. He said that I would have to make an authentic deal with you. So how do we do this?"

"Mutual disclosure. You share with me, and I share with you. Small things at first, and then if we learn to trust each other, the bigger things. There's a reasonable chance that if we put all the intelligence out there together, we can figure this thing out. Lives depend on it, and not just ours."

He nodded and smiled.

"That seems fair to me. As a matter of fact, I'll begin."

He walked over to the desk and crossing his arms, stood across from Destiny.

"First of all, Agent Martinez told me he has reasons to believe that your husband, Bryan Osaka—he has reasons to believe that your husband is part of the cover-up. Osaka was hired by a Washington insider, a man named Nathaniel Driscoll, for containment purposes. His job is to debrief you and make this all go away as a last-ditch effort. He was pressured into doing it, and he's doing it only to save your life, and the life of the reporter."

"Who *has* a name," Kiyomi interrupted.

Destiny paused, becoming angry.

"Agent Martinez never shared that notion with me. You make it sound like the government's involved. So, if that's the case, why should I trust you? You're a government suit."

"You've known all along, haven't you? You've known that your husband has not been honest with you."

"What I know is that he loves me and he's trying to help me in whatever way he feels is the best way to do that. Do I think he's told me everything? No. He's already said it. There are things he is not sharing with me and there are things I haven't shared with him, or anyone, but Kiyomi here."

"So, she knows *everything* you know?" Agent Easton West asked, settling into a seat. "Well, Martinez shared. He told me that you believe the prison deaths have something to do with a 'viral vector' and some kind of gene alteration?"

Kiyomi approached Destiny and stood behind her, facing the agent.

"You're telling us something you *think* we already believe? How about giving us something real, for starts? —something *you* know. How about giving us something useful?"

West raised his eyebrows and shrugged.

"Sure, useful. What can I give you?"

"We need information on a man they call 'Mr. Cotton,' who either works for the government or for some dark government agency. And we need to find a Dr. Irene Spagnola, who used to work at San Quentin. I believe she was the health care manager doctor there. Ring any bells?"

"Dr. Irene Spagnola? As a matter of fact, yes. She's in custody awaiting trial for suspected fraud. When the Inspector General's Office finished their investigation at the prison, they uncovered some irregularities that apparently made the doctor nervous. Once she realized they were onto her, she left her job and tried to flee the country. Already suspicious, the OIG alerted us, and we caught her at San Francisco International, in disguise, headed to Trinidad with a suitcase full of cash."

"Has she talked so far?" Destiny interrupted. "What did they have on her?"

"That's the funny part. They really didn't *have* anything. They just wanted her to come in for questioning. But her behavior, quitting so suddenly—it sent up a big red flag. They—we *all* need for her to explain where all that cash came from. It was a half million dollars."

"Is she in FBI custody?" Kiyomi asked. "We need to talk to her. Can you make that happen, like today?"

"Ms. Mitchell can possibly talk to her, but you can't, Ms. Yamakita. I got notice on the way up that you are a *person of interest* in the murder of Dr. Hussein Rashid. Your bloody fingerprints are on a knife they found lodged in his stomach. We've asked the Newark District Attorney to delay making a statement or releasing any information about you and your involvement for a week. I hope you have a good explanation."

"It was self-defense. He attacked me."

"You were at his house. *You* broke in—the security cameras show it. And do you always carry a knife?"

"Lately, yes."

"Well, you left it in the doctor. Why were you there?"

"Security cameras?" she sighed. "Do they show anything else? Do they show me leaving? Ask your bosses *that* question."

"I will," West nodded, thinking, "but where's the significance?"

"Because I left the next *morning*. Rashid came at me with a towel soaked in ether or chloroform. I stabbed him in self-defense before I passed out. In the meantime, someone came in and cleared the place out—Rashid's body and everything else in the apartment. I woke up in the morning, feeling drugged, and left at about nine, in *daylight*."

Her resolute eyes met Destiny's, and then she looked back toward West.

"These guys are pros. We knew that going in. The cameras were obviously tampered with so someone with connections to authorities would have something on me. If I'm in custody, I can't operate, and they can come in and kill me. Your people saw what someone wanted them to see, but the FBI should know better. Whoever it was that came in there, this Cotton, *he* could have killed me, but he didn't, which leads me to believe that we're dealing with more than one agency—one that wants us dead, and a separate one that obviously let me live. They're hedging. They don't know what we know or what we plan on doing with it."

"That's why we want to know who Mr. Cotton is," Destiny cut in. "Is he a good guy or bad guy? So far, you haven't given us anything. Have you ever heard the name before, Agent West?"

"Well, no," he answered. "I can't say that I have."

"Then we've given you something, a name. He's clearly involved in operations or containment for whatever went on at the prison. Cotton could be the key to unraveling this thing."

"Okay," West nodded. "I will look into it, and we will see if I get an answer. I just hope it will be something I can share with you."

"Excuse me?" Destiny insisted.

"Miss Mitchell, you have to understand. If the federal government is somehow involved in this, directly or indirectly—when it comes down the line, I could be ordered to withhold vital information from you, or I could be given intentionally misleading information to share. At that point, I will have a decision to make."

"You will! Whoever's doing this *murdered* Jake Martinez, a federal agent, your friend, who said you were closer to him than his own brother!"

Destiny stood.

"Martinez isn't dead yet, but she's right, Agent West. You have to make that decision *now*! Jake did it. Either you're in this thing with us one hundred percent right now, or not at all. Yes, or no?"

West shut his eyes and took a deep breath, his lips held tight as he exhaled.

"Yes."

Destiny, ever the closer, stood.

"Good, because I have a feeling this thing is ready to take turn for the worse, and when it's all over and if we survive, it'll be bigger than any of us had ever imagined."

Chapter 16

"Does anyone know we're meeting tonight? Does anyone know you're even *out* here, on the East Coast?"

Driscoll sighed. He had given up cigars, but he had become irritated. The premise for the meeting was ridiculous. He took a drag and exhaled with a groan.

"I had to fly. Of *course* people know I'm here. I'm a man on an itinerary. But this meeting, when we're done, it never happened. Do you understand that?"

The governor nodded.

"I do, I do." Gordon paused to compose his thoughts. "And I wouldn't have asked you here if this weren't absolutely necessary."

Driscoll glanced at his watch.

"Getting cold feet, Governor? I'm sure you know you blew past *the point of no return* over a year ago. I can't believe you had the audacity to call me out here to talk about this."

Gordon was quick with the correction.

"Oh no! I'm still on-board! One hundred percent. There's no question about that. I just had some questions and concerns, for my own peace of mind. It's something I needed to do person to person, and I trust you."

Driscoll placed the stogy in an ashtray.

"That's a good thing. If you had gone to anyone else with any sign of indecision, you would have become a liability rather than the beneficiary of all this work, expense and risk."

He leaned toward the governor, speaking quietly.

"When this is all over, you'll be the President of the United States. Isn't that what you want?"

Gordon backed.

"I do. That's *exactly* what I want. The President is ruining this country. He can't be allowed to serve a second term. That would be disastrous and irresponsible."

"Exactly. So where is your problem, Governor?"

"I can beat him in the election outright. The country is a mess—high unemployment, looming deficit, depressed economy, low approval numbers, congressional gridlock. I can beat him. We don't need to risk an undertaking so extreme. For a fraction of the money, and most of it from PACs, we can achieve the same result!"

Driscoll reared back, laughing in derision.

"Come now, Governor. You think you can beat *this* president, economy and jobs aside, in the general election?"

"I certainly do."

"Then you obviously think more of yourself and your chances than you should. No one on the board would agree with you. The die is cast. You don't have a choice at this point. That's what I am here to tell you. If you *should* become a liability, the board will take the appropriate action, with my full support. Do I need to make myself any clearer?"

The governor smiled, seeking appeasement.

"Oh no! I'm in this to win this. I just thought I could win on my own popular support."

"You *can't*," Driscoll interrupted. "He'd win by a landslide. We knew that going in."

"We *did*," Gordon nodded, "we knew it back *then*, but according to several national polls, it's very likely I can win this election outright."

"The pollsters, the media—they all have their jobs to do. They need the appearance of a race, the semblance of a contest to keep their readers and viewers engaged, but they know it too. We're outmatched, but we've found a way to win. We've found a way to save our country, and you're an essential part of that solution, Governor."

"So, you don't think I'm the better *candidate*?"

Driscoll scoffed, his eyes narrow, anger beginning to overwhelm his typical unflappable demeanor as Gordon continued.

"I take it you don't think I'm better qualified than the President to turn this economy around, create an environment conducive to job growth and restore the freedoms he's taken away?"

For the first time during the meeting, Driscoll seemed to give the governor's words serious consideration. However, he laughed to himself before answering.

"That doesn't matter, Governor. What does matter is that you're *our* candidate, and we *also* have a job to do. You look presidential, you've got the pedigree and you were chosen because we know we can count on your commitment to *Country First* and to our agenda, even if that makes you a one-term president. Right, Governor?"

Unsettled, Gordon forced a smile.

"All for the greater good, or course. Yes, I'm committed to do whatever I have to do. You know that. I *swore* it."

Driscoll gazed across the table, skeptical, and nodded.

"*It is not the oath that makes us believe in the man, but the man that makes us believe in the oath.* I've always had my doubts about you, Governor, but so far I've kept them to myself."

An uncomfortable silence followed, and then Gordon cleared his throat.

"You have no reason to doubt me. I only called you because of the things I'm reading and hearing. I'm the better candidate. America is coming around."

"You know, good men have no place in politics. Stop listening to your friends and family. *Stop* seeing yourself as the good guy and the President as the bad guy. In politics, you're *all* bad guys. At least that's how a man in my position sees it. And once you realize you're the bad guy, then you have to make sure you're badder than the other guy. *That's* the man who wins the election. Whatever it takes."

"Whatever it takes," Gordon nodded. "Thanks for taking the time to speak with me."

"Your *religion* doesn't matter, Governor. Do you understand me?"

"Yes, I think so."

"Think so? Then let me make myself clear: any oath that you have sworn to your religion or to God takes second position to the oath you swore to *Country First*. Do you understand that?"

"Yes."

"Then understand this. Any oath you swear as President of the United States, any promises or commitments you make, any duty or responsibility you owe, are subject to the oath you swore to *Country First*. Your oath to us takes precedence. Are we clear on that?"

Hugh Gordon swallowed hard, his throat protesting the words even as he tried to speak them.

"I, I understand."

"The simple truth going in, Governor, is that we *own* you, but you'll be the President of the United States."

"I get it. I understand," Gordon nodded. "So, is there someone who owns the *other* guy?"

Bryan arranged the meeting in the back room of a restaurant in Monte Rio, near the Bohemian Grove, where a member assured him privacy and discretion. Earlier in the week, he had made contact with Cornell Cotton, who reluctantly agreed to the meeting. There were conditions. Cotton would get complete copies of Sutter's backup computer files and notes from Osaka's sessions at debriefing Destiny Mitchell and Kiyomi Yamakita. In return, Bryan would get Cotton's assurance that he would intervene so that the women would not be harmed.

Cotton was Jettson Turner's point man for U.S. domestic containment at INWA (Industrial New World Army), a private military corporation, financed by major international corporations who contracted private military and security services. According to black ops insiders, the company's board was populated by the world's brightest military minds, who undertook great risks and expense to procure the services and loyalty of elite forces trained by government militaries, principally from the U.S. and Israel, but also from the British SAS and MI-6, the Russian Spetsnaz and French Naval Commandos. Despite its international diversity and New World based agenda, it was the best run and most disciplined military outfit in the world.

Thirty minutes before the meeting time however, Cotton phoned Bryan to tell him that he would be meeting instead with Cotton's surrogate, Colin Boyle, a captain who had been authorized to negotiate and deliver on Cotton's behalf. He assured Bryan that the meeting as originally proposed could have never officially taken place, though he admitted that the proposed deal had already been preapproved by higher command.

Bryan tried to phone Destiny as he waited. They had argued earlier in the day. He told her he was meeting with Cotton and insisted that she and Kiyomi cease investigating the matter. He warned that FBI agent Easton West should not be trusted because he was reporting to Driscoll, and he insisted West had somehow been involved in neutralizing agent Martinez. Bryan did his best to frighten and overwhelm Destiny, and though she was visibly shaken, she remained stubborn and insisted she would feel safe only after she and Kiyomi had a distinct advantage in information leverage.

Destiny asked him about Dr. Spagnola, the former prison health care manager at San Quentin, and what information her records provided. Under pressure, he shared the doctor's electronic files with his wife, even those he had not yet read, vetted and redacted. In turn, she promised that neither she nor Kiyomi would contact agent West or pursue the investigation until after his meeting with Cotton. With a guarantee from Cotton's bosses, Bryan hoped to assure both sides that a standoff would be the best outcome going forward.

He had a file on Dr. Spagnola. Before working at the prison, she was a researcher for fifteen years at *Genengine*, a new technology company founded by Dr. Benjamin Rosecrans. Prior to working at the prison, she had never held a management job. In her tenure at San Quentin, the overall health and data tracking for prisoners improved, except that two years earlier, thirty-three Death Row inmates had died of "natural causes," along with the recent year's forty-two—seventy-five "natural deaths" in twenty months, all specifically within an isolated section of the prison.

Of the seventy-five, fifty-six had visited the infirmary in the six months prior to sickness and death. The other nineteen had not visited or received medical attention in more than two years. Sixty-seven of the deaths involved complications resulting from congestive heart failure, while eight were from major organ shutdown. Seventeen were African American, thirty-eight were Hispanic, six were Asian, one was Native American and thirteen were white.

When the first investigation began, the doctor cooperated with perplexed state health officials from various agencies as they tested for a possible link to air and water contaminants, for lead or other toxic elements in the paint and cement of the cellblocks, and for food borne pathogens. The investigation did not begin until fourteen months after the first series of deaths because Dr. Spagnola never reported the heightened death rate to the prison CEO, who in turn would have reported it to the Receiver.

As inmates died, families were discreetly notified, and the bodies were either quietly transferred to relatives or sent to a cremation contractor who picked up bodies late at night. Forty-eight inmates died in the prison infirmary, while the balance died in hospitals outside the prison. All the while, Dr. Spagnola insisted that although the spike in inmate deaths was unusual and "somewhat disconcerting," the inquiries were unnecessary. Investigation results and autopsies confirmed all the men had died of natural causes.

The containment problems began in the Death Row section when the prisoners, becoming aware of the growing number of deaths, began voicing suspicions and complaining to guards. The guards were slow to acknowledge the inmates' concerns, but the sheer reality of the dying was unmistakable. Many of the inmates suddenly became ill and went to the infirmary, never to return. Others seemed to just go missing—one day in the cellblock, and the next, replaced without mention. Most were in their thirties to forties and had become sick a month or two after an initial infirmary visit.

Perseus Grant was an inmate trustee working at the infirmary with Dr. Hussein Rashid when the men started dying. Suspicious of Middle Eastern people, he initially believed Rashid was an Arab terrorist intent on launching a diabolical plot from the prison. Garnering the doctor's trust over time, he accessed the doctor's computer at every opportunity available, copying files onto a 64G zip drive supplied by his friend and brother in the Lord, Guard Robert Sutter.

After two months, both men realized that Rashid was not part of a terrorist plot. Rather, he was secretly collecting data on inmates who visited the infirmary, vital health information and DNA samples. These were being sent out via a courier service that collected on Sunday evenings. On Monday mornings, this same service would deliver a large box package, addressed to Dr. Spagnola. Perseus was never able to determine what those packages contained, but the manifest attached to tracking on one item the doctor received contained the names of seven Death Row inmates who died thirty to forty-five days later.

When Bryan learned Irene Spagnola was in FBI custody, he tried to set up a meeting with the doctor, to which she agreed, but Agent West interfered, setting up a false pretense to deny the visit. Immediately after, West tried to barter access in exchange for information. As a result, Bryan called a contact with the agency for background information on Agent West and found he had a secret bank account where he deposited three checks that he received from a dummy corporation owned by Nathaniel Driscoll.

"You can't trust him, Destee. Don't even *talk* to him again," Bryan warned.

He checked his watch as he glanced up at the serious and circumspect man who came through the door. The man's face and hair were reddish, his nose keen, his lips barely perceptible, seeming a mere slit in his face. He was thin, about five ten. Colin Boyle, an Irish name for a man who definitely looked Irish. After scanning the room and deciding on a seat that offered the best strategic advantage, the man approached the table and sat.

"Mr. Cotton extends his regrets. Remote as this location might be—and we are confident that you are careful—he cannot afford the risk of meeting with you in person. We are in a rather... delicate situation with this containment breach, as I'm sure you understand."

Bryan nodded.

"I understand."

"Mr. Cotton has assurances from our highest command that Destiny Mitchell and Kiyomi Yamakita will not be harmed now or at any later time by us, nor will they be subject to threat or danger from any other agency or organization. Two conditions: one, you turn over all materials you have collected in this investigation, including all files received in connection with acquisitions by Perseus Grant and Robert Sutter; and two: an assurance that Destiny Mitchell, your wife, and Kiyomi Yamakita, a news reporter with *The San Francisco Chronicle*, the assurance that they will cease and desist now and in the future all efforts to investigate this matter one step further... beginning now."

Bryan nodded, contemplating.

"They will not be harmed in any way, and all this will be over?"

Colin turned toward Bryan, never smiling.

"Yes. If you will, what does your wife *know*? She was on the phone with Perseus Grant for two minutes and fifty-seven seconds. What did he tell her?"

Colin Boyle was impossible to read. Bryan had researched Cornell Cotton prior to the meeting, but he knew nothing about Boyle. The man did not smile. He seldom made eye contact. He was all business. Yet Bryan proceeded with his best guess.

"He told her that someone was murdering Death Row inmates at San Quentin, had murdered them over a two year period. He told her Dr. Spagnola was involved, along with *Genengine* and possibly even Dr. Rosecrans, its founder. He said it was all part of experimental testing of a biological weapon purposed for clandestine assassination."

"Is that all? Did he tell her anything else?"

Bryan forced eye contact. Shifting in his seat, he adjusted himself to a place before Boyle, staring directly into his eyes.

"Look, I've been doing this for a while, been around the block a few times. You, someone I've never met or talked to before, you just gave me an assurance that Destiny and Kiyomi would not be harmed. But you're not even a player in this business. No offense intended, but your assurance means nothing to me, or my wife."

Without emotion, Boyle dialed a number on his cell phone and handed it to Bryan.

"Osaka," the confident voice on the phone began. "When you next check your cell phone, you will find you have received a document from Jettson Turner, my director, with an assurance that your wife and her friend will be protected by INWA for life from all unnatural threats, domestic and foreign, resulting from the call to her by Perseus Grant, provided that she has shared, without reservation or omission, all relevant disclosure in her conversation with Grant. I take it you know who Jettson Turner is?"

"Yes."

"And have you shared everything she has told you with Mr. Boyle?"

Bryan looked up from the phone in his hand as he dragged a package onto the table.

"Yes."

"And do you realize that any discovered withholding or admission, willful or unintended, will result in the immediate forfeiture of Mr. Turner's protection?"

Bryan looked toward Boyle.

"I understand."

"Osaka," Cotton continued, "we are aware of measures your wife and Ms. Yamakita have taken to protect themselves, but since we've already prepared counter measures, which will render their media threats meaningless, you will want to warn them against further exacerbating a delicate situation that could result in the likely elimination of all three of you."

Bryan sighed aloud.

"I can already tell you, Mr. Cotton, they're not going to take my word on it, and they don't trust any of you. Someone shot her daughter. Whatever protections they've set up are purely conditioned on their safety. Destiny and Kiyomi are innovative. They're well connected and they're desperate. If they continue unharmed, you and Mr. Turner have nothing to worry about there, but if someone *above* Turner decides their continued existence provides too great a risk and goes after them, I assure you, any counter measures you've prepared will be useless, and this business will have to be contained on *your* side of things, on Turner's level and above."

Cotton paused for a while, considering Bryan's words.

"Something doesn't sound right here, Osaka. I get the sense they have something else, some other information that neither you nor they are sharing. Is there something you are not telling us?"

"I've shared everything. I wouldn't waste your time or mine... or risk my wife's life by being anything less than forthcoming with you today."

"You're a detective and she's your wife. What do your *instincts* tell you? Has she told you everything she knows?"

Bryan bowed his head, becoming impatient.

"Instincts don't work with wives. She *said* she told me everything. Do I believe her? I think so. Look, the reason I am here is to try to settle this thing without having to bury my wife who, by the way, didn't ask for any of this. Grant called *her*. So, all she's doing is trying to avoid becoming collateral damage."

"If she and the reporter hadn't started digging and making people nervous, we wouldn't be going through this."

"Because she would be dead. Containment failed at the prison. I know how it works, and she obviously knows. To whoever's behind the prison murders, it doesn't matter *what* Grant told her, or if he told her anything at all. She's a liability against their investment, a loose end. In order to clean things up, they would have killed her just because she answered a blocked call at four in the morning."

Bryan pushed the package across the table toward Boyle, speaking again toward the phone.

"I've just given you everything I got from Sutter's computer, everything he and Grant were working on at the prison. They're dead. Destiny and Kiyomi know what they know, but no one else will know anything as long as they stay alive. When I walk out of here, I need to be able to tell my wife that she, as well as the people she loves, are no longer in danger. Is that what we've accomplished today, Mr. Cotton?"

"I'll have to do a final debriefing, just me and her. You can be near, but not present. You understand?"

"I just want to put an end to this. You work for some assholes," Bryan sighed.

"As long as your wife and the reporter put a stop to their prying, they will have nothing to fear from us or anyone else involved, but they must cease and desist at once. That condition is non-negotiable. You make sure they know that."

"I will."

"To think of it, it is a devastating thing, the prospect of losing a wife. I understand your concern. But as for you, Osaka—we know who you are working for, and we know you have to turn in a report about what you've discovered. My advice to you: understand the politics, look to the end game, and above all, tread lightly. There are already people who think you know too much."

Chapter 17

James Cassie slipped quietly into the prison under the pretense of addressing a dispute between a group of disgruntled rank and file correctional officers and two supervisors. The true purpose of his visit, however, was a meeting between concerned guards and inmates. For three weeks, Cassie had worked with a dozen defiant guards who, behind the scenes, were investigating the series of Death Row murders.

Slowly re-tracing the thorough research amassed by guard Robert Sutter and inmate Perseus Grant, Cassie was convinced beyond doubt that the deaths were not random, that rather they were part of a pattern involving a drug, virus or procedure that could create and accelerate heart disease in inmates and make their deaths the seeming result of natural causes.

Initially, Sutter had been unable to convince guards that the risk at the prison could impact the health of correctional workers and their families. However, each inmate death served to reinforce the assertion and warning. When Sutter got sick, he showed images of his clogged heart and MRI scans to fellow guards and sent them, along with his and Perseus' stories to their Internet mailboxes. When he committed suicide outside Grant's cell, all the correctional officers at San Quentin took notice, even the guards beyond Death Row.

Guards had been calling Cassie to express concerns and fears and to demand an investigation at the prison since the first ten or so inmates died mysteriously, and the number of calls tripled after the inmate deaths exceeded twenty. By the time Perseus Grant died, guards and inmates were convinced that prisoners were being murdered as part of a government experiment and guards and their families were at risk. Sutter's final statement before Grant's cell caused an outright panic, as more than sixty percent of the guards in the Death Row section requested transfers to other areas of the facility or out of the prison altogether.

The meetings with guards and inmates were part of a secretive, guard-initiated investigation, led by Denora Reed, an outspoken sergeant who had been a good friend to Raymond Gutierrez. She was convinced Raymond had been murdered and that CCPOA President Donovan Baker and the warden were part of the cover-up. Denora was relentless in her pursuit of clues and information from anyone who was brave enough to speak up, and she predicted she would be among the next to die.

James Cassie and Denora had been friends for more than fifteen years, dating back to his early days as a guard. She was well aware of Baker's warning to him and tried to discourage her former colleague's involvement, and Cassie was ready to back off, until he learned the guards were being threatened and intimidated. He warned his wife, Marybeth, that he could lose his job for something he could not tell her about, but he swore to the guards involved that he would unravel the mystery and expose whoever was behind the murders.

That night, three inmates joined the eight remaining guards for the secretive discovery session. One of the prisoners, Farouk Miller, was a trustee who had access to the infirmary at the height of the killings. He had kept notes on the courier pick-up and delivery schedule as well as times that the dead bodies went out, either picked up by the cremation contractor or sent elsewhere.

Another inmate had collected shipping labels and addresses from letters and discarded boxes from packages shipped into the infirmary. While the return addresses for most of the packages were post office boxes, there were a few physical addresses included. He had even created a graph, showing dates of package deliveries, superimposed against a chart displaying the death dates of prisoners.

The third inmate was an older man, Raoul Garza, who turned over a small notebook he claimed belonged to Dr. Irene Spagnola. He said he had swiped it from her desk when she was distracted on a lengthy phone call. He initially went in to request medication for his upset stomach, but he left untreated, afraid the doctor would discover the random theft.

The book contained almost twenty pages of notes and scribbling, mostly indiscernible, though there were a few names. Some of these were inmates, all deceased or murdered, and there were other unfamiliar names, one that seemed to be Thomas Hancock, who had an association with Rosetta Biotech. This person seemed to be Spagnola's direct contact for many of the suspicious packages sent and in some manner of coordinating tests and results. There were even a few personal notes and comments by the doctor, a smoking gun, actual proof that Spagnola was involved in experiments that caused the deaths of seventy-five inmates and two guards.

After intense scrutiny of the notebook, Cassie announced that Spagnola had been arrested and was in FBI custody. Given the secrecy and ruthlessness on the part of the group or agency responsible for the murders, no one expected the doctor to live for long. While no one felt sorry for her, most felt she might be willing to leverage details about her involvement and the identity and participation of others involved for a chance to live. When they asked Cassie about the possibility of someone going in to help her save herself, he said he already had someone on the inside.

Denora's questions were more aggressive than eloquent.

"What did you say his name was, this elite, private espionage guy you got?"

"He's an old friend I worked with when I as was a detective with at SFPD. His name's Bryan Osaka. He's been working the State OIG investigation at the prison for the last three months, and he knows the FBI guy who arrested her. We've got a shot there, and we've also got this notebook, which no one else has, and we've got the stuff Sutter and Grant uncovered, if we can just get through it and make sense of it.

Garza wagged his head.

"Spagnola's already dead. There's no way in hell they're gonna let her talk to anybody. They'll kill her, and it will be like none of it ever happened. So what if seventy-five fuckin *inmates* are dead, right? Just a bunch of worthless bastards who people wanted dead anyway! Who the hell will care?"

"There were also two guards," Cassie maintained. "And an FBI agent, as I understand. Guys, I'm not saying any one life is better than the next, but it's not just inmates, and these people are being *murdered*! Right now, as we speak!"

"But is it *murder* if the government's doing it? They make the laws and enforce whatever they want. The government can get away with murder. They do it all the time."

Cassie sighed.

"No, no. Laws are laws, and they apply to everybody. The government is just the people we put up there to make, interpret and enforce those laws. We pay them and give them power, but they're people, just like us. Any law that applies to anyone applies to them. So, if someone in the government is murdering people, we can get to them. We can use the law *against* them."

Garza laughed.

"Not if they merk us first. Inmates, guards, wives, babies— all of us. That's how it works. It's how it's always worked. It's why they're the most powerful government there's ever been. They'll never let us use the law against them, and we know it. It's David and Goliath, but David's got a slingshot, while they got fuckin Uzis."

Murphy, one of the guards, agreed.

"I gotta tell ya. If we find out it's the government, I'm out. I got a wife and kids. It's an unfair fight against a bunch of ruthless fuckers. Patrick Henry I'm not, that's for sure."

Inmate Farouk Miller sneered and spat on the floor.

"Right. What he really means is, 'it's just a bunch of worthless inmates who's dying. Oh, and a coupla meddlin guards! They ain't worth riskin my life over.' Right, Murphy?"

"Fuck you, lowlife!"

Denora stood, taking a place between the men.

"Now y'all need ta quit. We swore to each other we were all in this together. We're takin this risk *together*. We don't know if it's the government, but it's gotta be some of the same people involved, someone inside. Cassie's right, though. The government can't outright break the law if people know about it, and that means if this gets thing exposed, they'll roll over on whoever's behind it and claim they knew nothing about it."

Cassie nodded.

"Unless they kill everyone who knows anything, but I'm thinking right now we've got enough to go public with this. We got seventy-five inmates murdered, two guards, an FBI agent, the doctor involved, a book of her notes, thanks to Garza, and all the documentation Sutter and Grant gave their lives to put together. We've just got to get it ready and determine who we need to go to with it."

Guard Harris laughed, shrugging.

"That's right. We can't go to the government. The U.S. Attorney might be in on it. So, we go to the media?"

Cassie wagged his head.

"The media's a joke. No one believes what they hear in the media anymore. We've got to get it ready and put the word out there that we're ready to go public, and then we'll see who's behind all this. They don't know what we know, so they'll come callin. One of us will have to deal with them and I think that should be me."

The room was silent until Guard Rodriguez spoke up.

"Fine by me, but you gotta know it's your ass."

"I know the risks, but since they won't know what I know, I'll have at least a little time to find out who they are and look for an enemy."

Denora interrupted.

"An enemy?'

"*Everyone's* got enemies, and the more powerful people are, the more powerful their enemies are. My father always said, 'Get a dog who'll eat a dog.' I'll just have to find the other dog."

Garza nodded.

"My *papa* said the same thing, but it sounded better in Spanish. I agree. There *is* another dog out there, watchin all this, waitin for its chance tear out a throat. Maybe Cassie and all this dirt we put together will be enough to take em out."

"That's all good, Garza," Farouk concluded, "but in the end you'll still be a Death Row inmate who people want dead. Am I right, Cassie?"

"And that all sucks because you're innocent. Right, Miller?" Cassie returned. "This is about saving lives and making whoever killed people in here accountable. It's about making sure it never happens again."

He smiled.

"Besides, this is California. You'll die of old age before they ever *think* about putting your sorry ass down."

"Destiny Mitchell? Agent West has been expecting you. Please turn around, raise your arms and hold them out."

Passing a detection wand along the underside of her left arm, down her body, along the insides of her legs, up her right side and arm, and then over the front and back of her body, the female agent nodded.

"You'll have to leave your purse with me, or you can return it to your car, and we can start this over again."

Destiny cringed. She knew better. She had planned on leaving the purse in her car, but she was reluctant and uneasy. Earlier in the day, she promised Bryan she would not have any contact with Agent West or pursue the investigation further until *after* his meeting with Cornell Cotton. During the conversation, Bryan seemed certain he would put an unambiguous end to the threat posed. He said he did not trust Agent Easton West and specifically insisted that she avoid his calls.

When Agent West called two hours earlier however, he offered a one-time opportunity for Destiny to meet with Dr. Irene Spagnola, the health care manager at San Quentin during the murders. Destiny initially tried to stall and schedule the meeting for the next day, but West insisted it was "now or never, and Spagnola said that she would only talk to *you* for some reason."

When Destiny called Kiyomi, the pressure began to mount, as Kiyomi insisted a Spagnola interview would be a breakthrough.

"I know, but I promised Bryan I'd wait..."

"Bryan's been great. Let him do what he can," Kiyomi countered, "but he couldn't get to Spagnola after three tries, and now you have a chance. She wants to *tell* you something! He's just going to have to understand."

Kiyomi, still considered a "person of interest" in the murder of Dr. Rashid, was not included in West's offer, and Destiny could not share any information beyond mention of the proposed meeting.

"I've been there for *you*. I've risked everything for you, Destee. You *have* to do this, if not for us, then for me!"

The rented FBI safe house was in Cow Hollow on Pierce, at the edge of Pacific Heights. It was a beautiful three-story, 1931 European design home with a main living residence and four attached apartments. An agent met Destiny at the curb and escorted her to a three-bedroom apartment on the second floor. A second agent, waiting inside the front door, briefed Destiny on the pre-approved parameters of the interview, warning that inappropriate questions would result in an immediate cessation of the visit.

"Do you want to leave your purse with me?"

"No!" Destiny recoiled, cursing herself for bringing it in. "No, I'll just put it back outside."

She didn't want the FBI going through her purse or planting listening devices. But this was the FBI. They would have no problem getting into her rented car if they wanted to, so it didn't matter. However, if she went out, she would lead them to the secluded spot where she had hidden it before she walked fourteen blocks to the house.

"No, wait—I'll leave it," she stuttered, deciding she would do the interview, retrieve her wallet and ditch the two-year-old Dooney & Bourke on the way to the car.

"Is Agent West here? He said he'd be meeting me here."

The female agent checked her watch.

"Agent West is unavailable at the moment. The doctor is scheduled to be moved to another location in thirty minutes. You'll have a little more than fourteen minutes to conduct your interview. Are you ready?"

Destiny hesitated. She was certain she saw West's car on the way over. Kiyomi had sent her detailed research about West, including a recent photo of his vehicle, a black Lincoln Towncar with a scrape along the passenger side and a missing rearview mirror.

"Ms. Mitchell?"

"I'm ready."

She felt small, vulnerable as she traveled down the narrow hallway. Something did not *feel* right. She regretted accepting West's offer, but her only option was to move forward.

Irene Spagnola stood when Destiny entered the room, desperately reaching out to clasp Destiny's hands in her own. Dark lines distorted her face as tears trickled from the corners of her eyes. She did not seem healthy.

"Destiny Mitchell! I *know* who you are."

"Dr. Spagnola, I'm sorry we have to meet under these circumstances. I don't have much time, so can we sit?"

Seated next to the doctor at a dining table, Destiny began.

"The FBI told me what I can and can't ask, and I am certain they're out there, watching everything we do and recording everything we say, but I'm going to take a chance here and go off-script. I need you know that you really *are* Dr. Spagnola, so can you tell me something right *now* that only Dr. Spagnola would know, something verifiable?"

"Well, I," Spagnola sputtered, straining to remember. "Well, when I was a little girl, I was obsessed with unicorns, blue unicorns. Any of the kids who grew up on my street could verify that, but you'd have to find them."

"Okay. Before we begin, is there anything you would like me to do for *you* when this interview is over?"

"*Yes!*" the doctor pleaded. "I have a daughter, Brittanie. Brittanie is pregnant with my first grandchild, a girl, who she's going to name after me... either after me or Bianca Maria. Somehow, I need you tell them I love them, and I need you to make sure they always *know* that."

Destiny bowed her head, tears filling her eyes.

"I will. I promise they will know."

"You know I'll *never* make it out of here. They're going to *kill* me."

"Who's they? The FBI?"

Spagnola wiped her eyes.

"No, the people I used to work for. I know you think I'm a horrible person, but I started working for them because I thought I would be helping people. I just got deeper and deeper in, and before I knew it, I was doing things I never thought I could have done. It wasn't real to me until they started dying, until I had to watch one kid, who looked like my nephew, lie there and suffer to the end. By then it was too late, and the rest became a matter of survival for me."

"You conducted experiments on human subjects at the prison, experiments that killed almost eighty people?"

"They weren't experiments. They were final tests for streamlining a process, for perfecting it."

Destiny sighed, her suspicions at last confirmed.

"A process for what?"

"For using human DNA as a murder weapon. We took samples from the inmates, mutated a gene that triggered rapid heart disease, and then reintroduced it to the subject. Genetic researchers have always known it would one day be possible, but the people I worked for spent over a billion dollars to speed up the progression."

"Using a viral vector?"

Spagnola wagged her head.

"A genetically enhanced vector we wouldn't have seen for thirty years under normal research circumstances, and gene therapy that shouldn't exist, results that defy science. It's scary. I know they've already gotten to me. I'm dying as we speak."

"Why? Why did they develop it? What are they trying to accomplish?"

"I don't know. I'm just a doctor, but I know it's advanced and it's one hundred percent effective. They can kill anyone they want, anywhere in the world, if they can access the DNA, and no one would know the difference. It wouldn't just *seem* like natural causes— it would *be* natural causes."

Destiny's hands trembled as she wiped a tear.

"Who's behind this? Do you know? Is it the government? You worked for *Genengine*—is *that* company involved?"

"Not the *company*, but all its best researchers were put on the project at a separate facility. There's someone big, a group of billionaires, who put it all together—some of the most patriotic guys you'd ever see."

Destiny nodded, focused on remembering every word and facial expression.

"Can you give me a name, anything that could lead me further up the ladder? Who were you working for? Who did you answer to?"

"He owns Rosetta Biotech Laboratories. Used to be a geneticist, one of the billionaires behind this, but you'll never get to those guys. They own an army. They're more powerful than the government. Believe me."

"Who owns Rosetta Biotech Laboratories? What's his name?"

"You've probably never heard of him. His name is Thomas Hancock."

"Thomas Hancock?"

"Yes, but the genius over there, the doctor who owned *Genengine*, his name is Benjamin Rosecrans."

Destiny thought for a moment. She had three minutes left.

"If you had to guess, Doctor, what do you think they're up to?"

"They're powerful men, and there's only one thing powerful men want."

"More power?"

"I think they want to use what they're doing to go in and selectively murder world leaders they don't like. If they're successful, they could shape world events so they would end up with exactly the people they want, people they can control, a New World Order. That's just my guess, but I've always kept that to myself. I've heard more than a few rumors and guesses."

Under two minutes remaining.

"Of all people, Doctor, why did you ask to talk to me?"

Spagnola grasped Destiny's hand.

"I knew who you were. And then, after Grant called you, I heard you were a loose end. I waited, and I was surprised."

"Why?"

"Because you're not dead. So then I thought, *the people behind this, they must have a big secret, some huge vulnerability, and they know you know it.* You have something on them. You must know what they're planning to do in the near future. They're afraid of you, Destiny, because if they weren't, you'd already be dead, you and the reporter."

She winked and smiled.

"So that's why I wanted to talk to you. I needed someone who would make sure my daughter and granddaughter know how much I love them. Grant was right, you know. Whatever secret he told you about, whatever you've got on them, guard it, Destiny! Use it to protect yourself. I'm praying you survive."

An agent opened the door, indicating the interview was over. Destiny stood, bowing her head.

"Thank you for sharing what you've shared, Doctor. I promise you, they'll know."

Irene's face became serious, a sense of desperation in her eyes.

"Thank you, Destiny. But I have to warn you. You're up against a group of extremely wicked and powerful men. They're going to make it rough on you. Things might get worse before they get better."

Chapter 18

It was a rare meeting of the principals, convened at billionaire technology stock trader Helmut Wolf's secluded manorial residence in eastern Idaho, situated in the mountains outside Tetonia in Teton County, on the Wyoming border. The remote castle-like estate, sixty miles northeast of Idaho Falls and four hundred fifty miles northwest from Denver, was designed to be inaccessible, excepting aircraft. Paranoid about security, Wolf rotated in a New World Army infantry platoon every other month.

Driscoll and Wolf hastily organized the gathering under emergency circumstances, as details emerged about a meeting between Destiny Mitchell and Dr. Irene Spagnola, which occurred during the previous day. A loyal FBI operative had provided a printed transcript and live streaming video.

Incensed, Wolf insisted on swift and decisive action, but cooler heads prevailed. While Wolf wanted both women killed at once, Nathaniel Driscoll and Thomas Hancock resisted, insisting Destiny Mitchell should be spared and closely monitored until after the vector was launched and results were realized. Driscoll feared the former prosecutor had intelligence that threatened the entire operation and organization.

Earlier in the week, former San Francisco prosecutor Mitchell contacted a former acquaintance at the U.S. Attorney General's office in Washington D.C., while *Chronicle* reporter Kiyomi Yamakita met in Virginia with a political reporter at the *Huffington Post*. Analysis of the Mitchell-Spagnola interview convinced Driscoll and Hancock that Mitchell and Yamakita knew enough to expose the operation and to implicate certain individuals involved, including Hancock and Dr. Benjamin Rosecrans.

"We have no idea how much she knows and what she's done with it. She and the reporter are obviously up to something. Until we know what it is, we should wait."

While Wolf wanted Destiny dead from the first mention of the call from the prison, the other four founding members of *Country First* were concerned that murdering a former prosecutor and popular women's' activist posed a much more profound risk than killing Death Row inmates. All agreed to launch a vector against her, if operatives could acquire an adequate DNA sample, but Destiny had been careful not to leave inadvertent sources of genetic material behind. It meant she knew something, or someone was helping her.

In recent months, Dr. Rosecrans and researchers had been working to expand applications relating to "trace DNA," which referred to the small amount of DNA left behind after casual contact, such as a handshake, a sneeze or turning a doorknob. By definition, trace DNA included samples that fell below recommended template thresholds at any stage of analysis, from sample detection through to profile interpretation. Depending on the quantity left behind, the source could be identified, as DNA profiles could be created, though trace DNA did not provide enough material for sequencing.

Researchers borrowed from work done by the Forensic Science Service in the UK, where doctors consistently amplified trace DNA by increasing the number of cycles during the PCR of the STR loci. Rosecrans' labs also experimented with the incorporation of synthetic nucleotides with stronger bonding capabilities into PCR primers. The object of the experiments was to amplify trace DNA to such a level that it could be sequenced.

Sequencing involved determining the precise nucleotide sequence of a DNA strand. Only then was gene therapy/manipulation possible. In the end, if researchers could find a way to amplify and enhance trace DNA to the level of sequencing and gene therapy, then no one would be inaccessible. Trace DNA taken from a clothing item, a personal effect or utensil could be altered/weaponized and used against its unwitting provider. It was a goal, but still months or years away, so Destiny remained safe and alive.

Rebuffed, Wolf instead directed his anger toward Operations Chief Jettson Turner, whose job it had been to handle the Destiny Mitchell situation. While Wolf despised Turner for crudeness, insolence and a lack of respect, he also feared the former White House Chief-of-Staffer for his political acumen and influence in Washington. Turner was hired by the group, but he never really worked *for* anyone. When he was in charge, he was totally in charge. No one ever *told* him what to do.

Wolf confronted Turner, whose face appeared larger than life on the video conference screen.

"Jett Turner, we trusted you, and you let us down. We just watched a feed of Destiny Mitchell interviewing Irene Spagnola, with the FBI listening in on the whole thing!"

Turner's face was angry as he took a final drag from the cigarette.

"Two hours before that interview, I cut a deal with Mitchell and her husband, and she agreed to a debriefing by me," he sighed as he exhaled smoke. "We cut a *deal*! She wanted this to be over. She went for it! But then you assholes let an FBI agent call her fifteen minutes later and set up that goddamned meeting, and with *your* fuckin doctor! And you tell me you guys didn't *know* about that! Don't you have a man over there? I mean fuck, guys! What did you expect? What did you *think* she was gonna do? She's a trained *prosecutor*! She caught you with your balls out, so she whacked em. You shoulda kept your doctor under wraps."

Nathaniel Driscoll raised a hand, interrupting.

"This Destiny Mitchell, do you know what she knows, or what she's up to now?"

"*You* saw the interview! She knows what happened at the prison. *That's* obvious. She knows some of the players involved. She's got your name, Driscoll, and Hancock's, and she knows there's more to this shit than killing a bunch of inmates. She's got credible evidence. And then, of course, she knows whatever *Grant* told her, which is why you brought me here in the first place. We still don't know what she knows for sure."

"We should have had her taken out a long time ago," Wolf interrupted. "I say we kill her now, her, the reporter and anyone else she's talked to. That is why we have people to do that."

"And then what?" Turner challenged. "*That's* when you find out what she knows? When this thing becomes a big news story, and the government has enough to come after each of you, one by one? All it'll take is for one of you to talk, and you'll all die. I know the other side. They'll take it personal. The President and his people, they will *kill* all of you."

"Well, Mr. Turner, what do *you* suggest," a concerned elderly woman's voice broke in. "The idea that any of us would be a target or killed was never part of the plan, certainly not mine. We're just investors in a cause, not part of *The Committee*. We were assured we would be insulated from any possible consequences."

All five investors in attendance were billionaires. Sixty-five-year-old Meredith Williams, heiress to an American shipping empire, was visibly nervous.

"Not if you start murdering well-connected prosecutors, reporters and other people involved," Jett countered. "You gotta figure, whatever they know, whatever evidence they've collected, they've got it rigged so that if anything should happen to one or both of them, they're gonna flood the media, prosecutors' offices and the feds with it. And no matter how many counter stories you put out there, certain people will know and investigate, and they'll see it as treason."

Thomas Hancock spoke to moderate Jett's negative tone.

"No need to invoke such provocative terms, Mr. Turner. We would all prefer a more diplomatic solution to the matter. You said she was willing to make a deal. Is that still a viable solution?"

"I believe so," Jett answered.

"No. You said you made a deal with her *before*," Wolf interjected, "before she went out and interviewed Dr. Spagnola. She went *back* on that deal. We have invested a lot of money and none of us want to be implicated in this. But we know *now* that Destiny Mitchell cannot be trusted. So we have to make her *know* we mean business. We know the stakes are high, and she should too. She exposed us! It's the law of retribution, so we do not have a choice. She must pay for what she did, for whatever information she got from the doctor and for whatever that will cost us!"

"What on Earth are you saying, Helmut?" Meredith demanded.

"You *know* what I am talking about," Wolf insisted. "We will not kill that bitch, for obvious reasons, but Destiny Mitchell has got to pay for her betrayal, *in blood*. I will see to that!"

"It would only be the biggest scoop of the decade, Sam, and if you were to dig a little, the biggest of the century by far, maybe the past few centuries. This is *scary* big!"

Kiyomi blew her nose and continued.

"And maybe a little dangerous. But we've put together enough evidence so that if it ever breaks, it will go down as the greatest conspiracy in world history."

Sam laughed. He and Kiyomi had been friends for two years, since a shared flight from Miami to Washington D.C.

"Either you're joking with me, or you've lost your mind, Kiyomi. Talk about an oversell!"

She did not laugh with him or smile. Taking a breath, she began.

"It's the truth, but this time the truth is every bit as spooky as it sounds. An associate and I stumbled on this story accidentally, and the evidence we have is the only thing keeping us alive."

Sam shrugged.

"Which of course means you can't tell *me*. So, if I may ask, what is the nature of the evidence?"

"Well, it's no accident I'm talking to you. It's a political scandal with global implications, though I don't know how far reaching it goes and who all is involved. All I know is they've murdered eighty people in California and their future targets will be political."

Sam sat perplexed for a moment, gauging her demeanor.

"My God! You're *serious*. And you can't clue me in on a little more?"

"Believe me, Sam. If I told ya, I'll hafta kill ya, unless someone else beats me to it."

They had met at the bar in the basement of a posh hotel on Sixteenth, just down the street from the White House. Seated in a dark alcove across from dark wooden tables, Kiyomi bowed her head, inhaling from a *Tea and Sympathy* in a snifter while Sam sipped a Grey Goose martini.

"My birthday is next week, and it's nice you came, Kiyomi. But you didn't make a trip all the way to Washington just to tease me with this story. What are you asking me to do?"

She closed her eyes briefly, sighing, and pushed an envelope toward him.

"Read this later. Now before you start thinking I'm sweet on you, I have to tell you you're not the only one."

She leaned in, quieting her voice.

"I need for you to be on the receiving end of a *dead man's*, or in my case, a *dead woman's switch*. If anything happens to me, if I am dead or otherwise incapacitated, you will receive a communication detailing everything I know about this conspiracy. If that happens, I'll need you to do whatever is necessary to make sure the world knows everything. I'll need you to send it to all the news people you know, all the bloggers, the reporters, bureau chiefs and television stations."

She detected a smidgen of fear as it developed in his gaze, addressing it at once.

"Of course, there is a degree of risk involved, but I swear you won't be the only one. I have fifteen other people, just like you, who have sworn to me that they would put it out there. Don't worry, they're not all reporters. And my associate, she has another twenty people in media, government and the legal profession doing the same thing."

Feeling a little light-headed, she wiped beads of sweat from her brow with a handkerchief.

"You okay? You seem a little peeked. Got a flu bug or something?"

"Yeah, damn summer cold!"

She blew her nose, by then feeling a little self-conscious.

"Please Sam, if you swear it to me and you do it, and everyone else does the same, no one will have anything to worry about. And like I said, if you dig a little, you'll have the scoop of a lifetime."

She had approached Sam about the matter because she knew he lived for reporting. He started his career as a blogger, investigating a political scandal in Baltimore. He had been so fearless and dedicated that he finished the story from a hospital bed with two cracked ribs and a concussion, after having been roughed up after an interview.

For the last two years however, his work involved less risk. He reported for an Internet political news bureau and was a walk-on political correspondent for a cable news network. Older and more adverse to risk, he hesitated, but curiosity got the better of him."

"*How* many reporters?"

"Three, but none like you."

He smiled.

"Come on, you're just sayin that cuz you love me."

"Of course I do."

"Of course I'll do it. One problem though."

Kiyomi's face showed concern.

"What's that?"

"If things get really slow in the news cycle or if I lose my job..."

He winked, pointing his hand in a gun-like fashion.

"I might want to throw that switch myself."

He stood, checking his watch.

"Gotta go. Can't be late for the broadcast. But I swear I'll do that for you. I give you my word."

"Thank you, Sam. It means the world to me."

He grasped her hand.

"I just hope I never get to write that story, not at least till I'm sixty-five."

With Sam gone, Kiyomi took a notebook from her purse and scribbled a few notes before turning to a table and writing his name in box 17. He, along with sixteen others, was her insurance policy, her guarantee that any action against her would be met with a retaliatory reaction. If they hurt her, she would hurt them, and they clearly had more to lose.

Her *dead woman's switch* operated on the principle that as long as she and Destiny were healthy and active with day-to-day life, the switch would remain off, but if either failed to log in to a secret, encrypted mailbox for seven consecutive days, the switch would be triggered and the damning emails, postal mailings and other notifications, complete with evidence attachments, would be dispatched. Another trigger involved the GPS tracking element of their smart phones. In the event that one of their cell phones did not move for seven days, the switch would activate, and the information would be dispersed. She had a third, more convoluted trigger and had paid a hacker to devise a clever fourth switch.

Kiyomi was just about to call Destiny when she saw the text message. Tears welled in her eyes as she read it:

Sad news Kiyo. Notification from FBI. Agent Jake Martinez dead today. God is great.

Chapter 19

When the hotel lobby attendant asked for an ID and credit card, Destiny provided one of the many sets Bryan made up for her, though she told the young woman she would be paying for the room with cash at checkout. Nervous after the meeting with Spagnola, she had driven out of the city, certain the interview was a game changer. An hour and a half on Interstate 80 and an unplanned diversion north on I-5 put her on Richard's Boulevard, just beyond downtown Sacramento. She was tired, so she pulled into the first hotel parking lot she saw.

Settled in the room, she called Bryan from one of the three stealth phones in her guarded *media* bag. When he gave them to her, Bryan explained that the phones were equipped to automatically reprogram their IMEIs after each call. The IMEI was the fifteen-digit code used to identify an individual GSM (Global System for Mobile Communications) telephone to a mobile network. The stealth phones generated codes randomly and never repeated, making interception of made or received calls virtually impossible.

As a private detective who specialized in the latest technologies, Bryan provided Destiny and Kiyomi with numerous aliases, complete with photo IDs, credit cards and Internet IDs. He gave them communications equipment and helped establish protocols—detailed plans involving computer logins, ping transmissions and phone calls to be performed each day. He provided procedures and regimens for electronic bug detection, making purchases, traveling, parking, hotel check-ins, attending public and private meetings, for identifying and avoiding threats and rules for cleaning up potential DNA residue.

He acquired the encrypted software for their *dead man's switch* and gave instructions about what to do if captured or tortured, or if either went missing. For emergencies, he provided guns, glocks with pink accessories, and shooting instruction. For their purses, he gave them low-profile protection kits, containing knives, pepper spray and lethal poisons. He even made emergency cash sources readily available. Both complained that he over-protected and over-worried, but neither underestimated his expertise or instincts, as they followed instructions to the letter, except for on the day before.

"I can't believe you *did* that, Destee! I don't even know what to say to you! This is bad. Why would you do this to me? To yourself!"

"Bryan, I'm sorry! We've been stalled for a week. We've been coming up with dead ends. They were going to kill Spagnola. I'm sorry! It was the only chance I had to talk to someone on the inside, someone who could provide details!"

"That's not the point and you know it! You promised me you'd wait, that you'd let me make this *deal*. And I had it made! We were done, don't you see! It was *over*!"

"Bryan—"

He exploded in uncharacteristic anger, his voice becoming shrill through the receiver.

"Why couldn't you just let this go, Destiny? Why couldn't you do what I asked for a change? I *begged* you to do it. For *me*! I begged you to do it for me."

It was late afternoon the next day as she sat at a desk in the hotel room, laptop engaged. She closed her eyes, concentrating while doing her best to reconstruct the Spagnola interview as she sipped from her second double martini. She typically drank a glass or two of wine two or three nights a week, but she defaulted to chilled vodka when she felt especially stressed.

Bryan was on flight in from Virginia after having met with a friend outside Langley. Reflecting on the conversation the day before, Destiny could not remember him ever being so livid. He said they would talk, but his voice—there was something ominous in his voice, and it scared her.

Butterflies in her stomach, she checked the time at the bottom right of the computer screen: 6:11. His flight was scheduled to arrive at Sacramento Metropolitan Airport at 7:43. Anxious about the looming moment when he would walk in the door, she breathed deeply, putting explanation upon explanation on trial in her mind, but it was useless in the end. Bryan was her husband. There was no excuse.

When Irene Spagnola pleaded, "make sure they always *know* I love them," it meant that she had money, either in a trust or a hidden account, and that her "love" would provide for regular payments to her daughter and unborn grandchild. At the *Aegis Foundation*, directors had prepared a book of code words and expressions to be used by abused women who spoke to workers while still under the threat of an abusers' influence, and Spagnola was speaking by the book. Only after Destiny promised to "make sure" did Spagnola begin to share information.

The name Spagnola mentioned, the alternative baby's name, Bianca Maria—that name would relate to the person or persons who Spagnola had entrusted with that "love." When Destiny asked the identity confirmation question, Spagnola mentioned blue unicorns and kids who grew up on her street. When and if the threat was ever over, Destiny would ask *Aegis* staff members to search for a Bianca and/or Maria who grew up on the same street as Irene, so that arrangements could be made to provide for Brittanie and little Irene, allowing her friend or friends to remain anonymous.

Unable to concentrate, Destiny phoned Kiyomi to check if she had returned from her East Coast trip.

"I'm back in the city, Japantown. Right now, I'm bundled up in bed. Caught a cold on the plane. You know how one person sneezes and it just keeps on getting recycled? Happens to me all the time."

"Is it more of a cold than a flu?"

"It's a cold. Tell me about what happened with Spagnola."

Destiny hesitated, reflecting on what the information had cost her as she poured a third martini.

"She confirmed that she was involved in the murders of eighty people at the prison. They were reprograming human DNA and turning it into a weapon that could kill a specific person. They were testing in the prison."

"Did she know what they were going to do with it?"

"She could only guess, but she said a group of billionaires were behind it, mostly, if not all American, I think. There's a Thomas Hancock who owns Rosetta Biotech, and the company who employed her before the prison—*Genengine*, owned by a Dr. Benjamin Rosecrans."

Kiyomi sat up in the bed.

"Dr. Hussein Rashid, he was a researcher at *Genengine* as well. What was her guess?"

"Well," Destiny sighed, "it sounds like it's taken from the plot of a modern James Bond movie. She said they want to use it to covertly murder world leaders in order to reshape and create a New World Order—the Invisible Hand. Theoretically, they will be able to kill anyone on Earth, as long as they have a DNA sample. It's the mother of all conspiracy theories."

"I used to make *fun* of conspiracy theories," Kiyomi rejoined. "Who would ever believe something so incredible? Sane people will think we're nuts."

Bryan's call interrupted the conversation. He told Destiny he had just exited the freeway, meaning he would arrive in minutes. Hanging up, Destiny panicked. She knew the exchange, at least early on, would not be pleasant. She fixed her hair, retouched her make-up and forced a smile, waiting.

"Hi Bryan, I *missed* you. Where are your bags?"

She embraced him and tried to kiss him, but he grasped her shoulders, gently pushing her away, turning his back toward her.

"I didn't think it was possible. If there was ever a single thing you could have done to turn the love I've felt for you all these years into pure anger and resentment, you managed to accomplish that yesterday."

"Bryan, you don't *mean* that..."

"Of course I do," he returned, stoic, his eyes averted. "I'm *through* with you, Destiny. Now you can finally do things your way."

She feebly reached toward him, her eyes clouded, tears ready to stream.

"That's not what I want."

When she embraced him from behind, he turned and pushed her away.

"*Don't* touch me! I came to meet you tonight because you deserve to hear this from me in person."

"What?"

"I *despise* you right now! You're selfish. I married you because I loved you. I knew you had a life before me, but I believed in *us*. I believed there was nothing our love could not overcome. We had something special, and what did you do with it? You threw it away. You pissed all over it. It was all about you, you and this important work you *claimed* to do, so important that you just stopped giving a damn about me and our marriage."

He turned toward her.

"I *begged* you. I was always begging you, and all you ever had was bad excuses. Everything you ever thought to do was more important than me. You claimed you cared about women you never *met* before, but what did you ever care about me? I sacrificed all for you—you sacrificed none for me. When I moved to San Diego, I thought that would wake you up, but all you ever paid me was lip service. Never once did you ask me to come home!"

"But I *did* ask you."

"You hinted, Destiny. You talked about it, but you never directly *asked* me. You never told me you wanted me, never told me you needed me. It was always about you and your precious, pretentious work. And what all your fans don't understand—you don't really care about any of those women you help. It's always been about *you* and your damn ego. So that's what you're left with in the end—your work, your ego and your disrespect. I deserve better. This is goodbye."

When he headed toward the door, she charged and leapt, wrapping her arms around him, clinging tightly.

"You can't *leave* me, Bryan! I told you I was sorry. You can't go. I love you!"

"Bullshit!"

He struggled for a half minute, trying to extract himself from her grasp, at last gaining advantage as he slammed her, pinning her against the wall. At some time during the scuffle, her face smashed against his elbow. Blood trailed from her nose.

"What? Are you going to *hit* me now, Bryan?"

"I bet you *wish* I would, so you could become one of those pitiful women you're so intent on saving. Yeah, you'd like that. You've always envied those women. Even though you want to think you're better than them, you know you're *worse* off than they are. At least they have passion, but you're just a cold, sanctimonious bitch! Tonight's the last you'll see of me."

Shoving her a final time, he broke free and headed again toward the door. Weeping bitterly, Destiny slid down the wall, back first, collapsing into a shivering heap on the floor.

"I'm sorry, Bryan! Please forgive me. I need you so *much* right now. I need you, Bryan. I need you and I want you in my life. I'll listen to everything you say from now on. I promise! Just please don't leave me."

Her pleading froze him where he stood. It was a rare, uncomfortable moment. In fifteen years, he had never seen Destiny so broken and vulnerable, not since Suziko's wedding reception. Doorknob still in his hand, he reentered and shut the door.

"Do you *mean* that?"

"Yes!"

"I meant the part about you *needing* me and wanting me."

"I want *us*. I'll do whatever I have to do. I'm *sorry* if I've been selfish."

Unable to resist his wife, Bryan walked over and slid down the wall to a place beside her. He took her hand.

"What you did was inexcusable. If it were anyone *else*, I'd let you hang out to dry! I'd say you deserved it!"

He bowed his head, his voice becoming low.

"No one's ever *done* this to me before. I put everything on the line for you—my word, my reputation, everything! You broke your promise to me."

Her face a mess of tears and blood, she caressed his cheek, turning him toward her.

"If I have to live a hundred fifty years, I promise I'll make it up to you. No excuses. No doubting you. No secrets between us. I will be your wife, I will love you, and I will be forever in your debt."

He sighed.

"I don't know what we're going to do, Destee. This complicates things. I saw the interview. Whoever these people are, you've already exposed them to their potential enemies. Now they might not *care* what you know."

"So what are we going to do? I need you." she sniffed, tears still streaming.

"Well, Jett Turner and Cornell Cotton are off the table. I'm sure the Spagnola interview burned both of them. But there is one other person I know who might be able to help us. His name is

Nathaniel Driscoll, and you'll probably have to talk to him in person."

"Do you *trust* him?"

"No, but he's all we've got."

Bryan bowed his head for a moment.

"Look, I'm sorry I lost my temper, Destiny. I can't imagine what *you* must be going through. But you have to understand how frustrated I was when I heard about the interview. I had confirmation from Jett Turner, who had authorization to make the deal. We had negotiated an impasse. It was all over, and now we're right back in it."

"I'm sorry," she sighed. "It's just that part of me didn't believe anyone could be capable of something so diabolical. I suspected it, but Spagnola finally confirmed it. All this time, I thought Perseus Grant was exaggerating or delusional. What if he was right?"

"Right about what?"

Destiny took a deep breath, ready at last to share Grant's final revelation.

"He said—"

Bryan halted her, fingers on her lips.

"I know I asked you to tell me everything, but that probably would not be the best idea right now. You were right not to tell anyone. It's all you've got. When the time comes to use it, you'll know want to do. Until that happens, I have an idea about how to settle this thing, once and for all."

Forty-five minutes later, Destiny and Bryan continued to talk while lying in the bed, nothing between them, sheets still damp from sweat as she listened to his heart.

"When this is all over, I'm quitting the foundation. Lyndsey's ready."

"Maybe she is," Bryan smiled, "but *you're* not done over there yet. Forget what I said earlier. You've found something in your life where you are making a difference, and I admire you for that. Just scale back, put in a regular work week. I can live with that. Home at night, home on weekends—it works. We love each other. Together, there's nothing we can't overcome."

Chapter 20

Cornell Cotton leaned forward, an elbow on the table, his chin cradled in his palm. It was the fifth time through the roughly ten-minute tape. This time, he focused on Dr. Spagnola's careful words, the deliberate pauses and her anxious facial expressions.

"It's out there. At least the implication is out there. If they were only guessing before, they *know* now. It's only a matter of time."

Easton West stood across the room at the bar, titrating the shimmering brown liquid into a crystal snifter.

"The Justice Department called our director to a special briefing in Washington yesterday," West offered, sipping. "Pretty sure it's related. Have *you* heard anything?"

"Well Jett Turner, my director—he's already in an exit strategy. He warned them ten months ago when they went after Sutter that this could happen, but they wouldn't listen. They're a bunch of arrogant rich guys who think they can do whatever they want. They're used to getting away with shit, you know."

"This morning, I got a call from the Associate Deputy Director's office. They want me in Washington tomorrow for debriefing. I guess this is where it gets interesting."

"It's *been* interesting," Cotton countered, as he restarted the interview. "All I have is a tiny piece of a big puzzle, and Turner has his own separate piece. You guys at the FBI have a piece, Osaka's got a piece. The more I watch this, the more I get the sense Grant really *did* tell her something, something specific. But how would he know it? What could a Death Row inmate know? Somewhere, *someone* knows how it all fits together."

Cornell Cotton and FBI Agent Easton West initially met at a Justice Department inauguration function in Washington D.C. three years earlier. At that time, Cotton was an Assistant Inspector General for Investigations, though he retired a year later. The men became acquainted, realizing only after that they lived less than twenty-five miles apart.

Cotton owned a large estate in affluent Montclair in the Oakland Hills, while West's modest home was in North Berkeley. West had visited Cotton's home for his exclusive summer and holiday season theme parties and his December 11 Birthday, and they had met on a few occasions for drinks, but their professional paths never crossed until investigations began for the series of inexplicable deaths at San Quentin.

Easton West was at the prison with Jake Martinez, while Cornell Cotton claimed he was there in an investigative capacity as a private health care company consultant. Over weeks of examination and inquiry, Cotton began to suspect West of leaking details of the investigation to questionable outside players, including billionaire Nate Driscoll, who had ties to secretive labs of a biotech company owned by Thomas Hancock.

When Jett Turner got involved, he offered to hire Cotton away from the health care company for twice the salary. Impressed by work Cotton had done with the Justice Department, Turner wanted the astute former Assistant Inspector to run on-the-ground operations for a highly sensitive debriefing and containment job requiring someone with access to the prison. Destiny's interview with Dr. Spagnola however, effectively changed the nature and urgency of managing containment.

"How many times are you going to watch that video, Cotton? Have you discovered something we amateurs with the FBI didn't catch?"

"Not me. I'm just an old, retired *has-been*," Cotton groaned, never looking up. "That being said, I heard a rumor *you* were the one who set up the interview. How did that come about?"

"Well, Spagnola was arrested three weeks ago, and she wasn't talking. Not a word, not even to a lawyer. Then one day, about a week ago, she just got spooked by something and started asking to meet with Destiny Mitchell. I didn't know Mitchell, but my buddy Jake worked with her before he got sick. He put me in touch."

"Sorry to hear about Jake."

"He's in a better place, but he really suffered at the end."

West bowed his head, remembering his friend. Glancing over, he continued.

"I guess we have to assume that somewhere at the Justice Department, they'll be investigating Spagnola's claims."

"If they don't already *know* what's going on," Cotton nodded. "You'd be surprised. How would *you* assess the tape, Easton? What did you see going on?"

"I saw two desperate women who both realize they've stepped in shit. Spagnola's in deep and she knows it. Maybe she thought Destiny could save her, or maybe her family. But she named *names*!"

"I see *desperate*, and I hear code. They're speaking in some kind of code. I'll tell you though, if I didn't know any better, I'd say that interview was not the first time those two women have met or talked. I mean, look at them. They've *met* before. So why pretend, unless they were staging the whole thing?"

West sighed, shaking his head.

"Well, you won't be able to ask Dr. Spagnola that question. She's *dead*. Agents had to break into her room this morning. It was barricaded—found her dead, blue in the face, nude, torn sheets, body dangling outside the window."

"No shit!"

"She hanged herself. We didn't see it coming."

Cotton seemed troubled by the news. He sipped the last of the cognac in his glass, crunching on the ice.

"Yeah, funny how that works out. It's just really convenient for some people—tidies up a loose end."

He paused, contemplating.

"So, now all that's left for them to tidy up is Destiny Mitchell."

"Destiny Mitchell," West laughed, "now there's a woman with balls. It won't be so easy with her."

"The last time I looked at Baby," Cornell smiled, "I saw some shapely legs, juicy titties and a nice ass, but I didn't see any balls. It's called self-preservation. Destiny Mitchell knows something no one else knows—obviously, intelligence that's *still* in play. But my guess: she has no idea what to do with it."

The area, called Billionaire's Row, was located in Pacific Heights and stretched from the Golden Gate, past Alcatraz, Fisherman's Wharf and around to Treasure Island and the Bay Bridge. Since the late 1800s, San Francisco's wealthiest families built their mansions on the hills there, with views of the San Francisco Bay, Golden Gate Bridge, Marina and Mount Tamapais.

Prices ranged from seven million dollars for more modest homes, to a whopping sixty-five million for a stunning 21,888 square foot French limestone mansion on Broadway.

Most of the homes were owned by one percenters and old money families, including hedge fund managers, private equity investors, Silicon Valley mega entrepreneurs, the Peter Haas family, the Gettys, Larry Ellison of Oracle and George Lucas. Despite having been born in San Francisco, Bryan Osaka still gawked as he drove past the overelaborate mansions, imagining how any single person or family could own something so vast, each home a rare glimpse of unimaginable wealth reserved for America's most privileged class.

Years earlier, when he was a detective with the SFPD, he responded to a call at one of the houses along Broadway. It was a gray and white four-story Victorian on a corner. Thinking back, he remembered feeling intimidated as he pulled up along the curb and embarrassed because it took him ten minutes to find the front door. The respondent was the head of a private security detail who had called the San Francisco police out to take a theft report for insurance purposes. Bryan never made it past the marble-floored foyer and never saw the residents. The reported loss: a blue Bvlgari diamond heirloom, valued at over fourteen million dollars.

Earlier in the morning, Bryan called Nathaniel Driscoll to renegotiate a deal that would save Destiny's life and keep crucial intelligence about *Country First* off-the-grid. Driscoll seemed amenable, but he was not available on such short notice. However, he said he had an associate in San Francisco who could negotiate on his behalf and suggested a time, while providing the address to a huge estate in the exclusive locale.

The tall, muscular servant who opened the door seemed stiff and awkward to service. As he served coffee, Bryan noticed his *Glock knuckle*, a massive callus that had developed on his strong hand middle-finger, resulting from the gun's poorly shaped trigger guard. Suspicious, Bryan found it irregular that the entire staff was male, large and exceptionally fit. While one of the four had his hair pulled into a discreet ponytail, all the others wore variations of *high and tight*. One of the men had a small tattoo on his neck, a vertical dagger, piercing a skull-and-crossbones, this over the words, *De Oppresso Liber*—the Special Forces motto.

Driscoll told Bryan to ask for a "gentleman" by the name of Helmut Wolf, who would handle negotiations in Driscoll's place. Outside one of the mansion's windows, two other dark suited men stood at the curb, glancing back at the house on occasion. In all, Bryan counted six men in the detail, though he guessed the total number to be eight.

"Mr. Osaka, good to meet you. My name is Helmut Wolf. Please make yourself at home."

Turning away from the window, Bryan laughed to himself at the irony of Wolf's hollow offer. Home? It felt more like a small military operation.

"Thank you," Bryan nodded. "If you don't mind, I'll stand."

"Suit yourself. I'll sit," Wolf sighed as he eased into a leather armchair across from the fireplace in the large private library. "Osaka—good Japanese name. Your people fought with the Germans in the war."

"No," Bryan countered, politely. "My uncles fought with the Americans."

The handsome older man nodded toward a servant standing in the background, who exited immediately. Helmut Wolf was a distinguished man with short white hair who was probably in his mid-sixties. His nose and lips were keen, his face more eastern European than American. Bryan guessed he was about five feet ten inches and in relatively good shape. He sported an Italian-tailored suit and designer shoes.

"We are both very busy men. We should get to the point," Wolf announced, his voice impatient. "My colleague Driscoll told me you wanted to renegotiate a deal involving your wife, Destiny Mitchell."

"Yes, that's true," Bryan nodded.

"Just what makes you think that I would *want* to make a deal with her? Is it *not* true that she reneged on the last deal she made? Tell me, why would I even trust her?"

"Because, as a wealthy man who's made billions investing in business and trading stocks, you're a man who definitely understands the nature of risk. To trust her, well, there is a degree of risk involved in that, but she doesn't want a fight she can't win.

She wants out, and she'll agree to whatever it takes to get back to her life."

Bryan paused.

"But then, what is the alternative? You kill her and whatever she knows is suddenly out there? Some in your group will be able to find cover, but not you—whatever your secret club is doing, it's *your* money and ideas that made it happen. So when the enemies show up, it'll be for you."

When Driscoll told Bryan he would be meeting with Helmut Wolf, Bryan only had a few hours to create a *dossier* and familiarize himself with Wolf's history and methods of operation.

Helmut Wolf was born in Nova Petrópolis, within the southern Brazilian state of Rio Grande do Sul. His wealthy parents immigrated to the U.S. with their only child when he was twelve, settling in Yorkville on the Upper East Side of Manhattan. Helmut spoke fluent German, Portuguese and Spanish as a child.

Considered a math prodigy, he attended Colombia University, where he received a Master's degree from the school of Engineering and Applied Science at twenty-three. He became fascinated with finance when, on his twenty-first birthday, his father took him to the New York Stock Exchange. Having found his passion, he remained and earned a Master's degree in Finance and Economics from Columbia's Business School, two years later.

Investing his parents' money, he was a multi-millionaire in his own right at twenty-eight years old. By the time he was twenty-nine, events of his life became indistinct. By most accounts, he returned to South America, where he got involved in the financial workings of several banana republic governments, returning seven years later with a net worth of over five hundred million dollars.

Still fascinated by science, he invested heavily in technology stocks throughout the global computer evolution of the 1980s-2000s, his trading company becoming an influential force in the industry. His political opinions favored a plutocracy, or rule by the wealthy, which in his opinion was the *de facto* form of government that suited America best. He donated to candidates and campaigns based on his ideas of establishing oligarchy control, regardless of political affiliation.

His arrogance and insensitivity were unmistakable. He carried himself with the confidence of a man who possessed a god-

ordained entitlement to privilege and power. Scoffing at Bryan, he
answered.

"Do you actually believe I have any reason to *fear* what your
wife knows?"

"If you didn't," Bryan countered, "it isn't likely we'd be sitting
here talking today."

"She knows nothing!" Wolf shouted, "And Grant knew nothing!
If it were up to me, your wife would have been dead long ago."

"You've obviously calculated the *risk*, Mr. Wolf. I'm here today
to try and settle this. I assure you that whatever Grant told my
wife will never be known. Further, as of this moment, my wife and
Kiyomi Yamakita will walk away from this and never ask another
question. And finally, I can personally guarantee you that none of
the findings from this investigation will implicate you or your
friends. I will make sure of that. You do what you are going to do,
and we all walk away."

"What good are your guarantees, Osaka?" Wolf sneered. "Your
wife is a troublemaker. She has already jeopardized more than you
could ever imagine or reimburse us. She threatens years of work
and the very future of our great country, the future of the world!"

Bryan closed on Wolf's position.

"I'm not threatening you, Mr. Wolf, but if you harm my wife in
any way, you and your friends will suffer serious consequences.
Make no mistake—I *know* what you're doing. I did not come to
you at a disadvantage."

"You are correct, Mr. Osaka. I *do* understand the nature of risk,
and I am willing to bet that indeed you did *not* come here at a
disadvantage, something rather unfortunate. We have been
watching you, listening to you, and I am willing to bet that
whatever your wife knows, then that is something *you* know."

He dialed a number on his phone.

"Victor, it seems we are ready to proceed with Osaka."

Seconds later, four large men entered the room, forming a
square barrier around the detective. Wolf rose in summation.

"Resistance is futile, as you already no doubt know. These men
will do anything I tell them to do. The die is cast. Whatever you
know, *we* will know."

Chapter 21

"Hello Destiny Mitchell."

"Yes. Who is this?"

"Do you recognize my voice?"

She hesitated, suspicious.

"No, I don't. How did you get this number?"

"Your husband asked me to call. My name is Cornell Cotton. I spoke with you one week after you spoke with Perseus Grant. Do you remember me?"

"Yes. You! Why are you calling me?"

"To re-introduce myself and to tell you that Bryan asked me to make sure you were safe and got help in case anything ever happened to him."

She cringed, a sudden chill permeating her body.

"*Has* something happened to him? Is that what you're calling to tell me?"

"No. Bryan's fine. He can handle himself. I'm just calling to let you know I'm here in case you need me. He left my phone number for you in your media bag."

"Kiyomi! Where are you?"

"In bed, still sick. Why? What's *wrong*?"

"Nothing. I'm just worried about Bryan. He was so angry when he found out about the Spagnola interview."

"You *told* me," she said, sitting up, "You *had* to do that interview, but that isn't why you're worried."

Destiny shut her eyes, a tear streaming down her cheek.

"Maybe I should have *listened* to him. He says if I had, this would all be over."

"That's what he hoped because he trusts these people. It was a mistake. They want to kill us! You did the right thing, Girl."

"Maybe not. I did what you pressured me to do. I'll never forgive you."

"Excuse me?"

"If anything happens to Bryan, I'll blame *you*."

The tiled massage room upstairs had been prepared for the procedure since morning. Victor and assistants had wrapped the table in cellophane and placed plastic around its base to keep the floor from becoming slippery. They brought in a deep recovery tub, several small glass ewers and a huge punch bowl, which they filled with water.

"Bring him in. Remove his shirt. Strap him to the table, arms and legs—zero movement."

Victor Collins had performed the procedure many times before, in Iraq, Afghanistan, Yemen, Guantanamo Bay and Virginia. As a former Army Ranger intelligence specialist, experienced at enhanced interrogation techniques, Collins had interrogated more than a dozen high value detainees. Under the CIA's expanded SERE program, he had been trained to administer specific physical and psychological interrogation techniques. Helmut Wolf was already seated in an adjoining room, on the other side of a two-way mirror.

"Invert the bed."

Hans Mehring, one of the two men assisting Victor, held a keypad, which he manipulated, simultaneously lowering the head of the bed while raising its foot. Bryan's supine body was positioned at a near thirty-degree angle, his lowered head positioned over the recovery tub.

"Place the cloth."

A second assistant placed a wet cloth on Bryan's face, covering his forehead and eyes. Victor leaned in and spoke in a low, gentle voice.

"Hello Bryan. My name is Victor. I work for Helmut Wolf. Please understand that I have nothing against you personally. The truth is I don't like what I do, but it's my job. Mr. Wolf has asked me to get some information from you. He wants you to tell me whatever it was that Perseus Grant told your wife, Destiny

Mitchell. If you tell me that now, neither of us will have to go through this unpleasant experience."

He uncovered Bryan's pleading eyes, trying to establish rapport.

"Can you do that? Can you tell me what Grant told your wife?"

Bryan shut his eyes, preparing for the torture.

"I don't know if he told her anything. I don't know what she knows."

"I'm sorry, Bryan. Mr. Wolf believes you *do*."

Victor unfolded the cloth, this time covering Bryan's entire face.

"Begin."

Hans Mehring knelt, holding Bryan's head in place. The other assistant filled one of the small ewers and, holding it twenty inches above Bryan's face, began pouring, slowly at first. Bryan's body tensed, fists clenched, as his first reaction was to hold his breath. In his mind however, he began to panic. As the water flow increased, Bryan got the distinct sense that he was underwater and could not breathe. The constant flow also caused temporal confusion, as he could not tell how long the water had been pouring. Desperate, he finally tried to take a breath, but he was drowning! The fact that he was completely unable to move made the experience all the more harrowing. And then suddenly, it was over.

The duration had been thirty seconds, but it felt like an hour. When the cloth was lifted, Bryan gasped, sputtering water, body shivering as he gulped several breaths of air.

"Breathe Bryan, breathe."

After ten seconds, the first assistant replaced the cloth, and the second began pouring water again. This time, the desperation returned at once. He could not think rational thoughts, reverting to the primitive urge to survive. Deprived of fight or flight, his body heaved, restraints unyielding, as he struggled for air. He tried to scream, but he got strangled when he opened his mouth and gagged as he tried to cough. He could feel Death pressing on his chest, his heart racing, pounding, ready to explode. And then, it was over.

Victor spoke as Bryan sputtered water, wheezing as he tried to inhale.

"Please Bryan, let me *help* you. Help me put an end to this. For your own sake, please tell me what your wife knows."

"I, I swear! I don't know! Please help me! Please not again! I don't know!"

Victor nodded, and the cloth returned, only to be followed by the water. Helmut watched the procedure from his seat with great fascination. He was amazed at the effectiveness of the technique. He had read a work-up on Bryan just that morning— "a highly-intelligent, focused, disciplined detective... stoic... unemotional..." And here he was, screaming, pleading, begging *like a woman*! Once again, the water stopped. Victor spoke.

"Bryan please, I'm trying to help you here. Come on, tell me what you know. It's okay. Just help me out here. Help your wife. Everything will be all right."

"I swear! Please! I swear she didn't tell me! Wait! I, I can tell you something else!"

"What's that, Bryan?"

"*White House Target*! I know what *Country First* is doing! They want to use their viral vector to kill the *President*!"

Victor glanced toward the mirror.

"Really? Give me a second, Bryan."

Two minutes later, Victor returned.

"You've done very well, Bryan. I told Mr. Wolf what you said. He wants to know how you know this. Did your wife tell you that? Is that what Grant told her?"

"No! Someone sent it to me! I swear. I never told my wife about it!"

"Who sent it to you?"

"I don't know. It was an encrypted upload, but it was a document, and it said they were going to kill the President using the viral vector they perfected at the prison!"

"Who else knows? Who have you told about this?"

After two additional waterboarding sessions, Bryan confessed that he had been working with James Cassie and two guards at San Quentin. After another, he admitted to sharing guard Robert Shaw's computer research and database with the group. Thoroughly exhausted, Bryan passed out on the table.

Inside the adjoining room, Victor and Mehring sat with Wolf.

"He's telling the truth. If his wife knows something, she never told him what it was. And I believe he's telling the truth about someone sending him some kind of document, accurate or not. This crazy bit about viral vectors and killing the President— in my experience, when you get to a certain point in an interrogation, the value of intelligence drops off. Subjects will literally tell you *anything* to make it stop."

"Wake him up and waterboard him again."

"Why? There's no further intelligence to be gained by doing that."

"You heard me. I said *waterboard him again*."

"Sir, there's no point. That would just be torture for torture's sake."

"Yes, *torture* him! I will watch from here. I think today I will indulge the crueler aspect of my nature."

It was late June. They began their climb at the Kawaguchiko Fifth Station, in the Yamanashi Prefecture, having come from Tokyo. It would be a seven hour climb up the Yoshida Trail. They began at 1:00 p.m. so they would be able to stop and stay overnight at a mountain hut that Bryan's cousin recommended. It was on the Eight Station, and the inn was owned by a friend of the family.

They brought along three bottles of wine, water, a large slab of smoked salmon, fresh *sato-nishikis* (cherries), dried *kaki* (sweet persimmon), and *onigiri* (rice ball snacks) in various flavors. Because it was off-season, the weather was cold and the wind bit hard, but the ascent was romantic as they held hands, exchanging proverbs and poems in Japanese.

The hut was modest, but there were few other climbers so early in the year. Bryan and Destiny stood against a rail outside their room, watching the sun as it set. Inside after dinner, they bowed and prayed a prayer of thanks for their good fortune. They were happy that *Unmei* (Fate) had been kind and generous, bringing their two hearts together.

"I am thankful that in all the world and throughout all time," Bryan prayed, "you brought me Destiny, who I will love with every breath to the last."

"And I am thankful," she added, "that you gave meaning to the word 'marriage,' thankful that you have sent me a man who is my best friend, my lover, my protector, my guide and best of all, my *husband*."

She smiled.

"I don't ever want this to end. You are my life."

Kilometers from the summit of the mountain, they made love on a mat in the little hut, taking their time. The setting was austere, creating a spirit that conjured primitive emotion and sensuality. Every touch tingled, every kiss titillated, every moment of ecstasy... rapture! They did not sleep at all. Instead, they lied together, pondering existence, musing on God's sense of humor, mourning the unfortunate, bemoaning the serious, condemning the arrogant and pitying the world not present. They laughed and giggled like childhood best friends until 1:00 a.m., when they rose and began their final ascent.

Bundled in heavy clothing to block the extreme cold, they adjusted their headlamps and trudged through snow and ice up the rocky trail, turning aside to avoid occasional blasts from wind gusts. They reached the dome at 3:30, almost an hour before the 4:25 sunrise. They walked the dome together and found an auspicious alcove along the eastern side and sat, prepared to watch the greatest glory known to humans, the rising of the sun.

"When I was a little boy, I came here with my *ojiisan*, and we came to this very place. He told me the name *Fuji* came from the Japanese syllables *fu* and *shi*, *fu* meaning 'never' and *shi* meaning 'die.' When we watched the sunrise together, he told me that he would never die, that he would always be with me. That is the only thing I can remember about my grandfather. He passed away a month after we went home."

"He's here with us now," Destiny comforted. "I can feel him. He's smiling at us."

As glory illuminated the appearance of the sun at the horizon, Bryan took Destiny's hand, squeezing.

"This is the happiest moment of my life, to have you here, to be with you, my wife."

"I will cherish this moment for as long as I live," she replied as they embraced, faces together, as they watched the sun ascend into the sky.

Bryan had passed out again after two additional sessions under the unrelenting water stream. His escape had been to that memory, to that moment in time. Ironically, in Sacramento, Destiny was remembering the same moment, the upwelling of love and emotion she felt as they sat there, the words of his grandfather.

When Bryan awoke, Helmut Wolf sat in a chair beside him, his face scowling.

"Today, I do not know what Perseus Grant told your wife, but I will know it. Destiny Mitchell has yet to live a few additional days on this Earth, but you, Mr. Osaka, unfortunately you do not."

Bryan tried to respond, but he could only groan. His voice was gone.

"I understand risk, but your wife does not. She made a deal to save her life. I did not like it, but I was willing to live with it. And then, without provocation, she broke the deal. The law of retribution says that she must pay for that betrayal. She damaged us, so we must damage her, and we must do this in a way that it will never come into her mind to defy us again. Your death will serve as a meaningful lesson to her."

Finally able to speak, Bryan's voice was hoarse from screaming, a haunting whisper, his mouth contorted in a wry smile.

"You will *remember* me on the day you die!"

Wolf scoffed, nervous, beckoning the interrogator Victor Collins, who was first-in-command in his elite guard.

"Ha! I will never waste another single *thought* on you!" he sneered as he rose, whispering to Mehring, who was his personal bodyguard and a distant relative.

"Quickly, Hans, and directly in the face."

Chapter 22

It started as a late evening news story, with brief footage of a
Coast Guard Cutter on the Bay near Point Diablo, its searchlights
scanning the choppy surface of the waters, and a brief statement
from the captain. By noon the next day, KRON and CBS San
Francisco were reporting it as a gruesome murder with bizarre
implications that were still under investigation.

*Former SFPD detective Bryan Osaka, born and raised in
Tiburon, had been shot multiple times in the face and his body was
thrown from the Golden Gate Bridge into the waters of San
Francisco Bay.*

At eight-thirty the previous night, the crew of an inbound
fishing boat spotted the body bobbing in the water near the
bridge, but it was not recovered until seven o'clock the next
morning. The Coast Guard spent hours trying to identify the
naked man, until one of the doctors discovered a microchip
embedded under the skin of the decedent's left hand. It turned
out to be a tiny radio-frequency identification transponder,
encased in silicate glass.

Within minutes of accessing the chip, the identity of the body
was confirmed. Yet before any notification could be issued, the
commander at USCG Sector San Francisco, located on Yerba
Buena Island, received a call from the Sacramento Regional Office
of Homeland Security. The supervisor, working in coordination
with the Department of Homeland Security-USCG at the
Interagency Operations Center at the San Francisco Sector Base,
directed a team to debrief the fishermen, the Cutter crew and
doctors, but its main purpose was to recover the microchip.

By the time the DHS team was able to complete its tasks,
however, the Coast Guard headquarters on the island was
besieged by reporters under a dreary, dripping sky, demanding
details about where the body was found, its condition and the
nature of the injuries to the face. The supervisor in Sacramento
was angry the identity of the victim had been shared with the
media, but there was no indication a leak had occurred. One news
anchor, noting the Department of Homeland Security's

involvement, suggested that Bryan Osaka, a well-respected private investigator and "American citizen," had stumbled across a terrorist plot and was murdered by conspirators in an effort to keep him from exposing it.

Even more interesting was the degree of nationwide coverage the story generated. It was not the first time a murdered body had been found floating near the Golden Gate Bridge, but news reporting on such events was usually limited to local television markets. That particular story, however, was reported on all the national television networks and affiliates, as well as on major cable news channels. There was something else to the story, as one commentator remarked, "something no one has yet been willing to talk about."

Kiyomi stood stunned next to the television set, trembling as she watched the story.

Bryan Osaka dead? How could it happen? He was so good at playing their game! There had to be a mistake!

She called a friend at the *Chronicle* and got confirmation of the story, only this friend repeated a rumor going around the bureau: when the microchip from Bryan's hand was activated, news editors nationwide, editors across the Atlantic as well as American government security agencies, received multiple communications and uploads from various sources, describing a powerful and well-financed confederate pact and a plot to murder the President of the United States.

When one of the phones rang, she was certain it would be Destiny.

"I was just going to call you. I'm coming to you there!"

"Kiyomi, this is Sam. Are you *watching* this? Please tell me it has something to do with what you were telling me about the other day. Some of the editors got notifications and a bombshell from this guy. No one wants to talk about it, but I can tell it's beyond huge."

"It is. Keep your eyes open, Sam, and remember what you promised me. I can't talk now. Bye."

She could only think of Destiny, and the last words her best friend spoke to her.

On the television, ABC7 ran a short biographical perspective on Bryan Osaka, piecing together a general narrative, interspersed with interviews by childhood friends, classmates, previous colleagues from SFPD, former agency clients and two former mayors. At the end of the piece, the reporter pointed out that private detective Bryan Osaka was the sometimes-estranged husband of San Francisco's famous women's rights activist and icon, Destiny Mitchell.

In a Sacramento hotel, Destiny sat catatonic in the bed, unable to move, initial reaction frozen on her face, her mouth still open. She was watching CNN when the story broke, unprepared for the unexpected shock to her soul when the anchor launched into the story.

San Francisco Police are searching for witnesses in the murder of a man who, a decade ago, was one of their own. The body of private detective Bryan Osaka, of Tiburon, was recovered by the Coast Guard from the fog-covered waters of San Francisco Bay early this morning, the victim of an apparent homicide. Osaka was recently involved in an investigation at San Quentin Prison. Police believe revenge to be a possible motive.

The phone rang every half hour for three hours as Destiny sat there, transfixed. She was numb, unable to feel, unable to even think.

The story she saw and heard on the television was unreal. She and Bryan being together, sharing a lifetime of memories, growing old together—*that* was real! The idea that someone had murdered her husband and thrown his body into the cold, churning ocean, it was unreal to her. The time they spent together two days earlier, when they reaffirmed their wedding vows and planned a winter trip to Morocco—*that* was real.

The thought that she would never see him smile or laugh again, would never hear his calm and comforting voice, would never feel his arms around her to reassure her, was unreal. But the determination she felt to track down the men who threatened her, shot her daughter and murdered her husband, the resolve she felt to make them pay even if it cost her own life, from then on—that was as real as it would ever get.

She was startled from the daze by the sound of someone pounding on the door. The voice screaming outside was familiar and annoying. She bowed her head, took a breath and rose.

"Destee! Talk to me! Are you okay? I've been calling for the last three hours."

Destiny responded without emotion.

"I'm fine, Kiyomi. Why'd you come?"

"Bryan! You heard about what happened to Bryan, didn't you? It's all over the news."

Destiny nodded.

"Yes, I saw. Yes, it's all over the news."

"You, you don't look well. Something's wrong. I think you're in shock."

"No," Destiny sighed. "I'm shocked, but I'm not 'in shock.' I just lost my husband. I'm sad, but they're not going to intimidate me any further. I'll mourn after Bryan's death is avenged."

"Brought you some tea. Oolong, your favorite. Sit down. We'll just turn this off."

Kiyomi shut off the television and sat across from her best friend, clutching one of her hands.

"The last time we talked, you said you'd blame *me* if something happened to Bryan. I'm sorry, Destiny—I feel this was all my fault."

Destiny squeezed Kiyomi's hand.

"No, it wasn't your fault. I said that because I was scared."

She paused.

"I'm not scared anymore."

She rose, walking stiffly to the desk, where she poured vodka into two small glasses.

"Bryan must have known what was going to happen when he agreed to meet whoever he did, and he made a choice—just like you and I have to make choices now."

She pushed a drink toward Kiyomi.

"I swear I'm tired of running and hiding, of being afraid, Kiyo. I think I've got enough right now to ruin *someone's* day, and I'm motivated. It's only going to get better. Bryan made sure we had our *dead man's trigger*, so I know he had his own. He's gone, but I'm sure he's going to make someone pay."

She raised a glass, voice breaking, "*Buraian no memori e!*"

Kiyomi followed, tears flowing, "To Bryan's memory."

Destiny threw the drink back and slammed the empty glass on the table.

"I'm making it my mission to see this thing through. What Perseus Grant started, I'm going to finish it—whatever it takes. So I'm giving you a chance to get out. You've already risked more for me than I could ever repay you. I can't ask for anything more."

Kiyomi sipped the vodka and twisted her face.

"You never *asked* in the first place. Look, we're in this together. I will be right beside you, to the death if I have to. It doesn't matter how clever or tenacious you think you are, Destiko. You can't do this without me."

Chapter 23

In an emergency meeting convened at the Arlington boardroom, members sat silently around the long conference table, awaiting the chairman. As always, it was close to midnight and the room was darkened. In keeping with tradition, each member wore a mask bearing the likeness of Thomas Jefferson. Governor Hugh Gordon breathed heavily and sighed on occasion, as he was tempted to seek a consensus opinion of others at the table, but the rule was unambiguous—no discussion before or after official meeting minutes.

Gordon was concerned about the Osaka murder and possible consequences, legal and moral. In his mind, the prison experiments existed in the abstract. The doctors were not actually *killing* the blood guilty inmates, who had already been tried, convicted and condemned to death by a state system, ill-equipped to carry out the will of the people. They were testing a process that would give America a decisive twenty-first century advantage in an increasingly complicated political/economic global community.

But the murder of innocent civilians, the murder of ordinary American citizens? Where was the justification for that? The group had been briefed on Osaka and his role at the prison. By all accounts, he was a patriotic American and someone who had helped the cause of *Country First*, murdered because he knew too much, or too little. And Dr. Irene Spagnola was murdered days before. Two prison guards and an FBI agent had also been murdered. How many more innocent people would be killed? Where would the so-called containment stop?

It was in direct conflict with Gordon's faith. His belief in God's law warned that *whosoever has sheddeth man's blood, by man shall his blood be shed: for in the image of God made he man*. On the morning that the broadcast and cable news announced that Bryan Osaka had been murdered, shot in the face, Gordon felt a sudden chill in his own blood.

And that night, he had a bizarre dream in which he was being nailed to a cross. *And fear not them which kill the body, but are not able to kill the soul: but rather fear him which is able to destroy both soul and body in hell.* In the dream, Gordon felt as if his bones were being pulverized with each time the stone struck the metal pins in his hands and feet. Gazing up at the burning sun in agony, he fancied he saw the *Eye of Providence*, and it was dripping blood!

Startled from the revelation, he nudged his wife awake. Susan Marshall Gordon, according to parents and friends, had been blessed with the gift of interpreting dreams with remarkable accuracy. Still groggy, she listened to her husband as he described what he felt and saw and responded without thinking, *"For ye were as sheep going astray; but are now returned unto the Shepherd and Bishop of your souls."*

All the next day, Governor Hugh Gordon meditated on the dream and the message. Yet he was a pragmatic man. He could go along with the methods and goals of *Country First* in principle and honor the oath he swore, though his true allegiance was to a greater power. He just hoped he would never be forced to choose between the two.

Over all the years of meetings, he never knew the identity of the others sitting at the table, or whether the make-up of the quorum was consistent or of varied representation. He believed he had guessed the identity of one or two members, according to vague references made by the chair, the only member whose identity was obvious.

Associate Supreme Court Justice Wendell Greene had taken a supreme risk in recruiting members to the executive committee of *Country First*, who were called *The Committee*. He let members know that any scandal resulting from his involvement in the plot would be precluded by his suicide or certain murder. For that reason, the vetting process he undertook for each member was thorough and exhaustive. Each had to submit to background searches and numerous interviews, along with random assessments in prefabricated public challenges on personal substantive issues. He trusted each member, though Governor Gordon, for his private and secretive nature, gave Justice Greene pause from the beginning.

When he arrived, the Justice called the meeting to order at once, beginning with prepared remarks.

"As you all know, we are presently embroiled in unfortunate and rather challenging circumstances in which difficult decisions have been made and perilous actions were required to be undertaken. You are no doubt aware of the result of one of these outcomes, or casualties, involving Bryan Osaka, a private detective from San Francisco."

Seeming to be out of breath, the Justice's eyes penetrated the darkness to study the reaction of one member in particular as he continued.

"It turns out the detective was in possession of a certain, sensitive document that could have only come from a person who is in this room tonight. We have no certainty of who it is, but we have ways to find out. It was a very damaging document to be sure, with rippling repercussions. As a result, we are all at risk. At this point, we must assume that certain unnamed government agencies are zeroing in on each of us."

The Justice paused to allow the weight of his words to reach bottom line.

"The consequences may be something difficult to consider, but tonight we must. We all swore an oath that we would die to protect the objectives and legacy of our cause. If the identities of members on our committee have been compromised, we have to expect they'll be coming after us. We must now strongly consider what we will do about the liability that *we* now present, the risk to *Country First*."

One member at the far end table spoke out, ignoring protocol.

"Liability? With all due respect, Mr. Chairman, it seems the only liability is the person who saw fit to murder that detective and the other civilians. I've sworn my allegiance, yes, and I'm willing to make the ultimate sacrifice, but not for light and transient causes."

"What are you suggesting, Senator?" the Justice sighed.

"Someone's got to take the fall, and the most logical person to do that is the idiot who authorized killing of a detective who we *knew* was investigating us. Who made the call?"

The woman at the table spoke up. It was the first time anyone had heard her distinctive voice.

"That person *and* the person who leaked information about us to the detective! —whoever he is! Who ordered the death of Osaka, Mr. Chairman? Certainly you know. Our lives are at stake."

Greene hesitated, reluctant to reveal the truth, but she was right. Everyone knew that he knew.

"It was Mr. X. He ordered it."

"Then I would have to ask *why?*" she returned. "For God's sake, from what I've heard, the detective got involved *only* to save his wife. He wasn't *interested* in us, and now *this*! I concur with the senator. Mr. X should take the fall."

Other committee members at the table voiced agreement. Greene sighed behind the mask and answered.

"I am afraid that will not happen. Mr. X was indemnified by each of you before we even began our enterprise."

"Indemnified?" Gordon broke in. "He *answers* to us, doesn't he? Or are you suggesting it's the other way around? I thought we were all in this together!"

"We are, and we *aren't*," the Justice answered, removing his mask. "Gentlemen and gentlewoman, when we began and each of you were being vetted—you may not recall, but you voluntarily submitted a 'whole saliva' sample to a technician. From that sample, your individual DNA was extracted."

The inference was unmistakable. The former senator slammed his fist on the table.

"What? We're being threatened! If we don't go along with what he wants, he'll turn his experiment against us! Is that what you're saying?"

The Justice raised a scolding finger.

"Mr. X has said nothing of the sort. What *I'm* saying is the security of *Country First* has been compromised, and we can't take chances that any of you are not fully committed to oaths you have taken as members of *The Committee*. One of you has obviously betrayed us. If the government comes after us and we have no other defense, ready vectors will be launched against each of you, the entire committee, myself included. The plan is still on. You see, we really *are* in this together."

Greene replaced his mask.

"To the very end."

Chapter 24

"My question to you, Mr. Cotton, is *do you know exactly what information Bryan put out there, and what happens now?*"

Cotton adjusted the glasses on his face and widened his eyes before answering.

"A bombshell! He revealed some of the most salient details from the Sutter and Grant files and pieces of a document that point to something else with profound consequences to the security of our country."

Destiny was unaware that her words and reactions were being recorded and fed live to a psychoanalyst at the Pentagon and to expert analysts at several other interested agencies. When she phoned Cornell Cotton to set up the meeting, he invited her to his home, but she refused. He then asked if he could come to her, but she balked, choosing instead a secluded place in the Sunken Garden area of the Japanese Tea Garden at Golden Gate Park.

The Japanese Tea Garden was one of her favorite places in the city, with its miniature mountain scene, including immaculate landscaping, waterfalls, goldfish ponds, flowering cherry trees and a wonderful tea house. Originally called the Japanese Village when it opened as part of the 1894 California Midwinter International Exposition, the exhibit was renamed the Oriental Garden in 1942, after California shipped its resident Japanese Americans to internment camps. The current name was adopted in 1952, years before Destiny was born.

She had visited the garden on regular occasions since she was a teenager. The sound of gurgling water and the essence of the *koboku* wood wafting from her incense burner brought tranquility in times of stress. On one occasion as she just finished her meditation, she met a relative of Makoto Hagiwara, the garden's creator and manager until his internment during the war. Mr. Hagiwara was the original inventor of the fortune cookie, which he introduced at the tea house on the grounds. Since he never patented the treat, Chinese restaurants in San Francisco copied it and popularized it, serving it after meals.

Despite Cotton's presence, Destiny closed her eyes and drew a deep breath, remembering how many times she had sat on that same bench with Bryan. For a moment he was beside her, breathing with her, until she opened her eyes.

Cotton seemed confused for a moment.

"Your husband obviously loved you. His enemies got to him, but in doing so exposed themselves, escalating a secret war that's been waged over the past two decades. This matter will be decided before the election I think, one way or another."

Destiny recoiled.

"Who are you?"

Cotton smiled.

"I thought you knew. I was a friend of your husband's. I promised him I would look after you if, unfortunately, he wasn't around to take care of you."

"I don't *need* looking after. Who do you work for?"

"I work directly for a man by the name of Jettson Turner. Who he works for, I haven't a clue, and I'm not sure if he even knows who they are, but we're the good guys."

"Jett Turner? You mean former White House Chief-of-Staff Jett Turner?"

Cotton laughed.

"The one and only. It's not like there are a bunch of Jett Turners out there."

The tiny sparrow flitting about had perched in a nearby tree. It seemed a bird, but actually it was a tiny surveillance aircraft, a winged *nano air vehicle*, developed by the Pentagon science division, DARPA, and controlled by an operator three hundred meters away. Directional microphone and camera engaged, the two-million-dollar avian replica zeroed in on Destiny's face as she spoke.

"Who was Bryan working for?"

Cotton leaned in.

"Do you want the truth, or do you want me to repeat something he probably made up in order to protect you?"

"I want the truth."

"I thought you would. He was a contractor for the Pentagon, and he was involved in shadowing a conspiracy operation—some kind of black-ops project. You only *thought* he was living in San

Diego, but he was mostly in Virginia and Massachusetts over the last three years."

Her face signaled confusion.

"And I imagine this conspiracy he was working on involved the murders at San Quentin?"

Cotton nodded.

"It did."

"I knew it! And the phone call I received from Perseus Grant? Did Bryan or someone else set that up?"

"Negative. He had nothing to do with the call from Grant. That was just a bizarre coincidence. The *last* thing Osaka would have wanted was to get *you* involved in something like this."

"And you were the second call?"

"Affirmative. I did everything in my power to scare you enough to keep your mouth shut, but you *told* people about it anyway, Osaka and the reporter. And someone *else* on our side knew about Grant's phone call to you, though we don't know who that is yet."

Destiny sat stunned, thinking back, still trying to process Cotton's words.

"Did your husband tell you *anything* about what he was doing? Did he share any *secrets* with you? Any cryptic message or information? A code word? A bombshell?"

"No."

"Did you ever share with him whatever it was that Grant told you?"

"No."

"Whatever Grant said, did it make sense to you?"

She sighed and answered, her face blank.

"It makes a little more sense *now...*"

Nathaniel Driscoll puffed at the *Cohiba* as the mini burner flared. He nodded, indicating satisfaction, as the young, brown-skinned female attendant replaced the ashtray.

"*Gracias, Bombón.*"

"*¡Ay, mi placer es servirle, Papi!*"

He sat in a secluded room in a smoke-filled restaurant at the end of *Calle Obispo* in Old Havana. The night was warm and humid, smelling of an impending storm. The décor was colonial, decadent, accented with deep reds and gold, polished wood, embroidery, flourishes and tassels, a throwback to the pre-Castro atmosphere of the 1950s. Just outside the room, a four-piece band with strings and Batá drums accompanied a pretty singer, who performed a medley of Celia Cruz songs.

A line of tiny bright red ants trailed along the bottom of the wall to his right, disappearing into a crack in the corner behind the Hemingway statue. Earlier in the night, a server smashed a scorpion by the door, and anole lizards occasionally scurried along the walls throughout the night. But the worst of the native pests were the ever-present swarms of black mosquitoes, which animated slapping gestures during customer conversations.

The cigar, a *Behike*, was individually hand rolled by Norma Fernandez, who blended and prepared cigars for the dictator when he was still smoking. At $420 apiece, each of the nine boxes of forty he purchased cost $18,846—a steal.

Across from Driscoll sat Helmut Wolf, a bottle of *Rhum Clement* at his fingertips and a shot glass cupped in the other hand. He was a little drunk as he sat across from shipping heiress Meredith Williams, who sipped occasionally from a daiquiri. The angry and agitated Thomas Hancock, who abstained from alcohol, sat next to Driscoll. Of 314,000,000 Americans, only 413 (one thousandth of one percent) were billionaires, and four (one-tenth of one percent of those) were sitting at the table. Together, they were worth thirty-five-billion-dollars.

The meeting was informal, as attendees were equals, though Driscoll was by far the richest, followed by Williams, Wolf and Hancock respectively. Driscoll had bought and refurbished a mansion outside Old Havana and invited select friends down to discuss the status of the operation and recent developments. After cocktails, the group had moved to a private room, where the chef provided an extravagant eleven-course seafood meal in exquisite Cuban cuisine.

The meal and desserts completed, the table sparkled with dozens of crystal snifters and wineglasses containing varied vintage cognacs and ports in colorful tints and hues, along with a hand-carved wooden humidor containing forty *Cohiba Behike* cigars.

After the last of the servants had left, the much-anticipated discussion began. Hancock was eager to vent his anger, pointing a shaking finger toward Wolf.

"Since *when* was there ever authorization, implicit or otherwise, for that asshole to go out and kill a government agent? One who we *knew* had some level of intelligence on what we were doing! Without any clear benefit to us whatsoever, he's put us *all* at risk!"

Wolf shrugged.

"I was dealing with a difficult situation. You were not. I did not have a choice."

Meredith exploded next.

"Whatever do you mean? You are a murderer! You had him under your control. Of *course* you had a choice!"

"I was protecting all of us."

"How?" Hancock injected. "By killing one of *theirs* and focusing attention on who we are and what we're doing?"

Wolf poured from the bottle and swigged from the shot glass.

"It does not matter. The die is cast. The vector has been launched. Our subject will be dead in four weeks, a full two weeks ahead of the election."

"And then what?"

Wolf smiled.

"Then there will be chaos, then we work like hell to get *our* man the job in a contest where he is suddenly eighty percent electable!"

He raised a glass, as if to propose a toast.

"And when Gordon is in place, then *we* will control the other side and the battle is won. We will destroy the opposition from the inside out. *We* will rule the world! It is what we have hoped for all these years!"

Driscoll and Williams raised their glasses in subdued excitement while Hancock resisted, still unsatisfied.

"And yet, what was the point of killing Osaka and drawing attention to ourselves? Was it personal? Are you operating unilaterally? I get that's your style. Is there something you're not *telling* us?"

Driscoll voiced his support for the questions.

"Those *are* fair questions, Helmut."

Wolf glared toward Hancock, resentful.

"Yes, it *was* personal. Osaka's wife has been a source of irritation since we silenced Sutter and Grant. We still do not know what Grant told her. She is the last loose end, the only person who threatens to ruin our grand ambition."

He drew an angry breath.

"I wanted to have her and the reporter killed right after Grant called her, but you, Driscoll and the others would not allow it and will not still. So, I had to make sure she paid a profound price for reneging on our brokered deal. Now she knows we mean business. If it were solely up to me, they would all be dead."

"When Osaka died," Meredith Williams countered, "he caused information to be sent out, linking all of us to the prison experiments and to a plot involving High Treason. It is not just *The Committee* anymore. Now the rest of us, more than ever, are subjects of government interest and investigation, and very possibly on our way to becoming enemies of the state. If you had not murdered Osaka, things might have been different. Quite the contrary, Mr. Wolf—*you* are the person who threatens to ruin our grand ambition. Frankly, I think you are a madman."

Wolf sighed.

"And you are a woman, a member of this confederacy, despite my protests. You do not have the capacity to understand the necessary expediency in such enterprises."

"I'm a man," Hancock interrupted, "and *I* don't understand your madness, Helmut. Destiny Mitchell is Osaka's wife. If he set himself up to have information released in the event of his *own* death, don't you *realize* he's done the same for her and the reporter? If she is sitting on a bombshell and you murder her, our grand ambition is dead, and our certain deaths will follow. Is that what you want? You've already devastated her. Leave her alone!"

"I know this is a rough period. Are you going to be okay? Do you need anything?"

Destiny recoiled when he touched her hand, drawing hers away.

"No. I'm fine. Still trying to figure this out. Did Bryan ask you to share anything *else* with me?"

Cotton bowed his head.

"He asked me to *help* you, but in order to do that, you've gotta meet me halfway."

"Halfway? You have to explain to *me* what that means."

"What did Bryan tell you about what he was doing? How much did he share with you?"

She glanced up, skeptical.

"Whatever he shared was between us."

"Well, what do you know about what he was working on?"

"I know a name, Nathaniel Driscoll, and I know who he is. He's somehow connected to the murders at the prison and directly responsible for what happened to Bryan."

"Driscoll is a powerful man, and dangerous, though he's worked hard to project a benevolent image. For the last three years, Bryan was shadowing a group calling itself *The Committee*, a secretive, private group that Driscoll helps bankroll. They were up to something, which somehow Perseus Grant dragged you into."

She rolled her eyes.

"That man is definitely burning in Hell."

Over the following thirty minutes, Destiny and Cotton traded bits of information back and forth, working toward a more substantive exchange.

"Let me tell you how this works," Cotton offered. "You've got *two* invisible governments in this country, always at war with each other, and neither gives a fuck about the people. Only one can be in power at a time—so you got your government with its representatives in power, the *active* government, and you got the faction on the outs, the *inactive* government. The active government, they do everything in their power to destroy the other side, because they know if and when they lose power, the same will happen to them."

"Is this Democrat versus Republican? Progressives against Conservatives?"

"Hell no! All that shit don't matter in the least. That's just what they put up there to make people think they can make a difference. It's all about wealth and power, one side or the other. It's about winning, and it's going global."

He paused.

"And here you are. Perseus Grant put you in the middle of it, and you have no clue about what you know and what's going on around you, do you?"

Destiny chose her words carefully.

"I know more than you think. This viral vector is being used to introduce some form of a DNA specific gene mutation that causes heart disease and organ failure. They were testing it at the prison, but you already know that. You said you saw the interview I did with Dr. Spagnola."

He raised his eyebrows.

"Okay, you know a little, but your husband was right. You and Yamakita have no idea about how high the stakes are and how much money's been spent. The price tag for the research alone was over one billion dollars."

She thought she felt her heart seize as she repeated the words.

"One billion dollars?"

"Yes. And when someone's spending that kind of money, and they've demonstrated they're more than willing to commit murder, they could care less about the lives of a disgraced former prosecutor and an old newspaper hack who are in the way."

Cotton's words disturbed her to the core, deep within her soul, as she better understood Bryan's reluctance to share and how much he had loved her. Yet unwilling to yield to emotion, she resorted to courtroom acting. Stiffening her resolve, she inhaled and re-buried the emerging sentiments.

"Okay Mr. Cotton, so *why* am I alive? Do you know?"

"Two reasons. One has to do with what your husband knew, half of which went out to their enemies when they killed him. In it he warned them. They know even more damning details will go out if they kill you. The second reason has to do with what Grant *revealed* to you. Whatever he said was enough to make them consider the consequences of you sharing that information. That's the *only* reason you're still alive."

He paused in order to let her process his words as he continued.

"Did you ever tell your husband what Grant told you, Destiny?"

"No."

"Did you tell the reporter?"
Incredulous, she could only wag her head.
"Really? I will neither confirm nor deny that."
Cotton nodded and sarcastic, he smiled.
"Any chance you might tell *me*?"

Chapter 25

"I appreciate you all for coming out, as I realize all too well the risk you're taking for even being involved in this. I just lost a good friend."

James Cassie stood before an empty room, save four guards and two inmates. News of Osaka's murder effectively ended active participation in the guard-inmate-initiated investigation. After all, the mysterious dying had ceased, and the prison had resumed the normal day-to-day routine. For most of the group, the investigation was not worth the jeopardy involved. Some had voiced their condolences and support while begging off. Even Denora Reed had lost resolve.

"I still say we have to do something with what we've discovered," Cassie continued. "Whoever's behind this, they came in here and murdered people, inmates and guards, and now an independent private investigator. If we do nothing, what happens when they decide to do something like this again? Maybe it'll be me, maybe it'll be you. Who knows?"

Denora answered from the first row.

"But nobody wants to *die*, James. We're up against someone, and we know what they've done, but we don't know who they are or what they even wanted. Maybe we're better off just leaving it alone."

Cassie's face expressed personal disappointment.

"Until when? Until they decide to come in here again? If we let them get away with this, then why not? Cleopatra tested poisons on condemned prisoners, Darius tested killing methods in their prisons and the Nazis did it! Don't you understand? They're doing the exact same thing at San Quentin! Only here it's inmates, guards and anyone else who's gotten in the way. Dr. Spagnola, Rashid, Agent Martinez, Bryan Osaka—they're all dead. If we don't do something about these murders now while we have documentation and evidence, who's to say it won't happen again next month, or next year? —when they have another killing technique that needs human guinea pigs. Come on! Who's still willing to *do* this with me?"

An older guard in the back spoke in a timid voice.

"I'm listening. What exactly do we *have* so far, Cassie?"

"Well, we have proof that seventy-five *murders* were committed here. Seventy-five! Okay? And we know through documentation that some quasi-government group came in here to test a genetic weapon on Death Row inmates. And finally, the record shows they've murdered anyone who's gotten in their way."

"I see, and *you* wanna be the next person to get in their way?"

Cassie raised a halting hand.

"No, I don't have a death wish. I'm not trying to put myself up alone against whoever they are, but I think we need to sum up everything we've found, including names and specific details, and we need to put it out there, on the Internet, and let someone else take it from there."

Denora contemplated, raising eyebrows, and nodded.

"That sounds like the best idea, but the problem with that plan is our claims and all our documentation will just get filed along with all the other conspiracy theories on the Internet. No one will believe it, and who knows—they might *still* come after us."

"*I'll* do it. All I need is a couple of you to help me narrow down what we're going to say. We'll put it up there anonymously, detailing specifics about the murders and mentioning San Quentin by name, and then we'll leave it alone for good."

"*I* got somethin to say!"

The voice came from an older black man at the back of the room. Nathan White was an inmate in his seventies who had attended only one meeting before. He could barely stand for the advanced scoliosis contorting his spine as he raised a hand with knobby, wrinkled fingers, twisted by arthritis.

"Since the young lady mentioned conspiracy stories, I figure I might as well include mine. See, I didn't wanna say anythang before because I thought no one would wanna *hear* it."

Denora spoke for the room.

"What is it?"

"I was a friend to Perseus Grant when he first come in here, so I musta known him for more'n twenty years before he died. What *y'all* don't know is Percy was part of a government experiment all along. He told me all about it. Not just me, but I was the only one who listened."

Cassie was incredulous.

"What government experiment?"

"He called it *Mind Kontrol Ultra*. It was some kinda CIA experiment where they used drugs and hypnosis and torture to turn ordinary people into weapons, he said. He said when he was in Viet Nam, they turned him into a machine ta commit political assassinations, killin enemies and they families."

The old man nodded in realization he had seized the moment.

"Percy said he was in that program for fifteen or twenty years, doing bad things to people. They made him inta a killer. And when they got through with him, he knew it was only a matter of time before he kilt someone, which we all know he did. That's how he end up on Death Row."

"He *told* you that?"

The old man nodded.

"He said they shattered his brain into like five different people, and one of em did that crazy, secret spy shit! That's the one Percy turned inta in the end. Real smart. He was hackin their computers and givin em all kindsa hell, just ta piss em off. They had ta kill im, especially after he called that bitch lawyer."

Cassie seemed annoyed by the outrageous distraction.

"By all accounts, Grant was *crazy* at the end. Besides being right, he was delusional, and now you, whoever you are, sound just as bad."

"When y'all was doin all that investigatin, did you ever take the time ta look up Percy's life *before* he come in here? He was a straight-A college kid when the government got im. Ya don't hafta take my word on it. Ya can look it up!"

The other five in the room seemed fascinated, though unsettled. They were the remnant of what had been an innovative, motivated team of fifty-two, determined to solve the prison murders. They had assumed risks of retaliation on themselves and their families. And unlike dozens of others, they had stayed the course, but they were clearly fatigued. For their good, immediate resolution was necessary.

"You should have spoken up sooner," Cassie lamented, "I'm sorry, but this investigation has to end today. Right here, right now. We'll take whatever we've got and put it up on the Internet Friday night and then we can all get on back to our lives."

"Sutter was part of that government experiment too!" the old man insisted. "That was their bond. This prison's a testin place for the government. Always has been! It happened before and it'll happen again. If you don't put the truth about Grant and Sutter in that report you're doin, then everyone that died in them experiments, then they all died for nothin!"

Inside the elevated temple, they sat on tightly woven tatami straw mats next to a fire pit and a pot of boiling water. The redwood structure sat on a mound surrounded by a well-tended, manicured garden of low shrubbery, growth-stunted miniatures and coordinated ornamentals. Destiny and Kiyomi had met in the morning at the Osaka family property in Tiburon, where Suziko and other relatives had gathered for the wake and funeral.

Across the room, a casket containing Bryan's body sat on a low stand. Earlier in the day, a priest came in to read a *sutra*, offer prayers and light incense sticks at the altar. Many friends and family members had come to offer condolences and to honor Bryan's memory. In the late afternoon, as beams of slanted light transformed the temple interior, elevating spirituality, the mats on the floor were covered with kneeling, bowing and weeping close relatives who prayed and paid final respects.

By nightfall, the temple was empty, as Destiny and Kiyomi alone had prepared to remain with the body on the final night. Both wore black kimonos as they knelt in prayer, pouring and sipping steaming green tea on occasion. For Destiny, it was hard to imagine that any portion of Bryan was contained within the casket, as she could feel his spirit with her, especially on that final night. In all the time since his death, she had not shed a tear. Funeral notwithstanding, it was not a time for grief. Rather, it was a time for action.

"I don't *trust* Cornell Cotton. He lied about his relationship with Bryan. I know for a fact they never met in person."

Kiyomi studied her friend's troubled face.

"But Cotton *was* telling the truth about Bryan working for someone at the Pentagon, and about a secretive group called *The Committee*. I checked it out with a friend over there. I think Bryan was reporting on something going on at Rosetta Biotech Laboratories. Apparently, he knew what they were doing with gene therapy and the possibilities, but he didn't know specifically how they planned on using the new technology."

Destiny stared straight ahead.

"Bryan *lied* to me. For three years he lied to me about what he was doing!"

"He couldn't tell you what he was doing! It was too dangerous. Just look at what's happened to your life since Perseus Grant's two-minute phone call. Bryan was *protecting* you."

"You're right," Destiny nodded, sighing, "but now we're on our own, and up against some secret group who've already put out a billion dollars and murdered probably hundreds of people to gain whatever advantage they did at the prison, and we're in the way."

Frustrated, Kiyomi exhaled aloud.

"Maybe Cotton told you that just to *scare* you. Bryan said he was negotiating with Cotton to establish a truce, right? Maybe that's what they still want. It would be *better* for both sides. I think we should ask Cotton if some kind of deal is still possible."

"Nathaniel Driscoll murdered my husband, shot my daughter and is trying to kill us. No deal could restore what I've lost. You don't have to follow me, Kiyo, because I know the odds are long and they'll probably murder me, but I'm going after Driscoll for what he did to Bryan."

"He's a billionaire, one of the richest men in the country. He's got fleets of lawyers and a private army working for him. What could you possible do to him?"

Destiny took a deep breath, thinking.

"I can expose what Grant told me. I still don't understand it completely, but I know it's something threatening to Driscoll and his viral vector plans, or else we'd be dead."

"You *still* don't know what Grant meant?"

"No, I don't," Destiny sighed, sipping from the teacup. "But I'm certain Cotton knows, and other people know. I just need to figure out who I can trust to help me use it. It's the only thing keeping us alive, so we've probably got one shot only."

"Bryan trusted *Cotton*," Kiyomi hinted.

"And look where Bryan is now. They're all in on it. They all know each other. Cotton told me Agent West was working for the other side. He gave them Martinez. It's hard to believe Cotton, but we have to trust someone. What do you think?"

"I say we *test* him."

"How?"

"We tell him we want to cut a deal with Driscoll and see if he goes for it. If he does and he's able to negotiate something in good faith, we'll know he's on the level. But if his involvement hinges on you telling him personally what Grant told you and we can't get beyond that issue, then we'll know he was involved in Bryan's murder and he's working for the people who want to kill us."

Chapter 26

"Mr. Driscoll and guest, we are now re-entering American airspace, altitude 23,000 feet, estimated flight time to destination—three hours, twenty minutes."

The Bombardier Challenger super mid-sized jet cruised in airspace hundreds of feet above the clouds at five hundred miles per hour. It was one of five Challengers owned by WPNS, the defense company owned by military contractor Nathaniel Driscoll. With a wingspan of sixty-four feet, the seventy-foot-long, dual engine turbo jet seemed more like a luxury limousine in the sky, with a full bar, a media center and two discreet attendants.

The jet was designed to seat twelve, though Driscoll had sacrificed eight seats for added amenities, which included two-fold-out beds and a small conference table. He sat across from Helmut Wolf, his sole guest on the return trip. Driscoll examined the cigar he had selected, admiring the handiwork, before removing the label and employing a double guillotine to cut off the end. Wolf sipped *Schwarztee* from a glass.

It was the first time they had an opportunity to talk privately in four days, as Wolf had chartered a private fight from Buenos Aries into Havana in order to attend the unanticipated meeting. Driscoll hosted the group at his home outside the city and spent three days entertaining his friends and reassuring them success was imminent, despite containment problems and dismal general election polling.

Meredith Williams was shaken by the Osaka murder, especially after his damning notifications went out to known adversaries. Until then, the idea of being involved in a high-stakes political conspiracy seemed swashbuckling and adventurous, but that was before she considered the consequences of losing. If the other side won, she and several key family members would most likely face an untimely demise.

An election had never been about life and death before. Sympathetic to her concerns, Driscoll took the time and effort to explain that the plan was still viable, and success was attainable, despite the risks. Meredith blamed Helmut, his arrogance and his callous disposition for the unnecessary exposure to increased risk, insisting he should not be able to take any action without expressed consent of the others. *"Put a muzzle on that dog!"* she demanded while leaving.

Thomas Hancock advocated for putting Wolf out of the group, or at least diminishing his role to one of insignificance. Most conservative of all *Country First* members, Hancock insisted brazen people like Wolf would be the ruin of the traditionalist government, currently out of power and public support. He never liked Wolf and became openly antagonistic after Wolf ordered Osaka's murder, ushering in a dangerous new front in the escalating war.

Hancock had only reluctantly agreed to Wolf's ambitious viral vector plan, directed by *The Committee*, while he was open about his criticism of Gordon as a weak candidate, warning that Gordon as president would not be as accommodating and loyal as he pledged to be.

"Our active president is a killer. So putting our trust in Wolf and Gordon," he warned, "places all of us on the brink of extermination."

One of the flight attendants lit Driscoll's cigar while the other refilled Wolf's tea glass.

"No one knows we're on this plane, save the pilot, and he didn't know until just before take-off. In our precarious predicament, one can never be too careful. Suffice it to say, Helmut, your decision to murder Osaka was problematic."

Wolf crossed his arms and angry, bowed his head.

"Must *you* condemn me as well, Nathan? I thought I would at least have your trust and support. Yes, I had him killed. It was my decision to make. I assumed the risk."

"And now you've put the *rest* of us at risk. You've put your plan at risk, as well as the research you advanced and the financial liabilities we all assumed."

"Great deeds are wrought at great risk, my friend. The rest of them *need* to feel what we're feeling, especially Hancock! *Beware of the man who urges action but incurs no risk.* It is why I never trusted that man. He does not know whose side he is on."

Wolf monitored the position of the attendants and lowered his voice.

"Someone on *The Committee* has betrayed us. Under torture, Osaka revealed to me that he received a copy file of one of our most confidential documents—the 'White House Target' document. He did not know the source, but it could have only come from someone on the inside. He planned to go public with it. That is why I had him killed."

Driscoll paid attention, but he remained unconvinced. As the CEO of a military weapons corporation, he had listened to many stories told by government leaders, agents and operatives who sometimes told the truth, and sometimes did not. He had learned to discern words, inflections, body language and several intangible factors, his mind keen to detect the ring of truth, something he did not hear in Wolf's words.

"Why would he go public with it? I talked to Osaka on several occasions. He was more interested in saving his wife's life than getting involved in a high stakes gamble in government affairs where he would receive no benefit. I don't know what happened in your torture session, but you're lying about his motive."

"He had the document. He was going to use it against us."

"To save his wife. And when you had him killed, you set in motion the release of that document and other damaging material to our enemies in power. And now the wheels are in motion. They're coming after us, and with the general election coming on, in full force."

Driscoll puffed on the cigar, blowing the smoke toward the glowing cherry before flicking the ash.

"We would have been better off striking a deal. Osaka and his wife would have been happy to walk away from this. I am certain he would have convinced Destiny Mitchell that the Grant phone call never happened. The situation *was* contained, Helmut. Neither wanted a fight with us."

"But you must remember, Nathan, we *had* a deal, for only three hours before she *broke* it! That same afternoon she combined with Spagnola to expose us and to further frustrate our planning!"

"There was something else to that, something beyond your supposed containment, but I suppose what's done is done. The question now, is how do we proceed?"

Wolf lowered his voice again.

"I believe that the best way to assure the viability of our plan is now to kill Destiny Mitchell and the reporter. Whatever she knows and exposes we will deny. We have an entire television network to do our bidding in this."

"I don't care about television and the people who watch it! You're so consumed by this scheme of yours, Helmut, that you're missing the point. Meredith, Thomas—they and the rest understand it, but you don't. The active president now has an idea of what we are doing, and if he believes he can get away with it, he's going to *kill* every last one of us."

For a rare instant, arrogance no longer contorted Wolf's face.

"He cannot *do* that."

"Of course he can. He has the levers of power at his disposal, and he's shown he's well inclined to use them."

Wolf contemplated Driscoll's words, pausing a full minute before he spoke.

"Then he has perhaps two weeks to do to us whatever he will. The vector is active. In three weeks, it will be too late for him, and we will own the man in the office. We will return to power, for good."

The mood was somber at the Osaka family home in Tiburon. Twenty-two men in black suits with white shirts and black ties stood talking in a reception area just outside the wooden temple. Women wearing solid black dresses were returning from the large house after the family meal following the funeral and cremation of Bryan Osaka. Some wore kimonos.

Much earlier in the day, with family members, close friends and Bryan's casket in the temple, the priest read the *sutra* and called relatives to an incense offering, during which time attendees, most wearing rosaries, approached the low table, bowed, placed a pinch of incense within the urn and bowed again before returning to their places. Only after relatives, in hierarchal order, had taken turns offering incense, were friends invited to participate in the ceremony, which was repeated twice.

Just before the incense ceremony, the priest stood and spoke as he assigned Bryan a posthumous name, or *kaimyo*, inscribed it on a wooden tablet and placed it before the altar. The purpose of this spirit name was *to help keep the deceased from returning every time the earthly name was repeated.*

Ritual complete, the deceased's relatives and close friends stood at attention as the pallbearers lifted the casket and transferred it to the hearse, which was a work of art in itself, resembling the temple on wheels. Hearse leading the way, the twenty-car procession wound along fifteen miles before arriving at the crematorium at a few minutes after eleven a.m. With attendees standing by, the pallbearers removed the coffin from the hearse to a sliding tray connected to the oven. All watched as the casket slid inside and the doors closed.

As they returned to the Osaka residence for a meal, they took an alternate route to prevent the spirit of the deceased from following the family home. Three hours later, family members returned to the crematorium, where the burned remains of the deceased were spread before them. Using chopsticks, they searched through the ashes, picking up bone fragments and placing them into two urns, one for interment in the nokotsudo at the Buddhist Church in Oakland, and the other to remain at the family temple in Tiburon. During this ceremony, the bone fragments were sometimes passed from chopsticks to chopsticks before being placed in the urns, while at other times, pieces of bone were shared between two sets of chopsticks.

Destiny, along with Bryan's sisters, Kimiko and Suziko, took one of the urns, wrapping it in a white cloth, and with close family members following, directed the limousine driver to the columbarium at the Oakland Buddhist Church. With a priest officiating at a private ceremony in a small room, they placed the urn in a niche next to the urns of Ichiro and Sadako Osaka, his parents. After the long day, the family returned to Tiburon for a final repast and closure, which was also a memorial service, which included Bryan's personal and professional friends and colleagues.

One of these personal friends wore a fedora and walked with a noticeable limp, despite employing a cane. Destiny noticed his occasional monitoring and recognized him only after Kiyomi reminded her. He had a distinguished look, with salt-and-pepper hair, glasses and a clean-shaven, handsome brown face, seeming every bit the legend he had become. He nodded as she returned his glance. They spoke in the temple.

"Professor Deuteronomy Saint Claire—it's an honor, but what brings you here today?"

Saint Claire unbuttoned his jacket as he sat.

"I worked with your husband, Ms. Mitchell, briefly when we were both inspectors with the San Francisco Police Department, and later on various other matters."

"So, you're *not* retired from detective work?"

He smiled.

"It's a lifelong passion for me, figuring things out, solving the unsolvable, unraveling tangled messes for the sheer challenge of it."

"Are you here to unravel something?"

He glanced over to the door, where Kiyomi stood.

"I'm here to help you in *your* effort to do that. I don't know how much you know, but you were married to Osaka, and your high-profile public persona seems to have disappeared overnight, so I have to assume you're involved."

Skeptical, Destiny did not answer. Instead, she began an interrogative.

"Are *you* involved, Professor?"

"Osaka and I were sharing information in two unrelated investigations, or at least it seemed that way. When they murdered him, several elements of our research converged."

"Are you a contractor with the Pentagon as well?"

"No. I work for a private group seeking to ensure the President will be reelected. They asked me to monitor the activities of the man who was responsible for your husband's murder."

Destiny paused, reluctant to reveal details of what she knew, but there was so much else she did not know, beginning with the circumstances of Bryan's murder. She glanced over at Kiyomi before turning back to the former detective.

"Who? Nathaniel Driscoll?"

"Never in a million years. Driscoll's too smart for that—too much to lose. No, it's more likely your husband was killed by one of Driscoll's associates, the man I was assigned to watch."

"Who is he?"

"A psychotic billionaire whose name is Helmut Wolf. Have you ever heard of him?"

"No."

Kiyomi interrupted.

"I have. Helmut Wolf is an American, but he's some kind of Nazi scientist, or at least he shares their racist ideas. He wrote a book about the potential of gene warfare in the twenty-first century and experiments in Africa during the 1970s. I read the book review and a blog about his work."

"So *Helmut Wolf* murdered my husband? Why?" Destiny asked.

This time, Saint Claire was unresponsive, proceeding to his next question.

"What did Osaka tell you about *Country First, The Committee* and their plan?"

"*Country First?*" she wondered aloud. "The conservative Super PAC? Driscoll is one of its big donors. Bryan was investigating inmate deaths at the prison. Are you saying *they* were involved in the murders? A Super PAC? Why?"

"Helmut Wolf is also a big donor. Your husband obviously didn't share the information in order to protect you, but yes, some of the members are involved—not as a Super PAC, but as part of an intrigue."

He removed an envelope from his jacket pocket and handed it to Destiny.

"Osaka's death triggered the release of a series of sensitive documents, and one of them links the experiments performed at San Quentin to a 'White House Target' in advance of the coming election. You have it there."

Destiny examined the document and gasped, letting it fall from hands that flew to her face.

"Oh my God! Now it all makes sense!"

"*What* makes sense? The message you got from Perseus Grant?"

"I'm going to need to talk to the President in person, as soon as possible. You have a reputation for being resourceful, Saint Claire. Can you or any of your friends make that happen?"

Chapter 27

It was four minutes after midnight on an otherwise quiet night above the suburban Boston medical research complex, eleven miles outside the city. The walls and fences around the facility were well-guarded, though the formidable army tasked with security was low profile. Hidden barracks housed fifty mercenary soldiers, most of them former Special Forces operatives from worldwide military operations.

Inside Rosetta Biotech Laboratories, doctors and researchers continued work, unaware of the approach of three top-secret U.S. Navy stealth helicopters that resembled Blackhawks externally, with design enhancements and advanced on-board technologies. Dr. Benjamin Rosecrans sat in a conference room with a team of gene therapy specialists, considering the implications of a new location-specific vector that would aggressively target organs and glands, reducing the exposure-to-result factor.

Security forces at the complex were unaware of the aircraft hovering above, even after thirty-six SEAL Team Six warriors fast roped into the heart of the fortified facility and took up strategic positions, preparing for the assault. The Navy teams engaged had spent the last three months rehearsing the coup and takeover of the strategic complex, along with the appropriation of all scientific research, data, records and technology contained there.

From the Situation Room located in the basement of the White House West Wing, the President sat with his arms crossed as he and his National Security Team watched the action unfold in real-time. His defense secretary gave the order, and the operation began. Since the President's SEAL team had the advantage of surprise, the earlier skirmishes were one-sided, as New World Army forces had retreated to defensible positions and dug in.

Numbers roughly even, the two sides exchanged fire as a separate SEAL platoon encroached to outflank the pinned-down defenders, according to a pre-designed plan. In the meantime, a separate team, dropped near the energy grid, worked to disable all power in the complex and block communication channels. Within minutes, the facility was dark. Over the next half hour, the SEAL

teams won the battle of attrition, offering the remaining fifteen
NWA soldiers alive the opportunity for surrender.

Once the complex was secure, teams infiltrated the buildings,
securing computer databases and documents, rounding up
research staff, assistants and doctors and assembling everyone
into a large, empty lab room. After SEAL technicians restored
power to the room, the menacing Officer-in-Charge stood before
the group, his voice stentorian.

"Please be informed: the *Viral Vector* Project at Rosetta Biotech
Laboratories is now under new management! All of you will
remain at this facility for debriefing, some for as long as seventy-
two hours. You will not be able to leave, and you will not be able
to phone home. During that time, you will cooperate and obey all
orders associated with transferring access of all research and
operations to our operators who are facilitating the completion of
the transition. If there are no problems, each of you will receive a
generous severance package. If you create a problem, the outcome
will not be a nice one for you."

He glanced at the image displayed on his phone.

"Dr. Benjamin Rosecrans—please rise. I need you and your
senior departmental research managers to follow me. The rest of
you, follow instructions from our uniformed personnel in place as
you proceed toward debriefing. Most of you will be able to leave
within the next twelve hours."

Outside the fences and walls of the *Viral Vector* labs, other
active government forces had set up a well-armed perimeter,
disallowing interference during the twenty-four-hour conversion
of the facility. To observers, clients and vendors, nothing would
change. A familiar operator would answer phone calls and former
management would seem to conduct business as usual, but no
one would enter or leave, save the dismissed workers. By dawn,
the helicopters, dead bodies and former military personnel were
gone, and the *Viral Vector* area of the complex was effectively
sealed shut.

Dr. Rosecrans was sequestered to a brightly lit private room,
where a seated interrogator waited on the other side of a bare
metal table.

"Please sit down, Dr. Rosecrans."

The nervous doctor scanned the room, hesitating a moment
before sitting.

"Don't I? Don't I have the right to have my lawyer present?"

"When you're in the dark, you don't *get* a lawyer."

The huge, muscular interrogator stood, reading from United States Code, Title 18, Chapter 115, Section 2381.

> *"Whoever, owing allegiance to the United States, levies war against them*
>
> *or adheres to their enemies, giving them aid and*
>
> *comfort within the United States or elsewhere, is guilty of treason*
>
> *and shall suffer death, or shall be imprisoned*
>
> *not less than five years."*

Lowering the thick document, he sat and removed his glasses, his intense gaze intimidating the doctor.

"In the interest of national security, there would be no substantial detriment to me if I executed you on the spot, right here, right now. I could make up any story I wanted to. Do you understand that, Doctor?"

Terrified, the doctor nodded.

"I understand, but I have not..."

The interrogator removed his Sig Sauer P239 pistol from its harness, pointing it toward the doctor's face.

"Are you telling me you are *not* guilty of treason, punishable by death, according to U.S. Code?"

Tears flowed from Rosencran's eyes as a dark, wet stain began to radiate from the crotch area of his pants. He pleaded.

"Sir, I swear to you! No! I'm a loyal American! I would *never* betray my country! I love my country! We, we were doing experiments! At the prison in San Francisco! That was all! This is a research facility! To *help* our country!"

The interrogator sat back, placing his firearm on the table.

"Oh yeah? What exactly do you research here, Doctor?"

Noting the doctor's hesitation, the officer re-gripped the handgun, pulling it closer.

"Time is of the essence, Dr. Rosecrans. Whoever you answered to, they can't help you. Now you're either going to talk to me and live, or I kill you and proceed to your next-in-charge. Your best option would be cooperation, which means divulging everything you know about your *Viral Vector* project and then coming to work for us. Decide *now!*"

The Internet launch was much more successful than expected, and the eleven-minute video, a narration of events at San Quentin and questions raised in the investigation, went viral. The story gained so much traction that the national news media launched their own investigations into the prison deaths, much to the displeasure of the state of California and Warden McGinnis, who took measures to shut the media out.

Notwithstanding, news bureaus and reporters converged on San Quentin State Prison with questions and suggestions that the state had taken surreptitious measures to reduce the number of inmates in its Condemned Unit, along with a renewed interest in the relative welfare of Scott Peterson, sentenced to death in the murder of his wife, Laci, and unborn son in 2002.

One network asserted the "alleged" murders of Death Row inmates had saved the state of California 6.75 million dollars per year, based on the cost to house seventy-five condemned inmates at ninety thousand dollars each annually. According to one reporter, if the state and U.S. government had to pay to have the same seventy-five inmates executed, it would have cost 22.5 trillion dollars, citing a study by two senior legal figures, a senior judge, Arthur Alarcon, and a professor at Loyola law school, Paula Mitchell, who had opined,

> *The full burden of the death penalty in California has been laid bare by new research that calculates that each of the 13 prisoners executed in the state over the past three decades has cost more than $300m (£185m).*

According to the news bureau reporting the story,

> *The study included costs incurred at both state and federal level in keeping 714 death row inmates*

incarcerated, as well as steering them through the tortuous judicial process all the way to the death chamber. The average length of time between conviction and execution in California now stands at more than a quarter of a century – double the national average.

Since 1978, California and the US government have together spent some $4bn on the state's death row, yet only 13 prisoners have been executed – an average of $308m for each one. The study, first reported by the Los Angeles Times, warned that the total figure would rise to about $9bn by 2030.

On the Internet, bloggers posted lurid scenarios and intricate theories about a state and U.S. government conspiracy. For years, it had been widely reported that California was mired in a trend of increasing debt, ranging from 22.5 billion dollars in 1999 to 612 billion dollars in 2012. Drowning in debt and strapped for cash, the biggest beneficiary of the prison killings was the state, and the motive was both financial and practical, since San Quentin's Death Row was a precarious area as a result of overcrowding.

After all, did it matter to the average Californian that the state was murdering condemned criminals who were gaming the system and costing taxpayers millions of dollars? Apparently, it did, as civil liberties groups statewide began to organize and protest the killings, calling the governor and the Department of Corrections into account and demanding answers. At the culmination of the protests, a riot ensued outside San Quentin's gates, resulting in police discharging rubber bullets and pepper spray. There were dozens of arrests and threats of potential lawsuits.

When private interest groups suggested the conspiracy included the powerful correctional officers' union, CCPOA President Donovan Baker issued a ban on media interviews, with an implicit threat of retribution against those who spoke, on or off-record. Enlisting the guidance of a PR consultant, he distanced the union from the scandal, portraying that any hazards to inmates was also a threat to guards and the union, detrimental to the interests of all three.

Privately, he suspected that if James Cassie was not directly involved in the launch of the Internet site, he was certainly responsible for much of the online content and conclusions. In the last week, Baker heard rumors from correctional officer informants that Cassie had led and organized the verboten investigation from the start.

It was one thing to say condemned inmates were being murdered and quite another to aver that the deaths of two correctional officers and an FBI agent had resulted from the lethal conspiracy. The website did not elaborate about *how* the murders were accomplished, though the narrator suggested the government was testing a biological/genetic weapon.

Baker took heat from the governor and individual members of the CCPOA State Board of Directors. One upstart director with an ax to grind saw an occasion to disparage Baker's management style as weak and indecisive. Three other directors agreed, and a query was initiated to determine if allegations were true that San Quentin guards were involved in the creation and distribution of the controversial website material. A day later, Baker was called before the board, grilled for ninety minutes and issued a reprimand. Executive Vice President James Cassie, seated next to him during the arduous session, was also scolded and admonished by the directors.

Still smarting for being called out and embarrassed, Donovan Baker called James Cassie aside under the pretense of happy hour at a bar in Old Sacramento. Maintaining an external calm, he waited until after he had sipped from the Bombay Sapphire martini, speaking in a threatening tone.

"I warned you weeks ago, Cassie. It was not your fight. But you just couldn't stop until you got the whole state in a panic. That was your damned website! That riot last week—*you're* responsible for that!"

"Sutter had a wife, Rodriguez had a teenage son. Who's responsible to them?"

Baker wagged his head in disgust.

"*We* are—that is—the union. In both cases, survivors are entitled to monthly survivor benefits. The system was designed to accommodate for unfortunate losses, which *happen* from time to time."

"But someone *killed* our guards, and they could kill more! We're just supposed to *ignore* that?"

"That would be for smart people, which apparently you *aren't*! Some things you just don't stick your nose into."

Baker sighed.

"You might not value your position and reputation, Cassie, but I value mine. I have a wife who loves to go out to eat, take exotic vacations and shop every day—all that while I'm paying for a kid at Berkeley and another at UCLA. I can't afford to lose my job."

He finished the martini.

"You were elected by the Board, but I am the President. I was elected because I have a lot of friends over there, friends who had to come out against me today. But they all know *you're* the problem—they know what you did. It's just a matter of time now, Cassie. Your ass will be *toast* within the week!"

Chapter 28

"Dr. Rosecrans, I'm going to ask you a series of questions, which we need you to answer completely and unambiguously. Your cooperation is the key to your fortune and to the fate of your research and breakthroughs from here on. Do you understand?"

The doctor nodded.

"Yes, I do."

Jett Turner and two other men sat across from the nervous geneticist and his chief assistant, Eli Zimmerman. Two days before the raid, Deputy National Security Advisor Lucius Draco contacted the man considered to be the best strategic operative in the world and asked Jett Turner if he would handle the conversion and debriefing of the *Viral Vector* project at Rosetta Biotech Laboratories. He agreed, requesting an overview of the project, the active government's proposal and real-time operational intelligence.

"There's none of that on-the-record/off-the-record bullshit going on today. You talk to me, and you tell me everything. The only ass you cover is yours, and you do that by impressing me with your willingness to share. On the project, who did you answer to?"

"Helmut Wolf."

"Helmut Wolf? Not Thomas Hancock, the CEO and President of Rosetta Biotech Laboratories?"

"The *Viral Vector* project was separate from RBL. Mr. Wolf leased six laboratory buildings from Hancock and put together his own team of researchers. We could access RBL computers, research and databases, but there was zero access the other way. Their doctors had no idea what we were doing here."

Jett nodded.

"Was Thomas Hancock in any way involved?"

"I do not know if he was."

"What is the *Viral Vector* project?"

Despite the context of the moment, the doctor's eyes widened with excitement.

"It was an opportunity to advance gene therapy and genetic research in ways we would not have seen for another forty years. It will change the world, in a *positive* way."

"How?"

"It will change the way geneticists and doctors treat many diseases and conditions. The vector we developed will make it possible to eliminate SCID syndromes and dozens of other rare disorders, to successfully treat heart disease before it begins, to cure many cancers!"

"Is that what they were doing over at San Quentin? Curing cancers?"

Rosecrans' excitement wilted.

"We, we were testing a process over there, on criminals, already legally condemned to death."

"To save them? Or to kill them?"

The doctor bowed his head in shame before answering.

"As in most cases, any great advancement is a double-edged sword. The same process we perfected to turn *off* harmful genes to save lives can just as easily be used to turn them on. In short, we sequenced the DNA in healthy inmates and made them very unhealthy. We turned the DNA into a murder weapon, one that could not be discovered or traced to its source."

Rosecrans sighed, his own words surprising him.

"I guess that makes me complicit in more than seventy murders. You probably think I'm a monster, but I didn't kill any of those men. I'm pacifist by nature."

He glanced toward his chief assistant, as if to share the blame.

"I—we, we at the lab—we just altered the DNA and prepared the vectors. It was out of our hands after that."

"But based on your research, you *knew* what would happen to the men once the viral vector was introduced? And as a scientist and doctor, you were interested in the results?"

"Yes, I am guilty of such curiosity."

Turner looked down at his notes, proceeding to another question.

"Who was controlling operations?"

"Helmut Wolf, everything from funding to operations to implementation."

"How big a project was it? Five hundred million dollars?"

The doctor crossed his arms.

"I'd say over a billion, maybe 1.2 billion."

Jett nodded, seeming impressed.

"And where did this money come from? Wolf?"

"And friends, a bunch of billionaires. I don't know who they are, but they're all in on it."

Jett paused, setting up the next question.

"This weaponized viral vector—do you know what they plan to do with it?"

"I think so. They want to use it to create a new front in the war on terrorism. They want to use it to go after high-profile terrorist leaders and organizations. Wolf calls it *a DNA drone attack, with perfect precision.*"

The man to Jett Turner's right was Lucius Draco, Deputy National Security Advisor. With Turner's assent, he asked a question.

"Dr. Rosecrans, over the past month, do you have any knowledge of a 'domestic' target relating to Wolf's *Viral Vector* project? Did you prepare a vector to that effect?"

The doctor was emphatic.

"No. The condemned inmates were Americans, but there has been no domestic target, unless that target was a foreign threat."

"Dr. Rosecrans, do you believe in the legitimacy of the U.S. presidency?"

"Of *course* I do! I voted for him. Why would you ask me a thing like that?"

The debriefing interview continued for an additional hour with the monotony of a deposition. In the end however, Jett was satisfied the doctor was not knowingly involved in the plot.

Two days earlier, Wolf had phoned Rosecrans and told him to prepare for the complete and immediate transfer of all research data, scientific advancements, and working and prototype vectors to another facility. If the raid had come a day later, crucial elements of the project would have been missing from the facility.

It took government technicians twenty-six hours to complete the technology conversion, replacing Wolf's security protocols and encrypted computer systems with their own. The active government also brought in their own researchers, doctors and a monitor, who reported directly to the Deputy National Security Advisor to the President.

On the night of the raid, New World Army intelligence informed Helmut Wolf and Thomas Hancock about the government invasion from the initial attack, but other than sending in outmatched reinforcements to battle the awesome power of the American military, there was little they could do. Within minutes of the assault, Wolf caused a cyber-order to be sent to lock out computers and dump sensitive data, but the order had been circumvented hours before it was issued.

The active government acted on intelligence primarily compiled by former operative Bryan Osaka, who spent three years gathering information about *Country First* in relation to Wolf's *Viral Vector* project. The government's action was expedited by Osaka's murder and the circulation of a document suggesting a "White House Target before the election." There were also rumors that the Chinese government was zeroing in on the project in order to advance its own gene therapy research project.

Eighty percent of personnel working on the *Viral Vector* project were briefed and released with severance packages, while the remaining doctors and researchers were assembled in a large conference room. All personnel in the remaining group had expressly requested to continue with the project under new management. In a government orientation session that followed, an NSA administrator instructed the group on laboratory procedural modifications, rules and practice. In a separate sitting, new hires signed stacks of government disclosure forms, acknowledgments and waivers related to policy. After fingerprinting, the new Project Director introduced Operations Chief Jett Turner, who finalized project conversion.

"Okay, doctors and researchers, based on debriefing, you've helped us determine who would stay and who would leave this project. Going forward, all research, discovery and advances related to *Viral Vector* are the sole property of the government of the United States of America. The government was aware of the project from its inception, but they allowed its development because the government was averse to becoming involved in experiments with humans.

"Further, and in the best interests of the United States of America, it is incumbent on all of you that no information or documents pertaining to this project will be released that refer to experiments with humans and might have adverse effects on public opinion or result in legal proceedings. All information about this project has been classified as 'secret.'

"Under the Security of Information Act, any unauthorized release of information about *Viral Vector* constitutes a higher breach of trust, with penalty of life imprisonment. And Doctors, if you've taken any clue from your experiments at San Quentin, you all know *exactly* how long your lives in prison will be."

"You seem like a decent guy. I'm sorry I have to do this, but I've got orders. On your knees, please..."

New World Army Commander Victor Collins held the gun directly on the back of Cassie's head. Grasping his shoulder firmly, Victor guided the startled man to the floor.

When he was thirteen, James Cassie made a decision to confront his most compelling conviction, the predatory injustice of the strong molesting the weak, the powerful suppressing the feeble. Since he could remember, he pitied her, tried to stick up for her.

His mother, September, was seventeen when he was born, and he was the second child of her fifth pregnancy. Her parents belonged to a religion that disallowed pre-marital sex and dating unrelated to marriage. Her strict father disallowed make-up, skirts, boots and all shades of red fingernail polish. And he was quick to slap her or knock her to the ground if she showed the slightest sign of disrespect.

Having been raised under such a rigid structure, she was attracted to boys who broke the rules, who defied authority and seemed to succeed despite being bad. Unfortunately, the same boys who flaunted convention and sought instant gratification loved her selfishly. She was used and abused so often that she grew accustomed to ideas and treatment most considered perverted and debauched.

When James was young, she had a repeating series of boyfriends in and out of her life, some nearly decent, with the majority made up of drug dealers, pimps, petty criminals and poor white trash. He and his older sister cringed, embracing in their bedroom, listening as their sloshy-drunk or drugged-out mother, argued, had unrestrained sex, whored, begged for meth or crank, was beaten and was arrested in the living room of their apartment. They ignored or made excuses for the black eyes and bruises displayed when she showed up for parent-teacher conferences and dreaded when she insisted on going to open house.

But at thirteen something changed in him. It happened the morning after he learned his older sister was being raped by the newest boyfriend. His sister and mother denied what happened, but he knew, and when he confronted the man responsible, he discovered he had an inner strength he never realized.

Denial came first, and then aggression, but his spirit was fueled by righteous anger and indignation. Despite a six-inch height and eighty-pound weight disadvantage, he beat the loser who abused his mother and raped his sister so badly that the man had to be carried out of the apartment and was crippled for the rest of his life. After that incident, men no longer came to their home, and James' mother rediscovered and realized her relationship with a more forgiving God. Until the day she died, she was a good Christian who called James her savior and God's instrument of her redemption.

Resulting from his childhood, he was always protective of Marybeth and his two daughters. Marybeth insisted he had a "victim complex," that he felt an unnatural compulsion to save people he saw as victims, regardless of personal peril. She called him *Robin Hood* and supported his sometimes "hopeless crusades" over the years, even when she disagreed.

His biggest regret involved the estrangement of once best friend, Bryan Osaka, whom he betrayed in an Internal Affairs investigation against him while they were both inspectors with the San Francisco Police Department. Bryan was stoic by nature, so there were no words after the trial that disgraced him and forced his resignation. There was only a sad, condemning glance that James Cassie could never get out of his mind.

During the investigation of the deaths at San Quentin, the friendship was renewed, and James felt closer to Bryan than ever before, despite his friend's penchant for secrecy. Bryan came over for dinner every other Sunday and took great interest in the girls, their college adventures and their career ambitions. In less than a month, they were back to calling him *Uncle Bry-Bry*.

On the night before Bryan Osaka was murdered, he called James Cassie, insisting that James should abandon the investigation and devote more time to Marybeth and the girls.

"You've gone as far as you can go, James. This is all going to come to a decisive battle, something you will have no power to change or enough information to make sense of it. Let it go before they consider you a liability so you can stay alive. I am your brother. Please do that for me."

If he had known those would be Bryan's last words to him, he would have thanked him for returning for Marybeth and the girls, for the redemption he conferred. He would have told Bryan he loved him. But the murder was devastating to James. It was senseless, overwhelming and demoralizing. He wanted to attend the memorial service to express condolences to Destiny Mitchell, whom he had never met, but he felt a greater need to expose Bryan's killers, avenge the prison murders and protect his guards.

He closed his eyes as he knelt, mocking divine justice in a flustered prayer as he thought of Marybeth and the girls and the grief they would feel. Thinking nothing of himself, he shuddered, feeling his connection with them, so strong, so intact.

"They murdered seventy-five inmates, two guards, an FBI agent and my friend. Why? Why are they *doing* this? At least you can tell me that, before..."

Cassie paused, his mind still reeling over how quickly he had come to his end. It was a bad dream! He tried to force himself awake to no avail. The reality of his predicament caused reality to slip. The moment became surreal—ethereal, with an ever so fleeting flash of divine omniscience and clarity.

"...before you *kill* me."

Collins cocked the gun, his quivering cold blue eyes displaying equal parts resolve and regret.

"I'm sorry, Mr. Cassie. I'm just a mercenary soldier. I operate on a need-to-know basis. It's nothing personal. I have no choice. Now if you just bow your head for me, I promise, you won't feel a thing."

Chapter 29

At the beginning of October, presidential challenger Hugh Gordon was essentially tied with the President for the popular vote, but he was conspicuously behind on most polls for Electoral College projections, with the election slipping away in the ten swing states of Florida, North Carolina, Virginia, New Hampshire, Pennsylvania, Ohio, Iowa, Michigan, Colorado and Nevada. The lackluster party convention produced little bounce for Gordon, while the President's convention served to re-energize his base and narrow the enthusiasm gap.

While many of Gordon's supporters saw the popular vote polls as evidence that the race remained close, vocal pundits and partisan media prognosticators on both sides criticized Gordon's effete campaign strategies, vagueness on policy and gaffes, characterizing him as the weakest presidential candidate in four decades. Yet Gordon ignored the naysayers and projected genuine confidence that he would overcome the incumbent President's increasing advantage and pull off one of the greatest political upsets in U.S. history.

During the presidential primary debates earlier in the year, frontrunner Gordon did not introduce new policies, nor did he follow the advice of political operatives who suggested he should "swing for the fence, hurl that risky sucker punch." Instead, he followed a course to affirm his ideas for the direction of the country, press the President for disappointments and failed promises, and above all, to *do himself no harm*.

In network interviews, Gordon defied critics who insisted on greater specificity and a new direction for the campaign. A full week into the month, the polls seemed to stabilize with the challenger solidly three points behind, causing one wry commentator to remark,

"Gordon is behaving like a candidate who understands something the rest of us don't know about yet. Spoiler alert—he's so smug I'm expecting some sort of *October Surprise*."

In the meantime, the President's private military detail quietly launched an offensive against *Country First* and its backers in an effort to determine the ultimate source and precise motive of the

"White House Target" document. The President viewed the attempt against his life as another conspiracy, but this design went *way beyond the pale* in its objective. The only way to deter such plots was to select the most strident conspirator and make that person an example about the danger and folly of challenging the government in power.

According to FBI intelligence, the members of *Country First's* secretive Board of Directors, called *The Committee*, included Associate Supreme Court Justice Wendell Greene, senior Virginia Senator and the Senate Committee on Foreign Relations Chairman Rex Andal, House Majority Whip Chris Matthews, former Wyoming Governor Steven Testor, former White House Senior Advisor and Deputy Chief of Staff Charles Love, and former Congressional Representative/former Homeland Security Advisor Helen Abercrombie.

The billionaires who supported the Super PAC were military contractor Nathaniel Driscoll, Thomas Hancock, who owned Rosetta Biotech Laboratories, investor/financier Helmut Wolf, shipping magnate Meredith Williams, hedge fund traders James and Gerald Baxter, and Richard and Beth MacArthur, private operators controlling one of the largest health care facilities in the world. Of course, there were a few donors who were not billionaires, yet the size of their donations compensated for what they lacked in wealth.

The FBI suspected most of the Super PAC contributors were unaware of activities and actions of *The Committee*. Except for in the case of Thomas Hancock, who owned the buildings and laboratories comprising the *Viral Vector* project, as special agents suspected he was the original designer and developer of the futuristic technology. During the 1970s and 1980s, Rosetta Biotech Laboratories specialized in virus research and worked with the government as part of the U.S. Special Virus Program. When the Human Genome Project began in the 1990s, Hancock and RBL launched a major expansion into biological research, leading the world in the development of viral products and genetic research.

Agents also investigated the background and recent activities of financier Helmut Wolf, an avowed "enemy" of the President and the man who by all accounts had ordered the killing of private investigator and government operative Bryan Osaka. Wolf had ties to wealthy and powerful families in Europe, South

America and South Africa. He considered himself part of a global community of billionaires and felt loyalty to that community and their shared interests, rather than to "lazy, uneducated, petty Americans."

Nathaniel Driscoll was another matter. He was a true operator, a business partner with the current administration and with former presidents and heads of states, regardless of party affiliation. He played both sides of conflicts and occasionally bet against himself, but he had an uncanny knack for winning. He was close to Jettson Turner, former White House Chief-of-Staff with a previous administration. At times, it seemed Driscoll *and* Turner played both sides of the equation. The President *liked* Driscoll, though he did not trust him.

Recently, Driscoll had provided crucial intelligence prior to the invasion of Rosetta Biotech Laboratories, and he suggested Turner as the best person to run conversion and new operations. The active administration accepted Turner reluctantly, fully aware of his previous relationship with *The Committee*. After Osaka's death, it seemed *Country First* contributors sought to distance themselves from *The Committee*, as Meredith Williams, in particular, put out a statement that her involvement in politics was purely recreational. A week later, her company quietly made a substantial donation to the President's re-election campaign.

The members of *Country First* and *The Committee* resented Wolf, who was irate about the government takeover of the *Viral Vector* project at Rosetta Biotech Laboratories. During the initial raid, he called for reinforcements, but in an emergency meeting, convened by committee members, Associate Justice Wendell Greene cast the deciding vote against additional engagement. Yet *The Committee* continued to back Wolf's plan, under the threat that failure would result in the vector being launched against individual members, including presidential challenger Hugh Gordon.

"You've performed much better in the debates than most people expected, Governor Gordon, at it seems the polls in some of the swing states are shifting in your favor. What do you say now to commentators and pundits who wrote this election off in August, September and even early October?"

"I say I've known all along the race would be tight right up until Election Day, and in the end, November is all that matters. You know that, Chuck. So I say to pessimists on my side who were so sure I couldn't win this election: *Back off.* Let me *win* this thing! Working together, we can reshape the world through the power of our ideas and strong leadership from the United States of America."

For two weeks they had been shadowing her, detailing her habits, collecting and sorting through her garbage and seeking an unguarded opportunity to take her unaware. On all six occasions, by following Bryan's detailed protocols, Destiny located and destroyed the electronic listening devices they had placed in her room. The primary object of the mission was to acquire an adequate sample of her DNA, yet if the opportunity presented itself, New World Army trackers were authorized to capture her and debrief her, employing torture if necessary.

Two days before he was killed, Bryan made arrangements for Destiny and Kiyomi to stay at Travis Air Force Base in Fairfield, fifty miles away, where Deputy National Security Advisor Lucius Draco assured him that they would be protected by military personnel around the clock. After two weeks of surveillance that yielded no results, Wolf grew frustrated and instructed his team to "take the shot" the next time opportunity presented itself.

By the time Kiyomi's flu-like symptoms disappeared, she made the connection. The fatigue she felt and the shortness of breath were unusual, and though she attempted to disguise her general malaise, Destiny had also made the connection.

"I talked to one of the cardiologists over at the Medical Center and made arrangements to have you screened for heart disease. He said they would also perform a coronary calcium scan to gauge if there is any significant plaque build-up. We'll *both* go, and we'll get screened together."

"Destiny, we've talked about this before. I'm not going. If they got to me, there's nothing doctors can do. It'll be just like Jake. I don't want to know."

Destiny batted her eyes, blinking back the tears.

"But what if it's something else? Maybe it's just that your body is still recovering from the flu. We don't know what it is. We've been careful, haven't we?"

Kiyomi nodded.

"That's what I keep thinking. But what about that time I was passed out at Dr. Rashid's apartment? They had me. I was out for hours. They could have sampled me then."

"No. Cotton told us his team was the one that went in and cleaned things up. He wouldn't have let anyone tamper with you."

"But Cotton wasn't there. Maybe it was one of his team members. Or maybe someone else came in after the team left me there. It must have happened that night."

Destiny reached toward her best friend, caressing her face.

"Please Kiyomi. You're tired yes, and you had the flu, but that doesn't mean they got to you. The only way to really know is to get tested. We might be getting ourselves all worked up for nothing. Please?"

"I'll kill myself first. I won't end up like Jake—wasting away, suffering, hoping for a miracle, waiting out the inevitable. I have a gun. I'll just kill myself first."

Destiny grabbed her best friend's wrist hard.

"Listen Kiyomi, you are *not* going to die. I can't lose you! I made an appointment with the cardiologist for tomorrow morning. We're going together and we're *both* getting tested. Whatever happens, we'll fight together. I won't let you die!"

They had been at Travis Air Force Base for five days, two before the funeral and for three days that followed. To Destiny's surprise, Carla Ettinger, Lyndsey's spouse, had attended Bryan's memorial service and greeted Destiny with kind, consoling words, uncharacteristic for a woman who usually spewed vitriol at the mere mention of her mother-in-law's name. Pressing a card with her phone number into Destiny's hand, she asked if Destiny would meet with her in a few days, after things calmed down.

Carla's name was cleared, and they met at the Officers' Club on the base. Carla arrived in a shiny, new black Jaguar, and as always, she was overdressed for the occasion. Her red-soled blue stilettos clicked as she walked toward Destiny, who stood at the front door. Destiny recognized the cobalt dress as a Jason Wu, similar to the one he designed for the First Lady. Her stockings were gossamer, barely noticeable, except for the seam. Auburn tresses, loosely curled, hung down to her shoulders, contrasting with bright blue eyes and alabaster white skin.

Destiny always thought Carla was pretty enough, though at forty-eight, she was much too old for Lyndsey. Carla had a son from a previous marriage who was twenty-four, only two years younger than his stepmother. But more than age, Carla was insecure and could be childish and unpleasant when she felt threatened. At the wedding rehearsal dinner, she threw a tantrum because Lyndsey wanted to sit next to her mother and warned that unless Destiny was "uninvited" to the ceremony, there would be no wedding at all.

More concerned for Lyndsey's happiness than her own, Destiny and Kiyomi did not attend, and went to dinner at *Skates on the Bay* instead. Over a pitcher of margaritas, they placed wagers on how long the ill-fated marriage would last.

Seated at lunch, Carla reached across the table for Destiny's hand.

"Thank you again for meeting me. And as I told you last week, I'm very sorry for your loss. I didn't know Bryan, but Lyndsey always told me he was a really nice man."

Destiny smirked, convinced that Lyndsey would rather eat a toad than say anything complimentary about Bryan.

"What do you *really* want, Carla?"

Carla took a deep breath and sighed, tears welling in her eyes.

"I haven't seen or heard from Lyndsey in over a month. I miss her so much. I need to *see* her, to know we're still okay. I know you talk to her."

Destiny nodded.

"Lyndsey is fine. She misses you too, but I'm afraid that's not going to happen."

Carla reacted without thinking.

"So how is that fair to me? You're not even her real mother and *you* talk to her! She's my wife and I *can't*?"

Destiny's first impulse was to punish Carla for being such a bitch, but she did not. Instead, she remembered Bryan and how much she missed him. She empathized with the pain and loss she knew Carla was feeling.

"I'm sorry, but it's too dangerous right now, and I'm certain you would rather suffer through it another two or three weeks than have to deal with what I've just been through."

Carla was weeping, trembling hands covering her face. After watching a moment, Destiny spoke in a soft voice.

"I'll tell you what, Carla. Why don't we use your phone to make a video from you that we could send to Lyndsey? You can send it to me, and I'll make sure it gets to her. And maybe she can do the same thing on her end. What do you think?"

Carla smiled, astonished by Destiny's thoughtful gesture, while wiping the tears from her eyes with a handkerchief.

"*Really?*"

Wolf's team, under the direction of leader Victor Collins, had already taken up positions outside the secured residence where Destiny and Kiyomi were staying. Neither woman had left the home in forty-eight hours, denying snipers the opportunity for a kill. But when Destiny risked protection and exposure in order to meet Carla Ettinger, soldiers were quick to coordinate a plan to accomplish their objective.

The Delta Force detail guarding the house consisted of six men, active soldiers who did not understand the degree of threat involved. They were at Travis under an arrangement Bryan set up with a contact at the Pentagon. Two soldiers escorted Destiny from the front door to the car before driving her to the meeting destination, leaving two others to protect the house. The sniper had taken a position so that he would have a clean shot when they returned—in the instant Destiny stood from the car. He would fire a single shot, right in the back of her head.

Other team members were stationed outside the Officers' Club to provide real-time tracking from the restaurant to the residence. The team at the house was poised to strike, awaiting confirmation that the target was en route. No one, however, expected that Destiny's meeting with Carla Ettinger would last more than forty-five minutes, but after three hours, Victor Collins began to grow concerned.

"What on Earth is she *doing* in there?"

"Looks like something involving cell phones. A video statement maybe."

"Well, can we take her down when she comes out of the building, or at the car? Does it work?"

"Negative, Sir. Too risky. Got too much goin on over here. Response would be immediate and overwhelming."

"Copy that. We'll stand by here."

Fifteen minutes later, Wolf called Collins again, repeating his new orders, summoning the soldiers immediately back to Boston.

"Are you sure, Sir? Another thirty minutes and we've got her. A shot through the head."

"You told me the same thing two hours ago. I am tired of waiting. Your team needs to get back here *now*! We will deal with the bitch later. You should have left an hour ago."

"Sir, we've waited a week to set up this shot. Fifteen minutes?"

Wolf lost his temper.

"Are you countermanding my orders, Mr. Collins? We are already behind schedule for tonight. Drop whatever you are doing this minute, assemble your team and get your asses back here right now! Do you hear me? Do not ever question me again!"

Not one minute after the leader called the sniper off and redirected the team at the house, a call came from his team outside the Officers' Club.

"Got a visual on the target. She and escort are moving toward the car. ETA seven minutes."

"Copy that. We have orders to return to base. This mission has been suspended."

"But she's on her way, Sir. Let's just finish this!"

Collins sighed.

"Negative on that. Wolf gave the order and he's all worked up because we're not already there. She must have prayed last night," the leader sighed. "Today just wasn't her day to die."

Chapter 30

"Oh, what a tangled web we weave! Good afternoon, Nate."

Jett Turner took a seat next to Nathaniel Driscoll at the long table in the empty boardroom. Driscoll toked on a stogy, blowing the smoke toward the ceiling.

"You left off the end, my friend, which continues, *when first we practice to deceive.* This whole matter has gotten out of hand. Who would have ever thought, after all we've been through, that you would have limited oversight on the *Viral Vector* project?"

Turner helped himself to a cigar from the lacquered humidor on the table, savoring the first few puffs.

"It's a transitional appointment. The President chose me, but not because he likes me. He chose me because I'm honest, a straight shooter, and I was the best man for the job. The conversion is complete. The government got everything, including Rosecrans and most of his team."

"All that money! Almost one and a half billion dollars and they just came in and *took* it. Incredible!"

Jett shrugged.

"You can *do* that when you're the Commander-in-Chief of the U.S. military, but it's still outrageous. I don't think anyone's thought to do it before, but it's done."

"And what do they plan on doing with it?"

"Official story? They're going to shut down operations over the next year and set the technology aside. Of course no one *believes* that. Word is the President's already got plans to incorporate this viral vector technology into his anti-terror program, along with the drones."

Driscoll shook his head.

"And of course he would *never* use it against political enemies, here or abroad. He would *never* do that!"

"Apparently the active government knew about the venture all along. They just let you guys spend the time and resources developing it so they could take it from you a soon as they knew it was viable. It was a secret project, so they knew no one could complain about the conversion. Wolf should have known and planned a better contingency. He didn't and you all lost your money."

"To the tune of more than three hundred million dollars here. Me, I can afford it, but Hancock lost his ass, especially after the assault at RBL. And Wolf stands to lose even more."

Jett tapped the cigar on the ashtray, resentful.

"That asshole Wolf! This whole thing accelerated when he killed Osaka. How does anyone achieve containment with that megalomaniac callin shots? He's made a shitload of money in his life, but he's not livin in reality. He's the instrument of his own demise."

"I hate to say you're right, but Wolf is blaming Hancock for the invasion. I understand he believes Hancock is the one who leaked a document to Osaka. He thinks Hancock plotted with the government and provided intelligence to make sure they got all the essential elements of *Viral Vector* in the raid and conversion. I've tried to reel Wolf in, but he's stubborn and arrogant. *The tangled webs we weave!*"

"That makes absolutely no sense," Jett sneered. "Why would Hancock do that? The invasion and conversion will cost him hundreds of millions in losses. Half his company is gone!"

"If he cut a deal with the government, maybe it involved *compensation* for those losses. Highly unlikely, but it's possible."

Turner reached for the cognac flask and poured a liberal drink.

"Recently, I've heard something about a 'White House Target.' One can only assume *The Committee* is planning on using the *Viral Vector* technology against the President."

"Not to my knowledge. An assassination plot against a sitting President would amount to terrorism and treason, punishable by death. I don't know that any of us would be willing to engage in something so risky."

Driscoll mashed the cigar, extinguishing the cherry.

"Besides, it would be unpatriotic, un-American."

The offensive began three days after the original assault to the very minute. Two Blackhawk helicopters hovered over Rosetta

Biotech Laboratories as thirty-six Special Forces soldiers fast-roped in. In this second assault, the army invaded only Hancock's RBL buildings, staying well clear of the *Viral Vector* area on the other side of the large complex.

Fighting was sporadic, as there were no more than fifteen guards assigned to the original laboratories. Over forty minutes, Special Forces secured most of the buildings and detained all personnel, herding doctors, researchers and staff into a large storage warehouse.

After an hour, soldiers remained unsuccessful at locating the main target of the raid. In a situation room eighty miles away, former Deputy Defense Secretary Kyle Carter wondered if the intelligence he relied on was faulty or deceptive. Undeterred, he ordered a second sweep of RBL buildings and had soldiers initiate a third when Victor Collins, the Officer-in-Charge, announced the high-value target of the raid had been located.

Within minutes, a stealth Blackhawk returned to retrieve half of the soldiers. Mission complete, the helicopter was just about to clear the perimeter when it was struck by a high-speed anti-radiation missile. The mid-air explosion above the complex was so bright that it could be seen in some parts of downtown Boston.

Outside the perimeter gates of Rosetta Biotech Laboratories, a separate assault had begun. Soldiers inside fought to slow the invasion, but they were forced to fall back, yielding to superior forces. The remaining twelve Special Forces coalesced in secure positions, guarding the entrance to a small, seemingly insignificant building.

Two soldiers were stationed inside, behind doors they had rigged with explosives. The building itself was a deception, a Visitor's Center above a much more sophisticated underground complex. Deep within the gut of that complex was a safe room, where the target of the invasion had retreated in panic. He placed repeated calls to outside friends for help, but he was trapped. Inside, he could hear the drills that would eventually allow the door to be removed.

Special Forces inside held off their attackers until 6:00 a.m., when the sun began to rise. By that time, the Internet campaign and media messaging began to yield results. Local news stations flew helicopters and small aircraft over the complex, seeking to confirm the U.S. government invasion of RBL that they were seeing in four graphic videos posted online. By seven o'clock, all fighting had ceased outside.

At eight-thirty, the door to the safe room yielded, slamming to the ground outside after it was pried off. Inside, Thomas Hancock cringed with three frightened staff members, who were immediately led away. Seeking to gauge the motives of leader Victor Collins, Hancock smiled to appear friendly.

"I don't know what you're being paid, but I'm a billionaire, and apparently my life is in the balance here. Ten million. Ten million dollars apiece if you can find a way to get me out of this. What the Hell—twenty million! *Thirty million!*"

Collins wore the uniform and insignia of SEAL Team Six as he approached Hancock, pistol drawn.

"If you haven't noticed, we're surrounded. That would mean the two of us and you going past two armies, and that's not going to happen. It's a tempting offer, but you'd never be able to deliver it and I wouldn't be alive to benefit from it. The deal I'm in is good enough for me."

He raised his gun, aiming at Hancock's forehead as he glanced over at his partner, who aimed a camera.

"Make sure you get this, because we can't do a retake."

"Tell your boss he's only making it worse," Hancock panted. "He's going to lose because they're all against him, from the beginning—every last one of them!"

Collins read from a note.

"*There are two sides to every issue: one side is right and the other is wrong, but the middle is always evil.* Helmut Wolf sends his regards."

The loud explosion reverberated in the room, followed by the hollow thud of Hancock's lifeless body on the hard floor.

Chapter 31

The weather in San Francisco was mild, owing to an early October heat spell in northern California. Two days before, Destiny Mitchell and Kiyomi Yamakita were tested for coronary heart disease at the Medical Center on Travis Air Force Base in Fairfield. Destiny's tests came back normal, but Kiyomi was exhibiting early signs of arteriosclerosis, unhealthy levels of plaque and fat that had begun to build up in her heart. The news devastated Kiyomi, who insisted suicide was preferable to suffering a slow, painful death.

Destiny was determined to save her best friend, even if it meant risking her own life. Considering all options, she called Cornell Cotton to tell him about Kiyomi's condition and ask for help at speaking directly with the President. Cotton was disturbed by the news and insisted her DNA was not sampled on the night she spent unconscious at Dr. Rashid's apartment.

"I knew someone might be trying that. That's why I personally monitored that apartment and her condition until she left the next morning."

When Destiny repeated her request for assistance at speaking with the President, Cotton was blunt.

"Look, by all accounts, there has been a recent plot on the President's life. He does not trust Jettson Turner, my boss. So, by extension, he wouldn't trust me. Your best bet is to find someone he knows and listens to. Didn't you tell me you were friends with the Attorney General?"

"I met him twice, but I don't exactly *know* him. I just don't know how I would be able to get him to believe me without sharing what Grant told me."

"So why wouldn't you just share it with him?"

"Because it's all I got, and the President is the only one who can help me."

Destiny met Saint Claire in a parking lot next to the Berkeley Marina. Cringing, feeling vulnerable as she left her military escort in the car, she hurried over and slipped into the open door of the professor's car, slamming it shut.

"God, this is nerve-racking! Thank you for meeting me, Professor Saint Claire. When you said you had found a way for me to talk to the President, I cried. This experience has been horrible for me!"

"I can only imagine, but I have to warn you—you're going to Washington. You're going to the lion's den. It doesn't get any easier from here."

A wave of panic washed over her face.

"Why? I thought I'd be talking to the President."

"It's not just the President. It's Washington. There's this place and people we think we know, and then there's this other place, this alternative universe Washington that those *outside the Beltway* never see."

"What does that mean?"

Saint Claire sighed.

"It means that even if you get the chance to talk to the President, you won't know which side he's on. In Washington there's bad—by necessity, and there's only worse. The only way to survive if you go there is to suspend morality."

"You've obviously had a negative experience."

"Do you understand the concept of cognitive dissonance, Destiny? A man who believes he's honest—he can do something he innately knows is wrong, but he will find a way to justify it, pretend it didn't happen, avoid reality or ignore the facts because he does not *want* to know. That's as good as it gets in Washington."

Destiny felt betrayed.

"Why are you telling me this? You said you had a way. You said you could help me gain an audience with the President."

"I can, but you are obviously not hearing me. Listen again Destiny—what I'm saying might not make sense to you now, but you'll understand after this is all over. The higher you ascend, the harder it is to tell the bad guys from the worse guys, *including* the President. They'll all look and sound the same. You'll never know the difference by listening. You have to use your heart, and *sense* it if you can."

She clasped the professor's hand.

"I appreciate your advice, Professor Saint Claire, and I am listening. But what I need to know is: did you find a way for me to speak with the President?"

He drew a breath and held it before sighing.

"One of his Senior Advisors was a friend of my deceased wife. She said she can get you in to see him, but you'll have to talk to her first. Fair enough?"

"I'm sure I don't have a choice. When do I need to be there?"

It was more than a viral Internet phenomenon. The major networks initially seemed to consider the story and video as newsworthy. The U.S. government raid of Rosetta Biotech Laboratories and the execution of Thomas Hancock was just another example of the active administration's arrogance and government overreach. The President's Press Secretary quickly released a statement saying the raid was a "False Flag" operation, perpetrated by one of Hancock's enemies. Its purpose was to disguise the murder of a billionaire. An FBI investigation had begun.

Strangely enough, the online furor was short-lived, as the Department of Homeland Security began shutting down or blocking Internet sites that aired the video and misleading stories related to the incident. Media owners were pressured to drop the story.

As a result, the effect on the election was negligible, as most Americans never saw the video or heard about the invasion and assassination. Others dismissed it as just another conspiracy theory cooked up on the Internet. Instead, the mainstream media spent the next few cycles preoccupied with *Country First* and the lurid lives of its secretive billionaire members.

Hugh Gordon decided to sit the story out, his office suggesting any comment by the candidate so early in the investigation would be un-presidential for being premature. He would make an official statement after the FBI released its statement.

Over the first day, Thomas Hancock was portrayed as a very wealthy and successful businessman who loved his country. The company he controlled, Rosetta Biotech Laboratories, was valued at ninety-eight billion dollars. Politically, he supported and contributed to traditionalist causes in America and policies that favored the wealthy, though he was progressive on the issue of gay marriage.

His only son had *a husband and a wonderful non-traditional family*. Thomas Jr., who ran the genetic research division of the company, was a good son and a moral, responsible spouse and father. The elder Hancock disagreed with all the fuss people made over a person marrying whomever they wanted to marry.

It was never meant to be a political issue. On issues involving gene therapy, genetic manipulation, cloning, stem cells, science and global warming, he usually sided with the progressives. Not surprising, he was unpopular among traditionalists.

Some company executives suspected inside involvement in the assassination, suggesting only a handful of people knew Thomas Hancock would be on premises at RBL so late on that night. It was a big news story for a day, fading the next morning as networks continued to hype the upcoming elections, poll changes, demographic quirks, candidate blunders and gaffes, all building up to the political orgasm that would be Election Night.

Members of *The Committee* watched events unfold in horror. Most had known Thomas Hancock for years and respected his lucid, objective approach on most issues. Because committee members were not briefed about the earlier assault and informed that the *Viral Vector* project had been converted to government control, most were willing to believe the administration was responsible for Hancock's assassination.

Associate Supreme Court Justice Wendell Greene, who chaired *The Committee*, was not fooled. He suspected that Wolf, ill-tempered and extreme, had staged the deceptive black flag operation to exact revenge on the person he believed leaked the document to Osaka and an FBI bureau chief. It also served as a distraction as the vector took its effect. Greene never liked Hancock, so he was not terribly disappointed by news of his death. Two weeks earlier, when he told Wolf he believed Hancock was the person who had betrayed the pact, the judge knew there would be deadly repercussions.

"I am surprised you were brave enough to meet with me in person, Justice Greene. It seems all the others want to distance themselves. I am anathema. Here we are, at the end of this enterprise, at the beginning of our New World Order, and they have all deserted us."

"They have not deserted us, Mr. Wolf. They're just waiting to see if your plan will work. They're nervous, naturally, because there is so much at stake. As we approach the end of the election and the culmination of your *Viral Vector* project, they're realizing just how ambitious a plan it is, a chance to control the world!"

Wolf smiled.

"You really believe this is true, what you are telling me?"

"History has shown: Fortune favors the bold, and the unambitious will follow loyally in cadence, fools that they are. As of today, how stands your plan?"

"We launched our vector two weeks ago. According to a source at the White House, our target began exhibiting flu-like symptoms some four days later, which means the launch was successful. The clinical latency, or incubation period for the vector we used, was three days, during which time the virus was actively replicating the altered DNA. Once symptoms manifest, the vector operates on an accelerated timetable. Our target will be dead in two weeks, twelve days before the election."

Greene nodded, eyebrows raised to indicate admiration.

"And you know in advance how all individuals directly affected will react?"

"Now that is the part of the plan we know best. It will be an overwhelming blow, and Hugh Gordon will be our next president, no question about it."

Chapter 32

"What if you never get the chance to talk to him? What if Saint Claire is part of a plan to distract you, to get you out of the way until after the election?"

Destiny paused, thinking.

"I *trust* Saint Claire. In my gut, I trust him. If I am able to talk to the President, at least we'll have a chance. It's the only chance we've got."

Her eyes studied her best friend.

"How do you feel?"

"I've just been so tired lately, and I'm out of breath just walking back to the bedroom."

Kiyomi shook the bottle, dumping two pills containing the antiviral DRACO into her palm.

"Does Saint Claire *know* about Grant and that phone call? Did you tell him?"

"No one knows but you and me. We *stuck* by each other, and we figured this whole thing out together. Now the advantage is ours. The President will *have* to believe me. Make sure you take the antibiotics, Kiyomi. Saint Claire said it should slow the progress."

Kiyomi placed the pills in her mouth, took a swig from the glass and threw her head back, swallowing.

"I've always hated taking pills, but I know it's for my own good."

Destiny grabbed the bottle from the table and took her own dosage.

"I think only Dr. Rosecrans knows at what point the process becomes irreversible. The sooner I talk to the President, the better."

"I want to go with you."

"No, too risky. We both know how stress affects the immune system. You need to right stay here and rest, let your body fight the virus and whatever gene therapy is going on inside you."

Kiyomi sat back.

"I feel helpless! This whole story sounds too incredible to believe! What makes you think the President isn't going to just pat you on the head, thank you and ignore what you've said?"

"Because once I get him to connect the dots, and he understands what the symptoms indicate, I'm sure I'll have his undivided attention."

In the Roslyn sub-market of Arlington, twenty stories above the black waters of the Potomac, members of *The Committee* had once again assembled in the darkened conference room. Justice Greene sat at the head of the table, mask in place and gavel at the ready.

To his right sat House Majority Whip Chris Matthews, who seemed anxious for the meeting to begin. Next to Chris, former Homeland Security Advisor Helen Abercrombie tapped on an unresponsive laptop. Across from her sat Senate Committee on Foreign Relations Chair Rex Andal, who sat to the left of political consultant Charles Love. The former governors sat farthest away, Steven Testor of Wyoming and Hugh Gordon of Massachusetts.

As always, the meeting began at one minute after midnight when Greene tapped the gavel.

"Once again, it is the Witching Hour, and we begin again. Let this meeting of *The Committee* come to order!"

After he tapped a command on his computer, all the laptop screens around the table came on in unison, displaying the white *Country First* logo on a bright blue screen.

"As we come to the *dénouement*, the culmination of five years of planning, the spilled blood of fellow patriots and billions of dollars we've spent, our words matter more now than ever. You, Governor, stand at the threshold of time and providence, poised to establish a New World Order and ultimate destiny for humans in Earth's twenty-first century. It is an awesome privilege we have earned, a responsibility we will share."

At once, the laptop screens displayed video from the attack at Rosetta Biotech Laboratories.

"As a matter of business, the assault you are witnessing is not what it appears to be. This attack occurred three days before what you no doubt saw and read about in the media. This is the active administration in a black operation resulting in the seizure and conversion of the *Viral Vector* project at Rosetta Biotech. The takeover was complete within twenty-four hours."

The Senator from Virginia spoke after being recognized by the chair.

"The United States government just came in and took over the *Viral Vector* project? What does this mean for our enterprise? How does it change things?"

"It was a secret operation, so it changes nothing. Once Governor Gordon becomes President, the *Viral Vector* project will once again be ours to control."

The former Homeland Security Advisor asked the next question.

"How can we be so sure the Governor will *win* this election? We've all seen the Electoral College math. The big game changer—is it still going to happen?"

The chair answered.

"The vector was indeed launched, and we have assets in the White House who have confirmed the flu-like symptoms and fatigue. We're on target. At this point, we expect it to happen seven to ten days before Election Day."

House Majority Whip Matthews raised his hand.

"Are we certain we know what his party will do in a case like this?"

"A week before Election Day? In the middle of a funeral? They won't have options. They'll have to put up the Vice President. After all, he's been all over the country on the campaign trail this summer and fall. They'd be foolish not to put him up."

Matthews followed up.

"And *our* candidate beats the Vice President?"

'By a fifteen-point margin, according to internal polls. It hasn't hurt that we spent the summer playing up his negatives and inability to lead. We have already created the ads we will launch during the first and last week of his Presidential campaign."

The chair recognized Gordon.

"That's nice, but I am the candidate, and our campaign has done its own set of internal polls. We're surging in the swing states, and we will have momentum going into Election Day. We can win this thing outright! Against this President! Why risk treason?"

Greene slammed the gavel in anger.

"Sit *down*, Governor! And no more from you! The die is cast. *No man who puts his hand to plow and looks back is fit for anything!* Forward. We must move forward!"

After nearly a minute of awkward silence, the Senator from Virginia sought to be recognized.

"I hope I'm not out of order by asking, but if the active administration has the *Viral Vector* project *and* the doctor, who's to say when the sickness is discovered, he won't just go and get the doctor to cure it?"

"Because the President has no idea what we've done, and by the time he realizes it..."

Justice Greene sat back, adjusting his mask.

"By the time he knows, it will be too late."

Chapter 33

"Are they still behind us? Who do you think it is?"

The driver checked the rearview mirror.

"I don't know, Destiny, but I know it isn't *me* they're after."

Headed west on Interstate 80, the driver accelerated to seventy-five miles per hour. In response, the black Ford Suburban only moved closer, maintaining a quarter mile gap as the vehicles sped past the weigh station just outside Fairfield. The series of clicks in the front meant the soldier in the passenger seat was locked and loaded. He studied the dark vehicle in the side mirror.

"They're just keeping an even distance. And there's a second vehicle, same make and model, an even distance behind them. Maybe they know where we're going. We'll try to lose them in Vallejo traffic and see if they're still with us when we get to the Carquinez Strait."

The driver, Clark, accelerated to eighty miles per hour coming off the hill at American Canyon Road, as trailing drivers tried to close before reaching city traffic. The sun was setting in the hills on the right, casting a shadow, a precursor of darkness. Clark flashed his headlights as he zipped around cars and weaved through a major slow-down at the Magazine Street exit. By the time they crossed the Carquinez Bridge, the pursuers were no longer visible in the darkness.

"Pull off at the next exit."

Waiting until the last possible moment, the driver veered off the freeway at the Hercules exit, continued for a mile, pulled onto the shoulder of the road and turned the engine off. No one had followed.

The soldier in the passenger seat peered back at Destiny.

"I know you were hoping it wouldn't come down to this, Ma'am, but it looks like you have to go through with it."

The second soldier, Ware, handed Destiny a case containing battery operated hair clippers and a razor, grinning.

"It'll grow back. At least we *hope* it'll grow back."

Destiny smiled.

"You ought to do it *with* me, Soldier," she laughed, "for solidarity!"

Twenty minutes later, both were bald, heads gleaming. Destiny gazed in a mirror in shock and found it unsettling that she hardly recognized the person staring back, but the transformation was not complete.

Unwrapping two elastic sports bandages, six-inches wide, she began under an armpit, and holding her breath, she began to wrap the first bandage around her chest, covering the end. As she continued upward with the bandage, she used her fingers to make adjustments to the position of her breasts, moving them outward and upward to create the appearance of a flat chest.

She pulled on a pair of loose, faded, tattered jeans, sagging and stained with oil, along with a Pendleton wool plaid work shirt. Her work boots were three sizes too big, the toes stuffed with socks. By the time the moustache and tattoos were in place, Destiny had disappeared. Clark had provided her with a Level III-A *Kevlar 29* vest, a sweater and a jacket to bulk her up. The man who stood before the mirror was Victor Abreu, complete with a state-issued California ID, an American Express card and a cover story.

"Rosie and her daughter are already at the airport, waiting for you so you can go through the baggage check line together. Like you asked, we bought tickets to New York and Washington at four separate airlines under your name, with all departures between eight o'clock and midnight."

She smiled.

"That should keep them busy. And you're sure I can get the dummy pistol past baggage check?"

"Someone at NSA already talked to the TSA director. They know you're coming. You'll be pulled aside checked separately. They'll let it go through. Let's go. You don't want to miss your flight."

Back on the freeway, the sports utility vehicle wound past Pinole, San Pablo, Richmond and Berkeley before reaching the Bay Bridge. As they exited the bridge and navigated past Ninth Street/Civic Center onto the 101, city lights to their right, Destiny wondered if she would ever see San Francisco again. So much had changed, but the city would always be her constant, would always be her favorite city in the world.

Halfway along the San Francisco International Airport exit, the black Ford Suburban reappeared and began to pursue the vehicle, this time at less than three hundred feet.

"Don't worry about them," Clark reassured Destiny. "I already called in the license plate and vehicle description. They'll be stopped when we get in the terminal. It should give us just enough time."

Clark slowed the vehicle as it entered the terminal for departures, slowly rolling past domestic airline brand symbols and law enforcement vehicles. The Suburban followed closely, until all at once, flashing lights shined around it and an authoritative voice directed the vehicle to stop. Instantly, Clark sped away to the pre-planned destination, where Ware yanked open the door and pulled Destiny to the curb.

"Please take care of Kiyomi for me!" she begged.

"We will. Get in there! You don't have much time. Good luck!"

"If she's headed here, there *must* be a reason for it. We were *right* not to gamble before. She knows. She's *always* known. It will be disastrous if she speaks with the President. Where is she now?"

Wolf sighed, angry.

"Somewhere at San Francisco International. I've got two teams at the terminal. If we don't find her there, we will catch her when she lands in Washington. She is just one person. She will never get to the President."

At a quiet Washington seafood restaurant, Driscoll stirred the last bits of salmon on his plate, dicing to separate the pink from the brown, though in the end, he ate everything.

"And how long on the realization of your viral vector?"

"Ten long days. Kiyomi Yamakita is dead by now, so when we kill Destiny Mitchell, there will be no more problems. With any luck, we will kill her at the airport, in San Francisco."

Driscoll studied the dessert menu.

"I don't believe in luck, and I only bet on sure things. You know that, Helmut. For that reason, I'm separating myself from any association with *Country First* and with you. The situation has become too perilous. I know how much money you invested and how hard you tried, Helmut, but I have a wife, sons, shareholders, friends and even world leaders to consider. I *want* to support you, my friend, but it's bigger than me.

"I'm a Doey-Don't player," Driscoll continued. "I have to look at long term repercussions and consequences, and right now, your plan has become a big gamble. At this point, I have to pivot to the center, at least until I am certain who the winners and losers will be—something you can't guarantee, and that doesn't work for me. Until you have a sure thing, you're on your own."

He handed the menu to the server.

"Crème Brûlée, with a side of that American alembic brandy—the one from Ukiah."

Destiny sat in the waiting area of Terminal 1, Gate A10. Rosie Abreu, Bryan's former office manager, was seated next to her, along with Rosie's six-year-old daughter, Serena. Holding hands, they appeared to be a typical Hispanic family, bound for San Juan, via New York. Destiny's skin was brown, but Rosie was nearly as dark, and Serena, with long straight hair, was darker than both.

With thirty minutes left before boarding, Destiny watched a suspicious man combing the terminal. He was tall, his face chiseled, his bearing military. As he walked past waiting passengers seated or standing at the gates, he occasionally glanced down at his phone, comparing faces to the photo of Destiny that Wolf supplied.

But when he used his phone to take pictures of section after section of passengers at Gate A10, she nearly panicked. She was certain the images were being sent to some computer workstation, where experts who focused on identifying nervous behavior and facial recognition specialists were trying to undermine her disguise. The best she could do was turn and bow her head.

The soldier continued to Gates A11 and A12, but he returned ten minutes before the call for boarding and seemed to linger, glancing over occasionally, and then he took a second series of pictures. By that time, even Rosie began to grow nervous. Both were relieved when the air hostess extended early seating, in consideration of the child.

Seated on the aisle, Destiny was a twitching wreck as she watched to see if the suspicious man got on the plane, and she did not calm down until after the Boeing 767 jumbo jet was safely in the air.

Chapter 34

"Of *course* she was in disguise! Destiny Mitchell is listed on the passenger manifests on four different airlines? She is on none of them. And since all those flights are going to Washington, I know she is not headed there. New York. She will fly into New York and try to arrange ground transportation in from there. *Find* her!"

Helmut Wolf left Washington in a hurry after the meeting with Driscoll. He was disappointed his old friend decided to cut ties, though he realized Driscoll made his success betting on sure things. In the last week, Driscoll and others had lost faith in Wolf and in his ability to salvage the *Viral Vector* project, especially after the government appropriated and converted it. They had lost faith his plan would work.

Wolf was becoming paranoid. Hancock was dead, but it appeared someone else was working against him, informing on him. He was determined to find and kill the traitor. Without Driscoll's backing, Washington had become precarious for its treachery, even more so than before. Earlier in the day, Wolf retreated to his hidden refuge in northeastern Idaho, near the Wyoming border, accessible only by airplane. In a control center on the second level, personal staff ran operations while he issued orders to New World Army soldiers on the ground.

He remained hopeful. Once his plan for the election worked and Hugh Gordon was President, Driscoll would return to him, along with the handful of American fools who doubted his genius. Vindicated, he would reward his friends and punish his enemies, but beyond that, through his *Viral Vector* project, he could access levers of global power and wealth. No one would be beyond his reckoning, not even Nathaniel Driscoll.

But Destiny Mitchell could ruin it all, and against overwhelming odds, she was on her way to Washington. Whether she could gain access to the President was questionable, but the risk was unacceptable. For the first time, Wolf realized he had underestimated Destiny, and by murdering Osaka, he had created a resourceful and fearless enemy who would stop at nothing short of revenge.

Panicked and paranoid, he spoke to his first-in-command, Victor Collins.

"They told me not to kill her before—at the beginning of this, and like a fool, I *listened* to them! And now look where they are! Gone! Hiding! Do you have any idea where she is?"

"We think we got a match through our facial recognition software. She's dressed as a man, a Victor Abreu, and she's on a flight to New York as we speak."

"Good. I want her dead tonight. Tell all your men I am offering a reward. Two million dollars to whoever puts a bullet through her face tonight. Fifty thousand a piece for additional bullets. I will pay two million extra if she is raped and beaten. *Sodomize* her! And I want her tongue—a one-million-dollar bonus to whoever cuts out that bitch's tongue and brings it to me! Yes, I will place it in my trophy case."

Seated next to Rosie, Destiny's eyes studied an older, single male passenger, watching his movements and mannerisms. When passengers were allowed to move about the cabin, she approached him and appeared to be flirting. When she returned to the seat, Rosie was puzzled.

"What was *that*? Does he know you're a woman, or is he gay? I don't get it. He doesn't even seem like your *type*, Girl."

Destiny bowed her head, tears in her eyes.

"Rosie, I just wanted to say 'thank you' for helping me on such short notice. You know I wouldn't do anything to put you or Serena at risk."

"Of course not. And I didn't mind. Serena and I got a free trip to San Juan to see *Abuela*. Besides, you and Bryan are like family to me. I loved Bryan like family."

Destiny smiled.

"Thank you, but I have to warn you, and you have to tell Serena. Before the plane lands, there will be a major commotion, and I'll be involved. The two of you cannot get involved in any way. Change seats. Pretend you don't know me. Do you understand?"

Rosie nodded.

"You will be *okay* though, right?"

"I'll be fine."

Destiny glanced at the television screen as she pulled on a black beanie.

"Ooh! What's that you're watching? Disgusting! Are they on an airplane?"

"Yes. It's *Snakes on a Plane*, the Samuel L. Jackson movie."

"You're *kidding* me! Someone should be *fired* for that! I like him, but what kind of genius would think to show *Snakes on a Plane... on a plane*! I don't see how Serena can even watch that gross stuff. It would give me nightmares."

The terminal at John F. Kennedy Airport swarmed with New World Army soldiers who could not be distinguished from commuting U.S. military personnel. While pretending to be circumspect, their eyes were on the gate where Destiny's direct flight from San Francisco was scheduled to arrive in thirty minutes. Collins positioned his soldiers at twenty-meter intervals, creating a loose net that extended from the gate to the street exit. The target was obviously unarmed, having been screened by TSA personnel in San Francisco prior to departure.

The goal was to approach Destiny and lead her away at gunpoint, once she exited the secured area of the airport. The team would employ the element of surprise, appearing friendly, helpful and unthreatening until she realized she was in custody. By mutual agreement, they had agreed to split the five-million-dollar bonus Wolf offered between the eighteen men in the detail, with Collins performing the final honors in a secluded gas station restroom outside the terminal.

Twenty minutes before the scheduled landing, Wolf was in a good mood when he called to check status. Being careful, he asked if the Secret Service or any other security team had appeared to meet the arrival. *Negative.* Then he asked if any details of the arrival had been changed in the late going, such as a last-minute gate change or unusual delay. *Again, Negative.* Flight plans? *Negative.* The woman and child traveling with her would also be detained and debriefed. If they knew anything, they too would be killed.

Minutes before the flight began to descend on metropolitan New York City airspace, Destiny returned to the seat near the front of the coach section and plopped down, dropping a shoulder bag on the floor between her feet. The man seated next to the window sighed at the sight of her.

"*You* again! I don't know what you *think* you know, but I am not—"

She pulled the dummy replica pistol discretely, her back to the aisle.

"I *know* who you are. For all intents and purposes, I'm a terrorist tonight."

"Excuse me?"

"Isn't it obvious. I've got a gun. *Now* you have to arrest me."

The older, balding sky marshal was instantly nervous, though more perplexed, as Destiny continued.

"If you think it's odd that I have this gun on a plane, you'll be blown away to know the bag on the ground contains a bomb that will obliterate this jumbo jet and parts of the terminal when we arrive at the gate. If you want to save lives, *call* this in! Be a hero."

Hands shaking, the federal agent, arms still raised, carefully reached for the phone inside the front of his jacket.

"What exactly do you want?

She whispered.

"I don't want a panic on the plane. And I don't want anyone hurt or traumatized. We *both* know that wouldn't be good. But I need you to have me arrested, and I need you to come with everything you've got. Get it? Bomb on a plane? Emergency. *Lots* of police and federal agents. Send an army."

"You're not making sense. All you want is to be *arrested*?"

The captain came on the intercom, announcing pending arrival at the airport and an on-schedule landing time. Destiny showed what appeared to be a detonation device.

"Look, we can do this discreetly, or we can do it the hard way. Your choice."

By the time the jet touched down, the area of the tarmac in front of the slowing aircraft was lit up in red and blue, like a Christmas display. Most passengers thought nothing of the lights, though a few were concerned.

The calm voice on the intercom was reassuring.

"Ladies and Gentlemen, this is your Captain speaking. As we taxi toward the gate, we will be making a brief stop on the tarmac to comply with a law enforcement request. Please remain in your seats. At this time, we continue to request that all mobile phones, pagers, radios, laptops and remote-controlled toys be turned off until we arrive at the gate. Thank you."

When the aircraft stopped, Destiny, detonator in hand, insisted on being escorted off the plane by four federal agents, who were surprised she was a woman, considering her appearance.

"There is no bomb," she confessed as she surrendered the firearm, "And the gun's not real."

Angry at her for the trouble she caused, agents slammed her into the wall of the aircraft and patted her down before cuffing her. The agent who yanked her up, straining her shoulder, slammed her again.

"So, what's in the bag?"

"A basketball."

Another agent felt through the fabric of the bag, estimating the weight of the hollow object inside and tapping before unzipping it. He shrugged.

"She's right, Sir. It's a basketball."

"This is a dangerous game you're playing, Miss, whoever you are. You've put every life on this domestic commercial flight in jeopardy. And by bringing a firearm onboard, you've threatened the security of the United States of America. You'll be going to prison for a long time."

"Natalie Sterling."

"Excuse me.

"Natalie Sterling—Senior Advisor to the President. I need you to contact Natalie Sterling for me. She knew I would be coming."

Destiny sighed and bowed her head, regretting the desperate tactic.

"But probably not like this."

Chapter 35

Inside the terminal, eighteen New World Army soldiers awaited the plane and an anticipated $275,000 bonus for each. As minutes ticked by beyond the plane's expected arrival time at the gate, team leader Collins grew uneasy and checked the terminal screen for arrivals, which indicated the flight was on-schedule. Five minutes later, when he called the airline to ask if the flight had been delayed, an airline representative told him the flight was on the ground taxiing and would arrive shortly at the gate.

By that time, Destiny had been pulled off the plane and placed in federal custody, headed to the Department of Homeland Security's Anti-Terrorism field offices, located at the airport. Concerned that a lengthy delay on the tarmac would upset passengers and create major media hysteria, federal agents were discreet as they entered and exited the aircraft. For safety measures, they also removed Rosie and Serena Abreu from the plane. In all, the delay time to the gate was no longer than fifteen minutes.

Eager for details, Wolf called during the wait, unhappy with the news.

"Something is wrong. I am beginning to *know* this Destiny Mitchell. She is clever, for a black woman. I will have someone check for any irregularity with that flight. In the meantime, have your team ready. I want to be rid of her tonight."

While the doors to the gate opened seventeen minutes late, it took three additional minutes for the first passengers to exit. After that, a steady flow began to emerge. Some, eyes fixed, headed directly toward the baggage claim area while others engaged in happy or stoic reunions. A photo of Destiny, in disguise, displayed on soldiers' cell phones, but even fifteen minutes after most of the passengers had exited, there was no sign of her.

According to Collins, any one of three things had happened: 1) She brought a secondary disguise onto the airliner, changed in the restroom and slipped by soldiers in a new disguise. For this reason, he ordered his men to snap photos of everyone who left the plane and send them to Wolf's face recognition technicians; 2) She was still on the plane, either hiding or disguised as an air hostess or as part of the cleanup crew. For that, Collins sent a soldier in disguised as a regulator, dispatched by the airline. A thorough search revealed Destiny was nowhere on the jet; and 3) She had de-planed during the taxi to the gate— something that would have required the aircraft to come to a complete stop.

If it had stopped, other passengers could confirm as much. At the baggage claim area, Collins talked to a couple who remembered the stop and red flashing lights. A woman from first-class remembered four "official-looking" men entering the aircraft, and five men exiting about ten minutes later. That was it. *Destiny Mitchell had de-planed!* When the leader called Idaho, Wolf was livid, beside himself, but he could not blame the team.

"That *bitch*! If they took her off that flight, she is in federal custody, which means they will take her to the Department of Homeland Security at the airport to debrief her before they let her go anywhere else. But we are still safe. She will not talk to them. We have to kill her before she goes to Washington, before she talks to the President. Take your three best men over there, and a sniper."

Collins hesitated, reluctant to bring up the subject when Wolf was already so agitated. But he knew his men would demand an answer, so he took a breath and asked.

"What about the bonus you promised. The situation has changed."

"*What* the hell! I'll *double* it! Ten million then! You have my word. I just want her dead, today! What*ever* it takes!"

"Well, you're obviously not Victor Abreu. We had your story checked out. You are Destiny Mitchell, for sure. I hardly recognize you without hair, but I've watched you on television, on Oprah and a few of the cable news programs. My daughter, by the way, adores you."

In a detention room belonging to the Department of Homeland Security's field office at John F. Kennedy International Airport in Queens, the site supervisor, in compliance with National Incident Management System rules, conducted the interview. He walked toward her and reaching, peeled the moustache off and smiled. He sat on one side of a metal table, while Destiny sat handcuffed, in a chair, across from him.

"Suffice it to say, my daughter and I have never exactly seen eye-to-eye, politically speaking, that is. We're on opposite sides of the spectrum."

Office Supervisor Shawn Tillis had worked at the site for nine years, since the early days of the DHS, though he spent only the last four in charge, just long enough to become comfortable with arrogance. He was a black man of average looks, with a medium build, middle–aged paunch, bald head and glasses. His tone and tenor reeked with sarcasm, but he made no apologies. Taking a swig from the water bottle he clutched in his left hand, he contemplated his first question.

"You were the cause of a National Incident tonight, Ms. Mitchell. Somehow you managed to slip a *gun* past TSA security in San Francisco, you threatened and thus distracted an air marshal in the commission of his duties, and you threatened to blow up a jumbo jet, loaded with over two hundred Americans."

He sighed.

"I understand you're a lawyer. Do you have any idea how much trouble you're in?"

Destiny sat back.

"I did what I had to do to stay alive and to deliver a message to the President."

Shawn groaned, bringing his palms to his face, and sighed again.

"The President? The President of what? The airline? The network? The PTA? What?"

She was irritated.

"The President of the United States."

He glanced over at his audience, a recorder and an assistant, who he invited to sit in on the meeting.

"*You* want to talk to the President of the United States? You, a person who tonight caused a national security emergency by threatening to blow up an airliner, with a *basketball*! Are you on crack? You've got to be *kidding* me!"

He wagged his head.

"What is it you need to tell the President? Why don't you start by telling me?"

Angry, she leaned forward.

"What I have to tell him—is a matter of National Security. It's very personal for him, and frankly, it's way above your pay grade. I don't have time for this!"

She crossed her arms.

"I'll need to speak with your supervisor."

New World Army team leader Collins and three soldiers had taken up positions outside the Department of Homeland Security field office at JFK airport and the sniper was in place, one hundred fifty meters away, with a clear shot encompassing an eight-foot area outside the front door.

After thirty minutes, one of the soldiers edged his way over to Collins, whispering.

"Are you sure you want to *do* this? This will be a direct attack on DHS. They'll consider it an attack on the U.S. government. Before, at the airport, it was just a job, but this would be an act of terrorism, and they'll make it a point to track us down."

"Return to your station, Soldier."

"Hear me out, please! What good will it do for us to have all that money, six hundred thou, if we're dead? And does it make any sense to make it an even split now, when the four of us are taking all the risk?"

Collins glanced toward the building and took a deep breath.

"It's what we agreed to before we came."

"I *disagreed*. Remember? So, what happens when the government starts hunting us down? If any of the others get caught, they'll blame us because there's no *risk* for them! They're nowhere around here! And for that, they get an even split of the bonus? A bonus is supposed to be for something you've *done*."

"What are you saying, Soldier?"

The soldier continued, his voice low and respectful.

"I say it's too big a risk for six hundred thou. But if we split it between the four of us—it's two and a half million dollars apiece! Now *that* would be worth it."

"Have you talked to the others?"

"We've all agreed."

Collins thought for a moment.

"Well, if it's all about risk, I'm the leader, the shot-caller. If we get caught, it's not the same risk all around. And Madrigal, the man who'll pull the trigger, it's not the same for him either."

"How about this? You and Madrigal get three apiece, and me and Ham'll get two. We can *live* with that."

Five minutes later, Collins called Madrigal to check status.

"I've got a shot, but it's not a good shot—right when she comes out the door, from about three to ten feet out, no more. If I don't get it, make sure Cunningham is close enough to back me up."

Inside, DHS office supervisor Shawn Tillis had retired to a private office, where he phoned his supervisor. He resented the idea of Destiny going over his head, and though he did not believe her story about having personal information vital to the President, he could not afford to be wrong. What if she was telling the truth? In his experience at Homeland Security, he could not suspend credibility on any possibility. Stranger stories and theories had proven true.

When he explained the story to his supervisor, Cheryl, she first wanted to confirm the detainee was Destiny Mitchell, women's rights advocate and director of the *Aegis Foundation*. He told Cheryl about Destiny's appearance, with a shaven head, dressed like a man, and about her explanation for causing the dangerous incident: a secret army had pursued her from Travis Air Force Base to New York to stop her from talking to the President, and members of this same army waiting in the terminal, ready to murder her.

As he shared Destiny's story about the secret murders of seventy-five San Quentin Death Row inmates and an FBI agent, about her husband working for the Pentagon and about how they were killing her best friend, Cheryl laughed to herself.

"Did you have her drug tested? She's obviously having an episode. Jeez, anyone can have a bad day, but my God—and it's *really* Destiny Mitchell? She needs psychiatric help."

Tillis returned to the detention room with further justification for arrogance and further condescension. Contemptuous, he smiled toward Destiny.

"Well, I talked to my supervisor, and she didn't think it was worth her *while* to talk to you. She felt *sorry* for you, actually. Suffice it to say, I don't think anyone is going to take the time to bother Natalie Sterling with this nonsense. And I'm sorry I have to break this to you, but there's no way in Hell anyone, in the interest of national security, would let a batshit crazy person like you get within fifty miles of the President."

"But I'm telling you the *truth!*"

He scoffed.

"You went over my head, and now the ceiling's come down on yours. You are under arrest, Ms. Mitchell. You have no further recourse."

Vindicated, Tillis smiled toward his audience.

"Let me tell you what happens now, Destiny. We're transferring you to our complex in Washington D.C., where you'll be drug-tested and evaluated before the government files formal criminal charges against you. We've got transportation in route."

Two hours later, at three a.m., the driver called Tillis to announce his arrival. Summoning four security guards, the supervisor gave final instructions.

"We'll take her out to the van where I'll sign transfer papers, and two of you will accompany her to the transfer location. Let's go."

Guards leading the way, the group had traveled only a few feet from the door when the rifle shot echoed in the distance, followed by a hollow thud and an explosion that spattered warm blood in all directions. Shawn Tillis, eyes widened, fell dead to the ground, blood still gushing from his skull.

In the panic and confusion that ensued, two additional shots rang out—this time from a position much closer, and Destiny dropped beside him. Acting on instinct, two guards drew their weapons, taking up defensive positions, while the others dragged the inert, mortally wounded bodies back into the complex, slamming the doors shut before making a frantic emergency call for backup.

Chapter 36

The response was immediate. Within minutes, the area around the Home Security field office was swarming with police cars, unmarked government-issued vehicles and two crime scene vans. The FBI was quick to set up a perimeter and strategic checkpoints, while supporting Homeland Security's Visible Intermodal Prevention and Response Team, as they began a systematic search within the terminal.

Within thirty minutes, the four remaining NWA soldiers had already transferred their weapons into a van in a long-term parking garage, exchanging duffle bags for luggage and camouflage gear for casual wear before entering the terminal. The strategy was to go *up* rather than out. In two to three weeks, after the initial investigation was exhausted of anger and outrage, a driver would come back to pick up the van.

There were tense moments in the night as the DHS team worked through the terminal and gates, questioning males of military age. A suspicious, aggressive agent questioned two of Collins's soldiers in separate instances, but their cover stories held until they departed early morning. Team leader Collins was the last to fly out. He was headed for Denver, where he would arrange ground transportation to Buckley Air Force Base in Aurora. From there, he would take a military hop to Gowen Field in Idaho and a helicopter from there to Wolf's estate outside Tetonia.

Collins and NWA soldiers did not risk conversations or phone calls during their time at the airport and would maintain communications silence for one week by protocol. They were certain the government was listening in for any conversation or text that would reveal information about the incident. It was a direct attack against America on U.S. soil that threatened the administration's confidence in the intelligence community.

Cheryl Sommerset, the DHS supervisor over Shawn Tillis, who was the supervisor slain in front of his field office—Cheryl struggled to answer questions from the Secretary of DHS and other administration officials, who wondered why she had not taken the warning from the detainee more seriously. While one investigator suggested Sommerset had been derelict in discharging her responsibility as a supervisor, another castigated her for gossiping about the incident to others in her office, reminding her, "Their blood is on your hands, and no one will ever forget that."

By the time Collins arrived at Gowen Field, an Army National Guard facility located next to the Boise International Airport, it was late morning. From the helipad, he returned Wolf's call.

"Mission accomplished, Sir."

"I am hearing disturbing news from friends, Victor. What happened?"

"Sir, I'd rather not. Not on the phone."

"I have waited all night! And this is a secure line. I am receiving questions from colleagues, and I have no answers! Talk to me now. The helicopter is on its way."

Collins hesitated. In his experience, every time he ignored protocol, the result was not a good one. But Wolf was volatile and irritable, so Collins could not ignore the order.

"It's a mixed bag, Sir. The bad news, we killed the office supervisor. He was bald and black, with a moustache—similar in appearance to the image we had for Destiny Mitchell. So, when he came out behind the guards, Madrigal, two hundred meters away, checked the image and thought it was her. Clean kill, wrong person."

"And Destiny Mitchell?"

"We had Cunningham stationed thirty meters away for backup. He got a better look, but the shot was limited. After the supervisor went down, Mitchell's body turned his way, and he *got* her. He hit her twice, center mass, one straight through the heart."

Her phone rang seven times at four in the morning, but she was too tired to answer. When it rang again at six, she picked up too late. Kiyomi was worried about Destiny, who promised to call as soon as she got to Washington. When they returned, the guards who drove her to the airport said she got away safely aboard her flight, but fourteen hours had passed with no contact. It was odd for Destiny.

When the phone rang again at noon, Kiyomi answered the unknown number with a degree of apprehension.

"Destee?"

"No, Kiyomi, it's Cornell Cotton," the husky male voice answered.

"Okay, so how did you get my private number?"

"Bryan gave me all your numbers, in case of an emergency."

She recognized the tone of unspoken condolence in his voice.

"What? Is there some emergency? Is Destiny okay? What's going on?"

"I hate that I'm the person to break this to you, Kiyomi, and I wish I were there to tell you in person, but Destiny is dead. She was killed last night outside the Homeland Security office at JFK. I'm sorry."

"No! No! You're lying!"

She had already begun to weep.

"You're lying, you *bastard!*"

"I wish I were. They're trying to keep it *hush-hush*, but people are talking about it all over the intelligence community. New World Army— they attacked a federal agency on federal property, also killing a DHS supervisor. Of course, that means the government will have to retaliate, hit them back even harder. It'll be a secret war."

Kiyomi could not even comprehend what Cotton was saying. She felt a sinking sense of *déjà vu*. Losing Bryan was bad enough! Losing him was hard enough to accept. *But Destiny!* To accept that she was dead was impossible. It just could not be true!

"How do you *know* she's dead?"

"I saw the video. The team that went after her—they taped it so they could collect a bounty. It's out there. I could send it to you—"

"No!" she sobbed. "No, I don't *want* to see it!"

"Kiyomi—"

"Why!" she blustered in a tortured, guttural tone. "*Oh God!*"

Cotton thought he heard the corporal thud of Kiyomi's body as it collapsed to the floor, and then there was silence."

The 60-S Knighthawk helicopter lifted from the pad with a jerk and climbed at a steep angle over ten miles until it reached a height of six thousand feet. The pilot chose a cruising altitude that would mitigate the effects of swelling updrafts rising from the foothills, which gradually morphed into mountains. Arriving a few minutes after two o'clock p.m., he was late picking up Commander Collins, who was irritated and fatigued, after having been awake for the better part of thirty-two hours. Strapped to the seat, he nodded as the aircraft changed course due east to fly directly across forests, mountains and a vast wilderness.

Between sleep and wake, Victor Collins thought of his ex-wife, son and two daughters, who had betrayed him. He thought of how much they would regret the choice they made, the Hell they had put him through. *Bastard!*

On his third tour of duty in Afghanistan, his former high school best friend moved in with his wife and kids. Victor had no idea how long the affair had been going on, and the home wrecker had no idea how close he had come to catching a bullet between the eyes. Yet, instead of being ashamed and sorry for cheating, his wife was brazen, calling him an abuser and a drunk while turning the kids against him. *The kids even started callin that back-stabbin asshole "Daddy!"*

But they would all be sorry, especially when Collins rolled back into his old Nashville neighborhood in a brand-new Centennial Edition Chevy Corvette, bought and paid for with cash, a mere fraction of the three million dollars in his bank account. And he would buy the biggest and best house in the county. He would get a better wife, younger, a former beauty queen, and raise a new, better family.

A former Army Ranger, Collins filed a Post-Traumatic Stress Disorder claim after being honorably discharged, but his receiving free government money made him feel like a loser, a taker. So, he joined the New World Army, a private international military personnel contractor, to work for a living.

For the last year, Collins and his men were on assignment to Helmut Wolf, who along with friends, paid the NWA an amount in the hundreds of millions to lease the equivalent services of a military infantry division, roughly 7,200 soldiers, including commissioned and non-commissioned officers, warrant officers and other administrative personnel. Collins would retire for a second time from the military in comfort and glory, as a multi-millionaire.

By the time the rotary aircraft entered Madison County airspace, however, the pilot nudged the dozing captain, concern evident in his voice.

"*Now* might be time to worry a little bit."

Startled awake, Collins glanced around.

"What?"

"Behind us. Gunfighters from the 366th, F-16s. They've been back there for at least a half hour."

"What do they want?"

"I don't know, but it ain't friendly."

Collins unfastened his restraints and looked back, spotting the fighters.

"Did you try to hail them?"

"No response. Where are you coming from, soldier? What was your last mission?"

Collins sighed. *He knew the phone conversation with Wolf was a mistake!*

"Goddammit! Gotta figure they're back there for a reason. Can't you set this thing *down*? Can't you turn around and fight?"

"No way! I'll just keep flying and hope it's just intimidation. They've done this before."

When the helicopter reached Teton County, the jetfighters closed to a distance of one mile.

"Uh-oh. They've never done *that* before!"

In the distance, Collins and the pilot were just able to see Wolf's estate, nestled on the eastern side of a steep mountain slope. It was less than five miles away. Just then, the pilot gasped and exclaimed.

"Oh my God! They're arming weapons! They're going to shoot us down! Just for a *show*? Goddammit Collins! What the hell have you *done*?"

Missiles away, neither had time to say another word. Frozen in fear, neither could even draw a breath.

The midair explosion was loud and spectacular, with a brilliant orange pillar of flames and huge plumes of snaking black smoke, which remained suspended in the sky for several minutes, a warning to Helmut Wolf below, who was no doubt watching the show.

"I came right away because I was concerned about you. Are you okay?"

"No, I am *not* okay! You told me that my best friend in the world, a part of my heart, my soul—you told me my best friend, my sister, is dead! Of *course* I'm not okay!"

Cornell Cotton sat in a chair next to the bed, head bowed, as Kiyomi continued to sob. He was surprised by how much weight she had lost, and apparently her face had been bruised as a result of her fainting. She appeared malnourished, sullen and pale, an ashen cast of her former self.

Cotton himself was sad. He did not know Destiny well, but he admired her for her unrelenting determination, tenacity and feistiness. She had fought a good fight, but she had been up against insurmountable odds. No one could have overcome the sheer power and resources of the hidden opponents she faced. But there was still hope.

Cotton reached over and clasped Kiyomi's hand.

"I came today because I was worried about you, but I also came because I want to make sure that Destiny, that Destiny *and* Bryan did not die in vain. I want to take up the fight where she left off."

Kiyomi paused, no longer crying.

"Why would *you* do that? Why would you insert yourself in the middle of this when you *know* how dangerous it is? *Every* person who's gotten in the way is either dead or dying. Destiny and I didn't have a choice, but you *do*. So why? I don't get it."

He bowed his head.

"Because I'm sick too. Somehow, they got to me. So it's only a matter of time before I'll be where you are. By trying to help Destiny, I got on the wrong side of these assholes. But before I go down, I want to do everything I can to make them pay for what they've done to all of us."

Kiyomi nodded, her eyes examining the man across from her.

"Okay. I get it now. I feel the same way."

Cotton smiled.

"Listen, Kiyomi. Destiny's dead. She can't fight any more. But you can help me fight these guys if you tell me what Grant told her. Whatever it was, it must have been some kind of secret that would make or break what all the bad guys are trying to do."

She sniffed and wiped a tear.

"Destiny told me there's only bad, by necessity, and worse. In this situation, there are no good people."

"Then I'm *bad*, which makes me a little better than worse. Kiyomi, you have to tell me what Grant told Destiny. If you carry that secret to your grave, you will hurt people and the future of America rather than helping."

He clasped her hand again.

"I'm going to Washington tonight to finish what Destiny started. We don't have much time. Please tell me what he told her."

Kiyomi bowed her head, contemplating. She was not sure if she could trust Cotton. Her gut informed against him. But with Destiny gone, it seemed all was lost. If there was any hope for her, it rested with Cornell Cotton, but...

"Okay, I'll tell you."

"You'll tell me what Grant told her?"

"Yes, and the truth of the matter is,"

She paused. Though Destiny was dead, could Kiyomi betray what she had promised her best friend?

"The truth is there *was* no secret. Grant was unintelligible that night, obviously incoherent and very sick, because he *died* two days later. He didn't tell her *anything*! The whole idea of this last moment revelation was a bluff. We bluffed all of you this whole time, so we could stay alive. Grant told Destiny nothing."

Department of Homeland Security Supervisor Cheryl Sommerset tipped into the room for the third time that afternoon. *Still no sign of life!* In all her experience she had never come across such an unbelievable story, with so many unexpected twists and intrigue. *Who in their right mind would have believed it?*

In the last twelve hours, Cheryl had to deal with a major aviation event at a busy New York airport, wild stories and an ultimatum from a lunatic, demanding to talk to the President of the United States. All that after a seditious attack on a field office that left a supervisor and close friend dead, and a reprimand—not to mention major job insecurity as a result of not believing it all.

In one day, she had gone from gatekeeper to goat, or scapegoat, as the day's big question involved the private message Destiny Mitchell had risked all to deliver to the President. What would happen if the message was never delivered? And in the wake of a resultant presidential assassination or some other national crisis, who would take the blame?

Cheryl knew the answer. For that reason, she left for work early and spent the morning at church with her pastor, praying for forgiveness and a good outcome. She was certain her prayers were on time-delay midway through the day. It had been her roughest day ever since she started with the department, probably the most stressful period of her life.

When she entered the room for the fourth time that day, a doctor was standing over the bed.

"How is she?"

"Heavily sedated for pain, but she's non-critical."

"How soon will she be able to talk?"

The doctor removed his glasses and squinted, thinking.

"Well, that depends on how much pain medication we give her. At this rate, twelve hours, eighteen max. If we scale back to half of what she's getting now? I would guess five to seven hours."

"What if you cut it *all* the way back, back to nothing?"

He flinched.

"*You mean* to *nothing*? She probably wouldn't *like* that, considering the nature of her injuries. I'm certain it's quite painful. Anyway, if we do that—when what's already in her system wears off, the pain will wake her up. It'll be an hour, maybe two."

"Then don't give her anything else, Doctor. Let her feel the pain. She *needs* to wake up."

The Secretary summoned Cheryl to the briefing room to take part in a conversation about the video recorded interview between Shawn Tillis and Destiny Mitchell. It took little research to confirm the seventy-five inmate deaths at the prison as well as those of the guards and Jake Martinez.

"Supervisor Tillis did not bother to check, and neither did you, especially in the wake of a major aviation incident at an international airport. What were you thinking?"

The story of deceased husband Bryan Osaka working with the Pentagon also checked out, and Jett Turner confirmed Destiny Mitchell and the *Chronicle* reporter had been in protective custody.

"I was going to personally check out everything she said, Ma'am. *That's* why I sent the transport to bring her here last night. It was just so bizarre a story, and she wanted to speak to the President. You *heard* her. She said it was a matter of national security, but something personal."

The Secretary, already three hours behind schedule due to the attack on the JFK Airport field office, seemed angry during closing remarks and finished with a warning.

"As it turns out, everything *else* Destiny Mitchell told Supervisor Tillis was the truth, and he mishandled the matter. Luck was on our side this time. In this business, second chances are rare..."

She made it a point to glance toward Cheryl, who cringed, humiliated, as the Secretary concluded.

"...for *anyone*."

Chapter 37

During the entire meeting, the tension in the darkened room was palatable. Justice Greene did his best to stay on script, but members of *The Committee* were understandably nervous. Two nights before, and at Mr. X's direction, NWA soldiers had attacked one of the offices of the Department of Homeland Security and killed a high value detainee, along with the facility supervisor. The wheels were coming off Mr. X's wagon, and members were desperate to take cover.

"Let's not rush to judgment, anyone," Greene advised. "We've been too patient all these many years to turn against each other in the end and miss the fulfillment of our grand ambition. It is a matter of *days* now, before we change and reshape the world, all of us. Mr. X has always been loyal to our committee, so rather than condemn or second guess his motives and actions, we should be grateful that he has been with us to see our *Viral Vector* project to fruition. The chair recognizes the gentleman from Wyoming."

"How many more people does Mr. X have to kill to before gettin this thing done? We've got a slew of dead bodies from California to New York."

Justice Greene raised his hand in a halting gesture.

"No one else has to die unnecessarily. As of this week, we have achieved complete containment, and the vector is working. In mere days, a profound dynamic of the presidential election will change. They won't know what hit them, and there will be too little time to react. *The Committee* will at last have its President and we will call the shots."

He nodded.

"Mr. R?"

The former White House Senior Advisor and Deputy Chief of Staff spoke in a supportive tone.

"I, for one, am excited at the prospect. It had been a long and arduous process, but the end crowns the work. I must ask, however, where is Mr. X *tonight*?"

The Justice paused for purpose, contemplative.

"I am sad to inform you, the government has trapped Mr. X at a remote residence he owns, accessible only by aircraft. By imposing a no-fly zone perimeter, they have in effect imprisoned him at his own estate. Of course, we're working on a solution. We're doing everything we can, but this latest incident at the JFK Home Security office has complicated things. They're holding him there as they try to build a case against him."

He sighed.

"All the more reason for a leadership change in my opinion. Mr. X is counting on us. Once we help elect Hugh Gordon, one of his first actions will be to free Mr. X, as well as righting a long list of wrongs perpetrated by the active administration."

Quiet all night, Hugh Gordon rose and removed his mask, clearing his throat, reacting to the gasps and sighs.

"Come now, all of you. This can't come as such a shock. I'm certain most of you knew my identity months ago, especially after the primary season began. I imagine you're more surprised I took the mask *off.*"

Anger actuated the Justice's voice.

"Replace your mask, Governor."

"I'm sorry. I just want to talk for a minute. I have an announcement to make to all of you. From the beginning, you've all thought we couldn't win this election based on a better candidate with better ideas. You've been cynical about the process and voters themselves, but in doing so you undermine the underpinnings of American democracy.

"I realize it's not a problem for most of you. After all, I'm one of you—we are all one-percenters, the best this country and the world have to offer. I believe in a plutocratic government, but more American people, somewhere along the way, have got to become involved. That means expanding and finding new ways to create more wealthy Americans at the expense of those who have no desire to better themselves. That is our biggest challenge over the next few years.

"I've been all over the country this summer and fall, talking to businesses and future entrepreneurs about how they can achieve wealth in America, and I was encouraged. These are the people who will make the difference in this election. These are the people responsible for my recent surge in the polls. I can win this election outright.

"If you abandon this plan against the President and believe in me and the strength of my ideas, we can accomplish the exact same goals, without the immoral implications of the *Viral Vector* project. Let the American people elect me, and I will lead."

Gordon bowed his head for a moment.

"But if you continue with this plan and elect me based on secret workings rather than faith, I will wait until one month after the inauguration, and then I will disqualify myself from my office. I will step down and allow my Vice President to serve in my place."

He nodded.

"*I know*. It's no surprise to me. It's what you had planned all along, Justice. Right? I didn't pick my running mate. You and your friends did—because you knew he couldn't win a national election based on his record and positions. It's your MO—the invisible hand. So, you don't have to murder me—I'll just walk away. I was just the necessary face and narrative."

He looked toward the other members.

"I *can* win this election on my own! *Your* choice."

Without replacing the mask, Hugh Gordon strode toward the door and, without looking back, exited the room.

Cheryl sat next to the bed where the patient writhed in agony and groaned aloud.

"Destiny, my name is Cheryl Sommerset. I work for the Department of Homeland Security. I was Shawn's supervisor. I understand you wanted to *speak* with me."

When Destiny turned toward the voice, it was obvious that the pain killers were wearing off and she was suffering. There were black circles under her eyes and her expression was blank. She wore a hospital robe over tight bandages, which bound her chest. She struggled to breathe.

"No, I need to talk to the *President*."

She cringed in agony as she inhaled.

"Uuhhh! I had a *bulletproof vest* on. It was supposed to *protect* me. What happened?"

"It *did* protect you. It's the only reason you're not dead. You were shot twice in the chest at near point-blank range. It's like a condom—you still *feel* it. You're lucky to be alive at all."

Destiny strained to find a comfortable position in the bed.

"So hard to breathe! Where am I?"

"Washington. You have four cracked ribs, a collapsed lung, a bruised sternum and diaphragm—a blessing compared to the alternative. You'll be recuperating for the next week or two. You need to rest."

Cheryl caressed Destiny's hand.

"I am so sorry this happened to you, and I'm sorry I didn't get the chance to speak with you that night. Honestly, I sent the transport because I wanted to talk to you in person."

She smiled, hoping to gain trust, and she leaned closer.

"What did you want to *tell* me that night?"

"I wanted to tell you Tillis was an asshole."

Cheryl backed.

"Now *that's* a rude thing to say. Tillis is dead."

"And he almost got me killed. Who is *your* supervisor?"

The very handsome and charismatic Devon Kirk, who replaced Sommerset, was not actually her supervisor, but was instead a Secret Service agent. Seating himself next to the bed, he offered a plastic cup containing ice chips.

"Nurse said you were a little dehydrated."

Destiny felt an insatiable thirst, a side-effect from the medication. Her lips were dry, peeling, as she grabbed the cup and filled her mouth with ice.

"Water?" he offered smiling, as he placed a clear, misted, ice water filled pitcher on the table.

"I read your file. You've been through Hell and back these last couple months. I don't know who else in the world could have handled what you've had to deal with. You're a hero in the truest sense of the word."

"No. I just need to talk to the President. Listen to me: I need for you to call Natalie Sterling—she's one of senior advisors and a trusted friend. She knew I would be coming."

Kirk nodded, indicating agreement, contradicted by his words.

"It's the end of election season. Ms. Sterling won't even be in Washington for the next few days, but I've arranged a conference call with her. I can set it up, and you'll be speaking with her in thirty minutes."

"No conference call. I need to speak with her directly. My message is for the President, and I'm not sharing it with anyone else. Natalie Sterling sent her upcoming itinerary to a friend of mine before I left. I saw it, so I *know* she's in town, which means you are a liar."

She gripped the bed sidebars, trying to pull herself up.

"I *need* to speak with Natalie Sterling! If you can't set it up for me, then *find* someone else who can!"

"Is that *it*?"

The President rolled down his shirt sleeve as he stood from the examination table, growing concerned.

"And?"

The doctor looked up from his notes.

"We've ran a battery of tests, based on studies conducted involving Rosecrans' research. Initially, we did not see any evidence of exposure, but the tests we ran today were much more sensitive at identifying the new vector used. Looks like there's been some exposure, based on antigens we're seeing."

"*Some* exposure?"

"Yes," the doctor nodded. "The viral vector he created—you've definitely been exposed to it, but so far, there is no indication of any DNA change on the genetic level."

"Okay, so what does that mean?" the President asked, glancing over at the chart in the doctor's hand.

"It means they tried to affect you with it, but they were unsuccessful. Your immune system apparently recognized the threat, destroyed it and created a backup file for future detection. You are not one hundred percent in the clear yet, but it looks like you'll survive the election."

He smiled.

"At least *physically*, that is."

Chapter 38

"Congratulations, Destiny Mitchell. The Secretary spoke with Natalie Sterling, and you will be going to the White House tonight."

Destiny sighed, relieved.

"To talk to the President?"

"No. To speak with Ms. Sterling, who you already know is one of the President's close senior advisors."

Kirk's voice took a playful tone.

"Don't look so disappointed. Isn't *that* what you were asking for? Isn't that what you demanded of Tillis, Sommerset and me? You wanted to talk to Natalie Sterling, and now you *got* that! You're *welcome*."

She rolled her eyes.

"Thank you."

"*There* you go! You're welcome. As I said, you'll be going to the White House tonight. Are you sure you're up for it?"

Destiny strained, groaning as she drew a deep, agonizing breath. Her face dripped with perspiration.

"Ready or not, I'm going."

"Easy now!"

Kirk caught her as she collapsed while attempting to stand.

"You're weak. You haven't eaten for two days. Come on, back in the bed."

He helped her adjust her position to lessen the searing pain in her side and chest.

"You just rest for now. I'll go out and get you something to eat. What would you like?"

"A sandwich. Maybe eggplant or portabella mushroom thing—something vegetarian."

"Sandwich, absolutely. You got it. Anything else?"

"I'll need clothes for the meeting, and shoes."

She caught a glance of herself in the mirror, prickly shadow on her scalp.

"And a wig. A decent outfit and a nice wig."

Alone and awake, Destiny located the adjustable bed hand controller, experimenting and eventually raising herself to a near sitting position. Without the medication, every movement was painful, and the catheter was uncomfortable. Straining, she tugged at the plastic tube *down there*, though it appeared something inside was holding it in place.

Another dose of morphine would have been helpful, but she could not afford the side effects, the nausea and dizziness. And worse, her mind felt foggy, as if there was a three second time delay between a physical stimulus and any possible reaction, except the pain, which had returned to real-time.

She did not feel hungry, but she thought eating would help strengthen her body and clear her mind for what threatened to be one of the most important conversations of her life. When she went for the phone, she realized she could not reach out or raise her arms. The pain was too intense. Four ribs were cracked, but her sternum and entire diaphragm were bruised. Instead, she pushed the "call" button and asked a nurse to dial the number.

"Kiyomi! It's me. How are you?"

"Destee? *Oh my God!*"

Kiyomi shut her eyes, saying a quick prayer of thanks.

"You're alive! They told me you got shot! He said you were dead!"

Destiny nodded toward the nurse, indicating she wanted privacy, and waited until she was alone to answer.

"I got shot twice, in the chest, but obviously I'm not dead. I was wearing a Kevlar vest," she whispered, straining to speak. "I have never been in so much pain in all my life! But I am safe. How are *you* doing?"

"Sleeping most of the day. I've just been really tired. On the real—I don't know how much longer it'll take, but I think I'm dying. How's the mission?"

"I have a meeting with Natalie Sterling tonight. She's the last step before I get to the President. I just need to make sure she understands how important this is."

Kiyomi cleared her throat, something she always did before speaking off record.

"Cornell Cotton—he's the one who told me you were dead. Said it came from the intelligence community, so I'm assuming people still think you're dead. Cotton came by here yesterday afternoon. I don't know if he was working me, but he said they got him with the viral vector too. Told me he was going to Washington to finish what you started."

"And he came all the way to Travis to tell you that? What did he *really* want?"

"He wanted me to tell him what Perseus Grant told you. With you dead, he said he needed to know that in order to continue the fight."

Destiny paused, concerned.

"What did you *tell* him?"

"I told him Grant told you nothing. I told him we were bluffing the entire time."

"Did he believe you?"

"I don't know, but you're alive. What Cotton does with it remains to be seen."

When Kirk returned two hours later with the red and yellow brand-emblazoned bag, Destiny knew she should have been more specific.

"What is that?"

"You said you wanted a sandwich."

She groaned.

"Since *when* is a hamburger a sandwich? I said I wanted *vegetarian*."

"It's *chicken* by the way, with lettuce, pickles, onions, tomatoes, ketchup—what are those?"

Based on his performance on the sandwich assignment, she was afraid to open the garment bag, but she was pleasantly surprised by the outfit that he had put together. JC Penny notwithstanding, it was a smart teal pantsuit, with matching loafers. It was even the right size. Kirk had even accessorized, probably because he had help from some salesperson on commission.

"Did you get the wig?"

"Right *here*."

She recoiled. It was platinum blond, designed in a Marilyn Monroe "Bob" style. Destiny thought it was a nice wig, *for someone else!*

"Thank you, but I can't wear that! You have to go back out and get me something else, something *black*."

"No-can-do. You have exactly ten minutes of Ms. Sterling's time, two hours from now, and there's traffic. We can't afford to be late. Besides, I think you'll look great as a blonde."

As Kirk ate across from her, Destiny got an impression she had met him before, and then it hit her. He bore an uncanny resemblance to Charles Covington III, her former fiancé, a former colonel who had jilted her, marrying another woman, during the middle of the Jordan Alexander murder trial.

She wondered if it was a mere coincidence or if someone had researched her personal history and put Kirk in place for strategic purposes. She thought he was good-looking and charming, but she raised her guard nonetheless.

"I understand you lost your husband. I'm sorry to hear that. I lost my wife about a year ago to lymphoma. Not the same thing, but a loss is a loss."

Destiny thought of Bryan, and her focus returned.

"When you live and die on your principles, there is nothing to regret. My husband was willing to die for something he believed, and so am I."

She recoiled when he took her trembling hand, threatening to draw the hand back, but his gentle, warm touch felt good to her, it comforted her, renewed her courage.

"I don't know you, Destiny, but I've read enough of your story. I believe in *you*, whatever you're trying to do, and I hope you're successful. When it's all over, if we're still standing, I would really appreciate the chance to be your friend."

She smiled. He seemed sincere enough.

"Thank you. Can I ask you a question?"

"You can *ask*."

"Do you think they'll let me speak to the President, in your honest opinion?"

"In my *honest* opinion? I've been at this for a while. You've got three things going against you: one, he's really busy with the election coming up, two, *you* can't be definite with anyone about this *thing* you need to tell him, and then there's the terrorist incident on the plane two days ago. Never in a million years."

Chapter 39

The outfit looked better on the hanger. It was the difference between designer clothing and store brands. The pants just did not fit right, especially in the waist area. Always the same problem: if they fit her butt, the waist was too big. When the waist was a fit, she was lucky to get the garment up her thighs, let alone over her butt. She was out of sorts. Kirk did not get any socks and she forgot to tell him she needed a bra. Fortunately, one thoughtful, plus-sized nurse named Jessie Pearl had an overnight bag in her car that contained undergarments and toiletries.

Destiny was growing accustomed to the pain of being in an upright position, though rotation in any direction or any major muscle movement sent shivers of sharp agony toward her spine. The nurse helped her take a seated shower and get dressed.

Because Destiny could barely raise her arms, she asked Jessie Pearl to help with applying deodorant, brushing teeth, putting on makeup and securing the wig. Standing before the mirror, she tried to clear her head and regain control of her thoughts, but her mind was still foggy. *She had to be on her game for the meeting!*

"Wow! Do you look stunning or what? Is this the same woman I left an *hour* ago?"

Devon Kirk circled, inspecting her. By this time, he had changed into formal attire, a silky black suit, a pink shirt and skinny black tie. He effused warm, musky essences from the cologne he wore.

"That's a nice look for you. It says, 'professional, serious, credible.' It says, 'you need to *understand the words that are coming out of my mouth.*'"

"It's, it's not me, but does it work?"

"It works for me, but I'm not Natalie Sterling."

Destiny sighed.

"What do you *know* about her?"

"Professional, serious, credible. She's known the President since before he ever considered politics, so they're close. She's fiercely protective and territorial. She'll probably see you as a threat— you know, that *woman* thing."

"How do I diffuse that? How do I make her see me as an ally?"

Kirk thought for a moment.

"I don't know. You might want to play to her protectionism. If she thinks you know something that threatens to injure him, she'll want to know, but any more than that, she'll move to protect him, whatever it takes."

"Is she proud? Or vain?"

"Practical is more like it. She's given you ten minutes, but if she doesn't consider you to be credible and relative, she'll have you out of there in two."

From the street view, it seemed smaller than she imagined it would be, set back three hundred feet off Pennsylvania Avenue. Destiny always wanted to take a White House tour, but she had always been too busy. Inured to public life and displays of wealth, there was not much that impressed her, but the experience that night was dreamlike, beginning with the motorcade ride through the tall gates. Maybe it was the drugs.

She had trouble standing from the limousine and walked slowly through the parking garage beside her tall, muscular and handsome escort. From the moment the elevator doors opened on the first floor, she was mesmerized, a sort of visual sensory overload. She stopped several times on the way to the Red Room, amazed at the intricate industry involved in the tiniest details of everything she examined.

The Red Room itself was so elaborate that it appeared virtual rather than real. Inside the rich, gleaming parlor, Louis XVI style clock, ticking in metronome fashion, there was not one speck of dust, not one smudge, not one fingerprint, not one item out of place. It was as if she had stepped into a computer-generated holographic world.

The manifestations of red and gold had never been so awe-inspiring. The Empire style sofa and other furniture was upholstered in carmine red silk, with a pattern of gold designs, complementing cerise red of the walls and draperies, elaborate swags and jabots of red, with gold medallions and tassels. A gold, thirty-six-branched   French   chandelier   hung   overhead, illuminating a large, gilded portrait of Angela Singleton Van Buren, which hung above the mantel. An elaborate, French bronze *bouillotte* lamp sat on a table, next to the place she stood. At Kirk's prompting, Destiny sat on the sofa, trying to still her mind.

Strangely, in that instant she thought of the moment she watched Supervisor Tillis' head explode, spattering her face with hot, bright crimson blood and bits of skull, the gold and scarlet in his bloody mouth, the glint from the gilded jewelry. She remembered the distinct smell of his dispersed brain. She next remembered the blow to her right side, feeling like she had been slammed by a huge sledgehammer, and then the blow that threatened to explode her chest, before she passed out.

Sitting there, she gave more thought to Deuteronomy Saint Claire's words. *In Washington, there's bad—by necessity, and there's only worse.* He had added that the only way to survive was to suspend morality. She considered his advice as she thought about what she would say to Presidential Senior Advisor Natalie Sterling to make her case. She had done more than a hundred closing statements in her career as a prosecutor, but this was the first time she would be arguing to save herself and everything she held dear. Never had the stakes been so high.

Destiny had been waiting ten minutes before she heard the distinctive cadence of unhurried high heels women's' shoes on the wooden floor. Upon her entrance, Natalie Sterling's bearing was serious, bordering on impatient. She wore a beautifully tailored burgundy skirt suit, probably a St. John's knit, with a frilled, ivory blouse. Her sheer stockings hinted a shadow, and the footwear was definitely Guiseppe Zanotti.

Natalie was an older woman, probably in her mid-to-late fifties, though she looked much younger. Her face was well-ordered, hinting that she had been very pretty in her youth. Yet she was quite accomplished. According to Destiny's research, Natalie received her B.A. from Stanford University and earned a law degree at USC. In her professional life, she worked in the banking and finance industry, eventually starting up her own lucrative enterprise called Pragmatic Solutions, where she was CEO.

Her political career began as chief-of-staff for the mayor of Los Angeles, where she made many powerful contacts and began lifelong friendships. While at the mayor's office, she met the future President, who had recently graduated Harvard Law School, *summa cum laude*. From the beginning, she called it. She saw the promise in him and correctly predicted that given time, a well-planned trajectory, a little polish and prominent backers, he would go on to accomplish great things.

She took great pains and risks, sacrificing to nurture his ambition, and when he became President, he asked her to work for him, to be the one person who would provide practical advice he could rely upon. It was a trust she took seriously, considering it an honor to be so respected by him.

As she entered the Red Room, she eyed Destiny's cheap, poorly fitted outfit and the obvious wig, at once scoring her low points in an initial assessment. And although she remembered Destiny from her work with *Aegis* and television appearances, she knew public images often belied private foibles and shortcomings. Destiny did not rise upon Natalie's entrance—another deduction. The White House policy maven took a seat in one of the chairs across from her guest, crossing her sculpted legs.

"Ms. Mitchell, thank you for coming. I am very busy. The President asked me to speak with you. Apparently, you think whatever you have to tell him is so important that it justified hijacking a Boeing 767 airliner, resulting in a federal employee shot dead and others wounded. What is it you have to say? Tell me, so I can tell him."

Feeling self-conscious about her appearance, Destiny adjusted her blouse and answered.

"Deuteronomy Saint Claire told me you knew his wife, that you could *help* me. Please, I know something that the President needs to know. You have got to get me to him to tell him."

Natalie sighed, incredulous.

"Yes, I knew Dr. Katrina Scott-Saint Claire—she was my best friend at one time, but Ms. Mitchell, that's not how things work here. You can't just walk in this place and talk to the President. No one can. He personally tasked me to find out what you are going on about so I can share it with him. The only way from here: you tell me, and then I tell him. Otherwise, you're wasting your time... and *mine*. So, you are either going to share what you know, or you're going to leave right now, and that will be the end of this business."

After a pause, Natalie concluded, irritation in her voice.

"Very well. It's obvious you have nothing important to share. Mr. Kirk, can you please escort Ms. Mitchell back to DHS? I have things to do."

Before rising, Natalie spoke in an undertone.

"And to think I used to *admire* you!"

Destiny held her place.

"You can get up and leave if you want, Ms. Sterling, but it's *you* who'll have to deal with the tragic consequences, especially when the facts come out and *you* are on the wrong side of those facts."

Natalie hesitated and relaxed back into her seat.

"What facts?"

"Three months ago, a dying inmate from San Quentin, a man by the name of Perseus Grant told me something that the President needs to know, and I've gone through *hell* getting here, so no—it's not something I'm going to just pass off to you so you can pat me on my head and send me on my way. I need to talk to *him*! The President!"

Natalie sighed.

"What could a condemned inmate possibly know concerning the President?"

"Look it up. Perseus Grant was a government *experiment* who eventually landed on Death Row, but he remained connected to a network of other 'experiments' with resources, some top secret, some underground. When Grant told the network that Death Row inmates were dying at San Quentin in unprecedented numbers, the entire network started doing research and came back with key details about a shocking plan. Based on what they sent him, Grant and a guard, Sutter, another 'experiment,' did additional investigation and uncovered a secret sub-plan. Grant shared the most important detail of that secondary plot with me alone before he was murdered."

Natalie thought for a moment.

"Two problems with your story: one, why would anyone trust information coming from a condemned rapist and murderer who is dead? And two, I already know about Grant's past experience with the government, but the idea of him telling you about a key detail, I think you're making that up. So, Ms. Mitchell, why are you doing this? What do you want from the President? You're only incriminating yourself."

Natalie glanced over at Kirk, reluctant to reveal personal information about her boss.

"And just to be clear: the President knows about the *Viral Vector* project, and he already knows he was the "White House" target. They tried to use the vector on him, but they *failed*. After three comprehensive medical examinations, doctors said he has no trace of heart disease. Trust me, he'll survive the election."

Destiny could feel her presence of mind returning.

"So *that's* it. You're going to walk out on what I have to tell the President, based on your smug perception of my credibility and what *you* think is true? That, after you *know* I was telling the truth about the murders at the prison? And about the assassins at the airport? *And* about my murdered husband working with the Pentagon? Do I need to go on here? You don't believe Grant *told* me anything?"

Natalie was cool.

"No, I don't."

"Why not?"

"Because I have it on good authority that you and the reporter have been bluffing all along, that Grant never told you anything at all relating to the President. He was almost dead when he called you. You were bluffing. Your reporter friend Yamakita admitted as much."

Destiny feigned an expression of betrayal.

"You have a *source* who told you that?"

"Yes."

"And you are willing to bank your entire reputation, your career and your relationship with the President on what that source had to tell you?"

Natalie's voice carried less certainty and confidence.

"Yes."

"I don't think you want to do that. First of all, I can tell you who your 'on good authority' source is. His name's *Cornell Cotton*! You can deny it if you want, but he's the *only* person in the world that information could have come from, which means that in the event of a national tragedy, *you* will definitely be on the wrong side of the facts. I'll make sure of that."

"Meaning?"

Upon Destiny's suggestion, Natalie asked Kirk to leave the room before the discussion continued. Destiny spoke in a low tone.

"Meaning that Cornell Cotton, like Jettson Turner, plays on both sides of the ball, for whatever reasons they do it. Maybe the government already knows, but maybe they *don't*. Saint Claire told me, *in Washington, the closer you get to the President, the harder it is to tell the bad guys from the worse guys*. He said they'll all look and sound the same. What do you think about that?"

"I think you have a very cynical friend in Detective or Professor Deuteronomy Saint Claire, whatever he is. Definitely a smart man, but trust me, he has issues."

"Ms. Sterling, I happen to know that Cornell Cotton at some time worked for the same people who are behind this plot *against* the President. So, if the plot is successful, then your association with Cotton makes you suspect, if not complicit. Tell me—are you in fact part of the plot? Are you one of the worse guys?"

Defensive, Natalie crossed her arms.

"That suggestion is ridiculous!"

"Kiyomi Yamakita only *told* Cotton we were bluffing to test his motives, and he went straight to you with it. But he's the same man who was part of *The Committee's* containment for the *Viral Vector* project and the White House plot from the beginning. I have proof of that. Kiyomi *lied* to Cotton and to Cotton alone yesterday, and just now you *repeated* that lie. Tell me, Ms. Sterling, how well do you know Cornell Cotton? Are you going to tell me you haven't talked to him recently?"

Natalie silent, Destiny sighed.

"Do you *really* want to go down that road? I might not be able to prove anything, but it'll be a bumpy ride for you, and for your relationship with the President—something we all want to avoid."

Destiny paused to allow contemplation.

"Believe me, Ms. Sterling, time is of the essence. I need to speak with the President right *now!*"

Five minutes later, seething Presidential Senior Advisor Natalie Sterling returned to the room.

"The President is very busy, involved in preparation for the upcoming debate. However, he is making arrangements to meet with you aboard Air Force One before he flies to Indiana for the contest. You will have three minutes to tell him about this mysterious secondary plot that only *you* can share with him. For your sake, it better be pretty damned spectacular!"

"It is. You'll thank me later, Natalie."

"And Destiny, if you're going to talk to the President, you need to get out of those tired clothes and that silly wig."

She glanced toward Kirk, mock rolling her eyes in disapproval, contemptuous of the fashion disaster she knew he had perpetrated.

"This time, we'll send out my *professional* shopper, to find you something more appropriate for the occasion."

Chapter 40

"I am beginning to believe I have been betrayed by you. You say the target has been infected and is ailing, and yet when I turn on the television, I see the opposite! I see good health!"

"You see the *appearance* of good health, for show, for political purposes. I assure you the vector is working on an accelerated level now. We will see results in eight days, a true October surprise!"

Helmut Wolf remained under siege at his Tetonia mountain fortress mansion in Idaho. He was trapped, along with his mistress, estate staff and sixteen New World Army special operations soldiers. His massive arsenal of weapons, helicopters and armored vehicles were no match against the United States military, who patrolled regularly and blocked outgoing and wireless communications twenty-four hours a day. Two soldiers had deserted a day earlier, while many others began to consider self-preservation.

Incoming calls were rare, as Driscoll and the other billionaires had abandoned Wolf altogether. Even members of *The Committee* who supported Wolf were loath to call in, risking further government scrutiny. Justice Wendell Greene had been the exception. He called at least once a day to check the status of his portfolio investment, which Wolf detailed in codes and language meant to covertly communicate information about the status of the plan.

Wolf had called for a meeting of committee members at his Idaho estate to discuss post-election considerations. Certainly, the government would not be brazen enough to shoot down defenseless planes or helicopters that carried influential former and current government officials.

Committee members, however, did not want to risk identity or the possibility that the President was actually angry enough to do just that, especially after Osaka's revelation that the President was the target of a seditious plot. None would take the risk, except Justice Greene, whose helicopter was closely followed by F-16 Gunfighters, but never fired upon.

Emboldened by the result, Wolf invited others to support and visit him at his estate. No one else, however, was foolish or bold enough to venture to the remote Idaho mountain location, especially since it appeared Greene was trapped as well. Unable to return to Washington until after the government's investigation of Wolf was over, Justice Greene was forced to tell Supreme Court associate justices and staff that he was taking a week or so off for "medical reasons."

Wolf had hoped to get enough notable people to his home to form a sort of human shield around him, so he would be able to escape within their mist. Even the active government was limited in its ability to retaliate and assassinate. In the event it did, no one would be able to explain the suspicious disappearances and deaths of so many influential people, all at one time. To Wolf's dismay, only one friend had obliged him, and Greene was irritated about the deception.

"You told me there would be others, and now I'm *trapped* up here, exposed, among other things, as the only person remaining who is foolish enough to associate with you. For your sake and mine, we better hope your vector does its job!"

Seated at the table across from Greene in the spacious formal dining room, Wolf sipped the last of the wine in his glass.

"I am now reminded of a quote by Goethe. It is something my father always told me, on the nature of risk.

Rest not. Life is sweeping by.
Go and dare before you die.
Something mighty and sublime,
leave behind to conquer time."

Justice Greene listened and shook his head, regretting much.

"And if *you* leave nothing behind, it will be because you were arrogant and rash. You underestimated the intelligence, resourcefulness and resolve of Destiny Mitchell."

"Yes, I underestimated her, but I finally *got* her. Thank *God* she is dead!"

Destiny was already dressed when Devon Kirk arrived with the courier, two hours before departure. After the meeting with Natalie Sterling, Destiny and Kirk had returned to the Department of Homeland security, where she had spent the night. At noon, she was scheduled to fly to Nellis Air Force Base in Nevada. Kirk would accompany her to a checkpoint on the tarmac, and Secret Service would escort her aboard Air Force One. In the conference room on the world's most sophisticated aircraft, she would have three minutes to change the course of history.

The courier held a Saks Fifth Avenue garment bag and a Neiman Marcus shopping bag, containing two boxes.

"Ms. Mitchell—compliments of Ms. Sterling at the White House."

Destiny halted the courier as she tried to enter the room.

"Stop right there. Please tell Ms. Sterling *thanks, but no thanks.* I'm already dressed."

Embarrassed by the perceived insult, Kirk tried to intervene.

"Destiny, you two got off on the wrong foot, but Ms. Sterling obviously went through the trouble and expense to help you look good for your meeting. The *least* you could do would be to acknowledge her gesture of goodwill. It's a *gift*—be gracious enough to accept it."

Ignoring Kirk, Destiny spoke to the courier.

"Tell Ms. Sterling I would rather meet the President barefoot and in gunnysack than trust the person who shops for her. I would rather take my chances with JC Penney or Wal-Mart than risk looking like her, which is tawdry, shameful and age inappropriate. *Exact words!*"

Kirk interjected.

"No, Destiny. That's just wrong! Natalie is a Senior Advisor to the *President*. You can't return her kindness with personal insults."

"But I can, and I just did. You obviously have a lot to learn about women."

She glanced toward the courier as she turned to exit into the bedroom, calling back to Kirk.

"You don't believe me? Just open the bag yourself. I need to go over my notes."

Upon unzipping the garment bag, Kirk discovered a velour leopard miniskirt, a sheer sleeveless blouse with a plunging neckline and bare midriff, and frilly crotchless panties. The bag with the boxes contained a pink wig, clear-heeled, five-inch stripper stilettos and black fishnet stockings.

When Destiny returned fifteen minutes later, the courier was gone and Kirk still seemed mystified. She smiled.

"I *know* women like her. If I had relied on her kindness, I wouldn't be meeting with the President at all, and I would have been stuck with whatever outfit she chose for me. Ninety minutes out, she knew it would be too late for me to get anything else. Instead, I took the time to make the best with what I had. I made adjustments to the outfit *you* bought, which is better than what *she* was wearing."

An hour later, Destiny and Devon Kirk sat aboard a mid-sized jet, headed for a private landing strip at McCarran International Airport in Clark County, Nevada. Destiny's trembling hands belied her calm demeanor as she closed her eyes, concentrating on her talking points. She worried that he would not listen, or that he would be dismissive. She focused her breathing, meditating before offering a desperate prayer.

An hour before landing, Kirk reached over and grasped her hand, smiling, an answer to her silent request.

"He changed his itinerary specifically to meet with you. He's going to listen."

The jet touched down a little after noon under overcast October skies and taxied to a location where three military jeeps awaited its arrival. Without luggage or a purse, with only the clothes on her back, Destiny followed Kirk to the middle vehicle and rode with him to Nellis Air Force Base, fifteen miles away. At the airfield on-base, the procession stopped at a remote, well-guarded security checkpoint. In the distance, the huge VC-25A, a Boeing 747 200B-series aircraft, emblazoned "United States of America," along with the American flag and the Presidential seal, sat on the runway, engines idling. At the edge of the horizon, the second of two C141 military cargo planes crept upward.

Kirk seemed notably more formal in his bearing.

"Ms. Mitchell, this is as far as I go with you. Good luck."

When she smiled, he merely nodded and stared straight ahead. Another Secret Service agent passed a detection wand along her body and used a second device for her face and head. A third agent helped her into the jeep, which took off with a jolt.

"I'm sorry, Ma'am," the driver said while accelerating. "We're two minutes behind schedule. Air Force One will take off in three minutes, regardless of whether or not you're on it."

Destiny was stunned at the thought of actually being *on* the flight, as she imagined the hurried meeting would take place on the runway in the final minutes before the President flew out. Jeep barreling toward the plane, she hoped the delay would not postpone the meeting for the day or even one hour! Very soon, the plot against the President would become unstoppable.

Chapter 41

Within a minute after the aircraft door was closed, the massive jet turned and began its sprint toward the sky. Sequestered in guest quarters aboard the plane, Destiny waited, practicing the words she would say. On the way to her seat, she passed a dozen reporters who were accompanying the campaign, one of whom she personally knew, but he did not recognize her as a blonde.

When she asked a steward for a vegetable sandwich, he returned with grilled portabella mushrooms and tomato slices on wheat. The plate looked great, but she was too nervous to eat. According to the jeep driver, it would be a two-hour flight. On-line, one network indicated the President was engaged in last minute preparations for the fourth and final debate. As the minutes went by and the first hour yielded to the second, she became less hopeful. Perhaps he would have time to talk after the debate was over.

"Ms. Mitchell, you will have exactly five minutes."

The Secret Service agent led her out the room and along a corridor on the left side of the aircraft.

"Where are we going?"

"The White House."

The President was seated at his desk writing when Destiny stepped through the door. Hearing her entrance, he looked up, smiled and motioned.

"Destiny Mitchell—please, sit down. I'm sorry to take you so far out of your way, but we were running behind schedule. We'll get you home. Welcome to my office."

She winced in pain as she sat, quickly glancing about the spacious presidential suite, an airborne Oval Office.

"Thank you, Mr. President. It's an honor."

"I've done a little reading up on you recently," he said, looking up. "You've obviously gone through a great degree of peril and personal sacrifice to reach me. I see here your daughter was shot, your husband, a federal agent, was murdered, you have lived under threats to your life... And you were shot, twice. By all accounts, you're dead. Yet in spite of all that, you've come here to tell me a 'condemned though now deceased' inmate from San Quentin provided you with some information that is very crucial to me?"

"Yes," she nodded. "What Perseus Grant told me didn't make sense initially, but when I heard there was a plot against the White House, with a White House target, I finally put it all together."

The President checked his watch and raised his hand in a halting gesture.

"Before you go on, we *knew* about the plot from early on, and we knew about *Viral Vector*. Fortunately, as President, I have access to the very best health care in the world. Acutely aware of the threat, doctors have checked me on a weekly basis to make sure this new weapon has not been used on me. It seems someone tried, but the attempt was unsuccessful."

Destiny took a breath and began, unintentionally sarcastic.

"I'm not surprised. I imagine a person would need to have a sizable ego to ever seriously *consider* becoming President in the first place, and maybe that's what they were counting on."

"I'm listening. Explain yourself."

"Well, you obviously thought *you* were the White House target, but when Perseus Grant called me, he said something that made no sense at the time. He said, 'It's the first *wife!*' It wasn't until after I heard about the White House plot that my friend Kiyomi and I put it all together. You were *never* the target of the assassination plot from the beginning. It was your wife! *They're trying to assassinate the First Lady!*"

The President appeared to be stunned at once, his face straining to hide flinches of terror, as Destiny continued.

"Has the First Lady been *sick* recently? Has she shown any signs of weakness and shortness of breath, beyond campaign fatigue?"

His face confirmed her suspicion. By then, his face had become stone.

"She's been sick, yes. She said it was her schedule."

"They knew you would find out about the plot, but they were counting on everyone being so concerned about protecting *you* that your wife's symptoms would go unnoticed amid the craziness of campaigning. They knew a plot against you as the President was too great a risk—it would be High Treason. Your wife, however, is a private citizen. A successful plot against her life would result in possible murder charges at best, which would never be brought and could never be proven."

"That's unthinkable! Why would they attack my *wife*?"

"They want her to die of a massive heart attack within one week before Election Day, which means you would spend the last week of the election mourning with your children and burying your wife. *That's* their October surprise, their game changer. You would face the challenging prospect of a second term as a single father, dealing with grief-stricken teenagers. It would be difficult for most men, but it would be a deal breaker for a man who understands the responsibilities and personal sacrifices required by the presidential oath, and a man who loves his children and wants to be the best possible father.

"They're counting on you to love your children more than you want to remain in your job as President, but if you were to decide to continue, despite losing your wife, they've got an ad campaign prepared to attack you for being insensitive, unloving and selfish. They expect you to suspend your campaign and allow the Vice President to run in your place. That is why they've spent the summer and fall campaigning against *him*. In the end, they'll get the President they want, Hugh Gordon—who could never beat you, but he easily wins against the Vice President."

The President sat dazed for more than a minute, his face at times displaying equal parts anger and fear. Taking a deep breath, he focused on Destiny's face, gratitude in his voice.

"Thank you for going through so much trouble to save my wife. Listen, I believe you. Thank you! This whole Viral Vector business makes sense to me now. Sick bastards!"

He pointed a trembling finger.

"*You* stay on this plane. We'll talk after the debate."

He stood.

"Now, if you'll please excuse me. I have a busy night ahead."

The widely anticipated final debate would be staged at the university in Bloomington, Indiana. Air Force One however, landed at Grissom Air Reserve Base, near Kokomo, fifty miles away. The motorcade unloaded and assembled before the plane, and the President, staff and security quickly exited to begin the forty-minute drive.

While Destiny remained secluded in her quarters, she was able to view the debate on television. It appeared, in her opinion, the President was unable to shake the initial shock of his enemies coming after his wife. He seemed dark, sullen, non-responsive at times, and out-of-character. Hugh Gordon, his opponent, capitalized on his rare off-performance, scoring points on aggressiveness and leveling shocking charges that went unanswered and unchallenged.

News bureaus and political pundits would later characterize the President's performance as "lackluster" and "uninspired." Party leaders offered excuses for the "failed" performance, while loyalists were baffled about the missed opportunity for an election "slam-dunk." Instead, the President had opened the door and left it cracked, allowing Gordon a long-shot opportunity for an upset.

On the way to the University, the President phoned the First Lady and asked her to watch the debate from the hotel, where she could rest, but she was determined to attend. When he insisted, she demanded to know why. Unwilling to broach the subject on the phone, he implored her to trust him on the call, but her mind was set. It was her job to support her husband.

On that same night, *after* the debate, the President sat in his private quarters with his wife aboard Air Force One. He was silent, brooding the entire time on the way over. She assumed he was frustrated by his poor debate performance, but he was seething over the thought that political enemies had gone after his wife. *What next? His children?* He was determined to put those involved on notice. *Someone* was going to pay!

"You know you and I have always been straight with each other. The real reason I wanted you to stay in the hotel tonight is that... *someone* got a sample of your DNA and has turned it into a weapon against you. The reason you've been sick, the reason for your fatigue—they've altered your DNA to make your genes induce rapid heart disease. They wanted you to suffer a fatal heart attack days before the election."

The First Lady sat back in her seat, covering her face with her hands. For five years, she had feared an assassination attempt on her husband without ever considering herself a primary target. Breathing heavily, she placed her right hand over her racing heart.

"The election's in two *weeks*! I'm gonna die? Is there a cure? Can our doctors *do* anything?"

"They're already waiting for us at home. They've set up a complete treatment regimen. We've sequestered the Lincoln Bedroom. The treatment will be intensive and long-term, but necessary at this point. Based on what Dr. Rosecrans believes, you've got a fifty-fifty shot of recovering, which is better than we hoped. If your condition had gone another day or two untreated, we wouldn't have had a chance."

Chapter 42

Financier Helmut Wolf was unaccustomed to the feeling of powerlessness. Cut off from his empire and resources, he struggled for ways to make his days relevant. As each day passed, he became more frustrated with his imprisonment, increasingly cynical and bitter about *The Committee* and its members.

He resented long-term friendships, feeling abandoned by those who proved disloyal. Like Timon of Athens, he scorned mankind, a diseased and impure race, cursing former alliances and his own unappreciated genius and generosity. While drunk, he railed against humanity and threatened revenge against all persons who had betrayed him, calling each by name.

His only true friend remaining was Justice Wendell Greene, like the character Flavius, who was trapped with him at the estate. When Greene first arrived, he was angry that Wolf had tricked him, intentionally inviting him into a trap. But upon realizing he would never leave unless there was an administration change in Washington, Greene rested his hopes in the viability and success of Wolf's *Viral Vector* plan.

Frazzled and unshaven, Greene wandered about the estate, though he was obsessed with election coverage and was never far from a television or computer. When he was not monitoring the news, he was in his room, writing his memoir about the clandestine revolution that changed the world and the players involved. In the work, he depicted himself as James Madison to Wolf's George Washington. Even more so than Wolf, Greene resolved himself to victory or death. *If you win, you need not have to explain. If you lose, you should not be around to explain!*

The estate itself was palatial, extravagant, modeled after a manor Wolf visited in Jelenia Góra Valley in Poland. High on an eastern Idaho mountainside, Wolf's home sat on a plateau, surrounded by a thick forest. Rectangular in shape, the 35,000 square foot, four-story building featured twenty-two guest rooms, a grand ballroom, a large dining room, three kitchens, a media center, a keep, separate housing for a full-time staff of servants, an extensive library and a well-stocked ammunition locker.

An enormous grassy lawn, a helipad and runway were located behind the home and a fifteen-foot-tall ivy-covered stone and mortar barrier lined the sides and rear of the property. The entire front wall, built on the slope edge, was polished granite, dark gray in color. From a glass-enclosed observation platform atop the wall, the view of the valley below was awe-inspiring, the sheer drop-off from the rocky ledge more than two hundred feet.

Wolf barked the order to Hans Mehring, his personal bodyguard and full-time escort.

"Bring them in here, and then assemble the rest. I want them all and all staff to come into this room."

Mehring led two shackled men, arms restrained, into the room, seating them in chairs against the back wall. The appearance of the men suggested they had been tortured by Wolf and the traitorous escort. Although one man's hand was in bandages, it was obvious two or three fingers were missing. The second man had a broken nose, a swollen knee and black circles under both eyes. When all were assembled in the ballroom, Wolf stood before the group.

"These two men were my soldiers. They swore an oath to me, to protect me, to follow all my commands. But these men are traitors. My *loyal* bodyguard caught them last night, trying to escape, possibly to render aid to those who would do me harm. In my life, I have always rewarded loyalty with great generosity, and that has only led to betrayal, an example of which you see before you now."

He withdrew a black Ruger pistol from a shoulder harness beneath his coat.

"It is better to be feared than loved, and in these difficult circumstances, it is time that I am feared!"

Standing before the first soldier, Wolf fired a bullet directly into his forehead, smirking, signaling personal satisfaction as he watched the body slump and fall from the chair. Smearing a spatter of blood on his brow, he took two steps to his left and fired two shots in rapid succession into the left temple of the other captive. When a remaining member of his loyal platoon stepped forward, seeming to protest the killings, Wolf fired a fourth shot into the man's throat.

"Victory or death! We are all in this together."

"No matter what—you *can't* let them win. If I die, you *have* to continue. You can't let them do this!"

The President, eyes swollen with tears, sat at his wife's bedside, holding her hand.

"No. You *have* to live. If you die, I can't go on. Without you, I'm not *fit* to be President. Come on, you of all people know what my job involves, how much time and sacrifice it requires. I can't *do* it without you. In four years, our teenaged children will be *adults* for all intents and purposes."

He wiped a tear from his cheek

"In life there are priorities, and nothing is more important to me than my family—not even the Presidency."

She struggled to sit up.

"But if they win, they've murdered me and gotten away with it. If they would do that, just think of what *else* they'll do. If you're not President, you won't have the power to stop them."

"No."

"And if you can't stop them, just think of the future our children will face. If not for me, do it for them. You have to... *Oh!*"

Suddenly cringing in pain, the First Lady slumped and fainted as the high-pitched alarm on the electrocardiograph monitor began to signal aloud.

All at once, the room was full of a dozen doctors and nurses, moving about, performing various tasks on the inert body in the bed. One doctor ripped open the front of her gown as another prepped the defibrillator. An older doctor stood between the President and the bed, partially blocking his vision and stepping forward until the President had backed out the door.

"I'm sorry, Mr. President, but you're going to have to wait outside. You wife's heart has stopped. We've got the best medical staff in the world at her bedside. We will do everything we can to save her."

An attendant came in at seven a.m., drawing the blinds in the Queen's Bedroom.

"For White House guests, the kitchen is open twenty-four/seven. What would you like to have for breakfast, Ms. Mitchell?"

Destiny struggled to sit up in the fancy, canopied bed, though not for pain. A nurse had given her a valium at bedtime. She wore new flannel pajamas, and the elastic bandages wrapping her chest were fresh and firm.

"Well, what do you have? Is there a menu?"

"You are a guest of the White House, ma'am. The menu is *anything you want.*"

Physically, she felt better. It was the first full night she had slept since leaving California. Nonetheless, she felt troubled in spirit, at ill-ease. She had met with the President. He listened, and he *believed* her. The First Lady was getting medical attention across the hall, and Destiny's bruises were beginning to heal, but she was unsettled.

On a sofa, desk and armoire were shopping bags, beautiful garments, shoe boxes and a card from Natalie Sterling.

Destiny,

We are all grateful for your concern and sacrifice for the First Lady. Please realize we spoke during a time of tension at the height of a hard-fought election, so forgive me if I appeared at all less than gracious. I hope we will find an occasion to talk soon.

There was even a wig, a cute black finger-wave doo resembling one of Destiny's favorite hairstyles. Yet, all was not well. She mulled over the brie cheese, sturgeon fillet Eggs Benedict, checking the clock every few minutes. She took her time getting dressed, watching a cable news channel on television. Nine a.m. meant six a.m. Lifting the receiver, she dialed the number.

"No, if she's asleep, don't bother her. She needs her rest. How *is* she?"

"Her energy is fading, but she's also been depressed, threatening harm to herself. We've had her on suicide watch. She's been asking about you."

"God is good. Tell her I love her, and help is on the way."

An hour later, Natalie sent a message to Destiny, advising her of an eleven o'clock meeting with the President in the Oval Office. "Be early!" the note said.

When Destiny arrived for her White House Blue Room appointment, a receptionist greeted her and advised her to sit.

"Busy place! We're *always* behind schedule."

Fifteen minutes later, an aide led Destiny into the President's office. This time, he stood—first extending for a handshake and then hugging her.

"I thank you, the First Lady thanks you and my family thanks you. We're not out of the woods yet, but if she alive, it's you who saved her life. I owe you an eternal debt of gratitude."

Destiny smiled as she sat across the desk from him.

"I am very pleased there's hope. Hope is a powerful thing."

He sighed, contemplative.

"It is. Destiny, I called you here to thank you, but I *know* what you've been through over the last two months. Even while you didn't know what you were up against, you were willing to endure great personal sacrifices in order to save my wife. For me, I admire your selflessness. But I am going to ask you to think of yourself right now. I am going to ask you to be selfish."

He handed her a large, sealed goldenrod envelope.

"Please accept this with my thanks. I cannot do anything publicly because this whole matter kind of flies under the radar, but I can make good privately. Please tell me what I can do for you to thank you for risking all to save my wife. I'll do whatever you ask, within reason."

Destiny had considered such an offer, and she was quick to respond.

"My best friend, Kiyomi—they got to her with the viral vector. As a result, she's dying right now at Travis Air Force Base in Fairfield, California. Whatever you are doing for the First Lady, I want you to do it for her. Wherever the First Lady is staying, I want Kiyomi in a bed beside her, with the *exact* same care and the same treatment."

The President thought for a moment and nodded.

"We'll send for Kiyomi Yamakita and bring her here immediately. She'll get the best possible treatment for her condition—the exact same treatment as the First Lady. Is there anything else?"

Destiny could not respond. She could barely breathe. She was overwhelmed that Kiyomi would also have hope. But Destiny had an agenda from early on. In her relatively humble position of power, she could never exact vengeance on the billionaire monster who murdered her husband, and yet he was the same man who had sought to assassinate the First Lady. In the spirit of common interests, she spoke quietly, though forcefully.

"Helmut Wolf. He murdered my husband, Bryan Osaka, and he tried to kill *your* wife. I want him to *pay*. I realize nothing will bring my husband back, but I want revenge, and I want him to *know* where it's coming from."

A rare flash of anger animated the President's eyes beneath a furrowed brow.

"Wolf will *definitely* pay. Good as done. Is there anything else?"

She nodded, seeming less certain about her final demand.

"The *Viral Vector* project—it's purely evil. It covets the power divine. I need you to promise me that you will never use it, not even if you think you're doing it for some greater good. Choosing who lives and who dies is a power that belongs only to God. You have your drones, and they all can debate about that, but this viral vector technology is too much power for a president or any other person to possess. It would only corrupt you. Promise me you will destroy the project or put it away and never use it. I need you to *promise* me that."

The President bowed his head, hesitating for what seemed like a minute. Destiny could not tell if he was strengthening his resolve through prayer, or if he was reasoning a legitimate rationalization for deception. When he looked up, he smiled.

"I promise to put *Viral Vector* so far away that those who would use it to do harm will never even know it ever existed. You have my *word* on that, Destiny."

Chapter 43

The most significant detail about Election Day was an element that never happened. As the final days wound down, members of *The Committee* and other expectant observers realized there would be no game changer. Certainly, the race would be close, but it was apparent the active President would eke out a victory by the narrowest of margins. There would be no sensational event, wrinkle or revelation to alter the inevitable outcome.

In the final days, there were a few news cycles of media-generated concern about the health of the First Lady. An alleged White House rumor suggested she was bedridden, under twenty-four-hour surveillance by concerned doctors and near death. Because the President generally avoided questions about his wife's medical condition, the gossip and stories persisted, with outspoken partisan critics charging that, in personal matters as well as in public affairs, the President had been secretive and dishonest with the American people.

When advisors informed that the President's non-disclosure about the First Lady's health had begun to affect several late polls, especially those conducted on likely women voters, she insisted on making a limited campaign appearance.

"So you want to collapse and just drop *dead* on the campaign trail? Give them what they want? I can't let you do that. The election will be close, but we'll be fine without risking your life."

The First Lady bowed her head.

"I'm not feeling well, Baby. I might die anyway, but my mother taught me to always have your husband's back. I'd rather drop dead trying to support you than waste away to nothing and die curled up in a bed. You don't want me to do it? Well, I respectfully disagree. I have something important to say."

At a campaign event in Ohio, the First Lady struggled even to walk, displaying true grit at a Columbus rally. Defying destiny before a crowd of twelve thousand, she extolled the virtues of her husband and the grand promise of his second term. Her stump speech resonated with deep conviction, personal flourishes and sincerity, but underlying all was a message to her enemies, summed up in her last words.

"I'm still *here*! I was on the ropes with the flu, but I beat it. I'm not going anywhere. For the next four years, I will continue as First Lady, proud to support my husband, my President—*our* President over the next four years!"

While the crowds cheered, news feed audiences tuned in and media pundits rejected the persistent rumors about her health problems, few knew she fainted in the limousine and had to be rushed back to Washington doctors. Almost no one knew her tired heart stopped again that night and had to be restarted with a jolt of electricity. And no one except the President knew he had just completed writing a speech, announcing the suspension of his campaign and his full-throated endorsement of the Vice President to step up and faithfully serve in his place.

Yet the First Lady's speech had an enormous impact on members of *The Committee* and others who had bet against a second term for the President. As the final days ticked down, key dynamics of a hard-entrenched partisan election began to change. Opposition to the active president began to soften as groups faced the inevitability of the outcome. Individuals and special interests began to hedge, repositioning themselves for challenges resulting from betting on the wrong horse.

Nathaniel Driscoll, the House Minority Leader, many business and industry leaders as well as several Wall Street players went on record in the last days with comments and predictions favorable to the President. In suppositional terms, various groups who were previously opposed indicated a willingness to cooperate with the administration on a range of policy and agenda items. Hugh Gordon however, continued to campaign to the end with admirable intensity.

In the mountains of eastern Idaho, Wolf and Greene cursed aloud the names of the traitors who had abandoned them. Surly and agitated, Wolf became increasingly abusive of his staff and soldiers. He pistol-whipped a female servant for bringing tepid tea and he hurled a crystal rocks glass at an attendant who smiled during an election report, striking him on the head. But the worse offense occurred on the morning of Election Day.

Suspicious of several of the remaining soldiers in his elite guard, Wolf had ordered Mehring to confiscate all weapons and firearms so that he could better manipulate the balance of power and the threat against dissention. Of the twelve soldiers, one in particular, *the black one*, infuriated Wolf the most. Though he spoke out against the President, it was clear he was lying.

On Election Day morning, Wolf entered the media center with an alleged copy of a communiqué between the black soldier and a U.S. Army intelligence officer, who was planning an assault for the morning after the election. Because most of his cohorts knew of Wolf's obvious animus toward the soldier, few believed the allegation and viewed the evidence with a degree of skepticism.

But because Wolf and Hans Mehring were the only persons at the estate with firearms, he insisted on an immediate execution. Once again, he summoned the remaining soldiers and staff into the large dining room, where the bloodied black man was standing, arms restrained.

"We have another traitor among us! This man, while living in our midst, has secretly plotted with our enemies, conspired against us even as we accepted him and extended our trust. For that, he must die!"

Instead of shooting the soldier in the head, as with the others, Wolf first shot him in the left knee, smiling as the man groaned. The second shot exploded the femur of the man's right thigh, causing him to fall to his face, writhing on the bloody floor, screaming in pain. Standing over the straining, quivering body, Wolf emptied the remainder of the clip, five shots, into the back of the soldier's head.

As Election Night wore on and news organizations began to declare victory for the President, members of *The Committee* launched protocols that would bring the group together a final time, despite the absence of Justice Wendell Greene. Concerned for personal security and political fallout after the election, a quorum of the body wanted to establish a non-incriminating exit strategy.

Three members and a fourth by proxy wanted to develop some efficient policy and procedure for disbanding the unsuccessful intrigue and the language for disavowing its purpose and its secretive plot against the President. Rex Andal, active Chairman of the Senate Committee on Foreign Relations, assumed the leadership role, calling the meeting to order at one minute after midnight.

"Committee members—of course you all know the outcome of the election, and given the President's propensity for cold, calculated assassination and revenge, I believe it in all our best interests to dissolve the political bands which have connected us together and either reconvene at some later time or pursue our protests independently. Is there any discussion before I call for a vote?"

Political consultant Charles Love cleared his throat, nodding to be recognized.

"Mr. R?"

"What about the oaths we took? We don't know each other beyond plausible deniability, but we *know* who we are. My concern comes in the event that one of us is discovered. That person could be turned on the rest of us, *and* our families. We all swore to take our own lives if our plan didn't work. That's exactly what we must do."

House Majority Whip Chris Matthews was quick to counter Love's comment.

"And I can honestly say I do not know who any of you are. But then again, *what* didn't work? We don't know, because we weren't *told*. Whatever went wrong was beyond our control. We haven't actually *done* anything! We shouldn't have to die for something we have no knowledge of. Besides, we're missing two members. Our elected chairman is not here, and the *governor* is missing."

Helen Abercrombie interrupted, unrecognized.

"Concession speech, no doubt."

Love returned to his point.

"But we are all bound by the same oath, and we knew what we were swearing to. If you lose, you should not be *around* to explain, or to derail a cause. I call on all of you to fulfill that oath on your own free will. Because believe me, if you don't fulfill your oaths, there are powers observing, who will make sure you die all the same."

The room was silent as members considered his words, desperation distorted faces beneath their masks. Former Governor Steven Testor's guttural groan was indicative of the general mood of the committee. Yet before another word was spoken, the computer screens lit up, displaying the words:

I KNOW WHO YOU ARE
AND WHAT YOU HAVE DONE

RIP
Colorectal Cancer

In shock, the members sat up rigidly in their seats, flinching, as if straining to test their individual sphincters. With the exception of the large bold words, the screen was empty, providing no clue or indication relating to its source. The words remained for thirty seconds before screens faded blank. Glancing toward Charles Love, acting chairman Andal shrugged, removing his mask.

"Powers *observing*? *Your* friends?"

Love only shook his head, sighing as he yanked off his own mask.

"Could be, but then again, maybe it's the *President*. Who knows? Maybe they're one in the same."

Chapter 44

"From what I've heard, Wolf *and* this entire place will be toast, and so will we, unless we *do* something!"

The man Helmut Wolf killed that morning had been the new first-in-command, well-liked and respected by remaining members of the platoon. No one believed he was plotting against Wolf, yet other soldiers were speaking with voices on the outside. One reported that the government was offering a reward on the capture of Wolf and Greene. However, there would be no immunity for anyone involved in the killing of Department of Homeland Security field office supervisor Shawn Tillis.

Matt Madrigal, the shooter in the DHS incident, was the new team leader, followed by Butch Cunningham, the team member who shot Destiny Mitchell. As the group discussed options, they realized that capturing and handing over Wolf would not be enough and concluded they would need something more salient.

By all accounts, Wolf had become unhinged from reality, an irrational and dangerous man, but the servant whose head Wolf injured described a conversation he overheard between Wolf and Greene. It was the reason Wolf exuded such confidence when faced with retaliation from the government. According to the servant, he told Justice Greene he had also managed to create an *antiviral* vector that would greatly improve attempts to slow, and in most cases, reverse the viral vector process altogether.

If Madrigal and Cunningham could get their hands on such a treatment or therapy, they would have a powerful tool for negotiating a deal with the government. After much discussion, no one could agree if this antiviral vector was a written formula, a vaccine, a prescription or if it even existed at the estate or elsewhere. All agreed, however, that the answer was in Wolf's head.

At nine-thirty that evening, a servant announced that Justice Wendell Greene had attempted suicide in his room with a large butcher knife taken from the kitchen. He had buried the eight-inch blade into his distended abdomen, though he had missed vital organs. Hands clutched on the hilt, he waited to die, but after fifteen minutes, he realized that while he was bleeding, his death would not be swift. By that time, however, the initial shock had faded, and the disabling pain began. His attempts at twisting the blade or removing it to stab himself again proved too painful, as the slightest movement of the knife produced monstrous waves of agony.

In sheer anguish, he began calling for the servant who monitored his room, groaning and spitting up blood for over thirty minutes. When the older man arrived, Greene begged him to finish the job, to stab him again or to smother him with a pillow. He even offered money, but the frightened man balked, running downstairs to report the incident instead. The nurse-practitioner on staff instructed the rest of the servants to transfer the Justice to a bed, where he administered treatment and provided medication to reduce Greene's pain. The knife was not removed.

It was the exact moment ready soldiers had anticipated. As Wolf, distracted with Greene's condition, spoke with the nurse-practitioner, two soldiers rushed Hans Mehring, Wolf's bodyguard, while a third tackled Wolf, pinning him to the floor. When both men were disarmed and restrained, the soldiers reinforced the tape and ropes bounding the traitorous Mehring, threw him in a closet and nailed the door shut, labeling it *A Special Place in Hell.*

Wolf threatened the men and protested as they led him down the hallway to a room containing an inverted bed, a deep recovery tub, several small glass pitchers and a huge bucket, which was filled with water.

"Bring him in. Remove his shirt. Strap him to the table, arms and legs—zero movement."

What made the preparation and lead up to the procedure most horrifying for Helmut Wolf was the memory of Bryan Osaka. As Cunningham's assistant covered Helmut's eyes with a wet cloth, Wolf remembered the diabolical genius of waterboarding as a torture method. It was an intriguing discovery. With rapt interest, he had watched the terror build as Osaka's arms and legs tensed against the restraints, again and again. He could only imagine what was going through the detective's mind, fully aware of the visceral torment that would follow.

The mind is its own place, and in itself
Can make a Heav'n of Hell, a Hell of Heav'n.

Yet it was worse for Wolf, who had great difficulty even comprehending the idea of powerlessness. As a multi-billionaire, he had possessed the power of a god. He had once been able to control destiny, to reshape the world and the lives of men, to demand sacrifice, obedience and honor. He could bestow grand blessings and mete out bitter justice and retribution.

But O how fall'n! How chang'd
From him, who in the happy Realms of Light
Cloth'd with transcendent brightness didst out-shine
Myriads though bright.

And how his *Viral Vector* project would have made him the greatest of all the gods on Earth, only to come to such a mocking end!

As Wolf watched Osaka being waterboarded, he realized the true nature of the procedure, which involved conditioning the mind to torture itself. In his estimation, *the greater a man's intelligence—the greater degree of terror he would experience.* Wolf's own genius would be overpowering. The water challenged the mechanical nature of his body, but the real torture began the moment that the water stopped, with his mind panicking, anticipating the onset of the next overwhelming experience of sheer powerlessness.

He tried to calm his mind and rationalize his thoughts, but all he could see was Osaka lying there at the breaking point, struggling, screaming and helpless. Prominent in his thoughts, he could remember Osaka's final contemptuous half-smile as his own torture began.

It took only two sessions to weaken Wolf's resolve enough, so that by the end of the third, he was sharing unrequested information and providing methods for confirmation. He cried like a baby. He screamed like a woman! The formula and vaccine were in a vault in his keep beneath the estate. Wolf provided key codes, passwords and combinations required to retrieve the items, cursing his captors while begging for mercy.

When the interrogator finished, the assistants unstrapped Wolf from the table and delivered him to three soldiers who waited on the grassy lawn. Madrigal had spoken with government officials who offered immunity in exchange for the formula and vaccine. When he was told to "put Mr. Wolf on ice," Madrigal conceived of a fitting method to do so.

Two of the soldiers had constructed a cross, made from cedar trees felled outside the estate's back gate. After first stripping Wolf of his shoes and overcoat, they strapped his wrists and ankles to the wood, nailing first his hands, arms outstretched, to the *patibulum*, and then driving a spike through both feet into the *stipes*. They took Wolf, attached to the structure, up to the estate's front wall observatory, opening the gate.

Attaching ropes to the horizontal member of the cross, soldiers slowly lowered Helmut Wolf, a crucified enemy of the state, six feet down the cold, glassy granite wall, a propitiatory offering to a wrathful government.

"You persisted. I realize that you put it all together, and I am thankful. But what I want to know is *how* you put it together. Certainly, you had help from your husband, but you obviously had other resources. While I'm impressed, I'd like to know what help you had and about what resources and processes you used to figure it all out."

For the second time in a week, Destiny sat across from the President in the Oval Office. True to his word, he had sent for Kiyomi at Travis AFB, and she was receiving treatment in a bed across the room from the First Lady. While the treatment they got from Dr. Rosecrans slowed the progress of the disease, neither woman seemed to be recovering well, and neither had more than a fifty percent chance for survival.

At times, Kiyomi was conscious and alert. In a conversation that stood out in Destiny's mind, she remembered her best friend sitting up, glancing over at the First Lady.

"We *did* it! We ran the gauntlet, and we saved her."

"We won't say it too loud, but my main motivation was to save *you*, and myself, and Lyndsey."

Reflecting on how much she missed her own daughter, Kiyomi began to weep.

"If I don't survive this, please take care of Natsumi for me. I really haven't been there for her these last few months. If I die, please become her mother, like you did for Lyndsey. And make sure Cedric finds someone special to make him happy."

Destiny leaned in, forcing a smile to contradict her teary aspect.

"*Only the good die young*, Kiyo. So you have absolutely *nothing* to worry about. Natsumi is my niece. I will always be there for her. And Cedric is my older cousin, so I know him. Special? You would be an *impossible* act to follow. You'll have to stick around if you want him to stay happy."

Destiny had watched election coverage up to the moment the President's re-election was declared by three major news organizations. There was excitement at the White House as champagne corks popped, setting off the first celebrations of what would be a long night. The President was set to fly to his campaign headquarters to deliver his acceptance speech, but he called Destiny in for a final debriefing.

"Besides your husband, where did the help come from?"

Grateful for the treatment both she and Kiyomi were receiving, Destiny did her best to cooperate.

"There was Deuteronomy Saint Claire, mostly for advice and then for access to Natalie Sterling. He's the one who told me about the White House plot, which made me realize your wife was the assassination target."

The President nodded.

"I understand. I don't know Saint Claire personally, but I understand he was working *for* us. Who else?"

"Well, there was Cornell Cotton. He filled in some of the details, and he helped get us to Travis, making sure we had the Delta Force detail protecting us. And according to Bryan, Cotton's boss, Jett Turner—he also helped us."

"Free radicals, not to be trusted, but they both came down on the right side of this one for us. Anyone else?"

Destiny hesitated before continuing.

"That's where things started getting strange. The night before I left Travis, I got a call from Nathaniel Driscoll, the billionaire Bryan knew. He told me I had to deplane before I reached any airport gate, period. He said Wolf would know where I was, and I would be killed if I got off at any terminal. He also said half of Wolf's soldiers sent over to *kill* me were under his orders—meaning Driscoll's orders—to *protect* me."

"Driscoll's a friend. We don't always see eye to eye, but he knows how it all works. He's never let me down."

Destiny seemed confused, though it was coming together for her.

"And the clincher—according to Saint Claire, the whole thing started for Bryan, while already investigating *The Committee*, when he got an anonymous phone call and information from someone with information and documentation about a 'White House target.'

"On the night before he died, my husband shared a few things he thought I needed to know. He wasn't sure how, but Bryan *knew* he would die the next day, so he prepared me for the fight ahead. He said the information that set all this action in motion, from Perseus Grant's access and the secret revelation Grant shared to Bryan's own evidence—it came from an unlikely source: your opponent throughout this election, Hugh Gordon."

The President did not seem surprised, though he appeared to be contemplating.

"Very good."

He smiled, taking the time to look her over, dressed in appropriate business attire.

"My children, by the way, have always admired you, and so have the First Lady and myself, but if you don't mind me saying, I thought you looked *foxy* as a blonde."

She bowed her head, embarrassed.

"Thank you, but with all due respect, Mr. President, I've truthfully answered every question you've asked. I have one question for you."

He smiled, his interest piqued.

"Please proceed."

"If so many of the people involved in this plot *worked* for you and you knew about almost everything that was going on, then you could have *stopped* it. You could have stepped in and *saved* my husband. But you let it happen! You let him die! *Why?*"

The President paused, his face becoming somber as he steepled his index fingers.

"I have a difficult job to do—*Hard Choices*. As you pointed out so appropriately the other day, Destiny—I am *not* God. I don't have the power to decide who lives and who dies out there. Often I might have the knowledge, or the intelligence on the ground, but I do not have the power to control real-time life and death outcomes. I only wish I had more control over certain things. I'm very sorry about your husband. Bryan Osaka was a national hero."

The President stood, checking his watch.

"Now, *you* should get ready. You'll be leaving in about thirty minutes."

"Why? Where am I going?"

"To the meeting you requested. Tonight, you get your face-to-face with Helmut Wolf, the man who killed your husband."

Chapter 45

She rode with members of SEAL Team Six from Andrews Air
Force Base in Maryland to Mountain Home Air Force Base in
southwestern Idaho, where she boarded a specially modified
stealth Blackhawk helicopter with the team. During the silent ride
in the dark night, no one spoke a word, as the soldiers seemed to
be in a trance, focused on their mission. She felt invisible.

Destiny bowed her head, considering for the first time what
she would say to Helmut Wolf, the person whose sick mind had
caused so much pain and death. For the first time ever in her life,
she envisioned taking a life, killing for revenge. She wondered
why the President had sent her, wondered if he was providing her
with the opportunity to exact vengeance on the man who had
murdered Bryan.

*Could the President have sanctioned it: the killing of a U.S.
citizen without due process? On American soil?* It was wrong. As
an attorney, as a sworn officer of the court, the thought of it was
unconscionable! Was *that* what the President meant when he
said, in such a peculiar manner, 'I have a difficult job to do?' What
would *Bryan* have done? What would he have wanted *her* to do?
Destiny's hands became clammy, and her mouth went dry as the
pilot announced the estate was in sight and the aircraft began a
descent.

When the helicopter touched down, the SEAL team leader told
her to remain in her seat while the site was secured. He returned
ten minutes later, escorting her inside the estate and up to the
observation platform where four team members waited. On his
cue, they pulled up the ropes, raising the body of Helmut Wolf,
impaled on a cross and still alive.

"Take him inside and lie him down."

As members obeyed his order, the leader glanced down at
Destiny.

"Ms. Mitchell, you will have exactly ten minutes."

She could hear Wolf's strained breathing when she entered the
room, his coughing. Taking a deep breath, she approached the
wheezing victim, realizing at once the monster he was.

"Helmut Wolf. It's me, Destiny Mitchell, and I beat you. I *won*."

His eyes slowly opened.

"You! No! No, Destiny Mitchell is *dead*. I had her killed!"

"No, I'm *alive*. I am alive to witness your fall, I suppose *literally* if I want to."

He strained, focusing his eyes.

"She is? *God* be damned! So, you are *not* dead. Why are you here?"

"For revenge. I wanted you to know that *I* am the person who beat you, in spite of everything you've done to me, in spite of all your money, in spite of your power. In this world, it shouldn't matter how much money or influence a person has, but it does."

He grinned in pain.

"I have known that all my life. Half of all Americans are lazy pissants—good-for-nothing and dependent on the government, victims, who feel entitled. The other forty-nine percent are ignorant, because they have sold their souls, and for what, they do not know. They have fooled themselves into believing they are successful, that they have power, when neither group is truly alive."

Arrogant to the end! When Destiny spotted the large knife on a nearby table, she imagined stabbing Wolf in the throat to cut off his words. This was also the man who had ordered Lyndsey shot, the man who was killing Kiyomi. He was responsible for the deaths of seventy-five inmates, for two guards and Jake. For Bryan! She reached over and grabbed the blade, placing the sharp point just under his larynx, drawing blood. If anyone ever *deserved* to die, Helmut Wolf did.

He smiled.

"Do it! Perhaps the President is testing you. He sent you here. Is that *not* what you came to do? Or perhaps you believe you came to *speak* with me? Well then, speak."

Destiny had dreamed of the moment, but she was ill-prepared for it. Angry though she was, she could not take his life, and it was obvious he had no regret.

Yet she had won. He would be punished. He would have to answer for his atrocious crimes.

"You murdered my husband, for *that* you deserve to die. But you're still at it—you're trying to kill the First Lady, you went after my daughter, you're murdering my best friend, and you ruined your billion-dollar project trying to kill me. What is it that men like you have against women?"

Wolf struggled to adjust his body on the wooden platform. The blood from the wounds on his hands and feet, nearly frozen outside, had begun to melt, and the numbness of the cold faded, allowing the pain to return. He grimaced.

"Is *that* what you think this is about? That I am engaged in some silly war on women? That is just a distraction they have fed to you. This is all about power. I never cared one thought for you. You were merely in the way. However, I did not expect you to be such a fool. You sacrificed everything to save the life of the First Lady, but it does not matter. Do you think the President cares at all about you, a low-born black woman? The President is the *consolidation* of power. It is his only purpose. You have not won at all. You have only helped *him* win."

Wolf's diaphragm heaved as he coughed.

"He now controls the power I created, and he will use it to destroy his enemies and ruin the world."

He smiled.

"Do not seem so surprised, Destiny Mitchell. Of *course* your president is a mass murderer! He is the most prolific fiend in the world! He has been killing the entire time, with the drones, with death squads and with other undisclosed methods."

Wolf nodded.

"Yes, the President *loves* playing God, watching down from the sky, watching everything we do, raining down judgment and death in fire and brimstone. Twenty-five hundred persons in Pakistan alone, but that is merely the official count. He has murdered ten thousand more across the globe. And now he can do it even more efficiently.

"You tell me, what would such a man do with the power of my viral vector, with such a weapon? DNA, Ms. Mitchell, is the true breath of God. It is the ultimate power over creation and destruction. It is *Godship Incarnate*, the authority over who lives and who dies, from the most fundamental basis of life. For him, for the President, such a power is irresistible! To control the very breath of God!"

His eyes dropped toward the knife.

"Kill me. This is your test. The President's test, or perhaps God's. The price of my blood? Your *soul*. Perhaps you will even get a presidential appointment? But killing me changes nothing. The genie is already out of the bottle. With this power, the President cannot be stopped. Be careful, Destiny Mitchell, mind what you do. If you get in the way, your president will kill you too."

Bowing her head, she returned the knife to its place, just as the SEAL team leader entered the room, followed by four men.

"Your time is up, Ms. Mitchell. Our orders are to put him back out there. Let's go."

Five minutes after they entered the estate, the SEAL team had acquired what they came to secure. True to Madrigal's word, the vaccine, formula and scientific research had been left in a suitcase placed beneath the desk in Wolf's private office in the keep. The team leader immediately called Washington to confirm procurement of the package, an announcement made directly to the President shortly before his acceptance speech.

Beginning with the main building, six other soldiers set about securing computer hard drives and storage devices, searching and boxing written records and documents and rounding up staff to prepare for evacuation. One soldier discovered Supreme Court Associate Justice Wendell Greene, locked in a bedroom, jaundiced, dehydrated and groaning in pain. The large knife was still lodged in his abdomen as they carried him out on a stretcher. He was delirious and near-death with a high fever when the helicopter medic started the IV.

A second team set heat-sensitive detonation devices in strategic locations. Curious about the door labeled *A Special Place in Hell*, one member pried the door open and looked into the pleading eyes of Hans Mehring, Wolf's personal bodyguard, bound and gagged.

"I don't know what you did, but I know why they *left* you here. I *spit* on traitors! You'll see Hell at sunrise—you *and* Wolf."

Back up on the observatory platform atop the front wall, four SEAL team members lowered the rope tethering the cross to which Wolf was attached. Destiny wondered why the team leader brought her up, and her intuition was true.

Just before his men tied the ends of the ropes to the metal supports of the platform, he turned toward Destiny.

"He murdered your husband. He's a wicked man. Just say the word. They'll release the ropes, and he'll fall. His fate is in your hands. *Your* call, Ms. Mitchell. You can just nod if you want to."

She did not move. She closed her eyes and exhaled, struggling to keep her head from nodding. Helmut Wolf was an evil bastard who *deserved* to die, and she had dreamt—from the first report of Bryan's death—of how she would slowly torture his killer. She had sworn to herself she would murder the person responsible. She imagined employing Perseus Grant's blowtorch method of depravity before stabbing him through the carotid artery to watch the gushing blood.

Yet it was fantasy. Taking a life involved more than anger or passion. There was a sense of morality involved, and thus the dichotomy of revenge. How could she condemn Wolf for being a heartless murderer after she had succumbed to the same paradigm? She could have nodded and turned away, but she believed in due process. She could not make that call.

"I can't. Not like this."

The team leader shrugged, disappointed.

"That's fine. Tie him up. It doesn't matter anyway. Drone at sunrise. He was going to die either way."

Chapter 46

Madrigal, Cunningham and seven other mercenary soldiers from Wolf's complex watched the Blackhawk helicopter depart as they descended to the valley floor. Employing night vision goggles, Cunningham focused on the front wall. The group stopped, taking turns to view, surprised to see the billionaire still hanging there against the wall. It simply did not make sense... unless it was a trap.

It was too good to be true. Madrigal assumed the government would have arrested Wolf to try him for sedition, treason or murder. Apparently, they came for the package, but they had asked to have Wolf put "on ice." They could have executed him or taken him away, yet they left him there. Dead or alive—no one could tell, but the prospect was enticing. *What would a billionaire pay in exchange for his life? How much would he offer to escape certain death?*

Unable to convince the group that the reward was worth the risk, Madrigal and Cunningham turned back alone. The arduous and treacherous journey toward Idaho Falls, the nearest city, stretched eighty miles ahead over rugged terrain, with Wolf's estate eight miles behind. The seven others were content to escape with their lives and immunity from the government. They saw Madrigal's scheme as "a fool's mission," one where Wolf was probably dead, and his body was booby-trapped.

Hiking upward by themselves, Madrigal and Cunningham became less confident about the plan, stopping twice to discuss abandoning the plot. Madrigal did not trust the government's offer of immunity. He argued that if he and Cunningham continued in their line of work, it would be easy for the government to create "an accident or two" to avenge the DHS shootings. As multi-millionaires, they could retire and leave the country, "maybe get lost in Europe or South America."

Cunningham had convinced himself that Wolf was already dead. *Why else would they have left him?* Halfway back up the mountain, he used the goggles to determine if there was any sign of life. *Negative.* One mile out, Wolf's head appeared to have shifted to a slightly different position. *The wind perhaps?*

Cunningham relented, though he continued to argue that if the government could not be trusted, then rescuing Wolf, an avowed enemy of the state, would only make matters worse. The President made it clear: *Those who provide aid and comfort to our enemies will also be pursued to the ends of the Earth, and justice will be done.*

It was four-thirty in the morning when they re-entered the darkened estate. Wary of tripwires and booby-traps, they proceeded cautiously through the building and up to the platform, hoisting the ropes suspending the man they had crucified. Cunningham gave Wolf water and examined his wounds as Madrigal sought to negotiate a deal.

"We want fifteen million apiece, half of it up-front, and the balance when you are free and clear."

Wolf readily agreed. Since the government was blocking data access and communications within a thirty-mile perimeter of the estate, he knew he would not have to comply with the first condition for at least two days, more than enough time for him to come up with a clever counter-stratagem.

"How am I to be sure that you will not discount the second payment and kill me as soon as you receive the first?"

"Because you'll have your phone. You can call whoever you want to call before you transfer the money. You can let someone know you're alive. We're soldiers-of-fortune, but we'd be crazy to *kill* a billionaire. Besides, seven million apiece is not enough for the risk we'll be taking. Once they know you're alive, the government will be pissed."

Cunningham extracted the nails through Wolf's hands and the stake through his feet. No bones had been broken. He wrapped the hands in gauze and elastic bandages. The holes through the feet would be problematic. Wolf could barely stand, let alone walk. After cleaning and draining the wounds, Cunningham wrapped Wolf's feet in tight bandages. Because Wolf's shoes would not fit over the wrapping on swollen feet, Cunningham went to the closet to take Mehring's boots.

At six feet six inches, Hans Mehring was well-muscled and agile. He had sat for two days planning some manner of escape. He pretended to be weak and listless as Cunningham opened the door and neared, only to sweep the soldier off his feet and lunge atop the startled man, head-butting him hard. He had nearly reached the tabletop with the knife when he heard an explosion, followed by a white-hot burning sensation on the right side of his buttocks.

Madrigal stood over Mehring, kicking him in the stomach to turn him over.

"You could have surrendered your boots voluntarily, Mehring, but now we're not taking any chances."

The next shot exploded into Mehring's left knee, causing the huge man to draw up, whimpering. A minute later, Cunningham, forehead swollen, came over and kicked Mehring onto his back, jerking at his ankles as he removed the boots, pleased that the traitor was suffering. It took both men to lift Mehring and slam him headfirst into the closet. After Cunningham shut the door, he heard a noise from within that sounded like weeping.

Madrigal discovered a pair of crutches in one of the servants' quarters and adjusted them to Wolf's height. He had also fashioned a litter, a make-shift stretcher, from two-by-fours and a one-inch-thick wooden panel he found in the warehouse. Pocketing a handful of codeine pills, the soldiers left the estate at five-forty-five in the morning, descending the mountain, with Wolf on the board between them.

Two hours later, as they walked along a plateau four miles away, Wolf looked up from a drug-induced gaze and called out.

"Drone!"

In the distance, a small, narrow silver aircraft with a rear propeller dipped its left wing as it leveled off and veered toward the estate. It was an MQ-9, designed by General Atomics. The Air Force named it Reaper, a larger, heavier and more capable version of the Predator. The turbo-prop aircraft, armed with two AGM-114 Hellfire II air-to-ground missiles, had loitered in the nighttime heavens at forty-five-thousand feet for twelve hours before beginning its steep descent at sunrise.

Madrigal, Cunningham and Wolf were on an ideal perch to watch as the remote drone operator fired the missiles. Seconds later, they watched the huge explosion on the mountainside as Wolf's estate disappeared in an eruption of flames.

Cunningham sat down next to Wolf, clasping his shoulder.

"You *see* that? We just earned the first half of our money! We'll expect the first payment as soon as we get within phone range."

After Destiny returned to the Washington, she got the distinct impression the atmosphere had changed. The servants continued to be friendly, and the accommodations were nonpareil, but the President and his senior staff were distant. A hall attendant explained that the White House was amid a transition toward the second term, with vast personnel changes, a redirection of policy, sad farewells and robust greetings for new hires.

Whereas in the week before she had met with the President three times and enjoyed rare access to White House areas reserved for the most adored and trusted visitors, she and Kiyomi were moved a day later to the luxurious *St Regis Washington DC*, two blocks away. The accommodations and décor rivaled the White House, and Dr. Rosecrans and staff had set up a bed in the suite so that the two would be together during the next phase of treatment.

Natalie Sterling's chief-of-staff explained that, because Kiyomi's private medical care would extend for a month or more, the nearby five-star hotel would be a better place for her recovery.

"The White House is simply an inappropriate place for such an extended stay. Here, you'll have *carte blanche*, courtesy of the President. All your expenses are covered, and you can stay as long as you like."

She explained that the doctor would begin a new and more aggressive stage of treatment that would greatly improve Kiyomi's chances of survival, and she indicated that Cedric and Natsumi, her husband and daughter, would be allowed to visit at the hotel.

Nonetheless, Destiny could not help wondering if the sudden change and distancing from the President had something to do with the "test" Helmut Wolf brought to her attention. If she had avenged Bryan's death by slitting Wolf's throat in that room, or if she had allowed SEAL team members on the platform to release the ropes, causing Wolf to plunge to his death two hundred feet below, would the outcome have been different?

Wolf called the President the most prolific mass murderer in the world, but the President had said something very different. When he said he had a difficult job to do, Destiny assumed he meant he would have to order men and women to their deaths in defense of country. By legal definition, that was not murder.

However, when a person or persons were killed as a result of pre-emptive actions taken to disrupt terrorist organizations that plotted against America, and in the effort of targeting individuals who would harm Americans, the distinction was less clear, though debatable.

But Wolf had suggested something more ominous. He told Destiny the President would use the *Viral Vector* project to consolidate and enhance his own power. Wolf predicted that the President would embrace the power to decide who lived and who died in much the same way he had advanced the use and technology of an expanding drone program to achieve his aims and motives—morality aside.

In a world growing more dangerous and deceptive each day, was the President going to bury the project away, "deep-sixed," as he had promised? Was he going to deny himself the formidable, transcendent power at his disposal, even during his most desperate moments? Or the country's most desperate moments?

Or would he succumb to the allure of that irresistible power by convincing himself he was acting for a greater good, for a *divine* purpose? Was there a discernible difference between drone weapons and DNA weapons? Was premeditated, preemptive killing self-defense, or was it murder?

If that night in Idaho was a test of her own immorality or bad character, then Destiny had failed. Despite Wolf's admission of guilt and his wickedness, she could not bring herself to take his life, either directly or indirectly, though she wanted to see him punished for Bryan's death. Yet it was not weakness or squeamishness on her part. Just then, she thought of something Deuteronomy Saint Claire said a day before she left.

The esteemed professor/detective told her the only way to survive in Washington was to "suspend morality," but it was something she had been unwilling to do in Idaho. He also explained cognitive dissonance in a person who believed he or she was honest, doing something he or she innately knew was wrong, but finding a way to justify it, pretending it did not happen, while avoiding reality or ignoring inconvenient facts. No, Destiny was not weak. If it was a test, it had only proved her upstanding character.

The knocking on the door was abrupt. When Destiny opened it, she backed and did a double take, surprised to see Natalie Sterling standing there, smiling. She handed Destiny a thick packet.

"It'll take you a while to get through that, but you'll want to start putting important information and documents together: tax returns, investments, financial holdings, all the typical stuff. The vetting process is fairly thorough."

Taking the heavy envelope, Destiny was honestly confused.

"Ms. Sterling. I suppose I *missed* something, because I have no idea what you're talking about. What *is* this?"

"Congratulations, Ms. Mitchell. You are being considered for a presidential appointment."

Chapter 47

They had journeyed nearly non-stop through the wilderness for three days, overnighting once in a cave and a second night in a cove by a fire. Earlier in the day, Cunningham shot an elk, a young bull, and he cut two five-pound fillets from the smaller end of the tenderloin. Carrying sixty-three-year-old Helmut Wolf between them, "Ham" and Madrigal had averaged ten miles a day southward through dense forests, over or around hills and across streams.

The days were cold, with temperatures in the mid-thirties. Nights were well below freezing. When Madrigal awoke that morning, his sleeping bag and everything for as far as he could see was covered in a blanket of snow. Ham stood south of Wolf's tent, binoculars aimed at the sky.

"What are you looking at, or for?"

"Drone. I swear I saw it twice yesterday, and once the day before."

"No way!"

Ham walked a few paces from the tent, speaking low so he would not be heard.

"It might be the same one or a different one, but I *saw* it. They're watching us. They know *exactly* where we are. And they know we have Wolf."

Madrigal reached for the binoculars.

"Can they see through clouds?"

Ham nodded.

"Those things can see clear as day in the dark. It's up there, eight miles or higher, out of sight. It's just sitting up there, watching us."

Madrigal sighed.

"And so are UFOs. Come on! Get your panties out your ass, Ham. You're bein paranoid."

The slushy snow and uphill slog slowed progress for most of the day. On the way down the one hill, Madrigal slipped, dropping the litter, which flying from Ham's hands, skidded downward for fifty meters, nearly missing a tree. Wolf tumbled thirty-feet downhill. He was bruised and injured further, but nothing else was broken.

Somewhere around one o'clock in the afternoon, after traveling through a densely forested area, the group came into a clearing and stopped for a ten-minute rest. Five minutes into their break, Madrigal looked up, suddenly blurting out the word.

"Drone!"

It was there for mere seconds, and then it was gone. Ham tried to relocate it with the binoculars, but it had disappeared, even in the clear blue sky. All three saw it.

At intervals during the day, Madrigal checked for a cell phone signal. Over and over, he got nothing, even after he hiked over to within a mile of the highway. As the third night fell, he became frustrated to the point of a cursing tantrum and discharging weapons into the sky, scattering the birds. Ham tapped him on the shoulder, pulling him aside.

"Do you get the feeling there's a *reason* you can't get a signal? It's that *thing* in the sky. They're controlling everything. Hell, they could take us out at any minute if they wanted—when we're out walkin, or especially when we're asleep. Wolf's a done deal. They ain't gonna *let* us save him."

The elk meat sizzled on the large stones heated by the bonfire, hidden under the cover of tall trees. Earlier in the day, Ham managed to spear a large five-pound German brown trout in one of the streams. The meat cooked quickly and was served along with a few dozen buffaloberries, a pocketful of juniper berries, six snowbank mushrooms and sedge stems.

Water and wood were abundant. As the men sat by the fire, it was obvious that Helmut Wolf's strength was fading. Though the outdoor temperature had dropped into the low-twenties, Wolf's face dripped sweat profusely, his eyes seeming swollen. Madrigal rewrapped the bandages, checking the wounds. The nails driven through his hands had not severed any tendons or damaged any bones. The wounds were tender to touch, but healing.

The holes through his feet were another matter. Even in the tightly tied boots, Wolf's feet had become swollen and inflamed. His toes were numb, indicative of neural damage. Pressing the edges of the wounds, Madrigal was able to express a teaspoon-sized dollop of thick, pungent, yellow-green pus from each foot.

Wolf cringed in pain the entire time, cursing Madrigal in colloquial German.

Later in the evening, as the men shared a bottle of *Kammer-Kirsch Birne Williams* pear brandy (an intact Bartlett pear within the bottle), looted from the estate, Wolf sipped and began.

"*Thirty* million dollars!"

Madrigal and Ham turned toward the older man, their faces inquisitive as Wolf nodded and spoke again.

"Yes, thirty million dollars, for *each* of you, if you can get me to safety! I saw that drone today, just like you did. But look—"

He parted the hair on the left side of his head, tapping.

"I have a GPS chip embedded in my skull under the scalp here. That means my people know *exactly* where I am right now. You two know how valuable I am. Some of these people stand to lose empires, political and financial, if I do not return. Someone will definitely come! Thirty million dollars for each of you! My associates will even help you leave the country and protect you. They will do anything I order them to do."

Sitting back, he feigned confidence.

"They will find a way to help us tomorrow, or the next day at the latest!"

The combination of alcohol and drugs caused Wolf to feel woozy, especially after Ham crushed an additional codeine pill to powder and added it to his drink.

Thus, with Wolf unconscious, Madrigal mused about the new offer.

"Thirty million dollars apiece, tax free? That is a hell of alotta money! In Venezuela, I could live like a king."

Ham sighed.

"They're never gonna let us take him out of here, and he knows it. That's why he's offering so much money. He's trying to buy time, but that drone could take us out at any moment. And even if his people *were* to show up, I'm sure they'd rather find a way to *off* us than shell out sixty million. To them, we're just two expendable military assholes who *crucified* their master."

At least Madrigal seemed to be thinking this time!

Ham whispered, turning his back to the forest.

"You've seen that gang of crows and ravens that have been following us since we left? Well, my grandma was a Cherokee. It's a bad omen. *Someone's* gonna die."

Madrigal looked toward the trees, which seemed to be animated with the cawing black birds. He nodded.

"My grandmother told me the same thing."

Ham continued.

"And the GPS chip on his skull he told us about? If that *thing* up there in the sky is blocking your cell phone and access to data, then whoever is looking for that chip will never see it. You haven't listened to me this whole time, but listen to me now. We can't enjoy the money he's promising if we're dead! We already have more than we need from that DHS job!"

"So, what are you *sayin*, Ham?"

Ham stood and placed his foot atop a hefty log and in a flicking motion, rolled it toward the fire.

"The name of the game is *survival*, Madrigal. We gotta do what we gotta do."

Wolf felt unusually groggy when he awoke the next morning. Crawling from the sleeping bag and away from the small tent, he could see the fire still burning. The healthy, nutritious meal from the night before had made a difference. He was feeling better, especially his hands. That morning, he could move his fingers well enough to grasp an object, in that case, a quickly scribbled note sitting next to a canteen and a compass:

Your offer was very tempting, Mr. Wolf, but we've decided to follow the first rule of engagement. We have to cover our own asses. We've left you plenty of food, fuel and water. That way, you'll be just peachy until your friends find you.

"No good bastards! The Devil's curse on them!"

Wolf's panicked eyes scanned the landscape for signs of Madrigal and Ham and the direction they had gone, but even their tracks were lost, covered by falling snow. He looked skyward to see if he could spot the drone, but the clouds blocked his view. Glancing toward the mountains thirty miles behind him, he saw the beginning of a squalling snowstorm. Ahead of him, he saw a vast, boundless and unforgiving wilderness, full of danger and certain doom.

Then he looked to his feet and instinctively tried to stand. Faltering from the moment he bore weight on them, he collapsed onto the wet snow covering a rock, face-first. Dragging himself along the ground to a place near the crackling fire, he spat blood and tooth fragments, rolled another log into the flames and bundled himself in woolen blankets. Rocking back and forth to dry and stay warm, he cursed the souls of the worthless men who had left him to such a bitter fate.

An hour later, he watched the drone descend in the distance, and then he heard two loud explosions that signaled the end of Ham and Madrigal. Wolf figured they had travelled maybe three miles before being targeted and incinerated. Sipping the last of the pear brandy, he raised first the bottle toward the heavens, and then an obscene gesture.

"Fuck you, Mr. President!"

Unable to travel or fight, he resigned himself to a disastrous destiny. Perhaps it would be a bear, a mountain lion, a few coyotes or a hungry wolf-pack. If he was lucky, he would freeze to death as he slept.

Alone in frozen Hell, he considered his fall and finally he raised his face and finger to the heavens and cursed God, realizing that if even he lasted another day, and despite his singular genius, despite his great wealth and the sheer power of his will—by the next morning, save a miracle, he would be nothing more than slimy carrion in the craws of scavenging crows.

Chapter 48

Two weeks later, Kiyomi Yamakita's chances for survival had improved. Tests by Dr. Rosecrans indicated the process had been reversed and some of the damage had been repaired, but there would be lingering symptoms and concerns that would not dissipate altogether for two to three years. The doctor recommended an endarterectomy, which would involve going in and surgically removing the obstruction in her left coronary artery, though he advised surgeons to wait a month to determine if the vasodilator and lipid-reducing drugs would yield satisfactory results.

The First Lady fared better. While there was still the risk of a heart attack, her overall physical fitness and diet had provided an effective firewall against long-term effects associated with viral vector induced arteriosclerosis. Her daily schedule was modified to include regular exercise, weekly electrocardiograph monitoring and a low-cholesterol regimen. To outside observers, staff, and even her own children, she was recovering from campaign fatigue.

Destiny remained in Washington at the *St Regis* with Kiyomi during treatment. After a reassuring call from Nathaniel Driscoll, confirming that all former threats against her had dissipated, and a similar assurance from the government, Destiny finally relaxed her guard.

When she called Lyndsey out of hiding, her daughter flew immediately to Washington and was able to hang out and shop for a day before Carla arrived. Carla did her best, pretending to be gracious, but "bitch" still showed around the edges.

Cedric Mitchell, Destiny's first cousin and four years her senior, was Kiyomi's husband. A pilot for a commercial airline, he had taken an extended leave of absence during the crisis. He and daughter Natsumi had gone to rural Mississippi, where they stayed with relatives. Cedric was unhappy in the arrangement and worried about his wife's health, so the reunion was bittersweet. Looking over at Destiny from where he sat at Kiyomi's bedside, Cedric scolded, half-joking.

"*You* two! Troublemakers! Always meddling into things, even back to junior high! But you're *women* now, with families! Kiyo can't help it—she *should*, though she can't. But you, Destee! You're *both* too old for this Nancy Drew shit!"

Destiny smiled.

"I swear, Cedric. This time, we were just minding our own business, and this thing just came out of nowhere and found *us*. We had no choice, except to go forward and finish it."

He wagged his head.

"Well, it almost finished you, *both* of you. And the takeaway from this?"

She sighed.

"*Never* answer your phone at four in the morning. Whoever's on the line and whatever they're saying, it definitely won't be good!"

Destiny had returned briefly to San Francisco to retrieve the necessary records and documentation requested by the President's vetting team. She was honored, but she was not sure she would accept the appointment. She did not trust the Beltway and its effect on decent and well-meaning persons. The President seemed kind and thoughtful, but there was an indescribable darkness underlying his calm and controlled demeanor, something possessed by most people she met in Washington, though at varying degrees.

It bothered her, but she could see it all over in the city. Sometimes, while in a conversation about issues, opinions or policy, it crept into a person's being, transforming his or her aspect. It crept into the soul, distorting the face, controlling mood, influencing speech and behavior. And strangely, it appeared the same in every person in Washington, again in varying degrees. It was unsettling. It took two weeks for Destiny to realize what she was witnessing: it was the corrupting effect of power.

Lyndsey returned to San Francisco after a week to resume duties at the *Aegis Foundation*. The near-death experience had changed her so that she showed a newfound confidence, perhaps even a bit of a swagger. She phoned "Destee and Auntie Kiyo" a few times a day, sometimes for advice, sometimes to complain about Carla, but usually to check on Kiyomi's progress.

Destiny typically sat with Kiyomi at bedside five or six hours a day, reading newspapers, magazines and occasional political biographies. Sometimes, when Kiyomi was up to it, they talked.

"Now that it's over, do you miss Bryan? Have you given yourself permission to cry?"

Destiny contemplated the question and closed her eyes.

"I miss him. But I haven't cried. Not yet. I feel like there is still something unfinished, something unresolved. I don't know what it is, but it keeps me from feeling any satisfaction or sense of peace."

"Have you meditated?"

"Yes, when I was home. I went to Japanese Garden. I don't know. It just seems like there's something *else* I have to do."

Kiyomi raised a feeble hand.

"Count me in."

Destiny laughed.

"Isn't it bad enough you almost died? I guess we wouldn't have to worry about it. Cedric would kill us *both*!"

When Cedric and Natsumi came into the room, Destiny decided to go to the downstairs lobby to read, allowing for privacy. As she sat on a plush sofa, reading *My American Journey*, by retired four-star general and former Secretary of State Colin Powell, a cable television news channel could barely be heard behind the background noise.

If Kiyomi died, Destiny would refuse the appointment and return to San Francisco to help Cedric with Natsumi, who had just turned thirteen. She saw so much of Kiyomi's spirit in the girl, which meant Natsumi would need special consideration. If Kiyomi *died* after Destiny was serving in the appointment, she would simply resign.

Closing the book, Destiny wondered how *anyone* could survive in Washington, sense of decency and morality intact. Just then, she heard key words from a news story that focused her attention, causing her mind to isolate the voice of the reporter, blocking out all other noise.

Again, we have this confirmed. Rafael Ramirez, the President of Venezuela, has just been admitted into Hospital de Clinicas in Caracas. The President, complaining of chest pains, was rushed immediately to doctors who are, at this very moment, performing a double bypass surgery on the Venezuelan President. Ramirez, while described as slightly overweight, has no known recent history of heart problems, though the President's medical history, like much about him, has remained private. We will continue to update you on this story as it develops.

Destiny stood. It was uncanny. She had just read a story about Ramirez, a leader who was perhaps the most strident voice against United States foreign policy and capitalism in South America. However, it appeared he had supported the President during the recent election. The last few months taught her to suspect that few major turns in world events were random, that *most* were manufactured, controlled by an invisible hand.

Minutes later, the news anchor returned with an update.

This just in. We are confirming now that Venezuelan President Rafael Ramirez has suffered a massive heart attack on the operating table. Doctors are doing everything they can to save him at this point. There is utter chaos in the Capital city. We now go to our on-the-scene correspondent in Caracas for an update.

Against her better judgment, Destiny decided her fate at that very moment. She would accept the appointment, fully aware that, over the course of time, she would learn Washington could not be changed. The President, though he denied it, was a part of it, and he would remain the most central character in it over the next four years.

During the election, the President said the "most important" lesson he learned was that "you can't change Washington from the inside."

If not from the inside, then how?

One week after the election, the people, the media and Congress had already gone back to distraction, distortion and hate, a disservice to themselves and the nation. And neither was it true that Washington could be changed from the *outside*, so what was left?

Helmut Wolf, for all his arrogance and bravado, understood the true nature of power, which in the beginning caused an angel of light to lust, casting himself in darkness and bringing about the fall of man. Ambition caused the first thinkers to covet the power of God, proving that *power corrupts, and absolute power corrupts absolutely*.

If he had already assumed *Godship Incarnate*, the divine power over who lived and who died, over good and evil, then the President would have to be stopped, and Destiny was perhaps the only force on Earth that could do it!

But then again, maybe it *was* just another random heart attack.

FINIS

OTHER TITLES BY MARCUS MCGEE

LEGAL THRILLER
(Suspense thriller, 439 pages paperback, eBook)
Murder mystery set in San Francisco

MURDER FROM THE GRAVE
(Suspense thriller, 425 pages paperback, eBook)
Berkeley professor-turned-SF police detective matches wits with a killer who wants to commit
seven murders after he is already dead

ALBERTA
(Suspense thriller, 318 pages paperback, eBook)
A chimpanzee with an Einstein brain, legal personhood, American Civil (Race) War

TWO MATADORS
(Novella, drama, 126 pages paperback, eBook)
An ancient Matador tells an epic story of living a life of love and passion!

FOUR STORIES
(Short Stories, 210 pages paperback, eBook)
Humorous collection of short stories

SYNCHRONICITY
(Short Stories, 298 pages paperback, eBook)
"The Club," "Anthropophagi" and other stories

THE SILK NOOSE
(Short Stories, essays, 217 pages paperback, eBook)
"Denouément," "On Niggers and Squirrels," and others

SHADOW IN THE SKY
(Suspense thriller, 263 pages paperback, eBook)
Asteroid threatens Earth, Last year of life

MOMENT OF TRUTH
(Suspense thriller, 265 pages paperback, eBook)
Societies deal with end of Earth, Book Two of The Last Year Trilogy

HOW TO EAT AN ELEPHANT
The Secret for How Ordinary People Can Accomplish Extraordinary Things
(Short Story, 8,870 words, eBook)

ON NIGGERS AND SQUIRRELS

An Examination of the Relationship Between Police and Black/Brown Males

#1 Amazon Best Seller for Two Years

(Essay, 11,030 words, eBook)

ON WHAT THEY CALL US

A Historical Perspective about the Illusion of Race in America.

(Essay, 11,050 words, eBook)

ON THE SEVEN-YEAR HITCH

A Discussion on the Efficacy of Long-Term Marriage in an Impermanent Society.

(Essay, 4,050 words, eBook)

WILLIE – THE MAN, THE MYTH & THE ERA

Texas Roots/California Dreams

Three chapters detailing Willie Brown's background and his earliest influences

(Biography, 15,760 words, eBook)

The Speakership Battles

Willie's ascension to the speakership and his efforts over insurmountable odds

Biography, 40,740 words, eBook)

California's Initiatives

Willie's influence on the history of the initiative process as practiced in California

Biography, 39,940 words, eBook)

Conspiracy and The Sting

Calculated attempts to depose or destroy the State's most brilliant politician

Biography, 17,540 words, eBook)

AN OLD NEGRO SPIRITUAL

(Inspirational, 425 pages paperback, eBook)

An African American "Scrooge" story, featuring Judge Thomas Dolittle

visit www.pegasusbooks.net

spend an afternoon or evening with Marcus

www.marcusmcgee.net

Acknowledgement

It is probably not widely-known that I managed an upscale Chinese restaurant for fourteen years. The establishment, a block and a half from the State Capitol in Sacramento, was called Frank Fat's, which opened in 1939. For many years, Fat's was called the "Third House," because it was the place where the legislators and lobbyists hung out, sometimes to work out landmark deals. Over that time, I bonded with the Fat family, and I was known as the darkest Chinese guy in the place.

I met Willie Brown, erstwhile Assembly Speaker, while working at Frank Fat's, and I wrote a book about him and the era of California politics in which he served. While there, I wrote a number of other books, drawing from all I watched and learned.

In 2001, shortly after the release of *Legal Thriller*, a Fat's customer, a medical doctor by the name of Del Wright, invited me to his table and suggested I should write a sequel with Destiny Mitchell about a nefarious group that had devised a way to murder enemies by weaponizing human DNA. We planned to develop the story, but we never got around to it, and then we lost contact with each other.

Such a story had always intrigued me, but it was not until 2005 that I set about researching and writing it. Ironically, I saw this book as a necessary commentary on the systematic killing of declared enemies of the state, foreign and domestic, in foreign lands and on American soil, and the larger implications of the debate over drone attacks.

Dr. Del Wright—wherever you are, I thank you! And I also thank all the legislators, lobbyists, insiders, friends and others responsible for my political tutelage, among them, Willie Brown.

What is legal personhood? Should humans feel threatened by nonhuman persons, which can range from cognitively complex chimpanzees to corporations that live in perpetuity? Are humans the only creatures with complex emotions, morality and culture? Are all humans entitled to equal rights and protection—even those suspected of crimes, whose freedom and lives are disproportionally forfeited?

Meet Alberta, a seventeen-year-old chimp with a brain resembling Einstein's brain in form and function. With an affinity for abstract math and an IQ of 131, she is arguably smarter than most humans. Alberta wants rights and protections—to become first breathing nonhuman person recognized by American law.

Yet American law has never treated all its human residents equally. Our Lives Matter is a community protest group focused on the police killing of unarmed civilians. When leaders learn that a secret police order is working to avert a nationwide race war/civil, war instigated by a group of selfish businessmen, unlikely allies learn trust and respect in the face of America greatest crisis and most defining moment.

Alberta (preview)

Chapter 1

"Stop! You do not have a legal right to progress beyond this point!"

The stern officer's face was indiscernible behind the gas mask as he stood before an intimidating phalanx of police officers clad in military riot gear. He spoke through a bullhorn.

"This is your final warning!"

When the front line stopped, the ranks marching behind began to swell and extend out at both sides. The setting sun glowed at the horizon as dusk settled on the apartment neighborhoods and the eclectic mixture of buildings in the progressive city. The chanting crowd continued to gather behind determined leaders.

No Justice, No Peace! No Justice, No Peace! No Justice, No Peace!

In the distance, an officer knelt, handcuffing a blonde with dreadlocks as two other officers threatened her black boyfriend. The air smelled of CS gas and smoke from an old Chevy Caprice, burning on Telegraph Avenue. Red and blue lights flashed from squad cars parked along 14th Street across from Ogawa Plaza in Oakland.

The protest began as a meeting in the public space at the center of the city, which many attendees had renamed Oscar Grant Plaza. That afternoon, the midday news reported the fatal shooting of an unarmed black teenager just outside the 19th Street Oakland Bart Station. Sandoval "Sand-Man" Sanders, a nationally recruited high school football quarterback, had been shot nine times when officers mistook him for a felon who had recently robbed a small community grocery store.

Angry Bay Area residents began to gather shortly after five o'clock, determined to make certain the city and the media did not ignore the event. The police chief had chosen to withhold the names of the officers involved until the investigation got underway, but local community leaders were incensed that the city was more concerned with damage control than justice for a wrongful death at the hands of the police... again.

"Turn around now! This is your final warning!"

Civil rights attorney Natsumi Mitchell stepped forward, presenting her card and legal documents as she approached the officer.

No Justice, No Peace! No Justice, No Peace!

"This is a peaceful protest, and we have a permit, signed by a judge, to proceed to Jack London Square."

"Why? So you people can burn and loot it? I'm sorry, but my captain has direct orders from the mayor to make sure this misunderstanding does not get out of hand. You're just gonna have to tell your judge to take the matter up with the mayor."

"We have the right to move forward. We have the right to march and protest. First Amendment of the U.S. Constitution. I'm sure you know how it works."

The officer sighed, disgusted.

"You might have the right, but do you see what's behind me? Do you think any of us care about your rights tonight? Do yourself a favor and go home before you're responsible for someone else getting hurt today. You're their leader. They'll listen to you. Take your troublemaking asses on home!"

Natsumi remained defiant.

"We ain't gonna let nobody turn us around. We are moving forward. So if you're going to arrest us for exercising our legal rights, you can start with me!"

The crowd cheered, following her as she stepped forward, but the police behind the officer had already reacted. Pandemonium ensued within seconds as the aggressive police force surged against the crowd, firing off tear gas canisters, pushing people to the ground and making arrests. Then without warning, a group of agitators at the left flank, separate from the protesters, converged on the scene, some intent on protecting people, while others attacked the officers, flailing with fists and trying to remove officers' gas masks.

It wasn't long before reinforcements arrived to help the officers under assault, which drew still more protesters into the fray. Television cameras rolled as police and news helicopters nearly collided overhead. Face-down on the asphalt, Natsumi heard cursing, screaming and gunshots fired.

It was never supposed to go like this! They'll never learn!

When the officer stood her up, she saw her friend and fellow attorney, Padmi Ravi, being restrained by a brutal, heavy-handed officer. Padmi was Natsumi's best friend through college and law school, and Padmi was seven months pregnant. *It was supposed to be a peaceful protest!*

Earlier in the afternoon, after the report of the Sandoval Sanders murder, Natsumi and Padmi sent out an email blast, encouraging friends and activists to meet at Oscar Grant Plaza to make a statement to the city, the nation and the world. They contacted a judge and managed to get a permit to march from the plaza to Jack London Square. If Natsumi had known the protests would turn violent, she would have insisted that Padmi stay home, but such admonition would have been unnecessary. Padmi would have never have knowingly exposed her unborn baby to such risk!

Natsumi recoiled at the sight of an officer striking Padmi on the back of her shoulders with a baton. At that point, it was obvious that Padmi wanted nothing more than to get out of harm's way—for herself, but more desperately for her baby. Yet once she fell, the officer continued striking her, on her back and shoulders and once on the head.

Desperate to get away, Padmi struggled to her feet and tried to run, but the officer shot her with a taser gun dart and dialed up the voltage. She fell, convulsing on the sidewalk as he maintained pressure on the trigger.

"Stop! You idiot! She's *pregnant!*" Natsumi screamed as she struggled against her restraints, only to be forced back to the ground. "You're killing her baby! She's pregnant! She's seven months pregnant, goddammit!"

By the time the officer who had pinned Natsumi to the ground made sense of her words, it was too late.

"Gates! Turn it off! She's *pregnant!* Kill the juice, goddammit!"

Padmi still convulsed on the ground even after the current no longer flowed through her body, with her spasms growing increasingly intense as she panted between deep moans of intense pain.

"I'm dying! Call 9-1-1! Help my baby!"

When the nervous, panicked officer turned her over, the crotch area of her pants was drenched with clear liquid and she foamed at the mouth.

"Oh my God! I'm sorry! Ma'am, are you okay? We'll get help!"

By that time, the officer who was restraining Natsumi softened his tone and posture.

"We didn't know she was pregnant. How far along is she?"

"Far enough! By the way, we're both civil rights lawyers. If you look to your left, this whole incident is being recorded by at least four people on cell phones! When will you guys ever learn? We're persons with rights. You can't do this to people! Our lives matter!"

As the police officer glanced over at the crowd toward the persons with phones poised, recording, a sick feeling flooded the pit of his gut. He knew the outcome would be bad, that he was helpless to halt the inevitable. Within hours, the recordings would go viral. There would be an investigation. He would be identified and condemned, labeled as violent and a racist.

And worse, Oakland's police chief and the city mayor, on the verge of succumbing to pressure from protesters and activists across the country, seemed poised to offer up a sacrificial victim, provided the circumstances were sufficiently egregious. It wouldn't matter to anyone that his favorite nephew was half-black.

"Is anyone a doctor?" one of the activists who crowded in screamed. "The ambulance won't make it in time! The baby is coming now!"

The officer turned back toward Natsumi.

"You have to understand, Miss. We were just doing our jobs. We didn't mean for any of this to happen."

"Of course you didn't!" Natsumi snapped. "You cops never do, but somehow we just keep on dying!"

****

On most days, Kendrick Vesey was a biological anthropologist, adjunct professor and lecturer at the University of California, Berkeley. He was the author of four renowned books relating to Animal Language Research, the Great Ape Language, Yerkish and case studies involving Washoe, Nim Chimski and Koko.

In recent weeks, he had appeared on *60 Minutes, 20/20, Nature, NPR Science* and as a guest on nightly news programs across networks and cable television stations. Yet the upcoming Wednesday would signal his crowning achievement, as he had flight reservations for Stockholm, Sweden, where the Committee and the King would present him with the Nobel Prize in Physiology or Medicine.

Kendrick repeated his words in American Sign Language as he spoke, a playful Jamaican accent flavoring his inflection.

"There is no reason to fear traveling to the ceremony in an airplane across the water. Yes, sometimes jets do crash in the water, but Kendrick and Alberta will not crash. It's no different than flying over land. Kendrick and Alberta will be safe. I promise."

Alberta frowned, unconvinced by his answer, and responded in sign language, which he translated aloud.

"Mi not happy to go to Stockholm inside airplane over water. Terrorist is on plane. Isis blow up plane! Boat is better. Better we sail on boat to Stockholm."

This time, Kendrick frowned.

"A boat would take too long. Besides, I've already booked our flight. We have to be there on Monday. Don't worry. We got this! Breathe easy now."

"What Tupac say? Mi no trust nobody. Maybe Kendrick get Mai Tai for Alberta, then mi fly."

After a moment of hesitation and contemplation, he sighed, amused at her toothy smile.

"It's a deal. Legally, you're under age, but who's gonna know? Maybe we'll even let you have the window seat."

Kendrick's fiancée, Jennifer Alvarez, was passing through the room as he finished the remark, leaving in her wake the fragrance of her sweet *parfum*. Jennifer was 5'3" with an attractive face, mocha skin and a thick, shapely body. She was an impeccable dresser and her voice possessed a musical quality, flavored in Spanish.

"I think this whole thing is ridiculous. She doesn't need to go to Stockholm. There are plenty of tapes and other documentation available. Besides, it's embarrassing. This is supposed to be a big moment for you—for us, and you're putting that silly monkey front and center in all this."

Alberta's reaction was instant and angry. She pounded the table, half-snarling at the woman, as she screamed something unintelligible.

"That's right. *Monkey*! I said it," Jennifer taunted as she snatched her designer purse off the black leather sofa in the luxurious Oakland Hills home.

"Come on, baby," Kendrick sighed. "You know the difference. She's an ape, not a monkey. You know she doesn't like being called that."

Alberta continued in the garbled tirade, and then she fixed her fingers in a sign that even Jennifer could understand.

"You see? She's flippin me off. I told you. She's always startin that shit with me. Monkeys belong in the zoo!"

"Where are you going?" Kendrick asked. "I thought we were going to dinner?"

"Last minute shopping for the trip," she announced over the sound of Alberta's protests while slipping into a sleek jacket. "One hour, max."

She kissed him, lingering, while eyeing Alberta.

"When we get married, we're moving to Millennium Tower in downtown San Francisco. You need to tell her the bad news. They have a no pet policy."

Alberta was still angry fifteen minutes after Jennifer left.

"Why do I let Jennifer come here?" Kendrick translated aloud. "Why do I not chase Jennifer away?"

"Well," he answered, signing, "because Jennifer is my mate—you know that... because Kendrick love Jennifer."

"Jennifer no love Kendrick," Alberta signed. "Jennifer no love Alberta. Jennifer love Jennifer everything. Too much perfume always. Jennifer is stupid monkey!"

"Look," Kendrick answered, becoming annoyed. "It not good for Alberta fight against Jennifer. After Stockholm, Jennifer will be my wife."

"Why Kendrick need wife? Why him want wife?"

"A wife is a mate. For human, wife is mate. You know that. Jennifer will be mate for Kendrick until him old and die. For humans, 'marriage' is law. It's human law."

Frustrated, Alberta wagged her head.

"Mi no like human law. Human law no like mi, no like ape. Human law no like chimp" she signed, and then she frowned in confusion. "Human mate till die? This true or lie? Till die?"

"Yes. One human is a mate for one human… for life. That's what marriage is."

"Alberta not have mate. Mi not free."

"No," Kendrick protested. "Alberta will be free. Human law says Alberta will be free. We're so close now. Alberta is not like other apes. Alberta will never go to zoo or lab. Alberta will be free, like humans. This month, I promise. Alberta will be the first legal nonhuman person, by human law! If anyone's going to change the legal status of nonhuman persons, it will be you, Alberta."

****

Fifteen years earlier, American billionaire philanthropist Davis Franklin read a scientific, scholarly manuscript for publication about a young female chimpanzee that some scientists were calling a freak of nature. She was born different. Her brain was different. CT scans and neuroimaging revealed a brain that was denser than normal chimpanzee brains, and it was fifteen percent larger.

Scientists used the Encephalization Quotient, the measure of relative brain size, defined as the ratio between actual brain mass and predicted brain mass for an animal of a given size, to get a rough estimate of the intelligence, or cognition, of an animal. While the EQ for average chimpanzees ranged from 2.2 to 2.5, Alberta's EQ, at 7.26, was higher than that of the tucuxi, a freshwater Amazon River dolphin (smarter than a bottlenose), at 4.56, but slightly lower than that of humans, who ranged from 7.4 to 7.8.

Alberta's brain was denser, due in part to the greater number of glial cells that fed her brain neurons. This meant the nerve cells in her brain needed more fueling cells because they consumed more nourishment, resulting from higher brain activity.

Secondly, portions of Alberta's brain, such as the cerebral cortex, were thinner, yet more saturated with neurons, than corresponding areas inside mainstream brains. Imaging indicated that she had an enlarged prefrontal cortex, and deep furrows divided her wider brain in the right parietal lobe and the left parietal lobe, and the Sylvain fissure seemed truncated.

In short, she was a chimpanzee born with a brain like Albert Einstein's, which neurologists had labeled an "Einstein brain," and thus her name was changed from *Kipekee*, which meant "unique" in Swahili, to simply "Alberta."

"It's like someone cut open her head and literally dropped Einstein's brain in it," proclaimed Dr. David Jacobs, the researcher who discovered her, "an exact match, except for the slightly smaller size!"

She was originally owned by the Southwest Foundation for Biomedical Primate Research Center in San Antonio, but Davis Franklin managed to buy her before the research paper and findings about her were published. By the time the scientific community realized how remarkable she was, Franklin and a fleet of his lawyers were well on their way to granting her relative emancipation, placing her in the moral category of a "person," rather than private property, meaning she would never be caged or studied.

Instead, Franklin sought out a sensitive, activist biological anthropologist who specialized in great ape language and/or Yerkish. After nearly nine months of vetting candidates, his team settled on a handsome, dark-skinned primate language researcher and adjunct Berkeley professor Kendrick Vesey, who welcomed the challenge of working with such an extraordinary primate subject.

When he was working, Kendrick and Alberta stayed in rooms at the opposite ends of the home that Franklin provided in the Oakland Hills, allowing the scientist access to primate facilities at Hlusko Laboratory in Berkeley. Kendrick returned to his upscale Midvale Drive Daly City apartment on his days off and for private time with Jennifer.

Over time, the scientist and his subject developed their own unique complex language that served for efficient communication in the home, though translated verbatim, it sounded unrefined and simple. The language was a fusion of Jamaican patois, literal ASL translation and Yerkish.

At birth, researchers selected Alberta as part of an animal language acquisition study, and a pair of primatologists raised her in an environment similar to that of a human child, complete with furniture, a refrigerator, dresser drawers and a bed, with sheets and blankets. She had access to clothing, combs, toys, books and a toothbrush. She had responsibilities in the home and travelled with a human family on car trips. Davis Franklin insisted on continuing the study in the Oakland Hills home.

Alberta was ten years old when Kendrick came to live in the home, so they had been together for seven years. During that time, she mastered American Sign Language so that she was completely conversant, marking a breakthrough in chimpanzee and human communication. Beyond signing and fully understanding human speech, comprehension testing confirmed that she could read and understand literature at or above proficiency for 12th grade student standards. She was also able to grasp and apply advanced math concepts.

Kendrick realized early on that Alberta was thirsty for learning, a quality that sometimes made his colleagues nervous. A few suggested that she was a monstrosity, created in a lab by the government, who would eventually return to claim their experiment. Others predicted that she would one day show her repressed animal side, resulting in a horrific bloodbath where some poor human would die. Undeterred by warnings and discouraging comments, Kendrick was a patient and compassionate teacher and friend, and Alberta prospered under his tutelage.

****

"Alberta make Kendrick proud in Stockholm," she signed.

"I'm already proud of you, Alberta. I just want the whole world to know how very special you are!"

As he reached over, rubbing one of her shoulders, she closed her eyes and tilted her head, relishing the feel of his fingers.

"One human mate one human? Till die?" she signed, repeating his words. "This human marriage law?"

"That's pretty much how it works," he nodded. "Why do you ask?"

"Mi ask to know," she answered, which was a response she repeated often. "Human marriage law is lie."

He laughed, scratching her scalp.

"Why does Alberta say that?"

"Mi watch movies and mi read news online. One human mate one human... till divorce—not die!"

An Old Negro Spiritual is Marcus McGee's take on A Christmas Carol by Dickens, with Judge Thomas Dolittle in a role comparable to Ebenezer Scrooge. The pharisaical Dolittle is visited by three haints: those of Injustice Past, Injustice Present and Injustice Yet-to-Come.

The herald to the three visitors is the haint of Thoroughgood Marshall, who has come to warn Dolittle that he has little time left to honor the legacy he inherited. Throughout the night, Dolittle meets the likenesses of John Henry, Etheldred Scott, Homer Plessy, Dick Rowland, Emmett Till, Barack Obama, Tamir Rice, Philando Castille, George Floyd, Breonna Taylor, Malcom X, Martin Luther King, Jr., John Lewis, Fredrick Douglas, Harriet Tubman, Miles Davis, the grandfather who raised him and many others in his journey from the past to the yet-to-come.

An Old Negro Spiritual was written to honor African American history, where song, music, the griot and oral tradition were a powerful way to tell our stories, express our joys or frustrations, and to honor God, each other and our shared culture and legacy. Rather than chapters, the work is divided into "Shouts," which are the divisions in a traditional Black spiritual.

www.ingramcontent.com/pod-product-compliance
Lightning Source LLC
Chambersburg PA
CBHW032225010726
47494CB00002B/349